Cover Designer: Najla Qamber, Najla Qamber Designs, www.najlaqamberdesigns.com

Editor and Interior Designer: Jovana Shirley, Unforeseen Editing, www.unforeseenediting.com

Content Editor: Christina Trevaskis, www.facebook.com/BookMatchmaker

Proofreader: Sue Banner

Silver Hummingbird Necklace: Blue Bayer Design NYC, http://www.etsy.com/shop/billyblue22

Cover Model: Thomas Gunter, Period Images

For my mother...

You should be here.

CONTENTS

PROLOGUE

ROMEO HAD SNAPPED.

Not body's death, but body's banishment, was the Prince's decree for the kid's crime, and Romeo freaked.

Exile. Abolishment. Banishment.

Much more than death, Romeo thought.

Banishment was purgatory, torture, doom, hell itself.

Yeah, that is what it's like, Romeo. You sure didn't live it as long as I did. Then again, you got yourself killed.

I'd first noticed the word banishment when we read *Romeo and Juliet* in high school.

Romeo had been banished from Verona as punishment for killing the man who'd killed his best friend. He kept repeating the word *banishment*, torturing himself with it, crying over his fate that was worse than any death he could imagine. He would have to leave his hometown and could never be with Juliet again.

Romeo went hysterical at the word, but none of us in that classroom had understood what the hell the big deal was. Instead of having to eat the death penalty, he was getting a pardon. We'd all shrugged because, hell, we all wanted out of our seedy little has-been town in northern Cali. Forced exile sounded like a good deal to us. Romeo was a lucky guy.

But, for him, it was a black word, a word the damned used in hell.

Our teacher had explained that, back then, banishment was a severe punishment, not just a move to the next town over. She'd made us say that word out loud over and over, just like Romeo did in the play. The sounds it made alone had a hushed power, an eeriness. An echo of loneliness.

Banishment meant you were alienated from everything and everyone you knew and loved. Romeo would be alone in the wilderness. Pushed out, shoved forth into the unknown. Naked, no property, no family. Everywhere he went, he would be a foreigner, a stranger, not to be trusted.

Oh, we'd all eventually nodded our heads, kind of, sort of getting it but not really. We had never comprehended the depths of what banishment really meant.

Me and Romeo—we had a lot in common.

But Romeo needed to buck up and get real. He had to own it.

No, he didn't have a cocaine addiction twisting him into the basest form of himself—an ass who made tilted decisions. He hadn't conspired with his enemies behind his family's back. Romeo hadn't tossed the match and had himself a good ole time while his house was on fire, the smoke singeing his lungs.

But I had.

I'd had a couple of Juliets along the way—my wife, then the Grace of my past, and the Grace of my present. I'd wrung myself over Grace, then and now, and still, each time, I hadn't been on my best behavior. No, I'd been no stalwart Romeo there. I'd been unable to step up to the plate, to be honest. I'd squandered my chances. Chances, really, I shouldn't have taken in the first place, but what the hell? I'd always jumped first and thought about it later. When I'd surfed as a kid, I'd always wanted to be in the pocket straight off.

Live and learn.

Somehow, I'd been lucky enough to meet my wife. We got it together and had it good, but then I lost her in a pool of blood, chrome, and regrets.

And that was where Romeo and I met again—on that road to Padua.

That pain, that monster on my back, that guilt drove me to do anything to forget.

And up it went.

Whomp went the fire.

Up in smoke, up my nose, in my mouth, across my tongue, on my cock, in my veins.

My shield and my weapon…against myself.

Money flowed in and out of my pockets, and the women—*ah, the women*—were an endless blur of, *Yes, yes, yes*, and, *What the fuck?*

Death was the end of all, but with banishment, redemption was still possible. There was yet a trace of hope. Even the Friar and the Nurse yelled at Romeo to cut his crying and stand up and be a man about it, to take his opportunities.

Hell yes.

Unlike Romeo, I wasn't going to steal back home in the shadows of the night, armed with a dagger or poison. I kept my nose to the ground. I got clean. I banged my head against the walls. I scraped my nails over the splintered wood. I ground my jaw to the bone.

Through it all, I rode my Harley and tended to her like she was my forever Juliet. And she was. She was my constant. Her roar over the road, our cutting through the wind, drowning the voices, the goddamn noise—that is my greatest satisfaction, my supreme indulgence now.

No, no more banishment.

I listened to my rough heartbeat through the black of the night. I worked hard, thought ahead. I was patient.

I would end this exile.

And, now, I had caught the prize, the token of war, and would deliver him to my club and lay him at my president's feet.

Creeper, former brother, cohort, traitor had been off the grid since things had exploded between the Jacks and a rival club, the Demon Seeds. I'd found him, and now he was my prisoner until the time was right. My carrot, my guarantee. Jump would need convincing that it was worth letting me back in, that I was worthy. Our National President had approved, but Jump was another story.

Finding Creeper was a deed I had vowed I'd carry out from the moment he'd shot me and taken off last year.

Catching Creeper was a pledge.

Killing Creeper meant the end.

Rather, the beginning of the end. Killing him would be a new beginning.

For all of us.

I used to wish I could go back in time.

Before I'd overstepped boundaries I never should've dared cross. Before I'd destroyed my brother, killed my wife. Before I'd held her as she bled out in my arms. Before I had drunk myself to sleep every night, the sound of her laughter a sting lingering in my ear.

Before I'd allowed my responsibilities to rust.

Alliances to splinter.

Friendships to crack.

To a time when the whiskey still burned down my throat. And I was still surprised by both good and evil.

But that was a long time ago.

All through my battle with my addictions—reliving the specters of my foul weaknesses, pathetic failures, and hollow ambitions—I had focused on one thing only.

Redemption?

Maybe.

Salvation?

Not really.

Revenge?

Useless.

I'd wanted to rectify. Put it all to rights. Repair the damage. Rebuild. Scrape off the rust. Fortify the bones.

That was what I'd wanted from the beginning, and I had vowed to myself I would make that happen. That was why I'd been working so hard for over a year now, taking risks other nomads wouldn't. And, now, the final cycle had begun.

There comes a time in every man's life when he must pay—pay for the wrongs he's done, the sins he's committed, the lies he's told, the misery he's wrought.

This was Creeper's time.

This was mine.

A new time.

ONE

BUTLER

I NEEDED MY BIKE.

I'd gotten used to getting on my hog and letting it lead me, leaving the question marks and shadows behind. Without the drugs or the booze to pull me up and do the tap-dancing for me, my bike was my lifeline.

Like going running every morning, if I didn't get a long ride in on my own, I would feel out of sync with myself, off my full capabilities, clarity diminished, all systems down. I couldn't fill that hole any other way. Well, of course, I could, but I didn't want to think about that now. That was what had gotten me into this mess to begin with, for fuck's sake.

I left Ohio behind, and opened the throttle. My bike surged underneath me, and a rush of sex and potency took over my body from the base of my skull, down my spine, to right between my legs.

I was going to stretch out the twelve-hour ride to Meager. I was excited to get home, but I wanted to savor these moments of freedom now that all my deals had been made and were ready to be put in play. My national president had told me I could go home. I'd earned it. The rush of adrenaline in my veins as I sped over the empty freeway made my lips curl.

The country here was bland to me, and I ignored it. Instead, I thought of home. What I truly considered my home. Meager, South Dakota. I couldn't wait to see it again, to breathe it in again. So many other brothers whom I'd hung with this past year had shaken their heads at me, knowing I came from the Dakotas. To them, it was only a wilderness where riding your bike was limited for a good chunk of the year. But I loved that hard, sometimes brutal country. Unforgiving, perhaps, but that land had taught me much and made me the man I was today.

I rode on.

Ohio.

Indiana.

Illinois.

Iowa.

I finally spotted the huge sign up ahead. *South Dakota. Great Faces, Great Places* along with a sketch of the presidents on Mount Rushmore. The sign flashed by me, and a grin split my face. I'd really been looking forward to this part of my trip. This was like fucking vitamins flooding my bloodstream. The Badlands were up ahead, the Grasslands, and then finally, rising above Meager was the glory that was the Black Hills.

The rolling hills of granite and spruce. Weathered ancient earth and stone and towering evergreens. The lakes and the reservoirs.

That beautiful, horrible stretch of road where I haven't been since Caitlyn died.

I adjusted myself in my saddle as I tore over the smooth asphalt, the wind whipping over me. Like today, it had been a gorgeous day then. Just the two of us swimming, being lazy, picnicking. We'd made the time for a whole day together; it had been a long while since we'd done it. And, on the way home, a car had bumped into us, and the driver, spooked by my rage, had taken off, leaving us alone.

Stranded.

We'd only been bumped into—a jarring nudge, really—yet that was all it'd taken.

She'd seized up against me and screamed.

A scream that stretched across the sky, echoed against the spires of eroded stone, shredding my soul.

Her body had slumped against mine. I'd stopped the bike, cursing a blue streak, and almost lost my guts right there at the sight of her mangled leg.

I'd held her.

Nothing else to do.

I'd shouted.

No one was on the road.

No one came.

I'd called 911.

She was in shock.

Cold.

Dazed.

Muttering. Trembling.

So pale.

The blood.

The sirens.

The blood. An ocean.

Too late. So fucking late.

I'd shaken her, calling her name, but she'd slipped away from me, her head knocking back over my straining arm.

I tensed at the memory, hitting the throttle and bracing as the bike flew harder over the highway.

Road, road, road.

She'd been laughing one minute, her body pressed up against me as we flew down that road. My old lady had been holding me tight for dear life.

My ma used to say that about the first time she'd ridden with my dad on his bike. *"I held on for dear life!"*

Made no difference—Caitlyn holding on to me.

My sore heart thudded dully in my chest; my gloved hands flexed around my handlebars.

Cait.

There was no ghost to speak to me or touch right through me and make me shiver. No graze of warmth over my thin soul. That was okay though; I expected none.

Would the same tree-filled mountains whisper back to me as they had then? Would the same sun lay its shimmering sparkle over the surface of the blue water of that lake just as it had five years ago?

I was on a different bike now. I had destroyed that one. Ripped it apart. Scrapped it to bits. Stomped on it, mangled it, hammered it. I'd removed most of my piercings after I'd quit using, piercings I'd gotten for her.

I wasn't high or drunk now. And my heart beat differently. Death was in my sight line, wasn't it? I'd finally admitted my vulnerability to mortality, my humility in its sneering face; that was finally real. I hadn't felt it then and certainly not all the years since. Then, all I'd felt was screaming shock, raw anger.

Pissing rage.

A mad thirst.

And I'd let that darkness suck me into its black pit of nothing. An aching cesspool of nothing.

There were no more illusions. No more grand gestures to make. I was going back to Meager to start a new life.

To show them that I could be an important part of the brotherhood once again.

To prove to my brothers that they could trust me, that I was worthy of that sacred trust.

To bring something of worth to our table.

Jump, my president, would know—they would all know—that I was serious, that I wasn't a has-been fuck-up.

I had one shot at this, and nothing and no one would stand in my way.

Not painful memories, not smoldering guilt.

I took in a deep breath at the road sign for Sioux Falls.

Yes, the air was sweeter, crisper here in South Dakota.

TWO

TANIA

I COULDN'T IGNORE IT any longer.

I took out the thin gray envelope with the embossed return address for the Alden Merrick Art Gallery in Chicago from my messenger bag. Carefully. Quietly. I didn't want him to hear. The letter had arrived yesterday, but I'd shoved it in my bag and let it simmer there.

If I got this job, it would be a game changer.

My husband, Kyle, had just heard that he'd gotten his dream job in Chicago, and last night, we'd gone out to dinner with his friends to celebrate. He was thrilled, but I wasn't. I didn't want to move to Chicago. I wasn't so sure I wanted *this* fresh start. A fresh start with him.

Last night, as usual, I'd learned new things about Kyle by listening to him talk to his friends, telling them all about his series of interviews for this new company. Once again, he hadn't shared details with me. Once again, I'd learned new information about him through hearing him enthusiastically tell other people. And there, at the table, with a full glass of Argentinian cabernet in my hand and eggplant rollatini on my fork, it had struck me. No, not like a bolt of lightning. More like a shallow flood of dirty cold water from old pipes bursting suddenly in your house. The flooding water had a sulfur-like, mildewy smell to it as it swelled up over my ankles, past my knees, rising up my belly to my chest.

He keeps things from me.

Not lies or secrets per se, but he simply didn't share with me, didn't feel the need to do so. Simple daily things, little occurrences, that, if he did share, maybe we'd be more connected. In sync. In my opinion, at least. Instead, we treaded the waters of indifference and disinterest and pleasantness for years now.

I'd brought it up later when we were alone in the car.

He'd shrugged and said, "Oh, I forgot to tell you."

But that didn't fly with me. Not anymore. I was so tired of it, beyond saddened by it. Numb.

He'd been waiting to hear if I'd gotten this job in Chicago because that would make our fresh start complete.

Applying for the director position at the gallery had been a fluke. I'd had my own freelance art dealer business going for years now, but even though I had made plenty of contacts with artists and collectors, a steady flow of income had proven elusive and required an enormous amount of legwork. Things were either going along nicely or dipping way down.

My specialty ranged from contemporary young artists to almost any kind of collectible from antique American pottery to vintage furniture and thingamabobs. I wasn't choosy. Good finds were good finds to me, and I was constantly learning. I loved that. My insides buzzed the same, be it over a rusty gas station sign from the fifties or a Mapplethorpe photograph of Patti Smith or a Gustav Klimt painting.

The Alden Merrick Gallery was breaking into the contemporary art business. My good friend Neil had set up the interview. Neil had risen high in the ranks of the Chicago art world where we had both started out as lowly assistants at the same gallery, fresh out of college, learning from one of the best eyes in the business.

Ever the restless Bohemian, I had eventually dropped out to do my own thing, but Neil had stayed the course, moved up the ranks, and become an assistant director as well as a sought-after freelance curator. Now, he had his own gallery. Over the years, he had directed work my way, invited me to all the right parties and events, and I had recommended artists and unusual finds his way.

I knew this job was an opportunity. A step in The Game. Consistent, good income. A stab at some sort of prestige.

Someone else would pay my cell phone bill and my health insurance. I would have regular mani-pedi appointments, and I would be able to afford a whole new wardrobe from Nordstrom or Neiman Marcus even—and not only one or two pieces a year—and more than the occasional new lipstick or eye shadow from my favorite designer makeup brands. That would be a kick for a change. I would be polished all the time and comfortable in that polish, like the women at Kyle's dinner party last night.

Kyle had certainly been excited about this job and had encouraged me to go for it. The plan was to leave Racine and move back to Chicago, back to where we had begun, the big city. According to Kyle, my getting a job there as well—a solid permanent job—would only make it perfect. Kyle hated my gypsy-picking ways. My on-the-fly/off-the-cuff way of thinking and doing business, taking off on my little field trips all over the country to hunt down finds or check out artists' studios and go through their works in progress.

"It's called inspiration! Passion!" I had argued once.

When things melded together—the business aspect and the art—it was magic. If they didn't, you would ride it out, riding it over every road you knew available. Kyle had never understood that, and he considered the lengths I went to—not to mention, the eccentric people I mixed with—ludicrous. He'd get irritated with the whole scene and avoid it. But I loved it, and I couldn't give it up.

Over two months ago, on my way to South Dakota to visit my mother, Rae, after she'd fallen down in her house and broken her hip, I'd stopped in Chicago for the interview. It had gone smoothly, and I'd promptly put it out of my head. Later, Neil had told me that they had hired someone else. But, now, since I'd returned to Racine, it seemed that had fallen through.

Now, they had sent me a letter.

I unsealed the envelope. I took in a tiny breath, my eyes flying over the printed words.

We are very pleased…

I'd been crowned homecoming queen. I'd won the lotto. Confetti rained down over me.

I'd gotten the job I knew deep, deep down inside that I didn't want.

My hold on the paper tightened.

So many things had changed since I'd first agreed to apply for this job months ago.

Mom had been officially diagnosed with multiple sclerosis after ten years of wondering why she was prone to tripping and falling, why her hands were numb off and on, why her vision was blurry for no apparent reason. There were so many other symptoms that no doctor had been able to connect their dots all this time. But, finally, one young resident at Rapid City Regional had decided to take the time to go through a two-hour consultation where my mother had to answer all sorts of questions along with having her umpteenth MRI, and voilà, we'd gotten the bitter diagnosis.

My sister, Penny, and I had felt so relieved and grateful that we finally had a diagnosis and could take a specific course of action. But then the grief and the anxiety from the unknown had set in.

Mom could no longer live at home alone. My sister couldn't take care of her full-time, as she was married and a mother to two young boys. Our baby brother was a biker with an outlaw motorcycle club down in Nebraska, and he had stopped communicating with us, except for a phone call on major holidays—God bless him. So, any help from ~~Drew~~ Catch was highly unlikely at this point in time.

Then, fate had introduced me to my brother's ex-girlfriend, Jill, who needed a way out and a place to land, and she had her own child—my niece—to consider. Something had uncoiled in my chest as I watched her bitch at my brother in front of his entire club about starting over and not putting up with his shit any longer.

I like this girl, I'd thought.

She had been determined to end the bullshit and start again. No matter what. She had been absolute in that belief, in her sense of purpose.

Would it ever be absolute for me? Why did I keep vacillating?

I'd taken Jill and her daughter, Becca, home with me and set them up with my mom at the house. A spur-of-the-moment crazy idea, but I had flown with it. Jill was a temporary solution but a good one. She would have a job as a general caregiver, my mother would be looked after, and my mother's only granddaughter would be under the same roof. Jill had ended up becoming a gestational surrogate mother for my best friend, Grace, in Meager, and I knew that, during the last couple of months of her pregnancy, I would have to be there to watch out for Grace, Jill, my mom, and Becca.

And the thing was, I really wanted to be there.

Kyle entered the kitchen, and I lowered the letter in my lap, almost under the dining table. He busied himself with his greens powder and the blender.

Kyle had a daughter from his first marriage, a daughter who lived in Chicago, so moving back there was right for him. Fortunately, I didn't have children to consider in my ongoing to-divorce-or-not-to-divorce years long inner debate.

"Why is there a mug in the sink again?" Kyle asked, my stomach tensing as it always did at his sharp tone. "No matter how many times I say it, it doesn't seem to make a bit of difference. You leave this unwashed crap here, and the sink starts to smell."

I wasn't going to acknowledge another rant yet again. Not this time.

When we'd first married, my eyes would water at the cutting tone in Kyle's voice, the dismissal in his eyes, the derision in his remarks whenever he expressed his disapproval.

The blender whirred loudly. I folded the elegant gray stationery back into the envelope and shoved it down into my bag.

Kyle poured his green shake into a glass and drank it. He rinsed out his blender pitcher. "Where are you going this early?"

I knew where. I just had to stand up and finally do it. No going back. If I didn't do this now, I would regret it for the rest of my life. All signs were leading me home to South Dakota.

Right now.

I braced myself. "I'm going to Meager."

Kyle stilled, water sloshing out of the pitcher in his grip from his sudden movement. "What?"

I met his bitter gaze. "I'm taking the last of my things from the storage unit, and I'm going back to South Dakota. Today."

He slammed the blender pitcher in the sink. "You're leaving? Again?"

"Here are the house keys." I tapped the keys on the table.

"You're being ridiculous. I thought we were trying here."

"We did try. It's not working. We need to be realistic and let it go, to move on."

He made a face. "Is this about the sex?"

I let out a heavy exhale. "No, Kyle, it's not about the sex."

"Right."

"Don't you see? Sex is not an isolated activity. The lack of sex between us is a symptom of how we don't work."

"There's been sex," he said, his voice raised.

I let out a controlled sigh. Kyle's form of sex was doing it and getting it done. There was no savoring, no delight, and that hadn't

13

changed really. Yes, the other night, he'd gotten aroused, and as he usually did, right after, he'd pulled out, tossed himself back onto the mattress, slung an arm over his eyes, let out a sigh, and drifted asleep.

He glared at me now, his jaw tight. I still found him attractive, his dark hair and eyes and lean physique still appealed to me. If I didn't know him, I'd want to go for him. But there was no palpable connection between us, and we disagreed on most subjects more often than we agreed. When we did actually have a sexual experience of any sort, he wouldn't even look at me. He certainly never said my name or kissed me with any kind of heat afterward. Maybe a peck but not an oh-babe-you-fucking-light-my-fire sort of post-sex kiss. Our sex, whenever we had it, lacked color; it lacked need.

Kyle had never been an affectionate person to begin with. In the beginning of our relationship he'd held my hand while we walked together, pulled me close on the sofa while we watched television, but after the first few years, that had withered away. I'd had to catch up with his long strides on the sidewalk.

Our chemistry, our way of being together, was not really together at all. Shit, I didn't even know how to describe it anymore, but I knew with certainty that it wasn't the kind of husband-wife relationship that I wanted.

I had chosen him though. What did that say about me?

"Kyle, sex is a form of communication, of intimacy, neither of which we share. Not for a long time now. It might not be important to you, but I need that." I sucked in a breath, my face heating. "It's taken me a long time to realize it, but I can't live without it. It makes you uncomfortable, and that's fine, but I can't go on like this. We've lived together as husband and wife for over ten years, and I've never felt lonelier in my life."

The silence between us was thick and prickly.

"Tania, I have a new job now, and it's just what I've been looking for all this time. We're moving back to Chicago. Have you heard back from the gallery yet?"

If I told Kyle that I'd gotten the job, he'd flip. He'd argue how it would be ludicrous for me to turn such an opportunity down, that we were meant to be back in Chicago, and that I should wipe the thought of starting my own business out of my head at long last. He would accuse me of running away.

"Kyle, moving back to Chicago is not a new start for me. With my mom sick now and Jill having the baby in a few months, I've decided to move back to Meager."

His brown eyes narrowed, and my insides chilled.

"I don't understand. You're being totally unfair. You want everything the way you want it, when you want it."

"That would be you, Kyle. You want the housekeeping done a certain way, your food cooked a certain way. To go out only when you want to. And when we do actually go out, you don't relax; you just want to eat and leave. You don't seem to have that issue with your friends or your basketball league buddies or your sister. You talk to them."

"What are you complaining about? We talk. And you know I can't live disorganized."

There it was again. Another insulting insinuation.

"I'm not disorganized. I don't like being disorganized either. You just don't like my kind of organized. I get to it when I get to it. And, after all these years together, you still can't trust that I have it all under control, that what I need to get done will get done. Your attitude is insulting."

His back stiffened. "Did you sleep with someone else when you were in South Dakota those two months?"

"What? No."

"You haven't been wearing your wedding ring."

"We're officially separated, Kyle, even though I came back and stayed."

"Officially?" His face tightened. "Right."

I stared at him. *Was it that zipped tone in his voice, the way his lips pressed together?*

"Did you have sex with someone else while I was in South Dakota?" I asked.

He planted his hands on the counter, his gaze averted, his shoulders tightening.

My pulse wrenched with a jolt. "Oh, shit. You did?"

His jaw twisted. "Yes."

My head jerked back, as if I'd been physically pushed. My mind blanked.

I'd let him talk me into trying again when I returned from South Dakota, my sentimentality getting the best of me. My never-give-up creed bolstering me on. I mean, I had to be sure. Triple sure. Ending a marriage was a big deal.

And he had found some other woman to fuck.

My blood jelled in my veins. I stared at Kyle, imagining him diving into someone else's body. Kyle groaning, kissing, pillow-talking, teasing, laughing, feeling satisfied, satiated, self-righteous.

Fuck my duck.

"It wasn't—it was just—"

I held up a hand. "Okay."

"That's all you have to say?"

The tide broke, and a flotilla of debris banked over me.

Unbelievable.

Unfair.

Fucking insane.

I rose from my chair. "The irony here is, I was the one complaining that there wasn't enough sex, any sex. And, at the first chance you got, you went out and got yourself laid?" I dragged out the words for a facetious effect for my own benefit, more than his.

"You left, Tania! You left me!" His face reddened.

"Yes, yes, I did." I curled my fingers into fists to steady the trembling. "So, tell me. Did you like it? Did it feel good? Was your dick happy?"

He only stared at me, his arms folded across his chest.

A wave of dizziness overtook me as I grabbed my bag and my car keys. "I have to get out of here."

"Sure! What the hell? That's what you do best, taking off."

"Holy shit, Kyle! Why didn't you tell me?" I charged toward him. "I came back here and stayed, and you touched me. You should've told me." I stepped back against the table. "Did you use protection with her at least?"

"Yes," he said through gritted teeth.

"Good job. Very organized of you."

I shoved myself out the screen door, and it slammed behind me as I charged toward my car, gulping in air against the rising tide of nausea.

"I want to live, not just exist. Not just shuffle along," I had said to him in a well-rehearsed, polite speech before I'd left for Meager the last time. I'd said it to give him something to think about.

He'd done more than think on it. He'd taken action, a step that said, *I'm alive! This is what I want!* That was for sure. He'd broken out, made a move. He had done it.

I was pathetic.

Fortunately, we lived in the no-fault divorce state of Wisconsin. In typical fashion, I'd jumped the gun and spoken to a lawyer about how to proceed. My enthusiasm always got the best of me—one of the things about me that, after a while, had annoyed Kyle—because I'd often retrace my steps and pull back. Now, I'd call that lawyer and put the process into fifth gear.

"Tania!" Kyle's voice rose from inside the house.

I climbed into the Yukon, slammed my door, and gunned my engine.

No, the waiting was finally over.

I swung out onto the road, but by the time I hit I-94 West, the anger had turned to a flood of hurt and regret and tears.

THREE

TANIA

"THANK YOU FOR THE DRINK, but I can't accept it."

"Why not, honey?" The older man peered at me from under his ratty baseball cap advertising a local car dealership. I'd lay down money that his seat at the cafe counter was his second home.

I had stopped for a quick bite at a small restaurant about half an hour outside of Sioux Falls, eager to get back on the road toward Meager.

"I do appreciate it, but I've got a lot of driving ahead of me, and I'm staying away from booze."

"Ah, naw, you can't leave."

A bony hand clamped around my arm, and my back stiffened.

"You should stay, pretty lady."

"I'm not staying. Now, get your goddamn hand off me."

He only laughed. "You gots attitude, huh?"

I picked up his bottle of beer. "Maybe you'd like this Bud all over your crotch to cool you down?"

"Let go of the lady," came a stern deep voice from behind me.

The older man's lax gaze suddenly tightened, training on someone over my shoulder, someone much taller than me. He released his hold on me, and I jerked my arm away.

A warm hand landed on my lower back. My body flinched at the contact, and I swiveled.

Pale blue eyes leveled at me, and a sculpted full mouth pressed into a firm line with wavy blond hair passing his angular jawline and gold scruff delineating the abrupt lines of a familiar face.

"Butler?"

"We'll leave you to your beer," Butler muttered to the man, his hand wrapping around my elbow.

"Don't git your hopes up," sneered the old man.

"She was waiting for me, buddy. No contest here." Butler led me to a table at the other end of the cafe.

"Thanks for the save. You didn't have to."

"I didn't have to, but I didn't think it would be wise to have him suffer at your hands." The edges of his lips tipped up, and he pulled out a chair, slanting his head.

Butler's aimed that cocky you-know-it's-true-sure-as-hell-can't-fool-me smirk of his. But that smirk was a more relaxed version from the acidic ones I remembered him constantly shooting my way years ago. I let out a small laugh and settled into the chair he'd gestured at, hanging my messenger bag around the back.

"Oh, so he was the victim?" I asked. "That's who you were saving?"

His smirk broke into a dazzling grin, and I pressed back into my chair, absorbing its potency like a shot of espresso.

"What are you drinking, Tania?"

"Nothing, thanks. I've got to get back on the road."

"You heading home?"

"Yes, finally on my way."

"You had mentioned it the last time I saw you and *Maddie* in Nebraska."

"Right. Maddie." I rolled my eyes, letting out a laugh.

Grace's little disguise when we had ended up at the Flames of Hell clubhouse several months ago, of course, hadn't fooled Butler, who happened to be there, but he'd kept our secret.

"I went to Racine to finish some business a couple of months ago and to bring back a few things that I had in storage," I said. "You?"

"Me what?"

"What are you up to? How did you end up here, ten miles outside of Sioux Falls? You look tired."

He rubbed a hand across his scruffy jaw. "I've been on the road for a few days now. Taking the scenic route."

"Oh, really? From where?"

"Ohio."

"Holy shit. On your bike?"

He let out a rough laugh. "Yeah, Tania. Of course."

"Where are you headed? Sorry, I probably shouldn't be asking, right?"

"Going to Meager, too."

"Really?"

"Really." His sky-blue eyes settled on me, and a giddy sensation fluttered through me.

"Have you eaten, or did you just get here?" I asked, my hands smoothing over the paper tablecloth. "I ate. I was just about to pay my bill actually."

"I just ordered. Stick around."

"Thanks again for before, with that guy."

"Sure. Maybe we should stick together until we hit Meager, just in case you get yourself into more situations you need rescuing from."

"Shut up."

"Remember what happened last time you were on the road?"

"Oh, I remember all right." *Kidnapped, almost sexually assaulted, found my niece, who was being held hostage…*"Did you ever find Creeper, by the way?"

"There's something you shouldn't ask me about."

The waitress brought over a coffee, plonking the steaming white mug on the table by Butler. He rubbed a hand up and down his arm, stretching his neck to the left and then the right.

"You want a couple of Tylenol to go with that?" I asked.

"You got a supply handy?"

"Always prepared." I unfastened my bag and fished a hand inside for the bottle. "I think you could use two."

"That good?" He chuckled.

I unsnapped the lid of the medicine bottle and put two caplets in his open hand. He popped them in his mouth, chasing them with a gulp of water.

"Thanks."

"Sure."

"How's Jill doing?" he asked. "Last time I talked to Boner, he filled me in on her being a surrogate for Grace."

"Jill and the baby are doing really well. She's almost four months along now. Grace is flying."

"Taking Jill in was really generous of you."

"She seemed like a good person to me. She was in a really tough bind, and she is the mother of my brother's daughter. The best part is, my mom actually likes Jill, and they get along great, which is huge now that they're living together and looking out for each other." I toyed with the fork before me on the table. "Yeah, it's all good."

"How about you?" he asked.

"Hmm?"

"You. How are you doing?"

"Me?" My eyes met his. Blue quartz. Clear, inquiring, dazzling. My fingers pressed down on the thin handle of the fork. "I'm good."

"So, why do you look like you could use a drink?" he asked.

I averted my gaze. "I could use some sugar actually." I flagged down the waitress. "Could I have one of those brownies with a scoop of vanilla ice cream?"

"Sure thing, hon," said the waitress before darting off.

"Thanks."

"Decisive and very determined." He sipped on his coffee. "That can only mean one thing."

"Says the expert on womankind."

Butler chuckled. "Yeah, that's me." He leveled his bright blue eyes on me again, eyes that made it hard for me to look away. "Come on, let's hear it. Maybe I can offer you some advice from my side of the high stone wall."

"I don't need advice."

"How about a new perspective?"

A new perspective?

Butler was a neutral bystander. He didn't really know me; he certainly didn't know Kyle. And I knew that Butler, the Lord of Shameless wouldn't judge me. He would be respectful of my confessions. I hadn't been able to discuss this with anyone. I hadn't even really wanted to discuss it with Grace in much depth, which surprised me.

An objective opinion, and from a man, might be a relief.

"Okay. I'm getting a divorce, and I went back to Racine to pick up the last of my stuff and check in with my lawyer, but I ended up staying longer than I'd expected." I bit down on the side of my lip and took in a small breath. "We made this last-ditch effort to try again, but it didn't work for me."

"I'm sorry."

"Don't be sorry. It's a good thing."

"Did he cheat on you?"

"No. Not really."

"What does that mean?"

"He slept with someone else after I'd left him, when my mom was in the hospital and I ended up staying in Meager for a couple of months with her and Jill. Kyle and I were officially separated, so...you know." I shrugged.

"Still sucks."

"Still sucks."

"Okay. Did he hit you?" he asked.

"No, it's not like that. We simply don't mesh, don't get along. We haven't for a long time, but he's not willing to admit it. We are the true definition of "irreconcilable differences." He's more than happy to keep rolling along. But it's pretending, in my opinion. I can't pretend anymore."

"That's good."

I let out a dry laugh. "Oh, yeah? Which part?"

"You not willing to pretend. There comes a time when you've got to stop and get some real air in your lungs."

My shoulders relaxed. "I pretended for a long while there. You figure, we're human, and things ebb and flow. But he and I have deeper issues, and he's just not willing to go there."

"To the deep?" he asked, his eyes pinned on me.

Butler was getting this. He was open to this conversation.

I leaned over the table. "Look, I'm not saying I need to be philosophical and intimate every second of every day, but it was enough for him to just be under the same roof. To exchange basic information. To get along. To keep house. Well, to keep house his way. After almost ten years, whatever spark had been there was no longer there."

A large fudge square with a mound of creamy vanilla ice cream slid before me on the table. "There you go."

A golden omelet with bacon and whole-wheat toast appeared in front of Butler. "Enjoy."

The waitress disappeared once more.

"Ah, breakfast for dinner? I like that, too," I said.

"One of my faves." He grinned as he moved his dish closer. "So, you've been putting in the effort with..."

"Kyle." I drove my fork into the large brownie.

"Right."

"I know it takes two to make it work, but he's content in his bubble. I'm not. Plus, I don't fit in that bubble."

Butler dragged his fork through his omelet and glanced up at me. "I don't suspect you'd fit into any kind of bubble, Tania. Or am I wrong?" He chewed his food as he watched me, a slow smile lighting his face.

Warmth swept through me at the sight, and I ran my fork into the ice cream. "Not wrong. Not wrong at all. One thing I realized was, I'd much rather be alone and lonely than be *with* someone *and* lonely."

He glanced down, wiping at his mouth with a napkin. "That's a heartbreaking place."

Something about the darker tone in his voice made me pause. That was certainly the voice of experience.

"I'm sorry. I didn't mean to get heavy and—"

"You're being real. Best way to be." He bit into a piece of buttery toast. "Lonely sucks."

"Maybe I expected too much out of the marriage." I swallowed down the gob of brownie and ice cream in my mouth.

"No, I don't think so. Marriage isn't supposed to be lonely and heartbreaking. It's supposed to make you a better, happier you."

I blinked up at him, my heart in my throat. "Exactly. In the best of all possible worlds, yes. You were married once. Grace told me about your wife. I'm sorry."

Butler's wife had died in a terrible bike accident five years ago, an accident he blamed himself for. A wife, Grace had mentioned, he'd never really gotten over.

He shifted in his chair. "Caitlyn and I had it good—while it lasted, that is."

"You were fortunate."

He wiped his fingers on a napkin and crumpled it into a ball. "I was."

"You never found anyone else? I mean, I'm sure you've been with plenty of women since, but—"

He pressed his lips together for a moment. "Not like that."

"Oh. Must get lonely."

"I do just fine."

I twisted in my seat. *I'm sure you do.*

Butler was, in a word, gorgeous. He had to be at least 6'3", and he obviously put in the time to work out. His chest and arms were defined, his torso firm. His blond hair streaked with gold was maybe a shade or two darker than what it used to be, but it was a showstopper along with those brilliant blue eyes. And I liked the lines around those eyes; with the years had come experience that had made its stamp. He still had that rugged rough and tumble exterior, but now, he was...intriguing. The kind of intriguing that was making my toes curl and my pulse jump at this very moment.

Butler's features creased under my scrutiny. "How's that brownie?"

I sucked fudge sauce from my fork. "Hitting the spot. Would you like to try it?"

"No, I'm good."

An awkward silence stretched between us, and the chocolate flavor dulled in my mouth. The idea of Butler and what he must be like in bed was a much more exciting subject to dwell on than my marriage or the flipping fudge brownie.

Much more exciting.

His playfulness was still there along with the cockiness in the flick of those amazing eyes and that volatile flare in the press of his jaw. But there seemed to be a settled core to it all now, not only that I-don't-give-two-fucks recklessness that he'd brandished twenty years ago when I had my initial taste of him.

Yes, accent on taste, not the whole enchilada. My choice.

Stupid girl.

Back then, I'd been young, barely experienced, and full of my own steam.

Hmm. Sort of like Butler at the time.

"What are you thinking about?" His deep voice interrupted my drifting.

"Huh?" I gripped my fork.

"You're scowling." His lips curved up as he speared the last of his omelet with his fork. "I remember that scowl real well."

I met his gaze, and my stomach fluttered. We both knew what he was referring to.

Over twenty years ago, we'd been different people, both of us raw, aggressive, full of ourselves, and full of shit. Both of us lashing out and using each other to do it.

Both of us.

FOUR

TANIA

PAST

THE SHORT CEREMONY HAD FINISHED, and Dig and Grace had been officially declared husband and wife to the roar of bike engines and cheers and whistles on the One-Eyed Jacks' property.

The loud party was in full swing, and I had drifted off from the raucous crowd. My spiked heel had ripped the hem of my dress, and I'd retreated into the repair shed to see to the damage. A good excuse to get away.

"Nice legs."

My head jerked at the sound. There was no mistaking that taunting tone, that sexy I-don't-give-a-shit ripple to Butler's deep voice. My back went rigid as my fingers let go of the hem of my dress, the silky wine-colored fabric sliding down my bare legs as I straightened.

Butler's icy-blue eyes were trained on me through a cloud of smoke, his long and thick pale golden hair its usual mess around his head, like he'd just woken up after a night of debauchery. Knowing him, he probably had and was up for more.

"What are you doing out here?" His gravelly, husky voice tightened my insides into a knot.

"Huh?" was all I could manage. Every cell in my body screamed, *Get the hell out of here!* But I didn't want to appear to be a scaredy-cat, not to him.

"Nice scowl. You're the maid of honor, Tania. Shouldn't you be out there, all smiles, making a toast or saying something…spectacular?"

I let out a small laugh, my shoulders dropping. "I don't think anyone would notice at this point, do you?"

Dig and Grace's wedding had been going on for over three hours, and it was definitely nothing like the country-club wedding I had attended with my mother, sister, and brother the week before over in Rapid City.

"What are you doing out here on your own?" I asked. "I thought you were a part of the inner circle or whatever it's called."

He exhaled another stream of smoke, his head tilting back, his hand falling at his side, those piercing eyes following my every jittery move. "Not so much anymore. As if you didn't know."

Oh, I knew all right. He'd gotten into trouble with Dig for coming on to Grace a couple of weeks ago, and he had gotten sent away up north to another chapter of the club.

"How's North Dakota?" I asked.

"It sucks."

"Oh. Sorry."

"You don't have to be. It's my fault anyhow."

"Yes, it was."

His eyes narrowed at me. A soft laugh rolled from his sturdy throat.

"They let you come back for this?" I asked.

"Mandatory."

"Ah, a show of good faith."

"Something like that."

"But you're hiding out in here to avoid everybody?"

"I'm not hiding. I don't hide." He exhaled a long, thick plume of smoke. "Just lying low."

"Right."

"And what are you doing in here? Too many bikers out there for you? You never hung out with us too much to begin with."

"The crowd is a little overwhelming."

He stared at me as he drew on his cig again. "Why is that?" He shifted his weight, his intent gaze bearing down on me with even more weight. The sudden silence between us pressed in on my chest. "We too low-class for you?"

"What?"

"Too rough?" He pushed back from the wall, dropping his cigarette butt to the floor. "Too dirty?" He mashed the cigarette into the cement floor with the heel of his boot and stalked toward me.

My breath hitched. "Give me a break, Butler."

He stopped before me, a hint of beer and cheap men's cologne hovering between us. That trademark lazy smile of his that made girls titter for miles swept his face. "Do I overwhelm you? No, seriously, Tania, tell me."

"You are so full of shit. Are you flirting with me now?"

He chuckled, his index finger flicking the end of my nose. "You're nervous. Have you been nursing a little crush on me all this time, and I've failed to notice?" His warm fingertip crossed down the center of my lips to my chin.

"A crush? On you?" I swatted his finger away. "Hell no."

"Oh, I'm such a freak, right?"

"Yeah, you kind of are, Blondie."

He grinned, his white teeth adding a dash of danger to his allure. "I'm such an asshole."

"A swaggering asshole, to be exact."

He stood two inches from my face. "A real pain in your ass then."

"Yep."

"That's a mighty beautiful ass, Tania." His fingers skimmed over the smooth fabric hugging my rear.

I jerked back, a cold shiver racing over my skin.

He gripped my hip with his other hand, pulling me closer to his body, right up against his erection. My insides went haywire at the shocking contact, at his presumption.

"No panties today?" he whispered roughly.

I only shook my head.

He lowered his head to mine. "You came here, to the club, to a party full of bikers from at least four different states, and you didn't wear any panties?"

I smacked his hand away. "It's the dress, Butler!"

His hand went to my ass again. "I'm talkin' about the body underneath the dress, Tania."

I rolled my eyes, avoiding the fact that he was admiring my body. "With this dress, you can't wear underwear." I squirmed in his hold. "It shows all the lines and the...if you..."

His hand slowly stroked the curve of my rear. Up. Down. My breath snagged. Heat radiated over my backside, seeping through my middle, riddling me with a series of explosions, like a minefield.

"Get your hands off me," I whispered.

He gripped my ass cheek, kneading it. "Ask nice." His voice was husky, that growliness of it more acute. Rough, playful, daring.

I raised my chin. "Why should I? You should know better."

"I don't know anything at all anymore."

Something in his words, in the raw edge in his tone, pulled me into him. The sculpted angles of his face and his square jaw were downturned. His usually gleaming eyes were now lackluster. Was this sadness, wistfulness?

I touched his arm. "Butler—"

He released me, snapping back from me on a slight shove. His laser shield had gone back up.

Asshole.

"What's the matter? They not letting you into the playground anymore?" I asked, a sneer shading my voice. "Not the tough guy you thought you were?"

He glared at me. "Fuck you."

"No, fuck you, Blondie."

He leaned into me, the edges of his lips curled. "You jealous your best friend found the man of her dreams and got hitched?"

"I'm happy that she's happy!"

His alcohol-tinged breath fanned my face. "Yeah, right."

"I am. He might not be what I wanted for her, but look at them—"

We both turned our attention toward Dig and Grace in the distance through the open main door of the shed. Dig was on one knee, his hands stroking Grace's thigh, as he tugged on her black garter belt with his teeth. Grace laughed, a hand on his shoulder, and the crowd whooped.

"If that's not happy, I don't know what is." I stared at Butler once more. "You wouldn't know what that was if it hit you in the head, would you?"

"Would you?" he shot back, his eyes fierce.

Would I?

I wasn't so sure actually. Blondie had a point. Truth had been spoken, blurted out into the hot afternoon air, and it stung like the jab of a needle, an inoculation a kid didn't want to have. The blinding light of those words scorched us both as we stood there, searching each other's eyes, waiting for the answer to a question that we both knew was utterly complicated and would not be given.

The door at the other end of the shed shoved open, metal scraped, and deep laughter gave way to a loud female voice. "Give me that cock now!"

The moment was gone.

Butler gripped my arms and pulled me back into his chest, moving us further into the shed, out of view, behind a towering tool chest.

Enthusiastic grunts and the heavy breathing of the busy couple echoed through the industrial space.

"I know what *that* is. Do you?" Butler whispered in my ear.

I elbowed him in the middle, and he let out a tight chuckle. I stiffened in his grip and pushed away.

He held me fast. "Shh. Trust me, Tania. You don't want us to be caught listening and watching those two. Ah, geez, look at her go."

My mouth gaped open. Pushing up her stretchy miniskirt, the woman had the guy on the floor and had scrambled on top of him. She was doing what I believed was called a reverse cowgirl. She held herself up on her arms as she pumped her pelvis up and down, taking him in.

Did she have gymnastics training in order to do that?

I let out an exhale. "Fuck."

"Yeah." His warm breath tickled over my neck as his arms tightened around me, and my hand squeezed his forearm.

An illicit thrill shot through me as we watched the live porn show together. I liked Butler's firm grip on me. I liked the insistent press of his rough erection through the thin silk of my dress up against my rear. I liked his presumption. I liked the smell of ash and tequila wafting from his breath, the incrementally slow rock of his pelvis against me, offering a crude sort of pleasure in friction, his hand pressing into my middle, sliding lower and lower where that ache bloomed.

Oh, what the hell?

I sank against him. A sound erupted in his chest as his one hand slid around my right thigh. My head fell back on his shoulder. I'd always been attracted to Butler. Who wasn't? Tall, muscular, blond, and blue-eyed, a sparkle of audacity and vulgar ever present in the lick of his gaze. Every girl's wet dream.

"What the hell do you think you're doing?" I breathed, the side of my face pressed against his.

"Whatever the hell I want, which is what you want." His lips sucked on the skin of my neck.

I turned and gave him my mouth, my fingers sliding through his thick hair. *Oh, that hair.* I'd always wondered what it would feel like. I tugged on it, its softness sliding through my fingers like thick silk, its almost fruity scent gave way to a forest fresh green, an edge of lemon. Energizing, elusive. Enticing.

I wanted more.

We kissed like enemies clanging swords on a battlefield littered with our dead. We were the only survivors locked in the final battle, both of us knowing there would be no victors.

He fisted my hair in his one hand, tugging my head back, and I let out a cry. His other hand gripped my jaw, tilted my face up. Strong, firm hands. Hands that I was sure had killed and tortured. Hands that knew how to use a knife, a gun. Hands that made a mass of chrome and steel zoom across the highway at a hundred miles per hour.

Hands that could hurt me now.

And it only turned me on more.

His fingers drifted down and circled my throat, pressing there. "After this, you gonna go crying to your friend, the bride, and bitch about how I fucked you and left you?"

"No," I breathed. "And you? You going to brag to your brothers about what an easy lay I was?"

One of his dark blond eyebrows slanted, his thumb grazing my lower lip. "No."

My tongue swiped at his thumb, and he hissed in air, his eyes glittering.

The biker fucking the Cowgirl just beyond us muttered a mile a minute about how hard his cock was. Loud moans and the sounds of slapping flesh filled the suddenly stifling space.

My fingers curled into Butler's black T-shirt. "This is for me. Maybe I want to see what all the fuss over you is about. And maybe I want something just for me. I'll be out of here in a few weeks anyway. Grace doesn't even know I'm leaving yet. What's your excuse?"

"I don't need an excuse." He turned me in his arms, smashing my back against his broad chest.

His hand found a breast and kneaded it. My insides twanged like overly tight guitar strings. I wanted him to tune me, pull music from me.

"This about getting back at Grace?" I asked, my voice hoarse.

"Maybe yes, and maybe no."

"At least you're being honest."

He laughed.

"Shh. Those two will hear us."

He pulled my head back, his mouth crashing down on mine. "Do you care?"

"Shut up, and let's do this already."

His hands yanked my dress up to my hips, and he moved us backward before pushing me onto a worn vinyl sofa against the wall. I kicked over a pile of magazines, and they tumbled to the floor in a messy heap.

"Get over here," he ordered.

My pulse leaped at his command, and I wiped my hair out of my face. I shifted into practical; that always steadied me. "Do you have a rubber?"

"Always prepared." He unzipped his leather pants and released a thick hard cock.

"Holy shit. Will it fit?" tumbled from my mouth.

He untucked a foil packet from his vest. "Did I just make a good impression?" He tore the small square packet with his teeth, and my heart banged in my chest at the *rip*. "I'll make it fit."

"You do that, but be gentle, okay? At first. Then...you know..."

He smirked as he fit himself with the rubber, stroking his length. "You really gonna tell me what I'm gonna do with my own dick?"

I bit my lip. "Can you do gentle, Butler? At least in the beginning?"

His eyes snapped up at mine. "Yeah, I can do gentle. And I'll let you know when my gentle is over. How's that?"

I made a face. "That's mighty kind of you."

He pushed me back against the ratty cracked cushions and ran his fingers between my legs. My back arched at the contact. He tugged the halter top of my dress down until my breasts spilled out.

33

He sucked on one breast then the other, his teeth scraping at my nipples, his hard erection slapping against my middle. My hands dug into his hair once more. It was really a beautiful blond. Silky, soft ribbons of silver, gold, and pale honey painted by the sun. Touching it could become an addiction, for sure.

"She broke your heart, didn't she?" I asked.

"Who?" came his muffled voice against my skin.

"Grace."

"Jesus. We gonna have a conversation now?"

My shoulders tensed, and my face heated all over again.

"Spread your legs more. Lift 'em up."

I complied as he nibbled on the underside of a breast.

"I don't have a heart to break anyway," he mumbled.

"That's bullshit."

"That's me. Take it—" He pushed inside me.

I gasped, tilting my hips up to meet him, and he thrust again, letting out a grunt.

His eyes met mine. "Or leave it."

"I'll definitely take it. Ah, shit."

He rocked against me and nudged deeper. "Where's a heart going to get me anyway? So, one of you can stomp on it?" He slowly thrust again, as promised. "So, one of you can turn on me and leave me hanging?" He dragged himself out and drove his hips in one motion.

My grip on him tightened. A painful invasion. A build of tight pleasure.

"Ah, fuck. I can't do gentle now," he said on a hiss. "Shit."

"Yeah. Go faster. Faster."

My hands slid over his tight carved-in-stone ass as he pumped into me. He raised himself up, extending his arms on either side of my torso.

"What do you want out of this?" he grunted.

"An orgasm would be good—oh, damn!" I adjusted myself on the cramped sofa.

He ground against my pelvis, his angle perfectly stroking my clit. "Guaranteed. What else?" His breath came fast and hard through his mouth.

I want something just for me, without my own brain telling me, Don't do that, Tania. That's not good for you, Tania. You'll regret it later, Tania.

I did want an orgasm. I wasn't joking. I never came while having sex. I was *difficult*, as one college boyfriend had labeled me, the one who'd actually noticed. Maybe here, now with Butler, it would happen. He was very sexy, I was pretty turned on, and he seemed to know how to make it happen. We were being spontaneous, and I needed to be spontaneous. This could work. I could get over that bump in my sexual highway, couldn't I?

Butler worked it above me, his head turned to the side, his neck rigid with the effort.

I pressed my lips together, trying to keep my pelvis relaxed under his assault, to go with it, to let go. I jammed my eyes closed.

"I knew it. You're a self-control freak."

My eyes snapped open and met his glaring ones. "Shut up!"

"You ever even come before?"

"Of course I have!"

"How?"

"What do you care?"

"Tell me."

"When I touch myself."

"Not during sex?"

I gritted my teeth, and he ground himself over me again, hitting my clit with his pelvis, filling me to the hilt.

"Oh my God!"

"Yeah. You're gonna come on my godly cock if it's the last thing I do in this town."

My lungs tightened, as if they would explode at any second. He pressed my legs higher against my chest and thrust deeper inside me. My flesh burned in his tight grip as the new angle ignited intense destruction in all my secret places. Places I hadn't known I had.

"You feeling it?" he grunted, his brow shimmering with sweat.

God, yes, I feel it.

That simmer boiled in my veins. An unfamiliar molten heat exploded between my legs, rising through me, lifting me.

Butler had his eyes closed. He was concentrating on getting the job done. I was trapped, at his mercy. I turned my head. Half-built bikes and huge tool chests and parts were scattered through the cavernous space, silently witnessing our debauchery.

Here I was, in a back room of the repair shop of the One-Eyed Jacks, getting banged, like one of their party sluts, in the most expensive dress I had ever bought for myself in honor of my best friend's wedding. Here I was, fucking the guy she'd had a kind of crush on, the guy who had had a thing for her and gotten punished because of it.

His breathing grew choppier, and his jaw stiffened as he thrust inside me over and over again. The impossible fullness reached up to my throat.

Butler worked his cock inside me like a pro. He worked it.

He worked me.

"Come on my face! Yeah, that's it! Oh, yeah!" Cowgirl's voice rang out.

My skin heated, and my chest constricted.

Wrong, all wrong.

My head spun. Too much cheap wine.

Too much. Too fucking much.

My brain took over, dousing ice-cold water on every inflamed tip of sensation coursing through me. My hips went rigid.

"Wait," I said through gritted teeth.

"Wh-what?"

"Could you—"

"What? You don't like it?"

I pushed against him, my eyes flaring.

"Quit moving. Fuck. Hang on—" He propped himself up over me at an angle now, firmly pinning my one leg back, and thrust even faster. "Oh, yeah, almost there—"

The slick sounds of our flesh made me cringe, his short breaths getting more intense. He was an animal in heat, moving to his own instinctual rhythm, and I was the prey.

My body tensed, every muscle stiff. I wanted this to be done. This…this wasn't enjoyable. This was—

"Yes, baby! Yes!" shouted Cowgirl.

Butler grunted above me, his grip on my leg burning, painful.

A deluge of crude.

My lungs fought for air. "No, really, Butler. Stop! Stop, goddamn it!"

He stopped moving, his ragged breathing clipped. "What the fuck?"

"Just get off me!" I pushed against him.

He grunted loudly as he jacked up, pulling his slick cock out of me. Dropping back against the sofa, he wiped at his damp face with his arm. His shiny, rubber-encased hard dick stood at shocked attention as my insides stuttered at the sudden hollowness.

"What the hell? What's wrong with you?"

"Sorry. This is just—I can't—"

The snap of the wet condom being pulled off sliced through the air. He lifted his pelvis and jerked his leathers back up over his bare body. "Shit. Just my luck. Serves me right. Cannot fucking believe…"

"I'm sorry. I—"

"You're a fucking piece of work. Piece of ice. As if I didn't know. Dig told me you were a ballbuster. Should've listened."

"What? What's that supposed to mean?"

"You're a hard-ass bitch. That's what that means! Uptight as fuck."

"Fuck you!"

"You're obviously not capable of that, so try again."

I pressed myself into the corner of the sofa. "I'm sure you'll find someone else to fuck out there. Big deal."

"Yeah, that's right. I will. Someone who can handle it." He slid his hand up and down the bulge in his pants, adjusting himself. "You can't start something and then just say no, like some innocent virgin. Didn't your mama ever teach you that fact of life?"

"I hate you, Butler."

"Feeling's mutual, little girl."

"I'm not a little girl!"

"I've had high schoolers begging me to fuck them, honey. But you're too damn uptight to take it on. Ice Queen."

I wanted to escape, run away, hide in the bowels of the earth.

I snapped the fabric of my dress in place, smoothing it over my shaking body. "I hope you enjoy your exile up north."

"I'm a One-Eyed Jack," he bit out. "It's what we do best—survival, making do, carrying on."

"Well then, Mr. Jack, I hope you grow up while you're at it."

"You're never getting this chance again, so you know."

"Woe is me! You deserve what you got, you know that?"

"Shut the fuck up!" He lunged toward me, his finger jabbing the air, his jaw sharp. "You don't know nothing about it! Nothing about me!"

"Oh, wait! You mean there's a real human being underneath that blond mop and leather jacket?"

"You deserve a smack for that, but I'm gonna be a gentleman here."

"A gentleman uses his mind, douchebag. You, however, think with your dick; that's what you do. Doesn't matter who or what gets in your way."

"We're done here." He rolled his shoulders. "Happy trails, Ice Queen. I hope I never lay eyes on you again."

His boots stomped out of the shed, the metal door swinging wide open and screeching on its hinges. I sank back down on the sofa, trembling. The cheering, the laughs, and the music in the distance grew louder, bolder, and only made me feel smaller.

FIVE

BUTLER

TANIA TRACED CIRCLES WITH HER FORK in the puddle of chocolate sauce in her dish.

She was remembering; I knew she was. I let out a heavy breath. So was I.

I'd pretty much made myself forget about our fuck that had never happened. I'd slung it on the pile of my greatest hits of all time. Grace and Dig's wedding was the last time Tania and I had seen each other—until I'd bumped into her and Grace in Nebraska three months ago.

And here we were now, having a swell time together.

Her shiny, long hair was a rich almost black color against her pale skin, and her dark eyes were huge and really expressive, almost startling. You could pick up a million different things she was trying to hide with every nuance and flick of those exotic eyes, and I was sure she didn't miss much as those eyes swept over you, leaving a trail of steam behind. Tania was a little taller than average, slim, but that curvy ass I'd admired once upon a time filled out those tight dark jeans she was wearing over a nice long set of legs. A thin gold chain with a green quartz crystal on it slid over her pronounced collarbone. She was a heady mix of high-class elegance and down-to-earth casual.

Chairs scraped against the pockmarked tiled floor of the small restaurant. Two elderly men settled in at the table next to ours, removing their jackets. I went back to my toast, and Tania continued to swirl her fork in her ice cream.

"I don't know what I'm gonna do, Floyd, but I've got to do something. The taxes on that property are going to come in now and bite me in the ass. Sadie is gonna have my neck for not dealing with this crap sooner. There's so much junk in that house. I swear to God, I'd rather just torch the whole damn thing and be done with it."

"Have a garage sale or something," said Floyd, scanning the menu.

"Ah, that takes a lot of work. I don't know shit about that."

"Excuse me. I couldn't help but overhear that you might have old things you'd like to sell?" Tania asked.

My head snapped up. Those spellbinding eyes of hers were riveted on the two men at the next table. The guy and his pal Floyd only frowned at her.

"My name is Tania."

"Dave," the man mumbled, his eyes wide. Yep, spellbound.

"Dave, I collect old used things, curiosities, heirlooms, furniture. Here's my card." She passed him a large-sized business card, and he took it. "I'm always looking for a variety of vintage items. If you turn the card over, you'll see a list of what I'm on the lookout for."

"Uh-huh."

"I'd love to see what you have. If I like anything, I could relieve you of it for a fair price. In cash. Is it your property?" Tania said, her tone light, easygoing.

"It's my great uncle's. I inherited his mess last year and still haven't done anything about it. I really want to clear the land and sell it."

"If you'd like, maybe I could help you get rid of a few things. Get the ball rolling. What do you think?" Tania's face was all lit up. Sincerity, pleasure.

Fuck, it was blinding.

Dave and Floyd exchanged glances.

She pointed at me. "This is one of my best clients—Rhett Childs, the country rock singer. He's the other half of that hot new duo, Scarlett and Rhett. Huge breakaway album this year."

What the fuck? Where does she come up with this shit?

She sent me a special twitch of that full mouth of hers. She was enjoying this.

Luckily, I wasn't wearing club colors, just a battered plain black leather jacket, new leather boots and pants, and my expensive sunglasses.

I remained motionless under the men's scrutiny, my leg sliding up against Tania's under the table. My gut tightened at the contact.

She blushed, her jaw stiffening under the polished smile she aimed at me.

Don't say a word, Blondie. Please, please, please, I could hear her pleading with me.

This could be fun.

Dave sized me up, and I remained silent. I only offered him a raised chin and a subtle lift of my eyebrows.

Dave grinned at Tania. "Oh, yeah? Pleased to meet you."

Score.

"I'm from around Rapid, originally. So is Rhett. He just bought a new house in Nashville," Tania rambled on. "I'm helping him fill it with interesting one-of-a-kind goodies."

Tania, Tania, Tania.

"I have a really good feeling about this, I have to say." Tania doused Dave with another sexy shower of positivity.

"That so?" Floyd pushed his cap higher on his head.

Time to catch her pass.

"That's right," I drawled, aiming a tight smile at Dave. "Tania's all about the feeling. She has amazing instincts. I've learned the hard way never to doubt her. She hasn't steered me wrong yet. I love scouting around with her on my free time between gigs."

I pressed my leg against hers. She didn't budge or squirm. She glanced at me. A quick flashback of our hot little past made a reappearance in my blood, and my leg brushed against hers again.

She aimed a dazzling grin at me, laying a hand on my arm. "Well, you've got great taste, too, Rhett."

I let out a laugh. "Thanks, babe."

"It's his cash anyway. He's the boss!" She removed her hand from my arm, leaving behind a ripple of heat.

Dave nodded, his gaze hopping from me to Tania and back again. "Yeah, all right then."

"Great. After you eat, we'll follow you over there?" Tania asked, this time flashing a sincere, warm smile.

"Sure."

Dave and Floyd settled back in their chairs and returned to their own conversation.

The lift in Tania's shoulders was unmistakable. Her dark eyes shone, but she kept her cool.

"You suddenly look a hell of a lot happier, or am I wrong?" I whispered.

She pushed the brownie dish to the side. "This is my excited face."

"Oh, yeah?"

"I hope I find something good. I could really use the boost. I'm thinking of opening up a store in Meager, and I need inventory."

"Are you? That's a commitment."

"It is." She met my gaze. "A good one. I have a few contacts who let me know if they hear of anyone selling off anything interesting. But most of the goodness happens when I'm out freestyling, looking on my own. Talking to people, listening. Like now."

"That's what you were doing in Nebraska with Grace, and then you two stumbled on Creeper and the kid he'd kidnapped, right?"

"The kid who turned out to be my niece, Becca. No, that time, I had gotten a lead from a friend of a friend. That pick was planned."

"Huh. Now, you just chatted up this stranger, and you're going to go to his out-in-the-middle-of-nowhere property with him?"

"Well, yes."

"Tania!"

"That's how this works a lot of the time. Either I get leads from people I know, or I find them myself. You've got to be willing to get in there and get dirty."

Tania getting dirty?

She wore fancy tight jeans and lace-up combat boots, the designer kind. Her wide-necked blouse was made of this flowy midnight-blue fabric that draped over her small tits and the curve of her waist and hips. It was casual; it was sophisticated. It was sexy as fuck.

"You don't mind doing that?" I asked, my voice coming out huskier than expected.

"No, it's fun."

"Fun?"

Her dark eyes lit on fire. "It might look like a heap of trash to you, but to me, it's a mountain of golden possibilities."

"Cash potential, you mean?"

"No." She leaned over the table, and a wave of her perfume hit me—an edge of spice rounded out with subtle sweet.

I steadied my elbows on the table.

"I mean, the possibility of finding something unusual," she continued. "Something interesting, out of the ordinary. A treasure from a bygone age. It may be rusted or broken, but it gives me a buzz."

"A buzz?"

"Yes, an actual buzz in my gut, my chest. You must feel that when you check out new Harleys or, better yet, really old ones, right? Especially the old ones. You imagine all the people who've ridden that bike and enjoyed her, all the roads she's traveled, what she could possibly feel like under you at high speeds, how she might hug a turn or plow through the wind."

My chest constricted. I hadn't thought she knew how that felt, but she had the imagination to know that I knew, that I could relate that way. Genuine enthusiasm was in every line of her features, lighting them up, making her come alive. I wanted to get her on my bike and *hug* a turn and *plow* through that wind with her right the hell now.

"Or whatever it is you think about when you look at a good bike," she added.

I rubbed a hand down my chest. "You got it. It's like that. You been on a bike lately?"

"No."

"Well, we'll have to do something about that."

She averted her gaze, her cheeks reddening, and a prickle sprinted through my veins. Tania being shy. Imagine that.

"Anyway, that's the way it is for me when I'm faced with the prospect of a pick," she said. "When the owner opens the door and that musty, stale odor hits me square in the face."

I sank back in my chair. Like me and the salty sea air. Like me and the burning smell of an engine and oil and metal.

"I get it." I flagged the waitress with a flick of my hand. "Good thing I'm going with you."

"You are? Is that okay? I know that was pretty damn presumptuous of me before with the Scarlett and Rhett thing—"

"I don't want to take any chances of you getting assaulted or abducted again. Jesus, woman, I'm not tempting fate."

"Oh, give me a break."

"Grace would have my head, and she'd be right. I wouldn't want to owe any explanations to that brother of yours either. I've got enough going on without the Flames on my back."

Tania's brother was a member of the outlaw motorcycle club Flames of Hell in Nebraska. Catch was a volatile, unpredictable man.

Huh, look who's talking.

The waitress ripped a piece of paper from her small pad and handed it to me. I glanced at it and gave her a twenty in return.

"You're not on some sort of schedule or anything?" Tania asked.

"No. For the first time in a long while, I'm not rushing to get somewhere. I wanted to take my time on the road, getting to Meager from Ohio. That's what I've been doing, enjoying myself on the road, taking in this beautiful country of ours."

"That sounds good to me."

The waitress offered me the change, and I raised a hand. "Keep it, hon. Thanks."

"Have a good one, you two." She took off once more.

"Tania." I lowered my voice, leaning over the table. "Why did you tell him I'm some rock-star client of yours?"

Tania edged closer to me. "I recognized his type right off. Doesn't trust a woman on her own. And if he heard that you were some rich celeb, we'd come off like a sure thing he wouldn't dare pass up. Anyhow, you look like an under-the-radar hipster. I couldn't resist."

"Terrific." I shoved the receipt in my pocket. "I need a smoke. You want to join me outside?"

"Sure." Tania turned to Dave and Floyd, who were finishing up their meal. "We'll be right outside, gentlemen. Whenever you're ready."

Dave nodded his head. "Right-O."

She swung her bag on her shoulder. "Let's go, Rhett."

I rose up from my chair, laughing. "Lead the way, Scarlett."

SIX

TANIA

"So, Dave, what do we have?" I asked.

The wood clapboard house looked more than dilapidated. Over time, it had not survived the harsh Dakota winters very well without much upkeep. The sagging house bore testimony to its weariness and age as it struggled to stand in a field of wild green and yellow grasses and dried brush.

"The thing is, I haven't been out here for decades," said Dave. "My great uncle Gerhard and my aunt Astrid lived here. None of us really knew them that well. He used to work at the local bakery, and when he retired, the two of them kept to themselves out here. I just want to clear this junk out and sell the place. I'm the only relative now. Got my own ranch two towns over. Don't got much time or inclination for all this. If you wanna go through this mess and you find something you like, I'll give you a fair price. How does that sound?"

"Sounds very fair, and I do appreciate it. How about me and Rhett take a look? We'll pull whatever catches our fancy, and then we can talk prices?" I handed Butler my extra Maglite as his free hand went to my back, slid down, and settled on my waist.

I glanced at him. *Was he being protective?* His face was relaxed, and he remained focused on Dave.

"Sure," replied Dave. "There's the house here and a small barn out back. I'll unlock 'em for you guys."

"Okay then. Rhett?"

Butler's lips tipped up. "Let's do this." He leaned in closer to me. "I'm too young to die just yet, Tania, and I'd rather not meet my maker under a collapsed roof in the middle of nowhere."

"You're telling me. I'll be quick."

"Famous last words."

Butler pushed at the crooked wooden door. I assumed there was no electricity, but luckily, a couple of good-sized windows on either side of the house filtered in sunlight.

I immediately gravitated toward a set of buffalo horns mounted on a deteriorated slab of wood, leaning against a table.

"This is a classic, huh?" said Butler. "You don't see much of these around anymore, especially ones that go way back. You want me to move it to the side?"

"Yes, please." I scanned the room, my pulse fluttering.

Half the walls were painted in yellows and blues and pinks— huge flowers, fruits, vines, and abstract swirling shapes. The other walls were collaged with odd architectural ornaments, sketches, and small paintings. On closer inspection, they were watercolor and oil paintings on all sorts of mediums—Only a few were on canvas. This man, Gerhard, had a need to create, and create he did, any which way he could.

A stack of photos in an old decaying wooden crate caught my eye. Some of the photos were embellished with washes of color. And every single one was of the same subject—a woman. A woman posing topless, her almost bare body adorned with long strands of pearls, and in a few shots, what looked like a gold tiara with a large dark stone at the top, making her appear like an erotic mermaid queen or a harem girl from an exotic fairy tale. A number of photos had palm trees superimposed over the image and a variety of tropical backgrounds.

"This must be Auntie Astrid, huh?" asked Butler behind me.

"I think so."

"His own fucking pinup. Fifties porn?"

"Yeah, but in every portrait, she has this sweet, genuine smile on her face. No lusty come-hither eyes, no pretentious or suggestive posing like the pinups of the day. There's something so sincere about this sort of sexy, right?"

"Just a woman in love, posing for her adoring husband."

My heart flipped in my chest. I turned to him and held his soft gaze. "Exactly," I whispered.

"You're zinging, aren't you?" Butler said, his warmth at my side, his hand touching my back, his breath hot against my face.

"Uh-huh."

"I feel like I'm intruding on them or something," Butler said.

46

"Me, too," I murmured, skimming through the hundreds of photos. "These are vintage gelatin silver prints. Shit, they're gorgeous."

Astrid had posed for her husband, and he had made her his queen. These were their fantasies, their intimacy, their tender, private world. Their unconventional delight. Gerhard had known what the hell he was doing.

"There's something almost naive about them but sophisticated at the same time, right?"

I blinked at Butler. "Totally."

A thousand volts of yes coursed through me. An orgasmic-like surge. A mix of enchantment, enthrallment. I was transfixed, and I was experiencing it with Butler in a ramshackle, dirty old farmhouse in the hinterland of Sioux Falls, South Dakota. I was glad he was here with me; I was so grateful to share this with someone.

"You're good at this," I breathed.

A slight smile touched his lips, the blue of his eyes positively aquamarine in this light. "Going with my gut never steered me wrong. The trick is to listen to it though, right, Scarlett?"

"That's right."

"Pick what you want, and I'll bring them out."

I took all the photographs and handed them to Butler.

He stacked them and wiped the dust from his hands. "This is not your typical living room, is it?"

I followed his gaze.

A raised platform, slumped with age, stood against one wall. Wildly colored floral fabrics were piled in heaps on it along with a number of boxes and wood crates. Furniture filled the center of the space in front of the platform. A threadbare red chaise longue was draped in a tattered satiny chartreuse coverlet. A curvy cushioned armchair in a mustard-yellow fabric stood next to it along with a number of sofas and stools and chairs of all shapes and sizes. Small and large handmade pillows with gold and silver stitching and brightly colored scarves lay bunched on the floor. I spotted several military trumpets and ornately painted ceramic bowls. One was filled with a heap of faux jewelry, and another was filled with glass and metal Christmas ornaments.

That beloved tingle of tension curled up my throat. My brain flashed with the possibilities. I could see Gerhard and Astrid moving about the space. I could see—

"You okay?" Butler's warm hand squeezed my arm, and the sensation brought me back to earth.

"This was their theater," I replied.

"What do you mean?"

I pointed to the yellow armchair. "He had her posing on this chair in one of the prints. Recognize the curve of the arms? And the backdrops?"

"You're right. Look, there's that tapestry with the big pink flowers he used in one of the photographs. I'll bet every single piece is in those photos. The bowls, the trumpets. Stage props."

I took out my cell phone and snapped photos of every angle of the room and the stage with close-ups of the props. A glint of brass peeked out from under the fringed bedspread, lit by my camera flash, and I leaned under the chaise and drew it out. My breath caught. The crown Astrid wore in the photos. The piece of hand-cut brass was heavy in my hands. The metal was engraved with swirls, and the faux black stone in its center was still intact.

"Jesus, you found her crown?"

I only nodded. I couldn't speak. The buzz inside me was overwhelming every sense, every flake of logic I possessed. Sheer clarity washed over me, vitalizing every cell in my body.

"Here, I'll take it."

I handed Butler the crown, and he took it and put it on my head.

He studied me, a grin spreading over his lips, and my face heated. "It suits you, Scarlett. Hmm. This is exciting, huh?"

Warmth spiked through my body. My veins sang with an indescribable sparkling sweetness I hadn't felt in a long, long time. Under the intensity of Butler's rapt gaze, I savored it now.

"Yes." I licked my lips as I carefully took off the crown and handed it back to him. "Very exciting."

I piled all the gelatin prints together and went over to the hand-painted ceramic bowls and the jewelry—long faux pearl necklaces and dangling beaded earrings, some of which I recognized from the photos. I sorted through the fragile glass Christmas balls in a variety of colors.

"Take these, too. I'll just bet he made those bowls himself."

"I think you're right. Check this out." Butler took my flashlight and pointed it to the far wall where he illuminated rows of brightly painted ceramic masks of gargoyles and clown-like faces trimmed with botanical motifs.

"Wow."

I chose four, and Butler reached up and took them down for me. I stacked them on the worn cushion of the armchair.

The strum of guitar strings in the thick silence made me look up. Butler had a guitar in his hands. His head was bent at an angle. He was listening as he plucked the strings, and they popped, snapped, and bent to his gentle will. The strains of his melody resonated in the lifeless dank space, hanging in the air.

"'Blackbird'?"

His eyes flickered up at me. He'd been in a trance, listening on all kinds of levels. "Huh? Yeah." His teeth dragged along his bottom lip, his gaze returning to the guitar.

"That was beautiful. You play really well."

"I haven't touched a guitar in years. A lot of years." The lines of his face were taut as he studied the guitar, holding it up to catch the dusty shafts of light, inspecting it from top to bottom with the flashlight. "Needs cleaning, of course. New strings, but the body is in good shape. I can't say I know what it's worth or what kind of wood it is, but it feels...right. There's a label here, but it's worn off."

"I think we've seen that before in one of Astrid's fairy-tale portraits."

"Yeah, the serenading mermaid shot," he said. "Do you want it?"

"I do, yes."

"Here's the case."

He lifted up its case and packed the guitar inside. I put the guitar against the chair.

"What the hell is this?" His voice rose from the furthest corner of the room.

I could barely make out his outline in the shadows.

"Over here." His hand stretched out toward me, and I took it. He pulled me in close, and that scent of man infiltrated my senses, distracting me.

"What the fuck?" He moved the light of the flashlight.

Lining an oddly decoupaged bookcase along the wall was a row of miniature creepy homemade furniture that could have been used in a Viking dollhouse. Ghoulish, grotesque, primitive medieval thrones made of—

"Chicken bones?" said Butler.

I leaned forward, picking one up. "Yes!"

A few were painted in deep hues of blue, red, and orange. On others, the paint had faded considerably. But they were all majestic, crazy gems made of common, ugly components.

"I have to have these," I whispered.

His hand pressed into my shoulder. "I saw some milk crates by the door. We can stash 'em in there."

Butler returned with two large dairy crates.

"Oh my gosh."

"What is it?"

Behind the thrones were a number of tiny skulls.

"Look at these," I said.

"Bird skulls." He leaned in close to me and took one in his hand, shining the light from the small flashlight. "This one's a hummingbird."

I touched it with my fingertip. "So strange, isn't it? A hummingbird is such a sweet, joyful creature, yet there's something harsh and scary about this skull."

"Always is when you're looking at skulls and bones, Tania."

A shiver raced up my neck at his remark. A shiver that reminded me of the life he led.

"Still beautiful though," he said.

"Still beautiful."

Butler carefully placed the small skulls in his large palm. "This is a hawk skull. This one's a falcon, and this is a crow."

"They're incredible. So delicate. How do you know this stuff?"

"My dad was a hunter and a hiker. I used to tag along."

We lined the crates with the colorful shawls and coverlets, and we carefully placed the furniture pieces in there along with miniature towers that I found on another shelf. I didn't have to tell Butler what to do. He handled all the material with care.

I added the photographs to another crate as well as small paintings Gerhard had made by swirling fat brushes, his own fingers, and objects through paint on pieces of Masonite. Each image was a bright detonation of color in deep space or a glowing underwater abyss.

"Every piece is a variation on the same image of an explosion, huh?" Butler remarked. "I bet he was obsessed with the H-bomb testing going on back then. I know my granddad was. Shit, those are wild colors. Like some sort of glow-in-the-dark octopus. This guy...baker by day and bizarre artist behind closed doors."

"It's called outsider art."

"Meaning?"

"He wasn't classically trained and worked outside the mainstream art world. He was obsessed with creating and worked with whatever material was available to him, often dabbling in unusual, unconventional subjects and elaborate fantasy worlds."

"He was good."

"Very, very good. I wonder if he ever sold anything in his lifetime. So imaginative. Really unique."

"Maybe he wasn't interested in selling. Maybe this was his and his wife's personal thing. Their world."

My eyes slid to his.

Their world.

"How's it going in there?" shouted out Dave from the open doorway.

"I think we're done!" I said.

"Let me take this stuff outside, and we can have a better look at what you've got," muttered Butler.

"Dave? Could I take a peek into the barn, you think?" I asked.

"Sure, sure," he replied.

Another hour went by with Butler and I sifting through the barn, which was filled with old farm machinery and tools, tattered magazines, and bakery equipment. Butler looked for any motorcycle parts but came up empty-handed. He pulled out an old iron bubble gum dispenser, and my eyes widened at the sight.

"Thought as much." He brushed past me, holding the heavy piece. "You need to see something." He pointed to a mass of rusty bicycles stacked against a wall.

"The bicycles?"

He pulled the second one out from the pile. "This one here is a Victory. Victory was one of the first bicycle companies in America. Has the original nameplate, clamp brake system, and pedals. Even the saddle looks original. You've got to take it, Tan."

51

His eyes beamed at me, his look intent. Butler was buzzing.

I bit down on a smile. "Okay."

"Hold it while I bring the gum machine outside."

"Yes, sir."

"Don't be a hard-ass with the prices, and let's get the fuck out of here."

I rolled my eyes. "What are you talking about? I might like a bargain, but I know a good opportunity when I see it."

"Okay, but don't be too hardcore about it."

"Stand back and learn, my friend."

Butler let out a laugh as he set the gumball machine on the ground by the crates. He came back and got the bike, and I followed him outside.

Dave and I bartered on prices, and I managed to quickly bundle several pieces, offering him a special price on those items, putting on my geez-you're-making-this-hard-on-me-have-some-pity face. I dazzled him with my willingness to compromise and my respect for the pieces, pointing out wear and tear to my benefit and knocking down his prices when I could. Butler agreed with my assessments and didn't interrupt, only making the appropriate faces as Dave kept glancing at him. Fortunately, Dave was eager to sell, and we quickly reached a mutually happy medium.

Butler packed my Yukon with our spoils.

Dave and I shook hands.

"Thank you for the opportunity, Dave. I really appreciate it."

"Sure thing. Glad it worked out." He tipped his hat at Butler. "You enjoy all that junk now."

"Oh, I will." He waved Dave off as the man headed for his truck.

Butler turned to me, shaking his head.

"What? Why do you look so damn smug? Did I miss something?" I asked.

"I'm not being smug, Scarlett. I'm admiring."

A rush of heat flared inside me, and I shifted my weight.

"You doing the math in your head now?" he asked.

I smoothed my hair back. "Actually, no. I'm thinking this sort of find might be art gallery-worthy."

"And you got here first."

"*We* did, yeah."

"Let's get the fuck out of here then before Davey changes his mind."

I touched his arm. "I'm so glad we got to see it the way we did. Untouched, virginal."

"Yeah, me, too. We pretty much got to see what they had seen, give or take a few decades of dust and decay."

"Thank you for coming with me, for—" I threw my arms around him and hugged him. I savored the fragrance of ash and soap and sweaty man. I held on to him and inhaled.

Shit, what's come over me?

"I'm glad I came," he murmured. His hand bunched in my hair, tugging, and my pulse quickened. He let me go, and I stumbled back.

Butler opened my car door for me, and I settled into the driver's seat.

"Thanks," I said. I started the engine and lowered my window.

Butler leaned in. "We're going back to Meager together, okay?"

"Okay. Let's go."

"You can't wait to get home and open your goodies, huh?"

"Something like that."

"Let's roll."

SEVEN

TANIA

BY THE TIME WE LEFT DAVE'S and got on the road, the sun was setting. Two hours of driving later, with me behind Butler on the highway, he suddenly pulled off into the parking lot of a steak house.

He tore off his helmet, a hand digging through his matted hair. "I've been riding since sunrise this morning. I need a break."

"Of course."

He tugged off his gloves. "We've still got five hours ahead of us. I say we call it a night here and pick it up in the morning."

"Oh, okay."

"I'm starved. How about you?"

My brain stuttered, my gaze hanging on his pale blue eyes.

Loaded question...

My eyes flicked up at the huge hanging sign emblazoned with an old-fashioned caricature of a smiling cow. "I could eat that cow."

Butler laughed and steered me toward the restaurant's entrance, a hand at my back as he opened the door for us. A sweet warm *ting* went off inside me. His tiny bit of chivalry was perhaps trivial, insignificant, but coming from a man like Butler—who, by all outward appearances, did not seem like the polite, caring gesture type—it made an impression.

We settled into a booth and ordered quickly. The waitress brought us our sodas.

"Thank you for helping me at Dave's property," I said. "I really appreciate it."

"I had fun."

"Did you? You liked it?"

"Yeah, I did."

"You didn't think it was boring?"

"No. I really liked it." He drained his glass, his eyes on me. "Is that so hard to believe?"

"A little. But I'm glad. You helped me a lot."

"You usually do this shit on your own, right?"

"I do, yes. It was different to have a partner in crime for a change. You were good. Your eyes kept moving, hunting. You weren't afraid to get dirty."

"Me?"

We laughed.

"We found some amazing things," I said. "Many times, it can be like a really bad garage sale. Or you find something good, but then it's moldy or damaged. The worst is when they're badly repaired, and then they don't have much value, which can be really disappointing."

"Every time, you go into it believing, with the same high energy and focus, don't you?" he asked. "Believing that the next thing you see or touch just might be an authentic whatchamacallit."

I laughed and clinked my glass against his.

He studied me as I drank, his eyes narrowing. "You've got a lot of fucking patience then, Tania. And an extreme level of belief. That's…special."

I squirmed in my chair, a stab of heat spreading through me. His good opinion actually mattered to me. "You have to, or you could miss out on something remarkable."

"Yeah, remarkable is the word."

My pulse ratcheted at his words, at the firm tone in his quiet voice that seeped under my skin, like it wanted to play there.

"I've learned in this business that good things happen when you least expect them. You never know."

His eyes leveled with mine. "No, you never know. Life fucks with you that way."

"Yeah, but some of those fucks can be good ones."

He laughed, a hand passing over his chest.

The waitress arrived with our dinner, and we both tucked into the chargrilled steaks and thick French fries.

"So, this past year, you've been working with different clubs?" I asked. "Is that how the nomad thing works?"

"No. I worked with different chapters of my own club. Only if our national president approves can I have contact with other clubs."

"That's why you were at the Flames of Hell when Grace and I saw you in Nebraska?"

He wiped his mouth with the large white napkin and crumpled it. "Right. How's your brother doing? Has he calmed his ass down since his girlfriend took off with his kid?"

"He's sort of calm. The last time he came up for a visit, my mom laid down the law about him being a consistent dad. He keeps trying with Jill, but I think he needs to give that a rest."

"You think?"

"She's done with him and all the club crap that comes with being some biker's old lady—sorry."

"I get it. It's a lot to take on for some. But if he still loves her, he should fight for her."

"You're right." I put my fork down. "But sometimes, the love crumbles into bits, and there's no putting it back together."

"Sometimes, yeah."

"Anyhow, I'm sure my brother is not a suffering monk or feeling lonely at his club without her."

"He's popular."

"You've spent quality time over there at the Flames' clubhouse?"

His eyes caught mine. "So have you."

"What makes you say that?"

"Something I picked up on that day you and Grace showed up at their clubhouse. You and Finger know each other, don't you?"

"He's Catch's President. Our paths have crossed."

"How much crossing?" His voice was clipped.

Why did he care if I knew Finger?

I shrugged. "I've met him a few times through my brother."

Butler said nothing. I held his gaze, chewing on the crushed ice cubes from my glass, chewing on the answer he wanted, but wasn't going to get.

"How are you doing with going back to Meager?" I asked. "Huge decision. You're not an officer anymore. You'll be seeing Grace again and Lock."

He pushed his dish away. "I'm glad they're happy together. They both deserve to be. It's great that it worked out for them."

I shot him a look. "Aw, that's so sweet."

"Excuse me?"

"Save that for the Jacks. How do you really feel?"

His large shoulders rolled as he leaned forward on the table. "You really want to know?"

"Yes, I do. Were you in love with her? Are you still?"

"You don't beat around the bush, do you?"

"That's part of my charm. Answer the questions."

"I've always been attracted to Grace. Everybody knows that, don't they? Last year, I thought it was our time, our moment. But it wasn't, and it isn't ever going to be. Even though we were together for that short time—forgetting that she was working me for Jump—it didn't click for us. I'd thought it would be a natural fit, but we were trying too hard. Then again, I was high for most of it."

"You didn't want to fight for her?"

The edges of his lips turned up. "I started to, but then I realized I needed to learn to fight for myself first."

My spine straightened. "Yes. Exactly! I couldn't agree more."

"I'd made enough of an ass of myself," Butler continued. "She and Lock were strung out on each other the whole time anyhow, and it was cutting them deep. You can't fuck with that. *That* would be a real sin. My pride got bucked, but I survived."

"Yep, you survived. Yet again." I went back to my food.

He stared at me. "Did you ever tell Grace about you and me?"

I pushed the potatoes to the side of my dish with my fork. "No."

"Really? I thought girls told each other all about that shit."

"Well, sometimes, we girls refrain from confessing inappropriate behavior that might disappoint or upset our besties."

"Inappropriate, I like. Disappoint? That, I don't like. I think you got that backward, honey."

"Don't *honey* me. And that's not what I meant. You boys always have your minds on one thing."

"Which *thing* is that?"

"How big and hard your cocks are."

"As if women don't have our big, hard cocks on their minds."

I chuckled. "Oh all right. I'll give you that." *Guilty as charged.* "What I meant was, I knew Grace liked you, and I didn't want her to think that, on her wedding day, I was trying to be some sort of backstabbing evil bitch, grabbing at her spoils, trying to make some kind of point."

"Were you? Just a little bit?"

"No, I wasn't. Grace and I never competed for guys, never crushed on the same ones. Sorry to let you down, but it wasn't about you either."

"Then, what was it?"

I let out a small breath. "I felt uncomfortable at her wedding. She was moving on, and I wasn't. She was doing something she really wanted; she had achieved a dream. I just graduated college—had done really well, too—but I still wasn't sure what I wanted out of life. I was in limbo. I didn't have many job prospects or a sense of purpose. Grace did though. She and Dig were flying. I felt stuck in the mud and left behind. Sounds stupid and immature, but—"

"No, it doesn't. Emotions are what they are. You can't help it."

"I was really proud of Grace. Really proud. Despite me, my mom, even her sister getting pissed at her over staying with the club and wanting to marry Dig, she did it. A life with Dig at all costs had become her new dream, and she went for it. I only felt buried under all my expectations for myself, my mom's expectations."

"So, at the wedding, you were letting your hair down with me?" He grinned, as if he were watching a replay of our hook-up with a new fascination.

"I guess so. I was frustrated with myself, my life. I wanted to slap myself in the face."

"I don't remember slapping you in the face. I do remember slapping you on the—"

"Shut up!"

He laughed a rich, throaty, unpretentious laugh that only made me laugh, too.

"Butler, I'm quite sure I was a minor blip on your screen."

"You want me to lie?"

"No, I don't."

His head slanted. "Yeah, you were a blip. A blip I wanted to forget. That was a long fucking time ago. We were so fucking young then."

"Yes, now, we're so fucking old." I rolled my eyes.

Grace and I were forty-three now, Butler was only a couple of years older.

"Jesus, she's laughing. Most women would punch me, slap me, tell me to fuck off for saying that."

"Nope, I like your honesty, Butler. Actually, I expected you to say something flip or charming to weasel your way out of this awkward moment."

"Oh, yeah? Like what?"

"Let's see…how about, *Oh no, babe. You were fucking unforgettable. That sexy bod of yours, that hot pussy—you made my dick come alive. Wildest piece of ass ever.*"

Butler laughed out loud, his chest shaking. An elderly couple at the next table glanced at us.

"You liked that, huh?" I asked.

His eyes gleamed in the light hanging over our table, his blond hair shining. "Ah, I didn't forget everything, Tania. I remember you in that dress. I remember you being pissy with an edge of self-consciousness. Then, we grabbed each other, and it was somewhere between angry sex and I-dare-you sex."

I bit down on the side of my lip. "I was mad at myself after."

"For what?"

"Not finishing what I'd started. That was bad form on my part."

"I was mad, too. My dick was even madder."

"I'm sorry."

"I forgive you."

"Shit, what a relief. Twenty-something years later, I can finally breathe easy again."

Butler squinted his eyes. "You going to go wild now?"

"What do you mean?"

"Now that you're getting a divorce?"

"No time for men, wild or otherwise. I've got so much good stuff going on with my work and settling into Meager again. That's what's important to me now. I'm going to focus on getting my business off the ground, being a good aunt to my niece and my sister's two boys, helping out my mom. And you?"

"Me what?"

"You must feed the wild need frequently."

He grinned at me, his fist lightly hitting the table. "After a while that kind of feeding is often just a step above jacking off on my own. Maybe that opinion is a part of me being in my forties now."

"Don't be an ass. We're not decrepit."

He eyed me. "Go for the wild, babe."

"Will do, Rhett." My fingers slid up and down my wet glass. "Do you have a type for your wild?"

"I used to." Butler stretched his legs under the table. "Blonde, blue-eyed, tall, skinny. You?"

Ah, yes, the complete opposite of me. Medium height, blackish hair, large almond-shaped brown eyes, and not heavy but certainly not skinny. Just…regular.

"Not so much anymore." I pressed my fingers along the edge of my napkin. "It used to be a specific look. But, now, it's beyond the beard or no, long hair or short, dark or light, built or lean, brown eyes or blue. Different things turn me on now."

"What things?"

"Mostly, it's an unexpected flare of feeling over an odd detail."

His bright blue eyes pierced mine. "A flare, huh? Like what? Tell me."

I cleared my throat. "It can be a smile or a…"

Or the way Butler's T-shirt was clinging to his powerful contoured shoulders right this second.

Oh, yeah.

Or the way he studied me as I spoke, totally focused on whatever crap was coming out of my mouth and then responding to it with irony or understanding—I was never sure which.

I like that. I really like that.

Or the way his hand had settled on my back as we walked into the restaurant earlier.

Yes.

Or that glint in his pale blue eyes every time I cracked a joke he hadn't expected, and I caught a fleeting hint of amusement and ease in them.

Yes, that.

All that.

His eyebrows lifted. "Or what, Tania?"

"Wh-what?"

"Here you go!" The waitress placed fresh drinks in front of us.

My hand seized the icy-cold glass, as if my life depended on it.

"You were saying what gets you hot for a guy now." His lips tipped up. "What is it?"

I drank greedily, but the burn in my throat remained. "Depends on my mood, I guess."

"Maybe a man bun turns you on today?"

"It's been known to happen."

"Your ex-husband have a man bun?"

"Yes, he does."

"Trendy asshole."

I laughed. "He is kind of a trendy asshole."

Butler grinned. "That's what I thought."

I wiped at the edges of my mouth. "You know what I want?"

"Tell me."

"Yes, being in love is beautiful—*blah, blah, blah*—and going wild is fun—*blah, blah, blah*—" I held up my hand as I crunched on ice.

He laughed. "I'm listening."

"However—"

"Yeah?"

"To be touched with intent. To be looked at. Really looked at. For a man to see me, truly see me. That recognition, acknowledgment, that appreciation. That's what I want. Where is that? Where did that go?"

"We let it go."

My lungs squeezed in my chest. He knew.

"Over the years, I'd learned to steel myself against Kyle's gruff manner, his flip way of talking to me, even the way he looked at me, which was not really looking at me. Put that in your man brain, by the way, because that truly sucks—when the person you're supposed to be closest to doesn't really see you anymore when he looks at you."

Butler took in a quick breath. "Yeah, I know what that's like."

I rolled my napkin into a ball. "After years of that, I don't think I'd know what the good stuff feels like anymore—if I ever do get to feel it again, that is." I let out a dry laugh. "Jesus, if I did feel it, I'd probably combust or just cry."

His brows drew together.

I snorted rather inelegantly. "There's a word without much intent."

"What word?"

62

"*Just.* When I lived in Chicago, after I'd left Meager, I took acting classes."

"Acting? Really?"

"It was fun. Anyway, my teacher once said that you couldn't play a negative. *My character doesn't want,* or, *She doesn't need,* or, *I'm not this or that.* You can only play a positive and a specific action through and through. That's what's clear, active, powerful. The *I want, I need.*"

Butler nodded. "Makes sense."

"He also said, you can't play the word *just.*"

"Just?"

"Think about it. What is that? Does it carry any significance in a sentence?"

"It can, but for the most part, it's a nothing word."

"Right. It's like a useless extra pillow on your sofa. Does it make things easier to express, to hear, to swallow?"

His lips curled. "We'd like to think so."

"Don't we though? What a great filler word to soften the blow. But there is no *just* anything. Things either *are,* or they *are not.*"

He grinned. "True."

"My marriage was being played on a negative and being excused with a just. Over and over again."

He slanted his head. "The sex must have been good then."

My face heated.

"Did I embarrass you?" he asked.

"Not for the reason you think."

Butler brought his head closer to mine. "What I meant was, if you two stuck it out so long even though things got mediocre, the sex was probably good. Right?"

"No."

"No what? The sex wasn't good?"

"No. There wasn't much sex the last few years."

"What?"

I sank in my seat. "Please don't make me repeat it. I've never told anyone."

"How could there not be—"

"Drop it, please."

"Hold on. First off, why haven't you told anyone, like your best girlfriend?"

"Because it's humiliating. And I'm sure Grace has never had that problem."

"You can't be sure about that. We all go through shit times."

"I just felt that—"

"You *just* felt?"

I chewed on my wobbly lower lip. "I felt that, if I told her, it would make that epic fail real."

"It is real, Tania," he said, his voice gentle.

"I know, but I didn't want to admit it to anyone or deal with how bad it felt," I breathed. My lip quivered, and I bit down hard on it, blinking away the water gathering in my eyes.

Don't be even more pathetic. Don't cry now. Not in front of Butler.

"Hey." His legs trapped one of mine under the table and squeezed.

I swallowed past the messy goop of embarrassment and emotions and met his gaze.

"You don't have to feel embarrassed with me. Trust me on that. I'm sure Grace has told you plenty of shit about how things were last year, and it's all fucking true."

"She hasn't. She can be a real lady when she wants to protect the people she cares about."

"This? What you're feeling? You've been burying it deep for years, and it's eating at you," he said. "It's raw. On top of that, you must be horny as hell."

I stomped on his foot.

He cocked an eyebrow in response. "These boots are way too thick for that shit, babe."

I really liked Butler's frankness, but oh, how the truth stung.

"I'm sure you've never had a no-sex problem or a boring sex problem," I said.

"Highs and lows of life, Tania. We all go through them."

"True, but over time, it's easy to lose that sense of awe with your partner. You let it go like a helium balloon you watch waft away from you, higher and higher toward the sky. You start saying to yourself, *Tomorrow, I'll make an effort. Next week, we'll go out to dinner, and I'll get dressed up. Next summer, we'll go on that vacation.*"

"Tania, I was married once, and it was plenty good. It isn't about dinners out and vacations. That shit's real nice if you can swing it, but either you stay connected, or you don't. It's either important to you, that giving to your partner, and essential to you, like breathing, or it isn't."

Essential.

A swell of ugly emotions rose up inside me, and I averted my gaze as I hacked them up and shoved the jagged pieces down.

Why did what he said make me so sad?

Because I wasn't, nor had I ever been, anyone's essential anything.

Butler had had that though. The man I'd once thought was nothing but a shallow, self-indulgent playboy had lived it; he knew.

"Hey, I'm sorry. I didn't mean to—"

"You're right. Absolutely right." I gulped down more soda. "Kyle would get mean a lot of the time, too, and then laugh it off, like he was only teasing. He'd never apologize. Saying *I'm sorry* was a sign of weakness, I guess. God forbid I talk to him like that though. He'd carry on about how rude I was and that I made it hard for us to communicate."

My heavy gaze fell on the elderly couple next to us who shared a plate of French fries, dipping into the same puddle of ketchup. "I couldn't sweep all those bad feelings under the carpet and open my legs for him at the end of the day. I couldn't." I expelled a deep breath. "I wanted something more out of marriage."

"That's good." His voice was low, quiet.

My gaze found his warm one. "What's good?"

"That you've taken a stand for what you want, what you need."

I rested my head on my hand. "I must not be good at relationships or marriage. Maybe Kyle was right, and I'm selfish. Even you, the reformed reckless bad boy, know what a committed relationship should look like, smell like, feel like." I raised my glass. "Here's to you!"

"You think I don't know about pushing shit away? Caitlyn died over five years ago, and I haven't been able to have anything real with another woman since. I've fucked everything in sight—which fed the need, as you said—but it didn't do much for me at the end of the day.

"When Grace came back, I convinced myself that she was my second chance. I saw her again after all those years, after all our pain—hers and mine—had subsided, and it was like I saw a light flickering in the dark, and I wanted its heat." His brow furrowed.

"Would've been so damn easy. We knew each other. The attraction was still there. But it wasn't easy. It isn't about easy, Tania."

"Attraction and chemistry should be easy."

"Definitely. But the rest of it—emotions, interests, the sharing—that shit takes commitment on a certain level. I'd figured, with Grace, it'd be real simple to coast through it all. She was my shortcut to having something real in my life again. I felt real good about landing the easy way." He rubbed a hand across his mouth. "I latched on to her for dear fucking life. What a jackass."

"Yeah, but you wanted it though, didn't you? You thought you were ready, so you were willing, and you reached out. That's a good sign, isn't it?"

His eyes bored into mine. "It was an illusion I was more than willing to believe."

"You were reaching out for a lifeline, despite yourself."

His jaw stiffened and released. "Anyway, back to you." He swirled the tiny ice cubes remaining in the bottom of his soda glass.

I sank back in my chair. "Not much more to tell. After a while, my and Kyle's personalities clashed, and we both let any sense of intimacy take a backseat. He was never into PDA anyhow, but without even hand-holding, casual hugs, a touch here or there—without that as some sort of happy glue—it all deteriorated fast."

"No kids?"

"He has a daughter from his first marriage, Celia, and he wasn't in a rush to have any more kids. We'd both decided to put off having them for a few years. We never had a big enough apartment anyhow. Then, a few years became ten years, and then there was a miscarriage along the way. I stayed busy with getting my business off the ground, and then I wasn't willing so much anymore. Didn't seem too important to him either."

"Did he say that?"

"No." I slid my wet glass along the smooth surface of the table. "Another thing that got swept under the proverbial rug."

"You regret not having kids?"

"I always figured I'd do it, that it was a part of life, but I don't feel terribly disappointed by not having done it. Living with Becca and Jill has been great though. And my sister, Penny has two boys, Nate and Carter. I love being their aunt. I enjoy it a lot."

"That's good then."

My fingertips shoved at the edge of my dish. "You want to hear something really pathetic?"

"I've got plenty of pathetic stashed in here." He tapped on his chest. "Lay it on me."

"A couple of years ago, I was shopping online on my favorite drugstore website, and they had a huge sale on condoms. I bought five or six mega boxes. I like a good sale. I'd just gone off the pill, so I thought I'd be prepared in case we got inspired one night. And I figured it'd make Kyle laugh when he saw it. Approach the situation with humor. Spur on some action."

"Did he laugh?"

"Yeah, he laughed. I put them away and kept a few at the bedside table. We used maybe four or five."

"Out of all of them?"

"Yes. Then, a couple of years after that, when I was switching our summer and winter clothes in our closets, reorganizing everything, I came across the stash. All those square boxes still sealed, and they'd expired the month before. *Expired.* That was when I felt it, like an actual punch in the fucking gut—the humiliation. It was ridiculous. Couldn't go on. And I'm not only talking about not getting laid by my husband."

"That is a huge problem. Could he not get it up?"

"That was part of it. He'd been stressed out about being unemployed for a while, traveling all over on job interviews. He got good offers in California and Texas, but he didn't want to go too far away because of Celia. He was frustrated. His life and career were flashing in front of his eyes."

"That shit affects a man down deep. His dick took a hit."

"I get that. But he was never willing to talk about it."

"You women always want to talk about everything."

"Why not? Instead, I felt alone and unattractive and—"

"You are not unattractive. At all."

My toes curled in my boots. "Thank you." I let out a small breath. "But that's how I felt. Rejected. Kyle behaved like I was being demanding and over the top."

"Were you?"

I shrugged. "He was protesting so much, putting it off, pushing me away, and I got the hint after a while. So, I turned my back on him, too. Then, he got a new job, a really good job, and he relaxed but not much changed. Anyhow, I was choking. A lot of time had gone by, and I was letting it go by. I couldn't ignore it anymore."

"Life's too short," he said.

"No, you're wrong. That's wrong."

He jerked his head back at my hard tone. "How's that wrong?"

"Life can be long, Butler. Way too long. And if you're not happy—really happy with who you are and whom you're with and what you're doing, fucking happy deep down in your soul, in your bones—then life is interminable. Life drags you along with it, shredding little pieces of you on its infinite winding, rocky road through time."

He was perfectly still, his eyes locked on mine.

"Standing in that closet that day," I continued, "piles of sweaters and T-shirts on the floor all around me, I couldn't breathe anymore. I knew it had to stop right then, or I'd be in the same exact place when I turned fifty one day, then sixty, then seventy. Then, I'd be dead.

"No. No way. No fucking way.

"God gave me a life to live, and I want to live it. *Live* it, not endure it. I can make choices. I can change it. Sure, it would've been more exciting to have taken off for Bali or Paris or New York and not crawled back home to South Dakota, but that's okay. My mom needs me now, and so do Jill and Grace."

"You like that, don't you?"

I raised my head at the sudden softness in his usually gruff voice. "What's that? Signs from the universe?"

"No, Tania." His eyes flickered at me. "Helping. Making a difference in the lives of the people you love."

My heart skipped a beat. We'd only spent several hours together today, yet he'd figured out what was important to me, what made me truly happy.

Butler raised his glass. "Here's to no more *justs*."

I raised my glass, willing the tears gathering in my eyes to stop. "No *justs*."

Clink.

Our eyes remained on each other as we drank.

"Looky what we have here." A sneering voice sliced between us.

A sour smell filled my nostrils as a heavy arm seized my shoulders. I coughed up my soda.

Butler's eyes glinted at the bearded biker who'd slid into the seat next to me. Every inch of Butler's massive body tightened. "Let go of her now."

The biker only grinned. A menacing ugly grin.

A threat.

EIGHT

TANIA

"WHAT THE HELL?" I rasped.

The biker gripped my shoulders tighter, and I winced. He cradled my head with his hand, and I grunted as his damp rubbery lips moved against my skin.

"Your boyfriend's famous, darlin'. Nothing like crossing paths when you least expect it."

My gaze landed on his free hand, which was planted on the table. A broken, jagged black knife was tattooed on the back of his hand. Letters tattooed on his thumb and each of his fingers spelled the word *Blade*.

A Broken Blade from Nebraska?

I'd heard a few of the One-Eyed Jacks mention them in passing. And I'd overheard Catch mention them while talking on his cell phone when he was at our mother's a couple of months ago.

"Um, I'm not his—"

"She's not my girlfriend, but trust me, douchebag, you don't want to involve her," said Butler on a hiss.

The Blade's thick fingers closed around my neck. "I don't give two shits. I'm here to tell you that Notch don't like you interfering."

"I'm not interfering in anything."

"You're a One-Eyed Jack, and—"

"I sure as hell am, and I sure as fuck don't answer to you or your club, only my national." Butler's eyes flared, his face as immovable as marble.

"Word's out that you've been working with—"

In a blur of movement, Butler flipped his steak knife in his hand and jabbed it down into the Blade's hand that was planted on the table. The Blade let out a grunt, but his greasy hold on my neck only tightened.

Butler's eyes lit up as he dragged the knife down the man's hand. Blood spurted from the slice. My breath throttled in my throat.

"Let go of the lady, or I'm gonna have to tell the Flames you messed with one of their own," Butler said.

"What?"

"You know Catch, the Sergeant at Arms of the Flames of Hell?"

"Yeah, yeah, sure I do." His voice was strained. He let out a tight grunt.

"This here's his sister. I'm doing him a personal favor and seeing her home."

"Ah, fuck." The Blade shoved me away, as if I were a burning pot on the stove that he had touched by accident.

My body smacked against the nearby wall. "Ouch!"

Butler's focus did not waver from the Blade, who winced and hissed. I sat up and flattened myself against the wall.

"Unless you want this knife all the way up your arm until I dig it into your neck, you best move along. Or I'm gonna have to call Catch and Finger." Butler glanced at me, his chin lifted. "You got your brother's number handy, babe?"

I slid my phone across the table toward Butler, and he caught it with his free hand, his eyes steady on the Blade.

Butler's eyes blazed with icy blue fire. "What's it gonna be?"

"My mistake. Huge mistake. Let me buy you two another round, huh?" said the Blade.

My eyes darted to his colors. The name Pick was patched on the front.

As in, ice pick? Or maybe for nose picker?

"It's up to the lady. What do you think, Tania?" Butler dug the knife in deeper in the Blade's hand, who let out a groan, his face twisting.

I cleared my throat. "Make that two shots of tequila, would you?"

"You sure that's all you want?" Butler asked, his lips tipping up.

"And an order of chocolate cheesecake. Oh, and an apology."

"You heard her," said Butler.

"Sorry," muttered Pick through gritted teeth. "Very fuckin' sorry."

Butler unstuck the knife from Pick's hand and wiped the blood off on Pick's sleeve. "Get moving."

I tossed a few napkins on the table before him, and Pick grabbed them, pressing them over his wound, as he trudged off toward the bar.

"I never thought my brother would ever come to my rescue, but there you have it," I said.

Butler slid the steak knife to the opposite end of the table. "You okay?"

"Peachy. What the hell was that about?"

He got up from his seat and slid in next to me, his arm around my shoulders. "That was bullshit. He recognized me and thought he could take advantage. Everyone's got a bone to pick these days."

"Terrific." I brushed my hair behind my ears, ignoring my pulse spiking at the touch of his fingers on my shoulder, the press of his warm, hard body next to mine.

"You sure you're okay?"

I glanced up at him. "How about you? Are you okay?"

"Me?" He dipped his chin, turned his head to the side, and fiddled with the paper place mat on the table.

I had asked a surprising question.

"Yes. Are you okay?" I touched his chest, and he seemed to wince as he took in a deep breath.

"I like your perfume. It's…"

"Peppery."

"Yeah, that's what it is." He shook his head, as if my perfume had gotten stuck inside there. "Pepper and flowers. What a combination."

"There are all sorts of peppercorns, you know—red, pink, white, green as well as good ole black. Each has its different charms."

"Very different." He leaned in closer to me, his nose brushing the side of my jaw, his heat fanning my skin, and I held my breath.

A waitress brought over two shots of tequila and two bottles of beer. Butler pulled back and adjusted himself in his seat.

"Thank you." I grabbed one of the small glasses and tossed it back. The sting roared down my throat, and I wiped at my lips with my thumb. "Ah, shit."

"Been a while?"

"Mmhmm." I nodded. "So, what was that with Mr. Pick? One of those never-ending crazy vendetta things?"

"Something like that. Notch, the Blades' president likes making waves and grandstanding. His hatred for the Jacks goes back to Dig's time. And the Flames and the Blades used to be friendly, but the past decade-plus, not so much. Word is the Blades aren't doing well financially anymore. They've been losing members and a few of their chapters have even shut down. Notch is outnumbered, and he knows it."

My eyes shot back to the bar where the Blade was sitting with another biker. A biker from another club.

"Look, he's hanging out with someone from a different club. No vendetta shit there."

Butler's head snapped toward the bar, his eyes landing on Pick sitting with a man who had a patch on the back of his jacket which read, *Smoking Guns MC, Kansas*. I pursed my lips at the logo of a skeleton with a satanic grin on his face, holding two revolvers in his bony claws.

I knew that image. I'd seen it before.

Butler muttered something under his breath.

"What was that?"

"You remember how I got my road name?" he asked, his voice curt, low.

"I sure do. You were a prospect. Another club was visiting, and one of their members was an asshole to you, making you his slave for the night until you couldn't take it anymore. You exploded and rammed a broken beer bottle in his neck, yelling, 'What do I look like? Your fucking butler?'"

"Good memory."

"Good story."

"Luckily, I didn't kill him, but I left him with a huge scar."

"That's good, I guess." I grabbed a beer bottle and drank.

He tilted his head toward the bar. "He was a Smoking Gun."

"Oh, shit. Is that him?"

"I don't think so. But the Smoking Guns are also the club that carved up Finger when he was a prospect."

My stomach tumbled. "You going to drink your tequila?"

"No." He slid his glass to me, his face drawn.

I knocked the liquor back, and the heat of the alcohol spread through my insides, quelling the riot there and inciting a new one.

Butler's face remained tight, grim. He was assessing.

I'd been kissed by danger, blood, and sudden threats, and all the while, I'd been under the shield of Butler's crazy cool.

He leaned into me. "We should go find a motel."

I choked on the fire in the back of my throat. "Wh-what?"

"A motel. There aren't that many around here, and I just hope we can find one with rooms available."

"Oh, right." My stomach clenched. "Good point."

A waitress placed two dishes of chocolate cheesecake drizzled with caramel sauce on the table.

"Can we dig into this first?" I asked.

"You got a thing for chocolate, huh?"

I slid a spoon into the wedge of lusciousness before me. "Chocolate is my answer for all of life's little ups and downs."

TANIA

"WE HAVE ONLY ONE ROOM LEFT with a king-size bed."

"One bed?" I asked.

The motel clerk shot me a look from behind his computer monitor. "Yes, one bed."

The first motel had no vacancies.

This motel had only one room available with *one* bed.

"Since when has South Dakota become such a hotbed of tourism?" I asked.

"It's still Sturgis season, ma'am," replied the clerk.

"Sturgis is all the way across the state, and the rally was last month!" I said.

"Be that as it may, people are still here, road-tripping from all over the country and Canada to see the sights in our great state." His eyes darted to Butler, then me, and then Butler again. "Will you be taking the room?"

"Yes," I said.

"You sure?" asked Butler.

"It's fine. I need to get lateral and soon. I'm sure you're exhausted. All I ask is that you don't smoke in the room."

"No problem. We'll take it," he said to the clerk.

And I'll take a few more tequilas to knock myself out pronto.

Moments later, we were in the room, throwing our bags on the floor. The door clicked behind us, and my chest squeezed. The room wasn't huge, but Butler was.

"You can have the bed. I'll be fine on the floor," he said.

"Don't be ridiculous. The bed's huge. Anyway, you don't have to be concerned about my virginity or reputation."

"Hell, woman, that's a relief."

I grabbed my messenger bag and slugged his side with it, and he laughed.

"Are you sure, Tania?"

"Yes."

He gestured toward the bathroom. "I need to take a shower. You want to get in there first?"

"Oh no, go right ahead. I'm sure being on a bike all day..."

"Yeah." He slid his gun from his back, his blond hair in his face.

My pulse skipped a beat.

Butler was beautiful and rough around the edges. Holding that sleek yet ominous chrome gun, he was a menacing rogue, a sleek mercenary, a brutal angel heralding danger, deliverance, and the fulfillment of dark vows and dreadful promises.

He placed the gun on the nightstand, settled on the edge of the bed, and took his boots off.

I'd enjoyed our conversations today. Tomorrow, we would both be back in Meager, jump-starting our new lives. Hopefully, we could continue with this new, improved friendship.

Within ten minutes, Butler emerged from the steam-filled bathroom with only a towel wrapped around his waist. His broad, defined chest was still damp. Water dripped down his smooth skin from his wet hair, which fell just below his ears. His long legs were contoured with hard muscles. I was in the presence of male greatness.

I shot up from the bed, beauty bag in hand. "I'm going to take a shower, too."

He let out a long sigh, his one hand stroking down his middle. "Felt great."

My breath caught in my throat at the sight of that small movement. He was like some sort of vibrant energy force filling this dinky, bland motel room. He checked his cell phone, and his skin glowed in the dim light given off by the small lamp on the nightstand, the shiny metal of his weapon glinting.

I scooped up my PJs and darted off to the bathroom.

After my shower, I smoothed lotion on my skin and put on my thin cotton pajama shorts along with a loose-fitting cotton tee on top of the camisole that matched the shorts.

Butler was lying on his stomach under the covers of the bed. The skin of his bare back shimmered in the soft light.

Is he naked under there?

Oh, shut up.

Taking in a deep breath, I turned away from the visual of Mr. Hunk of Blond Steel in Repose and deposited my clothes on top of my duffel bag on the floor. I trotted off to my side of the bed, sliding under the covers. The air-conditioning was set to perfectly cool.

"Tania?" His gruff throaty voice made my insides jump to attention.

"Yeah?"

"That thing with the condoms?"

"What about it?"

"That really is pathetic."

I grabbed a pillow and threw it at his head.

He roared with laughter. "Hey! Being honest."

"Are you enjoying my humiliation?"

He grabbed the pillow and propped his head on it over folded arms. Arms that screamed strength. Arms that were muscular, defined, and emitting gamma rays of pure male power.

What would it feel like to be held by those arms? Held tightly?

"No, I'm not enjoying your humiliation." A small smile played on his lips as he raised himself up on an arm, resting his head on it. "It sucks."

"Ah, you're showing your support then? Your compassion?"

"That's right."

"Great. Now, shut up. I don't want to talk about it ever again." I stared at the ceiling.

"I'm glad you shared it with me." His voice had softened.

"Why? So, you can continue to tease me? Fantastic."

"No, I meant, because you trusted me. Means a lot."

I turned to face him across the bed. Butler was thanking me for a gesture of friendship. For my frankness. My fingers curled in the top sheet.

"You want to hear more?" I asked.

"Sure."

"Kyle used to change the topic of conversation anytime things got too real between us or if I tried to delve too deep. Handling emotions took a lot of effort. When I got upset at the news of my mom being diagnosed with MS, he only patted me on the back. I guess it made him uncomfortable to reach out and support me while I skidded."

"Maybe he doesn't know how."

I lifted my head up on my arm. "But that's what I wanted. What I needed. Was I asking for too much?"

"No, you weren't. Is that what you think? You weren't. What's the point if you can't be there for your partner?"

I only let out a sigh.

That's over now, and I made that happen.

"I appreciate you listening to my whining."

"You aren't whining. You're not a whiner. I think you're a shut-up-and-put-up-with-it kind of girl. And you know what, Tania? You shouldn't have to be that way."

No, I shouldn't. And he knew that. *Butler* knew that. But I'd made it a lifestyle, even before Kyle.

I smoothed down my pillow. "Thank you for listening."

He touched my arm, a lock of his blond hair falling in his eye with the movement. "Glad I could help." The warmth of his fingertips on my skin lingered.

"I'll shut up now and let you get sleep." I let out a sigh. "I'm exhausted myself. What a long day."

He turned over, facing me, his hair falling in his face once again. "It was fun. Except for Pick coming at us, of course." His hand curled lightly over my upper arm. "How are you doing with that, by the way?"

"I'm fine. Once that tequila kicked in…"

"And the chocolate?"

"Definitely the chocolate," I murmured.

He released me, and I reached out and flipped the switch on the bedside lamp. The room was engulfed in darkness.

"You want your pillow back?" Butler asked.

"Yeah, actually, I do."

The pillow landed on my head.

"Hey!"

I punched him with the same pillow right back.

Butler laughed, and so did I.

BUTLER

THE WATER RUSHES OVER MY FEET, around my ankles, and I let out a sigh. That feeling will never get old.

I glance over at him. His eyes twitch as the water surges around his bare legs and then recedes once more. He doesn't care that the bottoms of his rolled up jeans are wet. He's transfixed by the water, the sight of Pacific infinity, the breaking of the waves over the rocks. He's an explorer who's reached the edge of the world.

"So, what's the plan?" His deep voice tears my attention away from the liquid sapphire before us. A roll of waves swells in the distance.

"Huh? What plan?"

He turns to me, his golden brown eyes glowing in the first light of dawn. "You looking for something out here?"

I shrug. "Um...nah, I'm just..."

He slants his head at me. "Why the fuck not?"

I woke up, struggling for air, the sheet in my grip, an acute pressure in my chest. *That* pressure. I gulped at air to push back the nausea. I wiped the sweat from my neck and chest, rubbed my eyes, but the image of *him*, like some biker Jesus beckoning me on the beach of my youth rattled through me. I breathed in, I breathed out, but he wouldn't go away. His question squeezed around my heart.

Tania moaned.

Again.

She twisted in the bed next to me. The rise and fall of her chest was deep and slow as she breathed through sleep.

I couldn't fucking sleep.

Even though my body was exhausted, my brain was wired. Pick coming after me through the woman I was with was all kinds of bullshit. All kinds of warning signs.

He had been drinking, but still, that was no fucking excuse. Creeper had been hiding out with the Blades, and they were obviously pissed that I'd taken him.

Too fucking bad.

But Pick hanging out with a biker from another club? A club that had never had a foothold in our parts. A club that I'd literally made my mark on as a prospect. A club that Finger had a bloody history with.

Shit, I need a smoke.

Another moan.

A deep sigh.

Tania kicked off the sheet, and a long bare leg made an appearance. Her shorts had ridden up her ass, and the curve of a full cheek was visible in the light from the bathroom that I'd left on.

I hated sleeping in the dark, and I'd gotten up and turned it on, leaving the door ajar, after Tania had fallen asleep in the middle of our conversation about our favorite rock ballads of all time. (Mine being Led Zeppelin's "Stairway to Heaven," hers being Pearl Jam's "Black.") Now, I had a view of skin. Smooth, sleek skin on a leg that was bending, the lean muscles flexing.

Maybe Pick's assault had freaked her out more than she'd let on? I should've talked to her more about it after. Instead, I'd gone on about club politics and club history.

Then, she'd asked me how I was doing. And that one simple question had a gutting effect on me along with the touch of her hand against my chest. I hadn't known how to answer.

When was the last time anyone had been concerned about me? About my fucking feelings?

Not for a long, long time.

Tania murmured in her sleep again, her head arching back.

I edged closer to her.

"Oh. Mmm," seeped from her lips.

More little moans.

She couldn't be dreaming about Pick unless he was some sort of fantasy come to life for her.

Huh.

She turned again, and her back pressed against my chest. The sudden heat against me, *her* against me, lit up my skin, and my breath shorted. I lifted the sheet a few degrees, unstuck my legs, and...*yeah, there*. Skin-to-skin with Tania's legs.

Fuck.

I wasn't supposed to be doing this.

Her neck arched again, offering itself to me. I ran my fingertips across the silky skin of her shoulders, her arms. She rolled over, a slight smile on her lips, an arm sliding up against my chest, around my neck, her fingers in my hair.

A current raced up my spine and choked the breath in my lungs.

My hand swept across that long throat of hers and cradled her face. My lips brushed her ear, down the hidden patch of skin behind it, and goose bumps rose on her skin. I smiled to myself and wiped her thick hair away from her neck, revealing more skin.

Always the conqueror of female flesh.

No, no, this is different.

She nestled against me, her fingers rubbing against my scalp. The fragrance of the soap we'd both used in the shower invaded my senses along with another far prettier, more delicate scent, something flowery yet clean. Something I liked a hell of a lot. Like unexpected gentleness on a take-no-prisoners determined Tania. There was plenty of soft and vulnerable underneath her hard shell.

My hips pressed against hers on a primal instinct for friction, and my cock heartily agreed with the move. It had been stiff since her first moan I'd heard over an hour ago. Now, it was full-blown bone.

I can't do this. I shouldn't be doing this.

Another moan.

Fuck.

I licked the side of her warm throat with the tip of my tongue. She let out a whimper, and it pulled on my insides.

"You like that, baby?" I murmured against her skin, following the angle of her jaw under her throat. I was rewarded with little cries and stretches, flexing, and hips searching for contact.

My fingers tucked under the warm cotton of her shirt, slid against her skin, down her torso, and over her hip. I hit elastic. Panty elastic. The final frontier. The border. Only, I didn't have a passport to cross over.

My heart clanged in my chest.

That's new.

This wasn't just turned on, ready to fuck. This was…anticipation.

She squirmed against my cock, another lazy smile tugging on the edges of her lips.

Tania, who always seemed bitter and sour, who I'd always enjoyed taking down a peg or two when the opportunity had arisen.

Tania, who, decades ago, had blown me off in the middle of fucking her, stomping on my inflated sense of identity and manhood.

But that was then.

This was—

"Yes, yes…" she murmured, her voice husky, low.

This was Tania, who hadn't gotten any in a long, long time.

The whole afternoon in that artist's house flashed in front of my eyes. The softness of her face. That was real pleasure, excitement. Those exotic dark eyes of hers alive with fire. That was intelligence, determination, appreciation. The way we'd communicated in the dark. I'd held my hand out to her, and she'd taken it. She'd handed me her flashlight, listened to my comments, asked for my opinions. We'd lobbed jokes back and forth to lighten the tediousness of the ginormous task of weeding through eons of junk, dirt, and cobwebs to find special somethings.

But there had been so much disappointment in those eyes when she told me about her marriage. Self-flagellation. For bad decisions, missed opportunities. I had seen it in her, and I knew. I knew. She was walking on burning coals.

Sex used to be one of my favorite outlets, but once I'd cut myself off from the drugs and the booze to fill the holes, the sex hadn't been what it used to be. It took effort. And being sober for it was new, and I wasn't sure I liked it that way. Being conscious, being aware, having to deal with the other person in the mix. Nothing like the aftereffects of high living.

At dinner tonight, Tania had asked me about other women. I'd caught the taunting smirk on her face, which she'd quickly masked with a laugh and a joke.

I'd gotten thrown out of my first rehab for fucking a fellow inmate over the copy machine. That was a new low because I couldn't even finish.

That was when I'd decided to button it up. Button it all up—at least for a while. A kind of fast. I'd figured, I'd gone the opposite direction, enjoying the ocean view from Party Town Heights. So, why not check out the desert now and see if I could get to the oasis at the end of it?

There had to be an oasis. And I'd be so ready to drink.

Now, with Tania here, in bed next to me—sexy, hungry Tania—after all her frank confessions of the day and night, after her trusting me with thoughts and feelings and insecurities she had trusted to no one else...I was hard as a fucking rock.

Tania's lips moved, her tongue peeking out against her bottom lip.

That tongue. *Her* tongue.

My fingers cradled her face, and I leaned down and kissed her. She moaned, her body pressing into mine. I tugged on her bottom lip with my teeth. I stroked her upper lip with my tongue. She raised her head a few degrees and kissed me back. She explored my lips with hers, sucking, nibbling. So slowly. So...

A moan escaped my throat, and her tongue invaded my mouth and stroked.

I got my fucking passport and got it stamped.

My fingers slid under that band of elastic on her hip and found *her.*

Warm. Wet. Irresistible.

Her body shuddered, and she cried out.

My head swam. I stroked her wet silk, finding her clit. I listened to her body with every cell in my being.

Tease her. Please her.

I went gentle, I stroked faster, I touched lighter, I rubbed harder.

Fuck, I love this.

I wanted her to come. I wanted to be the one to give it to her. I wanted my mouth on her tits, my fingers in her pussy. I wanted her crying out my name on those swollen lips.

But that would be going too far.

I took in a breath.

Cool it. Enjoy the small shit, goddamn it.

85

The small gifts in the dark. The ones you couldn't see, but you knew were there.

I rubbed my cock up against her, and she pressed back, enjoying the friction I offered and offered me more of the same.

I wanted to give her pleasure, relief. She deserved it. She obviously needed it. I wanted to be the one to give her that. I was peeling back layers. A flower was blooming in my hands.

Her body stiffened in my hold as her fingers dug into my scalp. "Wh-what the hell are you doing?" she choked out, her eyes wide open.

She'd woken up, and her logical brain had kicked in.

"Shh."

"Shit." She twisted in my hold and planted her hands against my bare chest.

Fuck if that didn't turn me on more.

"We're both here, so we might as well?" she asked, her voice tight.

"No. No, it's not—"

"I don't want to be your *might as well*," she blurted.

My hand gripped her jaw. *I don't either.*

A noise escaped from the back of my throat. "It's not that. You aren't that."

"Then, what? Are you doing me a favor, taking pity on me?"

"Fuck no." My fingers stroked her skin. "You ever touch yourself? Make yourself come?"

"All the time." She breathed hard.

My dick jumped at the husky sound of her voice. Stubbornness laced with need. Images of her touching herself in a stolen moment in a bed, the shower, on a sofa, her head thrown back, lips parted, fired off in my head.

"Good. So then, you can appreciate this." I increased the pressure of my fingers. "A man touching you. Now, stop talking and feel this. Enjoy it."

Her breath fanned the bare skin on my chest. "Butler—"

"Let me touch you, Tania. Let me give this to you."

Her legs rubbed against mine, and a fever rushed through my veins. I didn't want to stop. We both wanted this bad. Whatever the hell this was.

"No, don't. This isn't…"

"Feel it, Scarlett. Just this. Only this. This is for you."

My fingers dragged through the soft flesh between her legs. I swirled them through her, back and forth and around. Her eyes widened, hanging on mine.

Whirlpool. I was in a fucking whirlpool.

Her breath snagged, and her fingers squeezing my arms.

"Vibrator better than this?" I whispered.

"Shut *up.*"

I grinned against her damp skin, my lips nuzzling her throat. She trembled.

"Tell me it doesn't feel good, baby. Tell me you're not liking it. Tell me you don't want to come." My raspy voice sounded jagged through the darkness as I slowly stroked her.

"Butler—"

"Let me take you there." My lips danced across the side of her face. "Fucking tell me, Tania. Say it."

She squirmed in my hold. "Harder."

Yes.

I intensified the pressure of my fingers, and she cried out. A helpless wild cry. A tide of unexpected sensation pulled me under at the sound.

Her hips rocked against my hand. "So good."

"Yeah?"

"I'm coming…"

The sounds of my fingers moving in her slickness made the heat bunch in the base of my spine. It had been a long time since I'd given to someone I really wanted to give to. That there had been a reason, a motivation to give, other than the woman was a hot piece of ass who was working me good and I was obliged to do the same.

Forget my cock. My fingers weren't even inside Tania now. I hadn't even seen her naked; she still had clothes on. I was only touching her, holding her, kissing her, watching her.

This is crazy.

Her fingers rubbed my neck as our eyes searched each other's in the half dark. Our lips touched.

I wanted to be naked with her. I wanted more from her. I wanted—

My fingers moved rougher, quicker, pressing harder around her secret flesh.

"Go with it. Take it higher, Tania."

CAT PORTER

She gasped, her mouth against mine. "Oh, oh—almost—
oh—"

"Get there, baby. Fucking get there for me."

"Butler!" She detonated.

The priceless bottle of champagne had finally been uncorked.
The sweet bubbly liquor flowed over the bottle and into my
fucking mouth.

And I drank.

She clung to me, and I held on to her as the orgasm tore
through her. I pressed my palm down over her throbbing mound,
prolonging the intensity, and she cried out at the further
stimulation. Her lips nuzzled my chest as the pleasure tumbled
through her.

"Feel all of it, Tania."

Her muscles finally relaxed in my firm hold.

Her hand slid between the press of our bodies to the steel rod
craning through my boxer briefs. Her eager fingers slipped past my
waistband and wrapped around the engorged wet tip of my cock.

My body seized.

All I wanted was to plow through her right this very second.
All I wanted was to feel her coming on me, moving with me.
Those huge eyes taking me in as I drove inside her. Her pleading
for mercy, a mercy I wouldn't give.

Holy shit.

I tugged her hand away. "Don't worry about me."

"Let me—let me do something for you. Let me touch you,
please."

"No, you don't have to."

Have I ever said that to a woman before in my life?

"I want to," she whispered.

"Shh." I buried my face in her hair, trying to get my breathing,
my pulse, under control.

That didn't help. At all.

"You don't want me?"

"I wouldn't be touching you if I didn't want you, trust me. But
I didn't do this to get laid."

"Then, what? Why not?"

"You were moaning in your sleep, making me crazy. What the
hell were you dreaming of anyway? You and George Clooney?"

"No!" She laughed.

"You and your vibrator?"

She only laughed harder.

"Just don't tell me it was your fucking ex."

"No, no." She pressed her face into my chest, and I held her tighter, skimming her chin, her jaw with my lips. "I was dreaming of Gerhard and Astrid. How they were together. Only…"

Jesus, this woman.

"What?"

"Nothing."

"Tania, I just had my fingers between your legs. We're past embarrassing. Tell me."

"I dreamed that I was Astrid, and Gerhard was looking at me the way I imagine he must have looked at her while he was dressing her for a photograph."

A sharp prickle laced over my chest.

"Were you naked?" I asked.

"Uh-huh. And he put a long scarf around my neck. Only that."

My fingers traced a curve up her throat to the slim angles of her face.

"I could feel him touching me. Kissing me," she continued, her voice breathier. "Then, he put the crown in my hair."

"Hmm. You looked good with that crown." My hand smoothed through her hair. "Even better if you were naked."

She laughed. A satisfied lazy laugh.

"I'm serious. And all this black hair swirling around your neck, like a scarf."

"You wouldn't put a cape or that fabric over me?"

"No, only your hair wrapped around you. Much sexier. You've got great hair." My fingers smoothed down the ends of her silky black hair over the swell of her breast. I stroked the full curve, and she let out a low moan. "You deserve a man crowning you."

She pressed a hand to the side of my face and held my gaze. Comfort and assurance flooded my veins like morphine.

"I feel really idiotic for saying thank you, but I feel like I should. Thank you."

"For what exactly? The compliment or the orgasm?"

She laughed. "For both."

"My pleasure. Really. Now, go to sleep." I tucked her further into my embrace and inhaled the warm musk of her skin, a blend of soap, lust, and sweat dancing in my nostrils.

Years ago, she had pulled away from me, rejected what I'd offered her, and I'd shouted at her, cursed her for being so hard to please, such a snobby bitch. Now, over twenty years later, all I wanted this very second was to beg her to ride my cock, to take me in as deep as I could go.

The groan building inside me was killing me. The words were on my fucking lips.

I bit down on them to stop it all from spilling out of me.

Fucking Karma.

She stroked the sides of my face and brought her lips to mine. A small groan escaped me as she kissed me, enticing my tongue in lazy strokes with her own.

I pulled back, sweeping the hair from her face, and kissed her forehead. "Tania…"

Look at me, considering the bigger picture, thinking of consequences. I'm all grown up.

"That was really good. Really, really good," she whispered. "And that sounded sort of lame." She let out a giggle.

My chest swelled at the sound of that relaxed soft laugh. She'd enjoyed it. Enjoyed me.

"Can't we keep kissing?" she asked.

"That'll only lead to—we'd better stop here, not complicate things."

She twisted a lock of my hair around her finger. "You're right. I agree. I don't want to complicate things either. Both of us are going back home now after being away a long while, and God knows what we'll find. Only kissing, I swear."

My hand cupped her jaw, and her mouth met mine. Everything spun on our tongues—her taste, her enthusiasm, invading and caressing, giving and demanding, playful and forceful, needing.

Needing.

Oh, I needed. Shit, I really needed.

But I needed to stop this more.

My fingers fisted in her hair, tugging her head back. Her chest heaved under mine. My erection was as hard as iron against her middle.

I raised myself up. "We should get some sleep."

Who was I kidding? I couldn't let go now.

I slid lower on the bed, taking her with me. On a sigh, she burrowed her face into my chest again. Her fingers played with the curls of hair there and traced over the bumps and grooves on my skin.

"New scars and old scars?" she asked.

"Yeah. The new one is from Creeper shooting me last year. The old ones are from a few memorable knife fights and from a car accident when I was in high school. Got a couple on my back and down one leg from that, too."

I rubbed her scalp, unwilling to let go of the thick mane. Not yet.

Her eyes closed, and her breathing finally deepened.

This wasn't a great idea.

Fuck it.

Outside of getting sober and staying sober, it was the best thing that had happened to me in so fucking long.

Goddamn it, the sound of her moaning my name was going to haunt me.

I sank back into the mattress. Making her come was gratifying. Yeah, I liked having given her that. A whole fucking lot.

I like Tania.

I'd spent hours and hours with her today, tonight, and I genuinely liked her. I wanted to know more of her.

Maybe this is just me blowing off steam before getting home?

No. I was attracted to her; I wanted her.

Tania was a meteor that had torn through the sky over me and blown up on my road, and I had to hit the brakes fast. But she didn't fit; there wasn't room for her. Not now. Even if I was ready to take her on, to go there with a woman like her, the specter of what I had done to Caitlyn, of what I had lost because of it…

No.

No.

Things were good the way I'd set them up now. Things were structured, stacked, and there was a reason for it. A reason for everything. My fucking impulses had only steered me wrong in the past.

Logic said no. Logic got busy in my brain, shutting this down.

But there were a thousand electric threads of Tania prickling in my veins right this very second.

My heart thumped in my chest, and I succumbed to its thrum, an inexplicable, bewildering, almost eerie rhythm.

ELEVEN

TANIA

"YOU DIDN'T HAVE TO PAY for the room."

"You bought breakfast," Butler said.

"Coffees and oatmeal raisin bars are not exactly going all out, Rhett."

"We need to head out anyway."

By the time I'd woken up this morning, Butler had already gotten dressed. There hadn't been any awkwardness.

At least not too much after we'd murmured the initial, "Good morning," to each other.

I had gone about getting dressed while he went to the front desk, and we were now packing our things into my car and on his bike.

"Are they expecting you at the club? Jump, I mean?" I asked.

He zipped up his leather jacket. "No." He tucked his gloves on.

"Is this going to be a good reunion or a not-so-good reunion?"

He winked at me. "That all depends on Jump."

Jump, the president of the One-Eyed Jacks, had kicked Butler out to begin with last year. Or had made him an offer he couldn't refuse. I wasn't quite sure how this club shit worked. Would Butler have to pay for his crimes, make some sort of ancient tribal sacrifice to the One-Eyed Jacks' gods? Whatever happened, I couldn't imagine it was going to be easy.

"Ah, so, we might have fireworks over Meager this evening?"

He let out a deep laugh as he swung a long leather-covered leg over his Harley and settled in his saddle. "Maybe." He shot me that I-don't-give-a-shit grin of his.

Butler pressed a hand on one of his formidable thighs, and my insides tightened for a painful moment at the memory of me squirming against that impressive thigh last night. I blinked and took in Butler on his massive bike. All man.

I adjusted my sunglasses and cleared my throat. "I just wanted to let you know—"

"Just?"

I let out a dry laugh. "I don't want things to be awkward between us. I'm sure we'll be seeing a lot of each other. Meager's a small town. Grace and I spend a lot of time together."

"I won't be spending much time with Grace, Tania."

"Don't be a jerk. You know what I mean."

"Yeah, I know. No awkwardness from me. It was good to talk, to hang with you." His teeth dragged across his lip as he leveled his gaze at me.

The unspoken hung between us.

"Get there, baby. Let me take you there."

The burn of his hand on my bare ass remained, the press of his rock-hard leg in between mine, the knowing rhythm of his fingers over my flesh, those small groans he'd made—

His lips tipped up. "You want to get in your car now, Scarlett?"

I shoved at his shoulder, and he laughed.

Heading west on I-90, we got into Meager over four and a half hours later. Following Butler on his bike was fun. Not only did he look amazing on his Harley, but watching him command his bike over the road reminded me of seeing Grace and Dig tool around town on his bike in the old days. Man, woman, and machine—one integral sexy unit roaring past, both of them relaxed, happy, enjoying those small moments together.

Seeing Grace on the back of her new husband's bike around Meager when I was last home had made my heart sing in a new way. My dearest friend had found real love once more with another man, a very good man, and a happiness she so deserved. The sight of them riding together was living proof to me that there was the possibility of that second chance for the rest of us.

My divorce from Kyle would most certainly not be the end of the road for me.

Fooling around with Butler had shown me that, and I was grateful for it. I could respond to a man. I hadn't shut down. I hadn't kissed or touched anyone else since Kyle and I had first gotten together, and that was almost eleven years ago. Kissing Butler, feeling his hands caress me, his fingers tease me until I twisted with need and exhilaration, had me feeling all sorts of good crazy.

He was right, of course. His touch was much, much better than my own fingers or any vibrator.

Perhaps it had been presumptuous of him and easy of me, but I'd liked it, enjoyed it, and I didn't regret it in the least. Although him not letting me go near his dick was odd.

Butler, the generous, self-controlled gentleman. With age comes wisdom? Or, maybe, with pain comes wisdom and caution.

The thin cotton of my tee had been as heavy as chain mail on my body. My shorts and panties had been shoved down, trapping my legs, and that constriction had only made me squirm, made me want to be utterly at his mercy. To feel his bare skin against mine, to fuse my rising heat with his.

I had come at the skillful, determined, and violent hands of a man who wanted to stop time and give me that moment of pleasure. With that hand, he'd guided me through doorways and defended me with a knife, and now, he had given me this sweet bit of wild. And afterwards, falling asleep in each other's arms—that had been a simple and unexpected pleasure in itself.

Stolen intimacy.

I'd been a flaming tide of liquid fire crashing in the dark.

Sipping on fire.

One night, when I was all of thirteen, my daddy had let me try his whiskey. I'd wanted to know what all the fuss was about, what made that bottle so special to him on a cold winter evening, sitting around the fire with Mom, talking quietly into the night, the stereo filling the room with music. I'd actually enjoyed the harsh caramel-like flavor, the heat seeping through my mouth and rising in my veins all at once. But I'd been in shock over the burning sensation that had lingered long after.

The whiskey had humbled me, spanked me on the butt, made my mouth pucker, and it'd made me realize that I wasn't ready for it, nor was I worthy of it just yet.

"You'll see, sugar cube. One day, you just might like it. You'll appreciate it then," Dad had said.

I was sure I would age and mature like the words on the bottle noted, and then the mysteries of that elixir would be mine. Then, I would understand the richness, the secret pleasure, the sage adult wisdom it had to offer.

Even though I had kissed and been kissed many, many times and very well in my life span thus far, last night with Butler had been something else entirely. There was a delicate thread of honesty to it, a savoring, an enjoyment of the little moments. There had been no race to a finish line. Our lips, our tongues, had spoken their own heady carnal language while our fingers had searched over each other's skin.

Butler and I had fooled around before, but that had been grabbing, grandstanding, jeering at each other.

This?

Oh, that stinging fire made sense right now. Only, last night, I hadn't wanted to sip. I'd wanted to gulp it down, swallow as much as possible.

And not think about tomorrow.

We stopped for gas and a quick sandwich, helping out several Canadian tourists decipher their maps and choose from the lesser-known local sights. I checked in with my mom and Jill, who were on their way to one of my mom's many weekly physical and occupational therapy appointments. I called Grace and let her know I was on my way.

"Good. Come by the club," said Grace. "I have Becca with me. The guys are working on my car, so pick us up, and I'll help you unpack."

"Oh, you're such a good friend. What did I ever do to deserve you?"

She let out a laugh. "Can't wait to see you!"

I didn't tell her about Butler. Let him make his grand entrance.

I shut down my cell phone and turned to Butler. "I'm going to follow you to the club and pick up Grace from there."

He raised his chin. "All right. Let's go."

Having sung through my favorite Fleetwood Mac CD earlier—sometimes, a girl just needed her Stevie Nicks on—I flew through another favorite CD from my other rock goddess idol, Carly

Simon, until we arrived in Meager and circled the town to get to the One-Eyed Jacks' property.

At a stop sign, I sent Grace a quick text that I was two minutes out.

Once there, the long metal gate slowly drew open, and the club member walking up to the gate waved me in. His eyes widened as Butler raced in front of me. The return of the fallen warrior from faraway lands.

I parked my Yukon away from the row of gleaming club bikes and to the side of all the other vehicles. When I got down from the truck, a smiling Grace charged toward me. We'd been close since we'd first met in kindergarten. Now, Grace and I were older and wiser, but her hazel eyes still lit up with that familiar genuine warmth, and we still hugged each other super tight the way we always had.

"Hey you!" She squeezed me.

"Hey!"

"Good to be home?"

"*Very* good," I replied, planting a kiss on her cheek.

"Didn't get a chance to mention it over the phone, but it's been a really interesting day so far," said Grace, sweeping her caramel brown highlighted hair out of her way.

"For me, too, actually. I bumped into Butler on the road yesterday." I gestured at him.

Butler had parked his bike on the other side of the line of Jacks' bikes, and a group of men strode toward him, huge smiles on their faces. Grace's husband, Miller "Lock" LeBeau, tall, dark, and austerely handsome stood apart from them, stock-still, except for the harsh chewing motion of his jaw. Grace had told me her husband had taken up a lot of gum-chewing now that he'd quit smoking, but this seemed to be something more than a sudden nic fit he was experiencing. The now very rigid chiseled angles of Lock's face along with his longish black hair, which had grown out since I'd last seen him, gave him a severe appearance. His heavy dark eyes were pinned on Butler.

Boner, a One-Eyed Jack who was a close friend of Grace's from the old days, held Becca. He immediately moved toward Lock, clamped a hand on his shoulder and handed him my niece. He then went over to Butler, shook hands with him, and gave him a big rocking hug.

"You bumped into Butler?" Grace asked, her gaze focused on the men talking and laughing, thumping Butler on the back.

Her tone of voice made me glance at her. "What is it?"

"Things just got extremely interesting then."

"Why do you say that?"

"Well—"

"It's about time. Where the fuck have you been?" shouted out a twenty-something thin blonde, who came out from behind Jump, marching toward Butler.

A scowling man stood at her side, sporting Flames of Hell of Ohio colors.

Butler froze, staring at her. She swung her long hair out of her face before her hands landed on her narrow hips.

"What are you doing here?" Butler's voice was low, controlled.

Jump shook his head as he crossed his arms. Everyone looked from the blonde back to Butler.

A prickle shot up the back of my spine, tightening an icy noose around my neck.

I leaned in closer to Grace. "Who is that?"

"That's Nina. She showed up the day before. *She's* the interesting part."

Jump sported an acidic smirk on his face. "Well, well, well. Not happy to see your old lady?"

My heart stopped. "She's Butler's old lady?"

Nina grinned at Butler.

Oh.

My stomach dropped. She was the epitome of how he'd described his type of woman.

"Nina got here with her bodyguard, Led, both of them acting like they'd expected the welcome wagon," Grace said. "She's some national officer's sister-in-law from a Flames of Hell chapter in Ohio. She and Butler got together out there, and now—"

My heart slugged in my chest.

"Now, they're here," I breathed.

Butler and Jump exchanged words. Jump turned abruptly, his long braid flipping off his shoulder, and charged back inside the clubhouse. Taking his arm, Nina led her old man inside, the Flames of Hell biker following them.

My gaze was glued to the doorway of the club through which Butler had just now disappeared.

Now, he was a different Butler than the one I had gotten to know the past day and a half. Vastly different.

Good-bye, Butler.

Was this why he hadn't wanted to have sex or do anything more than touch me? So that, technically, he wouldn't be a cheater? So that I wouldn't have to feel too bad about it once I found out the truth?

No penetration, no oral contact on private parts. No orgasm for him. No guilt—sort of.

How very Bill Clinton. *"I did not have sexual relations with that woman!"*

Smart. Neither of us would have to lie. I wouldn't want to be dragged through adultery court at the One-Eyed Jacks, that was for sure, or hunted down by his old lady in a fit of jealous biker woman rage. No, thank you. Clubs had rules, and I certainly didn't want to be involved. Not to mention, the old lady in question was from another club and had brought backup with her.

I tore my gaze away from the clubhouse.

"Shit, he did *not* look happy to see her though, did he?" The sudden tension in Grace's voice disengaged my reverie. "Not at all. She's young, too. What the hell has he gotten himself into this time?"

"Maybe what she has to offer him in the bedroom is so extraordinary that he put a ring on it."

Grace glanced at me. "They're not married, just—"

"Oh."

"I'm not liking this," she murmured.

My heart plunged and dragged through sludge. "It's not for us to like, is it?"

I really wanted to go now. Get the hell away from here. Away from all of them.

Away from Butler.

Away from my daydreams that had no place in reality.

I shifted my weight and pulled my thin shawl jacket around me.

Last night's thing with Butler had been about him feeling sorry for me. He wasn't attracted to me. *How could he be if he's hooked up with Miss USA over there?* No, he had touched me because we had gotten along, we'd had a laugh, I had been there in the same bed, and, yeah, why the fuck not?

Whirring loopy feelings went off inside me, ugly feelings I needed to slice, dice, chop up, and throw away.

Lock strode toward us with my niece in his arms. Becca clapped her chubby hands together and babbled loudly at the sight of me. An intense contrast with Lock's dour expression.

I leaned into Grace. "Your hubs doesn't look too happy. You need to talk to him before we leave?"

"Hey, Tania. Good to see you," said Lock.

Becca reached out to me.

Thank God for you, my little puffball.

"Thanks. Good to be back." I took Becca in my arms and squeezed her, kissing her face over and over again. "Hi, Becs. Hi-hi!"

She leaned her forehead on mine and giggled, drool sputtering out the side of her mouth. "Tah-nee!"

"Yeppers, I'm back!" I kissed her nose, her cheeks, her chin, and she giggled again.

This was why I was back. Family. Reconnection, rebuilding. *This* was real. The scent of apple juice and baby shampoo. The tug of my niece's fingers in my hair.

Grace wrapped her arms around her husband and peered up at him. "That was interesting, huh?"

Lock scoffed, brushing her mouth with his. "You two headed to Tania's?"

"Yes. Can you swing by and pick me up later this afternoon?" asked Grace, smoothing a thick strand of his ebony hair behind his ear.

"I'll be done by then. I'm not sticking around here for the sideshow."

TWELVE

TANIA

GRACE HELPED ME UNPACK my car and get my stuff into my old room in my mother's house. The artwork I'd unload in the garage later on. We fed Becca, and she went down for a nap right away.

Grace and I toed off our boots, and we finally stretched out on the sofa and enjoyed tall glasses of iced tea.

"How was Butler when you saw him yesterday?" she asked.

"He seemed good, but he definitely didn't mention being in a relationship."

"My brain is still whirling about that."

"Why? He's hot. She's hot. End of story." I swallowed more iced tea, but it tasted flat and watery. "He came on a pick with me."

"He did?"

"He was very helpful and interested. He even found that antique bicycle for me. We had dinner, talked." I shrugged. "It was nice."

Grace laughed.

"What's so funny?"

"I'm having a hard time imagining the two of you spending a *nice* time together and enjoying it."

"I know. Years ago, I was a jerk to him, and he was always a jerk right back. But we've both grown up since then."

"I'm glad." She put her glass back on the coffee table. "You stayed at a motel last night?"

I went back to my tea. "Yeah, so many tourists around. The place was hopping."

What would she say if she knew what had happened?

I'd never told Grace about me and Butler at her wedding years ago, and I was just too tired and stressed out right now to get into the latest development. He belonged to someone else. And that someone else was a sexy twenty-something girl who was definitely old lady material.

My body seemed to have its own memory of events, no matter how my brain tried to shut it down. My flesh remembered the press and stroke of his fingers, sending a jolt right through me, and I crossed my legs, squeezing them together. Butler's sexy murmurings seared me fresh. His smoky tone of voice, his raw words, his gentle caresses, which slowly, slowly had become more and more intense.

My grip tightened on my cold glass. There had been more carnal sensuality, eroticism, and intimacy in those brief moments with Butler last night than in a long number of years with Kyle.

"Tania? You seem really tired. Why don't you go lie down? We can talk more tomorrow."

I sat up. "Oh, I'm fine."

"Divorce going through? Obviously. You're here—"

"It's going through. And don't say, *I'm sorry*, because I'm not sorry. It's a good thing."

"I'm glad for you then. I really am. I'm just so happy that you're back in Meager with me."

"Me, too, Grace." I sank back into the sofa, bringing my cold glass to my chest.

"You are really distracted. What are you thinking about?"

"Touching," I blurted out.

"Touching what exactly?" Grace asked, a hint of a smile on her lips.

She wasn't sure if she should laugh or give me a hug. Neither was I.

"Men and women touching," I replied, adding a wicked smile.

"Ah, there is nothing like someone touching you. No, correction—someone *you want* to touch you. And badly."

"Abso-fucking-lutely. Here's to that!" I raised my glass of iced tea in the air. "Oh, by the way, biker lady, there was a little incident with a member of the Broken Blades when Butler and I stopped for dinner on the road."

I told Grace about the encounter at the restaurant.

Her eyes narrowed. "Are you okay?"

"Yes. It wasn't fun, but Butler handled it swiftly. Of course, that must have been nothing for him. My brother's name seemed to be my bonus ticket out of that mess. Imagine that."

"I don't have to imagine."

We shared a look.

"No, you don't, do you?"

"Change of topic."

"Yes, please." *Enough about men.* I drained my glass.

"Are you still interested in opening a store here in town?"

"Yes. Why?"

"I think I've found a great space for you. Dillon's is up for rent."

"The old five-and-dime smack in the middle of Clay Street?"

"Yep. Right in the center of town."

I sat up. "But Dillon's is a huge space, isn't it?"

Grace got out her cell phone, her finger sweeping over her screen. "The owners are about to divide the store into three separate retail spaces for rent. Brick walls, wood flooring, pressed copper ceiling from its turn of the century days as Meager's one and only General Store."

"I remember."

"I think you're going to love it." She held her phone out to me.

I peered at the photo, and my muscles tightened. A bell tolled in my distance, the sound unmistakable. "I want to see it now."

"That's enthusiasm."

"That's determination to do what it is I really want to do for a change."

"Amen, sister. By the way, Miller has most of his brother's stuff in a new storage facility that the club just built on the property, so you can come over anytime you want and start going through it."

"He agreed?"

"He's thrilled."

"Oh my gosh! Terrific! Okay, first thing tomorrow, let's meet at Dillon's and check out the space together, and then you can show me Wreck's stuff in the storage unit."

"You sure you don't want to take a day or two to relax and—"

"Hell no."

"Whatever you say. Sounds like a plan then."

Yes, it was a mighty good plan. I would focus on me, getting my business off the ground. *Yes, yes, yes.*

The front door shoved open.

"We're home!" Jill exclaimed as she stood behind my mother, who used her walker to slowly and carefully maneuver herself into the house.

"Hey, you two!" I darted over and hugged my mother. "How was physical therapy today?"

"It was a pain in my ass." Rae kissed my cheek as she squeezed my arm with her free hand. "Good to see you again, baby."

Jill slid her sunglasses onto her head, pulling back her wavy strawberry blonde hair from her freckled face. She held up a familiar white bag with the Meager Grand Cafe logo on it. "Rae made me promise to stop on the way home and get her a cappuccino and doughnuts."

I hugged Jill and turned to face my mother once more. "Rae, you know what the doctor said about your cholesterol."

"I know what he said, but that's what those pills are for, aren't they? I need a treat after all that torture this morning."

Jill raised her hands in the air. "I tried to talk her out of it."

"That therapist boy is so pushy," Rae continued, smoothing a hand through her sleekly bobbed jet black hair. "Putting me through the ringer like that. Honestly."

Jill laughed. "Aw, Rae, Matt's pretty sweet to me."

Grace steadied the walker as I helped my mother into her reclining chair.

"I'm glad someone's getting something out of those visits. Sure isn't me." Rae let out a deep sigh as she pushed the button on her electric chair. The reclining motion went into full swing, lifting her legs up and out. "Ah. My cappuccino, please."

Jill opened the bag and removed a coffee cup for herself and handed another to me, along with a glazed doughnut wrapped in waxed paper.

"Go ahead, Mother, have your poison," I muttered, taking the coffee and doughnut from Jill and handing them to Rae.

"This is my only vice, Tania." Rae took a sip of her coffee. "Yesterday Jill did lots of food shopping at that new health food store co-op and got us all sorts of grass-fed veal and buffalo meat, free-range chicken, brown rice, strange greens, and milk that isn't milk. Didn't you, honey?"

"Yes, I did," said Jill. "I'm going to go start on that chicken cacciatore you showed me how to make. Grace, are you staying for dinner with us?"

"No, Miller is coming soon to pick me up. I've got braised beef that's been in the slow cooker since this morning. I'm going to make some homemade mashed potatoes once we get home."

"Oh, yum, that sounds good," said Jill, absently rubbing her curved belly. "Shoot, I've got to go take my iron pill." She darted into the kitchen.

"Have half this doughnut, Jill!" said Rae.

"No way!" Jill's laughter rose from the kitchen. "I gained a lot of weight with Becca, and it was hard to lose, so I'm determined not to overdo it this time around. A glazed doughnut? Evil!"

"See what a temptress you are, Mother?" I said.

Rae rolled her eyes. "Oh, Jill's a tiny thing, and she needs her strength now."

"Strength is found in fruits and vegetables, nuts, and lean proteins, not in sugar and flour." Jill's voice rang out from the kitchen.

"Killjoy!" Rae hit the button on the remote control of her lounge chair, and the chair hummed as it eased back further. "Time for my cooking show, girls. Hush and admire Tyler Florence with me, or leave the room. Those are your options."

Grace grinned as she leaned over and planted a kiss on my mother's cheek.

Yes, it was good to be home.

THIRTEEN

TANIA

"DID YOU GET ANYTHING GOOD?" I asked Jill over the phone. Once again, I was at the Jacks' new storage unit, up to my ears in Wreck's belongings. Jill was on her way home from the mall in Rapid where Boner had taken her and Nina so she could shop for maternity clothes and Nina could get her hair done at a salon.

"Yeah, I did," Jill said, her voice flat.

"Something wrong?"

"Nope."

"Was Nina a bitch again?"

Nina had picked a fight with me and Jill earlier, and Boner had broken it up.

"Nope."

"Everything good with Boner?"

Boner was always a bit standoffish with Jill, so I was surprised he had offered to take her to the mall today. He'd invited Nina to go along with them in an effort at making friends with the new girl on the block. She was his buddy's woman, after all.

"Yep."

"Jill, you sound weird. What happened?"

"I should be home in twenty minutes or so," said Jill in her fake relaxed voice.

"You can't talk now, right?"

"Hmm."

"Do I need to punch anyone?"

Jill only let out a dry laugh.

"That's better," I said, still not convinced. "Don't worry about cooking anything, okay? I'll bring food for us. Mom and Becca are staying at Penny's for dinner."

"Okay." Jill clicked off.

Jill was usually super chatty and blabby, what the hell could have happened at the mall, for Pete's sake?

Half an hour later, Boner pulled up on the Jacks' property in his truck, and a glammed-up Nina hopped out and strode into the club. She cast a cursory glance at me and kept walking.

"Hey, Boner!" I said. "Everything good?"

"Yeah. Great." He shot me a dark glare, his green eyes flashing as he swung out of the parking lot once more.

I think I needed to get home sooner rather than later.

Within an hour, I'd brought home a bottle of red wine for myself and a small lasagna from the new family style Italian restaurant in town for me and Jill to share.

"Jill?" I swung open the back door, which led to the kitchen, plopping the wine bottle and the heavy bag of food on the table. "Jill? I'm home!" I took off my messenger bag and dropped it on the nearest chair.

"Tania?" Jill's panicked voice rose from down the hall.

Moments later, Jill shuffled into the kitchen in her bathrobe, bare feet, hair mussed, blue-gray eyes dreamy, face flushed.

I bit my lip. "Oh…"

Now, it all made sense. Boner's cool attitude, yet overly protective behavior. Jill's usual skittishness in his presence, yet her eagerness to spend the day with him. Every instance of their awkwardness together over the past several weeks suddenly fit into place.

I wasn't the only one under this roof with a crush on a One-Eyed Jack.

"Shit, sorry. Did I interrupt you?" I asked.

Jill's face reddened again.

And I wasn't the only one who tended to her own needs to deal with her intense feelings for her crush.

"I have an idea," I said. "How about you take a cool shower, while I open my wine and pour you a glass of chocolate almond milk on ice, and then you can tell Tania all about it."

Jill let out a heavy sigh as she drew open a kitchen drawer, grabbed the wine bottle opener, and tossed it on the counter. "Make it a tall glass."

Early the next morning I stopped off at the Meager Grand and got a triple turbo cup of Americano to battle the post-Cabernet cloud that had taken over my brain cells, then shot straight to the club and got back to work on Wreck's collection. I was committed to going through as much of it as possible as I prepared to open my store. I had already found quite a number of pieces that I wanted to re-sell for Lock.

"Morning," a choppy voice rose behind me.

I spun around, clutching a box of rusty handlebars.

Sweat ran down Butler's flushed face, his wet hair pulled back in a short ponytail. He'd been to battle with himself and won. The sheen on his sculpted arms shone in the early morning light in the small courtyard to the side of Eagle Wings, Lock and Grace's custom-detailing and repair shop at the club. The club's new storage unit where I'd been going through Lock's brother's mountain of worldly goods was to the rear of the shop.

Weeks had passed since that day we'd arrived in Meager together, and I had managed to stay out of Butler's way.

Until now.

I took in a short breath. "Hi."

"What the hell are you doing here?" Butler's voice was sharp, his eyes cold, hard aqua stones.

Is he annoyed to see me?

He took the earbuds from his ears. "I mean, I'm surprised to see you here this time of day."

"Lock gave me the key to his unit. I try to get here early. There's a lot to get through."

"You're brave."

"So I've been told."

"And how's it going?"

"I've been able to plow through a good section of Wreck's eagle collectibles of all varieties, and I organized the piles strategically around the room. Now, I'm finding non-eagle items and trying to organize those. Next, I plan on cataloging it all and taking photos of certain pieces that I feel need a specialist's appraisal. I'm hoping Lock will let me sell some really nice pieces at my store or keep a few on permanent display there, if he doesn't want to sell them."

"Store? You moving ahead with your business plan?"

"Yep. I found a great space in town, and I signed the lease yesterday. It's official."

"Holy shit, woman. Congratulations."

A huge grin split his face, making him even more handsome than he already was, an almost boyish enthusiasm racing over his features. The tense version of this man had its own appeal. I had to admit, I liked that, too.

His hands hung on his hips. "That's great news, Tania. There you go, taking off. I'm really happy for you." The lines around his mouth deepened, the hollows just under his cheekbones making an appearance.

I cleared my throat. "Thank you."

"Let me get that for you." Butler took the box from me and set it down on top of two other boxes in the vast storage unit. "Jesus, look at this place. It's packed. Wreck used to find all sorts of stuff everywhere we went; he was always buying something."

"Yeah, it's quite obvious."

"He could get the toughest old coot to sell to him, I swear. Find anything interesting yet?"

A whiff of hard man and determined exertion wafted over me. It wasn't the clean soapy scent of him from that night in the motel but raw, wild natural, and it set off a raw, wild urge spinning inside me.

I stepped back and let out a breath. Bending over a box, I busied myself with ripping the yellowed tape off the ends. "I found a few interesting things, but there's plenty more to go. I'll be here a long while yet."

He held up an ice cream company sign from a now defunct chain in Wisconsin and studied it.

"Wreck was a good talker but genuine, you know? Not a bullshitter," Butler said. "He gave a shit about the regular guy on the street. It came through when he talked to people."

"I remember."

"People responded to him."

Like I was responding right now to the visuals of post-workout Butler?

"You went out for a run?"

"Yeah."

"Good for you."

"Running keeps me sane."

I smiled.

"What is it?"

"I run for that very same reason. Well, that, and it keeps the love handles at bay."

He lifted an eyebrow, his gaze locked on mine. "You don't have love handles, Tania." His growly voice curled around those words, making my stomach flip.

Why is he reminding me of his familiarity with my body, of his touch over my skin?

My face heated, and I mentally kicked myself for having said such a thing.

"Tania, look, I wanted to tell you—"

Oh God, please no! Don't tell me! Don't say anything!

"What's that?" My voice came out overly chirpy, a desperate attempt not to be awkward.

"You must be wondering. You must be—"

"It's none of my business. It certainly explains why you didn't want to *complicate* things, and we didn't, right? Things didn't get out of hand—I mean, out of control." I threw in a shrug to make myself seem casual and unruffled. "We didn't go far, so things are fine."

He only stared at me, his jaw stiff.

Ohh, harsh Butler.

Gah!

"Actually, I'm grateful," I continued.

"Grateful?"

"Yes, grateful. I'm just getting out of a bad relationship. You're newly in one, um…not a bad one—well, I guess—" *Ah, shit!* "Anyway, what happened between us showed me that part of me is still alive and ready to…" My face heated yet again. "You know what I mean. I'll shut up now."

"Right. I get it."

I crossed my arms. "That's very exciting for you—your new girlfriend. I mean, old lady. Although why you didn't mention her, yes, I do find that odd, especially since you initiated—I mean, it was unexpected. But good. I'm good."

His eyes narrowed slightly. "Unexpected that something happened between us or unexpected that it was *good* with *me?*"

"Do you care?" I shot back.

"Answer me."

I returned his glare. "All of the above."

He held my glare. "Huh."

I shifted my weight. "Nina is really…"

Searching…searching…buffering…

He tilted his head at me, the edges of his full sexy-as-hell lips— lips I'd enjoyed, lips I'd been daydreaming about—twitching.

"Nice," I said. "Nina's very nice."

And now that you're all hot and sweaty and raging with cardio endorphins, you can go wake her up with demanding kisses and wild beast sex, and while you're banging her, I'll most likely hear both of your orgasmic moans and satisfied grunts from all the way over here.

"Tania?"

"Hmm?"

His eyes were trained on me, and a ribbon of thrill rippled through me.

My body was having orgasmic flashbacks.

Down, girl, down.

"If there's anything here that you have a question about, ask me. I was on plenty of runs with Wreck, and if I haven't obliterated those particular brain cells, I might remember where he found something or why he got it."

"Oh, that would be great. Thanks."

His pale blue eyes lit up. "Good. I'd like to help you if I can. It'd be fun. I had a good time helping you in Sioux Falls."

I held his aqua gaze, and something kindled in my chest. "Me, too."

My messenger bag slid off the top of a box along with a pile of Wreck's Louis L'Amour paperbacks.

"Dang." I picked up the yellowed books and stacked them against the wall.

Butler scooped up my bag, which had fallen on the other side of the box.

"This yours?" He held out a piece of gray paper, glancing down at it. The acceptance letter from the gallery.

"You got a job offer in Chicago?"

"I did."

"A fancy high-paying job?"

"Yes."

"You still considering it?"

"No. I told you, I'm getting my own store together here."

"You're hanging on to the letter though."

"Souvenir."

"Of what? What might have been?"

"Yes. But it's not what you think."

"Tell me."

"That job is not my dream come true. It would've been in another life. I came back to Meager not to escape, not to lick my post-separation wounds, but *to do*. Firstly, I came back because my mother needed me, but then I realized that I needed to help her, too. And I needed to stop ignoring how really unhappy and unfulfilled I was. My mom's MS diagnosis was a wake-up call. I had to make a change, to live my life to the fullest, because I could get run over by a bus this afternoon or get an autoimmune disease tomorrow."

I took the letter from him. "This job in Chicago? Yes, it's glittery and attractive and sexy all right, and it would have been easy to say yes to it and move to Chicago with Kyle and carry on. But the job doesn't turn me on, not really. It's kind of like what you were to Grace when she was with Dig. A sexy, flirty crush."

An eyebrow jumped. "Thanks. Nice metaphor."

"Think about it. Even though she had a girl crush on you, Grace's feet were solidly rooted in Dig's earth. Rooted—and that's no metaphor. That's the way it was. There's no denying your essence, is there? I realized that when I had dragged Grace out to Nebraska to look at that old man's property and we ended up finding Becca. I hadn't gone on a pick in months and months. Those trips were cocaine to me, and I loved them."

He chuckled. "You're putting real effort into these metaphors just for me, aren't you?"

I let out a small laugh. "I'd like you to understand, Butler. Cocaine isn't right though. That day in Nebraska, I felt in tune, alive, like myself, the me I'm most comfortable with, happy with. There was nothing temporary or artificial about it, and I'd missed that. I didn't realize that in my twenties when I was bopping around or in my thirties, convincing myself I had finally found my groove with Kyle and my freelance work, which I'd fit in here and there. Underneath it all, I was still searching, still restless. But that one afternoon in Nebraska—before Creeper blew it all away—that was all mine, all me. Everything *fit*, and it was so good and right."

I folded the letter. "Getting this gallery job freaked me out because it spelled convenience. Yes, it's flattering, tempting. Yes, it's a perfect fit but for the life I don't want to have anymore. I keep this letter in my handbag to ensure that I don't turn my back on what's right for me ever again. That I don't uproot myself from my earth for an existence that only makes sense on paper." I folded the letter over. "That's not me. I tried to make it me, thought I should for a while there. But I realized, maybe a little late, that you couldn't function on *shoulds*. I want to function on my desires. What makes me feel alive, what—"

"What gives you that zing." His eyes were gentle, his voice soft, clear.

I averted my gaze. "Yes. And although it's supremely rotten that my mother is suffering with this disease and will until the end of her days, it's shaken me and made me see the essentials clearly."

"In your gut."

"In my gut. Everything fell into place because of it, and crazy as it sounds, I'm grateful for it. I'd much rather be out meeting colorful people all over the country, trying to find a rusty worn-out treasure, and I'd much rather run my own eclectic country store to showcase what I want, the way I want. And I don't want to have to wear high heels and a dress and blow out my hair every goddamn day anyhow. Yes, running such a prominent art gallery is a great opportunity—"

"But it's not *your* great opportunity. It's not your truth."

"No, it's not." That warmth went off in my chest again. "My store here is my truth. That, and being with my mom and making her comfortable, spending time with my niece and nephews, and reconnecting with my sister and my brother and the best friends I've ever had. Those are the golden opportunities to me. Making a difference in my community, my hometown. The hometown I'd always thought I needed to get away from in order to find myself."

"Full circle."

"Yeah. I guess I had to be selfish to do it though."

"You're doing it right." He nodded at me, taking in a deep breath. "I miss this."

"What? Dust?"

"No. Talking with you, like this. About important things."
Butler held my gaze for one torturous, speechless moment. He
quickly turned around and shoved a box to the floor and then
another.

My shoulders fell. I missed it, too. I missed him. I hadn't
expected to, but I did. Every day.

Could we be friends? Or would it be too hard for me, too
annoying, seeing him with Nina? Even though he and I got along
so well, and I was attracted to him, at the end of the day, I was not
what he wanted or needed in a woman.

Butler leaned over and ripped open another box.

I did want to have him as a friend. I needed to stop making
mountains out of molehills and get on with it.

"I have something for you," I said. "I kept meaning to bring it
to you, but I never had a chance."

More like I felt awkward in front of everybody else, especially
Nina.

"What's that?" He glanced up at me.

I went to the corner of the room and got out the guitar case. I
brought it to him, my heart racing in my chest. "This is for you."

He stilled, his eyes slid to the black case.

"Open it."

He unlatched it and opened the cover, revealing the acoustic
guitar that he'd found at Gerhard's house.

"Tania." His voice was just above a whisper.

"I had it cleaned and restrung. It's a Martin Company guitar,
Butler—top of the line, made in the USA, going back to the
nineteenth century."

"I know about Martin guitars," he murmured.

"Isn't it exciting? This one is from the fifties."

"Tania—"

"I want you to have it, Rhett. Consider it my thank-you for
coming with me, for helping me so much at Gerhard's house, for
making sure I was safe—"

"Baby…"

My breath hitched, and my stomach dropped at the
endearment. I had to say this quickly before I lost it because that
look on his face, his shaky voice—all of it was yanking on me,
twisting me.

"But, most of all, for listening. That meant a lot to me. A hell of a lot. I had fun, and I liked getting to know you. Again. Better."

"I did, too, but this, it's too much."

"No. It's a gift, and you have to accept it. Please. Anyway, you see, my instinct was right about you being a musician hipster. I'm a witch that way."

He dragged his teeth across his bottom lip. "Thank you doesn't seem enough," he said, his voice low.

No, it didn't.

I wanted to throw myself at him, take him in my arms, hug him tightly. I wanted to sit with him and hear him play. I wanted to watch him get mesmerized by the music he made, and I wanted him to mesmerize me with his music.

But that wasn't meant to be.

"Thank me by taking it and playing it. I hope you can pick up wherever you left off with the guitar. Enjoy it."

His dark golden brows drew together as he latched the case again. "I will. Thank you."

I let out a breath. "You're welcome."

"I'd better get going." He rubbed a hand across his chest. "I've got to get in the shower, start my day."

Shower. Images jangled in my head—that chest and those shoulders with the scars I had explored with my hands and mouth slick with soapy water, his large hands rubbing over himself, up and down—

Stop, stop, stop.

Nina would probably be joining him in that shower, getting herself a custom-designed jolt of adrenaline and sex endorphins instead of caffeine to start her day. I was sure that was their morning ritual. *What a healthy girl she must be.*

I raised my hand at him, as if staving off the flow of images. "I've got to get on with this, too. I guess you and Nina are staying here at the club?"

"Actually, I found a place in town. We'll be going there this weekend."

"That's good. You have a good day then." Cheeriness was encrusted over my voice like cracked icing on a stale doughnut.

"Yeah, you, too." He stood still for a moment, the guitar case in his hands.

I shot him a quick see-ya-later smile and busied myself with pulling open the flaps on a new box, but the heat of his stare smoldered over me.

He turned and stalked off toward the clubhouse.

I peeked.

The muscles in his broad back clung to his sweaty cotton tank, and his running shorts were molded over his rock-hard ass. His long stride was forceful, aggressive. He was marching back to his new life, his new girlfriend.

I released my grip on the edges of the dusty box and picked up my coffee cup and took a slug.

"Get back to work, Reigert. Get back to work."

FOURTEEN

BUTLER

"WHAT ARE YOU DOING?"

Nina rubbed her bare tits against my back as I yanked on the laces of my running shoes, her hands squeezing my shoulders. "What do you think I'm doing?"

"Get off me."

"Oh, come on."

I kicked off my sneakers and ripped off my socks. "Get the fuck off me!"

"This is one of your responsibilities isn't it, old man?"

She thought that was funny, that line, poking at our age difference, the irony of it with our *titles*.

I pushed her off my body, and she fell back onto the mattress.

I put my hand at her throat. "Don't you ever fucking talk to me like that again."

She bit her lip. "Sorry. I was kidding. You know what I meant."

"Yeah. You're incredibly articulate, as always." I released her throat.

"You're so fucking sensitive. What's wrong?"

I pressed a hand into my chest, my eyes darting to the guitar case I'd propped in the corner of the room. "I'm tired."

"You just got back from a run, didn't you? Shouldn't you be feeling energized and ready to tackle your day?"

"I couldn't sleep last night."

She sat up and moved toward me. "Let me rub your back. That always helps."

Her fingers dug into my shoulders, and a burning warmth went off in my muscles. I exhaled. She was good at massaging at least. My head sank forward as she kneaded my knots.

"Lie down, so I can work your lower back."

I turned around and spread over the mattress.

"Bet if I were someone else, you'd be in the mood," Nina muttered on a laugh.

I turned my head. "What's that supposed to mean?"

"I've noticed the way you look at her."

"What the fuck are you talking about?"

"Tania. The way you look at Tania."

"Tania's a friend from a long time back. Nothing's going on with her."

She ran her fingers down my spine. "What's the big deal? I mean, I wouldn't care. It wouldn't be cheating. Give me a fucking break."

Jesus, shut the hell up already.

Her thumbs worked my shoulder blades. "We both know I don't do it for you."

That was bordering on insulting, and she knew it.

I gritted my teeth. "Unlike you, getting laid is the least of my concerns right now."

"I'm just saying, I can tell you like her, so do what the hell you want. I know I can't wait to do the same. Led finally went home, so we don't have any eyes watching us anymore to report back to Reich."

"Don't be fucking naive." I turned over and shoved at her with my hips. She climbed off me. "You can't be sure. Your brother-in-law is never satisfied."

"Well, I made sure that Led would be convincing once he got back to Ohio."

I eyed her. "What does that mean?"

"Nothing." She grinned, like a kid enjoying a little white lie. "In the meantime, can't a girl get laid around here? Even by her own old man?"

Her cool hand cupped my balls and stroked.

I smacked her hand away, and she only laughed. She sat up and straddled my left thigh, sliding a hand inside her panties. She worked herself, grinding against my leg. Her eyes hooded, her tits swaying with her motion, her jaw slackening, her face a come-on.

I recognized the desire on her features, the sensual distraction, the heightening degrees of satisfaction ratcheting up, one by one.

Her hand moved faster between her legs, her face registering every flick, every vibrating stroke. Her upcoming orgasm was to her what hits of coke had been to me.

My cocaine in all its fervor. My cocaine in its promise of the ultimate pleasure high, always promising more and more.

I am Superman. I am roaring. I can do no fucking wrong.

My cocaine had wiped out all my thousand and one failures, obliterating that mudslide of self-loathing, that glittery golden revulsion I hoarded in a special treasure chest just for me. The blow had offered that superficial surge of fullness, of blasting through all my yesterdays, todays, and tomorrows.

I thrill, I want, I need. More. More. More.

Oh, one big hungering need. Right here, now in Nina's face.

Her features morphed as the sensations hit her, dragged through her. She panted harder, her nipples standing at attention. She grabbed my hand, pressing it over a breast and squeezing it there. Her other hand rubbed faster over her clit as she rocked her pelvis back and forth over my thigh.

I squeezed her tit, her hand pressing over mine, as she rode my leg.

But it was Tania's body that filled my hand, her unhurried moans and whimpers that I could still hear as I'd sunk my fingers into her wet heat, lavishing her smooth skin with kisses. Her flesh trembling as I held her.

How long had it been since a man satisfied her?

I remembered feeling the goose bumps racing over her flesh, her body calling out to mine with every moan and press and twist, wanting more of what I was giving. I'd smelled her excitement, her hunger.

"Oh, yeah. Oh, yeah…" Nina chanted, breaking the spell.

Ah, shit. Let's get this done.

I tugged on her nipple, twisting it hard, and smacked her other tit. She let out a high-pitched cry, her back arching up. She liked that shit.

I pressed my thigh against her, and her body stiffened.

"Fuck! Fuck yes!" she moaned loudly.

She finally shoved off my leg and laughed as she dropped back onto the mattress. Her hair was over her face, a hand rubbing down her throat to her middle.

"That'll have to do for now, huh?" she said, brushing her hair from her face before her hands flopped back over her head.

"Give it a few more months, and then you can go find yourself a fuck toy."

"Anything you say, honey." She let out a groan as she leaned over the edge of the bed, her hand searching through a tote bag. "In the meantime"—she unzipped a pouch and brandished her hot-pink two-pronged vibrator in the air—"I have this fuck toy. Next best thing to a cock. There are times when it's even better."

"I'm happy for you." I shot up from the bed and ripped off my shirt and shorts.

"You know, I read on the Internet that if you get used to getting off with the intensity of a vibrator, ordinary touching and fucking just won't do it for you anymore. You get desensitized or something. Imagine that, huh? Kinda freaky." She dropped back on the bed again and bent her legs. "But, a girl's gotta do what a girl's gotta do." She positioned the vibrator between her legs and let out a whimper. "You can watch if you want. You used to like to watch."

"I've got to take a shower and get moving."

I headed for the bathroom. I showered, jerked off to the Tania-coming-on-the-motel-bed video clip I had on constant replay in my head, washed up, dried off, and went back into the room where I threw on a pair of my jeans that lay crumpled on the floor.

Nina—her face flushed, a sheen of sweat over her skin—lazed, naked, on the bed, tapping on her cell phone. The vibrator was tossed at her side on the mattress.

Young girls today. They had an orgasm or two, and immediately, they've got to text about it.

"You going to do some laundry?" I asked, stretching my last clean T-shirt over my head.

Nina remained focused on her phone, her fingers tapping away. "Huh? Oh. Yeah, sure."

"I'm off. Call me if you need anything."

"'Kay," came out of her mouth without her looking up from her phone. "Oh, hey, what's with the guitar?" she asked, glancing up at me.

I flung open the door. "Don't touch it. It's mine."

FIFTEEN

TANIA

"MY TWO BEST FRIENDS are meeting tonight. End of story. One of you is either out of town or in the thick of work. So ridiculous. Lenore's finally back from visiting her son in LA for several months. The first ladies' night at the Tingle needs to be celebrated. What could be better?"

"What could be better?" I muttered as I raised my apple martini at her. *How can I possibly turn down the event of the century—male strippers at the club-run titty bar?*

"That's more like it!" Grace clinked my glass with her beer.

"Absolutely!" Jill clinked her tall glass of cranberry and soda and lime against ours.

Jill was a month away from delivering Grace's baby, and her baby bump was now huge and very round, stretching her clingy dress. We'd surprised her and Grace with a baby shower last week, and now, this would be the last girls' night out for a long while, so the timing was perfect.

Grace, Jill, and I had arrived first. The other old ladies—Mary Lynn, Suzi, Dee, Nina, and Alicia—had arrived soon after. The nightclub was packed and very loud. The women of the Black Hills were ready to party.

My stomach twinged at the sight of Butler talking in Nina's ear as he gripped her upper arm. Nina made a face and mouthed off at him, twisting her arm out of his hold. *A tiff?* Maybe tonight would prove to be far more interesting than sitting at home, crunching numbers while listening to the television blaring in the background or wandering around the Internet. Again.

Nina marched over to our table, her face tight, and threw herself in the last empty chair.

I leaned into Grace. "What's Butler doing here?"

"He's been managing the Tingle. He took over for Kicker."

"Seriously? The man had a serious drug and good-time addiction for years. What the hell is he thinking?"

"It wasn't his idea. It was Jump's. A test for good behavior. Otherwise…"

"Oh."

"Yeah."

"And how's he holding up amid all the booze and boobs?"

"Great, from what I hear."

"Good. I'm glad."

"You're glad?"

"Of course." I drained my glass. "He's come a long way."

"Yes, he has."

The last thing I wanted to do was be at a peen-ogling party with Butler present.

Grace and Jill had repeatedly invited me to club get-togethers, but I always had a ready-made excuse. The first one I'd gotten out of was that big club party months before when Butler and Nina had been officially welcomed back into the One-Eyed Jacks. I'd found a couple of estate sales just over the border in Wyoming and made it a weekend trip.

Although I should have been at that particular party, seeing as how my brother had screwed things up between the clubs by manhandling Jill when he'd found out she was pregnant, dragging her from our house to the club at gunpoint to mouth off to the Jacks. I could barely believe my ears when my mother had called me first thing the following morning and told me all about it.

The rest of the parties were the usual barbecues or community charity events, and I had managed to be busy for almost each one. The less distraction, the better.

Of course, I had attended Jill and Boner's wedding a couple of months ago. It had been a beautiful morning at Sylvan Lake, the two of them so emotional, so very happy. And then the party afterward at the club under a white tent in the middle of the track, just like Dig and Grace's wedding.

Butler had brought me a glass of wine. He'd held a can of soda in his other hand.

"You're not taking off after this wedding, are you?"
"No, I'm not, Blondie."

He laughed. "Good."

"Are you taking off?"

"Here to stay." He raised his chin at me. "Same as you."

We clinked drinks, our eyes on each other.

"There she is!" A grin lit up Grace's face, her focus trained on a dark-haired woman snaking her way through the tables to us.

Lenore had severely dyed black hair streaked with pink, pinned up into a sort of retro beehive do, with several thin hairbands at the crown of her head. She sported a dizzying web of colored tattoos all over her chest and up to the base of her throat with more around her arms.

"Lenore!" Grace hugged her.

"I finally made it! The traffic was really bad on the way over here," Lenore said on a throaty laugh. "There's a line outside."

My scalp prickled. I knew that sexy voice. I knew that spiked rose tattoo laced on the top of her breasts, peeking out of her fantastic black bustier. Black eyeliner along with dark red lipstick gave her a stark, intriguing look, and long turquoise earrings reflected the startling color of her large eyes. I knew those incredible blue-green eyes. I'd never, ever forget them for as long as I lived.

My stomach clenched.

"Lenore, this is Tania. And, Tania, this is Lenore, who has the lingerie store in town you love so much—Lenore's Lace. Finally, you two get to meet."

Lenore's grin faded, a dramatically defined eyebrow arching high.

Yes, it's me.

I raised my chin and pushed my lips up into some sort of a smile. *Lenore* was Rena.

I remembered those amazing eyes once fraught with terror and flooding with ugly tears. I remembered those long hands, not manicured, not laced with tattoos, but bloodied, scabbed, and clawing at me.

"Please help. Please," she'd pleaded with me when we'd first met.

"Lenore?" I asked, a tentative quality to my voice that I just couldn't stop in time.

She nodded slightly, her matte-red lips parting. "Yes."

125

My face blazed into a grin. "Grace has told me so much about you. I love your store."

But my first words to her, to *Rena*, over twenty years ago had been, *"Yes, yes, I'll help you."*

"Oh, thanks," said Lenore, standing next to Grace. "It's good to meet you, Tania. Finally. Grace has told me a lot about you, too. Congrats on your store. When are you opening?"

We were smooth. Yes, we were.

"Next month, hopefully."

Tricky slung an arm around Lenore's neck, planting a kiss on the side of her face. Her extraordinary blue-green eyes remained on me.

"You want a drink, hon?" Tricky asked Lenore.

"Geez, Tricky, it's ladies' night. We've got this covered! Stand off," said Grace, laughing.

Lenore flashed Tricky a smile and kissed him. A raunchy deep kiss.

I swigged my martini. I was envious of such a simple act of intimacy, envious of that shared affection. I forgot what that felt like. I'd stopped expecting it. Worse, I'd stopped getting sad by the lack of it in my life.

Tricky smoothed a hand down her hip as he whispered in her ear. He sauntered back to the bar where I'd spotted other club members loitering.

Lenore's eyes slid back to mine. Serious. Stealthy.

A topless waiter stud brought a tray of shots to our table, and Grace and Dee helped distribute them.

Lenore leaned in to me, a hand on my elbow. "Nobody knows. Nobody here knows anything about who I really am," she whispered. "Have you ever said anything to Grace?"

"No. I didn't even realize you were here, that you were...*you*."

"Good."

I lowered my voice. "I've never said a word to anyone. I'm sticking to that."

"Okay." Her eyes shifted around us. "Thank you."

"How are you? You look great."

"I'm good. Things are very good."

"You and Tricky?"

She shrugged. "We hang out off and on. It's fun."

"Good for you."

"Grace told me you're getting a divorce."

"Almost there."

"I got myself one of those a few years back, too, and I survived just fine."

I only nodded. *You always do, it seems.*

I'd first met Lenore over twenty years ago. Two months after Grace and Dig's wedding when I'd finally left Meager. When I'd met *him.* An escapade, an experience that was burned in my memory and was so pivotal to me, yet at the same time, disturbing, heartbreaking.

"How long have you been in Meager?" I asked.

"Right after we last saw each other, I came here. I liked it a lot. I stayed."

"Have you seen…" I asked in a whisper.

"No." Her voice was firm, her tone blunt.

"Oh, I have," I blurted.

Maybe I should shut the hell up.

Her eyes widened at me. Was she surprised or scared?

"You two getting to know each other?" Grace asked, an arm at my waist.

"Lenore was just telling me about her divorce," I said.

"I was. Stay away from musicians, Tania, whatever you do." Lenore raised her drink at me, and I clinked her tall glass with my martini as we held each other's gaze. "Fuck them, but don't marry them. Ever."

I laughed. "Ah, I'll keep that in mind. So, what kind of musician was your ex-husband?"

"He was the bassist for this band called Cruel Fate," Lenore said, sipping on her drink.

"No way! They were huge for a while there. Aren't they from our parts?"

"They are. In fact, Grace here played a part in their success," Lenore replied.

"Not really." Grace waved a hand. "When I managed Pete's, I booked them a few times when they were first making it around Rapid. They returned the favor later on after they'd hit the big time, and they played Pete's on a few special nights. They brought in big crowds and good attention for Meager and the bar."

"That's fantastic," I said.

Grace bumped my shoulder with hers. "See what you missed out on?"

"I guess I never should've left town," I replied, my tone dry.

Lenore's eyes slid to mine. She sipped her drink.

I know, Rena. I know. It was a good thing I left. Otherwise, we never would have met. Otherwise…

I licked the traces of sweet apple and vodka from my lips, fighting to block the visuals.

If I'd never left Meager when I did, I never would've crossed paths with Lenore, and she'd be dead right now or worse. And me? I would have bumbled and stumbled along on my merry way and been a much different Tania than the one I was now.

But here she was, best friends with my best friend, a successful small business owner, and most importantly, healthy, confident, and happy as hell with herself.

Sounds good to me. All good.

I raised my glass at her again and smiled. A true smile. A we-did-good-girlfriend smile.

"Ladies, ladies, ladies!" boomed a woman's velvety voice over the microphone.

We settled in our seats as Cassandra, the gorgeous and very elegant African American talent manager of the Tingle, started off the evening with a warm welcome and introductions. Butler stood at the side of the stage, his arms crossed.

The lights flashed and dimmed, and the crowd applauded as Cassandra swept off the stage. An electronica song pounded out its pulsing beat, and three men in shiny black cowboy hats and impressive black chaps appeared onstage. Each of them thrust and pulsed their hips to the rhythm.

I grabbed a fresh apple martini.

These crazy cowboys were wildly talented dancers. We roared and clapped furiously.

One of the dancers came forward and headed for Mary Lynn, taking her hand and raising her from her chair. This hunk of man was all shiny-skinned with ripped muscles to hell and back, which he somehow managed to make flutter and pulsate on their own in a display of testosterone gone mad.

"Spartacus of the Wild West," I muttered to myself.

Mary Lynn squealed as he twirled her around and led her away from the table toward the stage, but she pulled away, shaking her head at him.

"Come on, Mary Lynn! Go!" I yelled, clapping.

"She can't!" Jill shouted over the blare of the music.

"Why the hell not?" I asked, my eyes still pinned on Spartacus.

"Because her old man is going to freak. He's here at the bar with the rest of the men," she replied.

I glanced toward the bar where Boner, Lock, Jump, Kicker, and Judge sat stern-faced, all in a row, like ornery bulls caged in a pen. Only, these bulls were clutching beer bottles and glasses of liquor.

"What the hell is the point of ladies' night then?" I asked.

Dee got the dancer's attention, and pointed me out to him.

Spartacus Cowboy shot me an I'm-coming-for-you-and-you're-all-mine grin, stalking over to me in his cut-muscled glory.

"The guys will leave soon, they're going to get bored!" shouted Grace over the din of the music. "But for now, you be our ice-breaker! Go!"

"Why me?" I asked.

"You're the only single woman at our table!" Jill clapped.

Nina laughed at her side, hooting and whistling.

Single woman?

Spartacus swiveled in front of me, his oiled up skin shiny and inviting under the lights. He took my hand in his, making a show of kissing it, his mouth moving up my arm. I laughed at his melodramatic expression, at the roar of the crowd.

"Go! Go! Go!" shouted and clapped all the women around me.

Hell yes! I am proud to be single, goddamn it.

I shot up from my chair, and a slick grin broke over Spartacus's chiseled face.

Let me enthrall you, his face said.

I grinned. *Give me your best, baby.*

He led me up the small set of stairs to the side of the stage, and we brushed past a familiar figure.

Butler.

I glanced at him. His eyes were shiny blue stones, his lips tilting in a lopsided grin, as the dancer pushed me down into a waiting chair onstage. I held Butler's steady gaze, and he raised his chin at me and smiled.

Spartacus danced in front of me, beckoning me with his pistoning hips and undulating pelvis. Each crazy move was greeted with cheers and whoops from the crowd. He took my hand in his and rubbed it along his ass as he ground against me, his oiled skin shining under the heavy spotlights. He popped back, executed a skillful spin and turn and tore off his chaps revealing the rest of his fantastic body and a tiny shiny thong, which sheltered a massive tool. We all responded wildly.

Lenore clapped and hooted, and I pointed at her and laughed, raising my thumbs in the air.

Yes, Rena was here. She was okay. More than okay. She was happy and had good people around her, had created a new life for herself. That counted for something. That counted for a hell of a lot.

And me?

Why was I hiding away, burying myself in work, making excuses? No, it made no sense.

So, I had a crush on Butler that hadn't waned in the many months since Sioux Falls. It wasn't the end of the world. It meant I was alive; it meant that blood was pumping through my veins, pumping through my heart. My crush wouldn't amount to anything, but it was okay. I actually liked him as a person. We were friends.

I glanced at Butler. His smile was huge as he positioned his fingers in his mouth and blew out a shrill whistle. The crowd whistled and hooted back over the crest of the throbbing music. I laughed and stood up.

Spartacus Cowboy offered me his hand. I took it and let him sweep me up into his arms and dip me low. He raised me up, and we danced, we grooved. He flirted with me with his eyes, his grin, teased me with his amazing hot body, and I flirted and teased him right back.

My girls shouted and cheered. "Go, Tania, go!"

SIXTEEN

BUTLER

TANIA WAS HAVING FUN, cutting loose, and it was good to see. Really good to see. She laughed as the fucker shook his muscled ass in her lap and then rolled his cut abs and pecs in her face, beckoning her to lick him. The sight of her moving to the music, laughing—her head tossed back, that long white throat arching, her black hair gleaming in the spotlight—had me rooted to the spot.

Yeah, you sure wanted to help her cut loose, didn't you?

And I'd done it.

Tania shimmied her upper body at the dancer, following him move for move, spurring him on. Once she was in, the girl gave it her all. I liked that.

I liked her.

She was probably seeing someone, fucking someone. I'd noticed Travis, Lock's army buddy from South Carolina and his hot rod specialist at the shop, checking her out more than once every time she was at the club, going through Wreck's stuff in the storage unit. Seeing that had annoyed me like a mosquito buzzing in your ear when you were just about to fall asleep and all you wanted was to hunt the fucker down and smash it.

But I can't do anything about it, can I?

Tania hooted and made funny faces as the dancer pretended to hump her.

What would it be like to take it all the way with her? She'd give as good as she got, really appreciate it, and tell me all about it with that mouth of hers that never stopped running.

I'd like to hear what Tania had to say as I got her up Come Mountain.

Let it go. Ain't gonna happen.

Getting back into business mode, I shifted my gaze around the crowded night club. The place was jammed tonight. My brothers were missing from their perch at the bar.

A touch on my arm.

Cassandra's pretty face was spoiled with a frown. "B, something's going on up front."

"What is it?"

"A group of men are outside, trying to get in. Men from another club."

I charged toward the front door, pushing through the people standing by the bar. The humid night air blanketed over me, making the knot in my throat stick.

With a group of men at his side, Notch, the president of the Broken Blades, leered at Jump.

What the fuck?

"We're here to celebrate," said Notch, his face in Jump's. "Everybody knows the Tingle is the best strip joint for miles, so we came here special tonight. Don't you assholes want our money? Same color green as everybody else's." His lined gaunt face suddenly burst into spasms of laughter.

"You know this is all kinds of wrong," I said, standing next to Boner.

Last time we had seen Notch in the flesh, he had tried to kill Boner, but thank fuck, we had gotten there first. Then, the Feds had raided, thanks to Finger's insider connections who had blown the whistle on the Blades and the Calderas Group working together. All hell had broken loose.

The Blades waited for us to retaliate for them trying to kill Boner, but you couldn't go crazy with Homeland Security riding your ass. Instead, we'd hung back, laid low and watched as the Feds chopped the Blades up into little bits and took away their property, broke their operations, indicting more than half of their members. It was a sad day for a decades old one percent club, but that was real life on the outside of society. There was always a price to pay, no matter how free you thought you were.

The Blades were jumpy. They should be; they were in pieces. A number of other powerful clubs, Finger's Flames chief among them, were circling, lapping at the trails of blood and torn flesh the Feds had left behind. Only Notch and a few other members were left, trying to recruit new members while desperately hanging on to whatever territory they still had.

Notch turned to me, his brows jumping. "What I know is that you and your friends all tried to destroy me and my club. Ain't gonna happen. Broken Blades are still standing. You all think you got us down when you blew us out of the water?" His dark gaze flew from me to Jump and back again. Notch was from Alabama originally. His Southern accent dragged out his words, giving their intent even more drama. "Blades don't go down easy. You tell your friend Finger that, huh?"

He came here to showcase.

"Tonight's ladies' night," I said. "You all here to dance for the women? We've got quite a crowd. All of 'em screaming for more. Dollar bills are flying in there. What do you say?"

Notch laughed. A decadent laugh. An I've-got-all-the-time-in-the-world-to-fuck-with-you laugh. His brothers sneered at us, including Pick, the Blade who had interrupted my and Tania's dinner that night outside of Sioux Falls. Boner's face twitched under the bright lights of the front entrance to the Tingle.

Notch knew that Finger had enjoyed smashing his club by destroying the Calderas Group and the Blades' union with them. He knew Finger was gearing up to take them over now that they had been broken so that he could expand his own territory in Nebraska and further south of us where the Blades had once ruled. And Notch also knew that the Jacks and Flames were suddenly friendly with each other.

"Tell you what," Notch said. "You set us up in one of your private party rooms with a couple of girls. We came a long way, after all."

"No girls working tonight," I said. "You should've called ahead. It's best you all find somewhere else to party."

"Ah, that's a shame. Real shame. What kind of hospitality is that, huh?" He tilted his head at his men. "Let's not waste any more time then." He turned to me and Jump once more, spitting on the ground. "Y'all have a good night."

Notch and his men stalked off and got on their bikes, revving their engines.

Jump's shoulders rolled, his jaw stern. "He's planning something. He looked mighty pleased with himself. This was just the intro." He eyed me and tracked back into the nightclub.

133

The Blades roared off, one by one. A blare of arrogance and conceit rumbled in the thick night air, hanging there long after they'd vanished in the darkness.

SEVENTEEN

TANIA

"OH, DAMN IT!"

An avalanche of tin oilcans, small metal post office box doors, and license plates tumbled down over me.

I hit the concrete floor of the storage unit, gasping.

"Tania, you okay? What the hell?" Butler stood over me. His hand reached out and pulled me up by the arm, and then his other hand circled my waist.

"I'm fine, I'm fine. Thanks." I wiped the hair from my face.

"Look at me a sec."

My gaze met his, and I steeled myself. I had to.

"Take a breath," he murmured.

I took in a breath, and his arms—those long, muscular, powerful arms—tightened around me. And, for one tiny second, I imagined what having this might be like on a daily basis, available to me whenever I wanted, needed. A centering, soothing feeling. An unbelievable turn-on.

His hand smoothed over my cheek, his thumb lingering along my jaw.

Sparks flew over my skin, my heart thumping, as I looked up into his handsome face concentrating over mine.

Those eyes. I'd never paid much attention to men's eyes before. I'd always liked smiles. But, here I was, in the presence of something utterly unique, and I couldn't look away. *A gentle sky at dawn, the Caribbean Sea, Roman glass.*

"I'm fine." My voice came out low, barely audible.

He didn't let go of me. His thumb rubbed the side of my face, his eyes serious.

"Wh-what is it? What are you doing?"

"You've got a smudge of dirt and a scratch."

"Oh. It's okay." I pulled back, but his hold remained steady. "Thank you," I mumbled.

He released me, clearing his throat. "Still going through Wreck's shit?"

"It's not shit, and there's a ton to go through."

I stepped back from the Butler ring of light, bumping into a stack of unopened boxes. My face heated again, and I quickly turned around.

"I wish I could sit here for hours on end, but I can't," I said. "I've got too much else to do. I usually steal an hour here or there to come rushing over to dig back in wherever I left off the last time. It's a bit frustrating. With the store opening soon—"

"You never did call me."

My head snapped up. "About what?"

"Helping you out here. I don't have anything going on now. I could stay."

"Oh. Sure. If you like."

"Yeah, I like." His eyes hung on mine, his hand brushing across his stubbly chin.

My pulse spiked. "You could open up those boxes over there and take a look."

He went over to the boxes and pulled them to the center of the space. His lat muscles flexed through the thin cotton of his tee with the movement.

"We're planning on another ladies' night at the Tingle since the first one was such a hit last month. We've been getting a ton of calls about the next one," he said.

"Well, I certainly enjoyed the very hard, very fine hunk of male jiggling his ass up against me in front of a hundred other screaming women."

"That was quite a show you got."

"And I have you to thank for it, don't I?"

"I'm glad you had fun. You're very welcome for the ass-jiggling. Anytime."

We laughed.

"By the way," I said. "That dancer gave me his phone number. I have direct access if I ever want a private show or whatever."

He raised his head and shot me a pointed look.

"You know, if I'm feeling that need to go wild. Like you said. Remember?"

"Right." His lips pressed together. "So, did you ever call him?"

"No. I mean, God knows where that dick has been, right?"

Butler laughed, his eyes gleaming.

I wanted to go wild with Butler right this very second on this floor covered in plastic bubble wrap, old newspapers, and wadded yellowed paper. Not with Spartacus boy. No, not with him.

Butler leaned over the crate, shuffling through the packing material.

"Ah—you'll like this one."

He held up a candelabra and handed it to me. Silver-plated, dented in a couple of spots, but castle-worthy, to be sure.

"How gothic of Wreck," I said.

"Can you picture Wreck having a candlelit dinner for two at his house with this?"

"No," I said, laughing.

"He'd gotten it for the Halloween Haunted House we sponsor every year."

"Fitting," I said. "But, still, very romantic of him. Maybe he did use it at home once in a great while."

"Wreck was a handsome dude. He was never wanting for female attention."

"I can imagine. I mostly remember being intimidated by him."

"Really?"

"He was never too chatty or smiley," I said. "Usually a very stern exterior. Unless he was wasted. Otherwise, he used to shoot me these blank looks."

"You were a civilian girl; that's probably why. Not to mention, Grace's best friend. He loved Grace, was protective of her like a real big brother."

"Yes, he was. And, now, here I am, all these years later, rifling through his hidden secrets."

"He's lucky that you're around to do it. Lock was never up for it."

"It's too difficult for him still, I think. Anyway, he doesn't have much time now, with his business taking off and the baby at home." Jill had given birth the week before. Lock and Grace's baby boy was finally home.

"I'm glad to do this for Lock." The backs of my eyes prickled. "More than glad."

"You okay? What is it?"

"It's nothing."

"No, it's not. Tell me. Come on."

I cleared my throat. "Doing this for Lock and Wreck is an honor, you know?"

He slanted his head at me. "Yeah?"

"I feel bad that I didn't really appreciate Wreck or Dig, even, when I knew them. Both of them are gone now, and…"

I pushed back at the sudden surge of emotion. Wreck had gotten his throat slashed at a bar brawl in Texas, and Dig had been gunned down on his bike here in Meager.

"They both died in such terrible ways," I murmured.

His hand wrapped around my neck, and he pulled me into his chest, his other hand at the back of my head. "They lived big lives though, baby. Big lives the way they wanted. We should all live up to that." His mouth brushed over my hair.

My arms slid around his waist, and I buried my face in his chest. "I don't want anything like that to happen to you," I whispered.

His hold on me only tightened. The breath squeezed from my lungs, and I relished the dizzying rush.

His shirtsleeve had ridden up his arm, and the tattoo on his right shoulder was splayed before me—a glorious splash of reds and golds and rusts giving life to a hawklike creature. Fire, sun, passion, energy. There was triumph in those colors, in the lines of the bird's proud stance, his magnificent feathers.

I cleared my throat and pulled back from his embrace. "Is that a phoenix? Your tattoo?"

"It is."

"I don't remember it on you in the old days."

"I got it recently—once I hit my one year of sobriety."

"Well, hell yes, that's an event to commemorate on your body."

"I thought so. Reborn from my own ashes."

"There's more to that story though."

He lifted an eyebrow. "Tell me."

"The phoenix perceives its own impending death and ignites itself into a big fire. Then, he reemerges from his own ashes, renewed and very much alive. The phoenix is brave. He takes charge of his own destiny."

"You know your mythology, huh?"

"I had to. I was an art history major in college. The phoenix myth is part of the big three of ancient cultures—Greek, Roman, and Egyptian."

"A very powerful symbol."

"Victory over death always is."

"Hey, what's up?" Lock's voice boomed from the doorway, making Butler and I break our stare.

"Helping out Tania here with Wreck's stuff," said Butler.

"Hey, Daddy. Getting any sleep lately?" I asked Lock.

"No. Thanks for asking," he replied, his voice clipped.

"Aw, poor thing!" I said. "How's he doing?"

"He's got a good appetite. Just needs to sleep at night more than during the day. He'll get there," Lock said. "Hopefully, sooner rather than later."

"Fingers crossed," I said. "Oh, hang on. There are a few things I wanted to ask you about. If you've got a sec, that is."

"Sure."

I brought Lock a box where I had collected a few of the more personal baubles I had come across in Wreck's grand collection this morning. Five pairs of eyeglasses, old club patches—including ones from other clubs, which I'd found rather curious—thick silver bracelets that were missing links and fastenings, and, oddly enough, an old lipstick, which seemed more solid than your usual drugstore brand.

"Ah"—Lock went through the patches—"these were spoils of war from when he first joined the Jacks. Lots of raids and double-dealings with the Demon Seeds in the eighties." He glanced at Butler. "He ripped off the patches and took 'em."

"Would you like me to put them in a frame? Or maybe an album is better—for private viewing, not visible to guests?"

"Yeah, much better idea," Lock said. "You can get rid of the glasses. Jesus, he never threw anything away. And this?" He held up the lipstick. "You open it?"

"No, I didn't get a chance."

"Open it." He handed me the lipstick.

I twisted open the wand, and instead of lipstick, a small knife poked up from the tube.

My eyes widened. "Holy shit."

"Nice," said Butler.

"He got into a fight with this woman at some party, and she used it on him, nicked him. He took it away from her, and by the end of the night, they were together, and they stayed together for a couple of years. Izzy was her name. Here." He turned the lipstick over. An *I* was scratched in the bottom of the tube.

"I don't remember him with an old lady or a steady girlfriend ever," Butler said.

"Yeah, never happened again after Izzy," said Lock.

"What happened with Izzy?" I asked.

"Izzy wanted more of Wreck, less of the club," Lock said. "But he couldn't give that to her, and she ended up leaving him. A few months later, she got killed in a convenience store robbery. You believe that?"

I gasped. "No!"

"Yeah. I never met her. All of that was right before Wreck came looking for me, found me on the reservation, and brought me to Meager. This knife was the only thing he kept of her—no pictures, no nothing else. Only this. He kept it in his top drawer with his socks and his rings, so he could see it or touch it every goddamn day. Who the fuck knows?"

I bit down on my quivering lower lip.

Butler stared at me, the muscles in his jaw flexing.

I closed the lipstick and choked down the urge to cry for a man I'd barely known and his broken love story. A man who, to me, had been an enigma, a closed book, a hard rock.

"Can I keep it?" I asked. "For myself."

Lock's dark eyes flashed at me. "Sure. Yeah."

"I'll give the bracelets to Jill. She can probably fix them," I said.

"Great. The glasses you can get rid of. Hey, you two seen Wes around?"

"I haven't, no," I replied.

"Me either," Butler said. "Something up?"

"He was supposed to be here an hour ago, so I could show him how to use the airbrush. First time since he started working for me that he hasn't shown without a word."

Jump and Alicia's son, Wes was a handsome, tall seventeen-year-old. His parents' severe falling out after Jump had screwed two club girls at a party when Alicia was out of town was an extreme blow to their only child. A son who spent a lot of time with his dad and at the club in between school and football. A son who loved his mother and was now very disappointed in his father.

"That's not good. I'll keep an eye out," Butler said.

"I'll try calling him again. Not sure I want to call Alicia, upset her."

"Yeah, give it another hour," said Butler. "Maybe he'll slide on in."

"I hope so. On top of the deadlines we got here, he's been on board to help with the kids' designs for the Go-Kart Championship. I need him. Beyond that, he made promises to those kids, and they look up to him."

"You're right," Butler said.

"And, hey, don't forget about your snowmobile, man."

"Will do."

Lock tipped his chin at us. "Later."

Butler pulled out his phone and dialed, waited, and shut it down again. He let out a huff of air as he typed out a text.

"Everything okay?" I asked.

"It's Wes. I'm concerned."

"That bad?"

"Not sure."

"So, tell me about the Go-Kart Championship," I said.

"Lock and Grace got the town to agree to a race for the junior high in town. It's part art project, part learning seminar on cars, practical teamwork. Mostly a good time. We're gonna have it here on our track."

"Oh, right. Grace had mentioned it to me a while back. You're going to raise money for a Moms with Cancer support group she helped put together in Ruby's memory at the hospital, right?" Grace's sister Ruby had passed away from lung cancer almost two years ago.

"Yeah, it should be good. I'm looking forward to it."

"You like working with the kids?"

"I do. I actually like helping them and teaching them. It's satisfying in a different way from just doing the work to make a buck."

"That's great. You must be a real car and bike expert after living and working here all these years?"

"I was before I got here, Tania. My dad had his own auto parts store and repair shop back in northern California. This shit's in my blood. It's funny because my dad and my brother were real close, but Stephan hated the work. I was the one who liked it, was good at it, but it didn't bring me any closer to my dad."

"Oh, that's too bad. What does your brother do? I'm assuming he didn't take over your dad's store?"

His head snapped up at me. He looked lost, like a child who hadn't realized he had wandered off in a store. His features tightened, and that lost child vanished. "Stephan died when we were in high school. A car accident."

"Oh. I'm sorry."

Time to change the subject.

"I saw that snowmobile Lock mentioned. That's yours?"

"Yeah. Boner kept it for me while I was away. I got to take it out of the storage unit and check it over. It had a few problems this winter, needs more work."

"You going to give me a ride?"

"You been on one before?"

"Let's see. Born and raised on a farm in South Dakota. What do you think?"

"I think yes."

"Who do you think gave Catch his first taste of speed?"

"You?"

"That's right. My dad had us on snowmobiles since we could walk. He taught me and Penny, and I gave Catch his first ride. He must have been no more than three years old. We'd go really slow, and he'd scream. He loved it. He loved helping me commandeer the combine, too."

He gave me a wide-eyed look.

"What is it?"

"Trying to picture you as a farm girl."

"My mother's got the photos, if you need hard evidence, mister."

"I believe you. You can show me what you're made of next snowfall."

"Deal."

He studied me, his teeth dragging along his bottom lip. "I'm sure Grace is gonna have you bake cupcakes or something for the go-kart event. You a good baker, Tan?"

I made a face. "Hmm. Not really."

He grinned. I was entertaining.

"You going to come root for my team? It should be good." His voice had quieted.

"I just might."

"You'd better."

A flutter swung through my tummy. I missed this—talking with him, laughing with him.

He's taken, he's taken, he's taken.

I took in a breath. "If you've got a minute, there is something I'd like for you to look at actually."

"Sure. What is it?"

"That wood crate in the corner over there." His gaze followed to where I pointed. "It's really heavy. If you could get it open? I haven't had a chance to tackle it yet. I don't think Lock's ever opened it either. It looks untouched."

He brushed a hand over the old crate. "I'll get a few tools. Be right back."

He left and returned a few moments later with a short crowbar and a hammer. I dusted off my hands as I watched him levy the crowbar in the wood, under the old nails. He pushed and pulled, his shoulders and arms straining with the effort.

Popcorn would be good about now.

Creaking and Butler's low grunts filled the room. Wood split and cracked.

"There we go," he muttered.

I stepped forward and reached for the top of the crate from his hands.

His brow furrowed. "Don't touch it. You'll get bad splinters."

He lifted the top, placing it against a wall, and we both peered into the crate.

Balled-up wads of yellowed paper separated different automotive parts, tanks, motors.

"Ah, fuck me." Butler leaned over and pulled out one large piece from the wadded paper.

"What? What is it?"

"It's a Harley motor." His fingers brushed over the thick metal.

"Oh?"

"But...um..."

"Is that a good or bad but?"

Butler lifted the heavy piece of crafted metal, setting it on the floor. "No wonder he had it crated and packed."

"Why?"

"It's from the twenties at least. A Harley J engine. It's got a generator, carb. No cracks. Could retail up to five thousand bucks at least." He went back to the crate. "Motherfuck, there's another one, too."

I bent over the crate. "There's a tank here. Two of them."

Butler put down the motor and joined me at the crate, shuffling the paper around the box. "Tania, go get Willy. He was cooking in the kitchen before I came in here. He's got to see this. He'll know exactly what's what. I'm telling you, this is precious metal you've got here."

Willy was the eldest member of the Jacks. He and Wreck had been very close.

Butler and I grinned at the crate, and we grinned at each other, like two kids who had just discovered a litter of puppies in their backyard.

"Jesus, there's another engine in there. Plus, four original headlights, pre-World War II." He shuffled through the wads of old paper. "And here are a bunch of Indian head badges, a few carburetor covers."

"Oh, Wreck," I murmured.

"Scarlett?"

"What is it?"

"I'm feeling the zing."

I leaned into him. "Feels good, right?"

"Oh, yeah." He grinned at me, slow, warm, and satisfied.

I soaked in the rays of that sun.

He reached over and carefully lifted one of the Harley fuel tanks out of the crate.

He muttered to himself, his focus intense on the tank.

"What is it?"

"This is original paint. Babe, go get Willy."

My heart squeezed. I could hear it in his voice. That zing. Our zing.

And I liked it.

EIGHTEEN

TANIA

THE ONE-EYED JACKS had landed in my art gallery.

"What's all this?" I asked.

Butler held the door open as Boner and Dready hauled toolboxes and cables and digital equipment. Willy strode in with Clip and their own tools and ladders.

"Butler, what is going on?"

"You're opening a business. We're here to help," Butler said, ripping off his jacket.

Speechless.

He leaned into me. "Dready and Dawes have a security business with the club."

"They do?"

"Yeah. Club's got a lot of businesses going."

"We'll be setting up an alarm system and your Wi-Fi," said Dawes, taking a large box from Boner.

"And a bitching sound system." Dready winked at me as he pulled his dreadlocked long hair back in a tie. "Shit's gonna rock this space."

Boner glanced at me as he flipped open a box, a you-better-believe-it grin on his face.

"And you know that Willy is a master craftsman carpenter," added Butler.

As if on cue, Willy came up to me. "What do you need, baby girl? Shelves? Display cases? Front counter for a desk? Talk to me."

"Um. Well…"

"It's an amazing space. You did good. Gracie told me all about it a while back. I'm going to take a look around, take some measurements. Then, we'll discuss." Willy strode off into the back of the space, glasses on, measuring tape in hand.

I turned back to Butler. "You don't have to do this. Really."

"We're here; we're doing this."

"Butler"—I took a few steps toward him—"I can't afford this right now. Not all of it." I lowered my voice. "I'm on a strict budget."

"Don't worry about that now. If it makes you feel better, you can pay for some of the materials at cost whenever you can, but the labor is free."

"But I've got—"

"You've got what, Scarlett?" Butler's lips twitched. His face was relaxed. He was enjoying this.

My shoulders dropped, my eyes darting around the space, to the men settling into working. "I've got good friends," I replied.

"Yeah, Scarlett, you do."

"Can I get everyone coffees? Breakfast?" I said.

"Sounds good," replied Dready, his white teeth visible in his wide grin. "Triple espresso for me."

"Got it."

Jill entered the store. "Hey, everyone." She went to her husband and gave him a quick kiss. She glanced over at me. "We all set?"

"Did you do this?" I asked.

"Me?" She fluttered her eyelashes at me. "All I did was express my enthusiasm for this new adventure in your life. This is all Butler."

My eyes slid to his and took in his grin.

"Tania! Come on back here. I have a couple of questions," called Willy.

"Jill, could you pick up coffees and breakfast for the guys? Whatever they'd like. There's money in my handbag."

"Oh, I already put in an order with Erica on the way over here," Jill replied, putting her thick mane of strawberry-blonde hair up in a fat ponytail. "She's having it delivered."

Always good to have a personal in with the owner of the best coffeehouse in the state.

"Sweet Lord." I turned to Butler. *Thank you*, I mouthed silently.

He raised his chin at me, those icy blues shining. Once again, those sweet, delicate strands of appreciation and positivity threaded between us, connecting us, taking my breath away, filling my insides with warmth.

"Tania!" called Willy.
"Coming!"

NINETEEN

TANIA

"TANIA, THIS LOOKS WONDERFUL." My mother stood with her walker before her in the middle of my store, her large dark blue eyes taking in every detail.

I was almost ready for tonight's opening.

I had artwork and antique pieces in specially designed groupings around the space. Willy was making adjustments to the custom shelving we had designed together weeks ago for one of the walls, the golden afternoon sun streaming over his gray hair and all down his back as he worked.

"Can't believe this is the old five-and-dime," Rae murmured.

"Part of it, but, yes, it's Dillon's. One and the same. The owners took longer than expected to separate the old store into three retail spaces, but the timing worked out for me."

Her face broke into a smile. "I used to come here with my daddy in that old Chevy pickup. You remember the one?"

"Of course I do. Dad used it, too, for a while. We'd come here together in that truck, tool around town, go to the luncheonette."

"Yes, you did."

Our eyes lingered on Lock's hand-painted mural on the wall behind the long front desk. A painting of a great big pulsing heart that was worn and rust-colored on the edges but a deep silky blood red at its living center. An original work of art that Wes had helped him with.

"Stunning," Rae murmured.

"The painting was Lock and Grace's gift. I still pinch myself every time I look at it. What do you think of the front desk, Ma? Willy created it out of an old vintage front door I had found in Iowa, and he made the legs using pieces from an iron gate I had found at a house demolition years ago."

"It's beautiful. He does amazing work," she murmured, a hand smoothing over the top of the desk.

"He does. We've had a lot of fun working together."

My mother's eyes roamed over every part of the store. Her shoulders rose and fell with the effort of moving with the walker as her guide, the walker bearing the brunt of her emotions.

"You did this, baby. You did. How I wish your daddy were here to see it. He'd be so proud of you. He always said you'd do great things in your own way, in your own time. You certainly have here."

"I wish he were here to see it."

"Oh, I think he can. I know he can feel it."

I slid my arm through hers as she wiped at her eyes.

"You think this is nuts? Doing this here in Meager?" I asked.

She turned to me, adjusting her grip on the walker. "A little bit of nuts can have its merits, Tania. You have that, and you used it wisely. It shows. Otherwise, you never would have gotten this off the ground."

"I had a lot of help from my friends. I couldn't have done it without them."

She gave me a pointed look. "Those are good friends to have."

"Yes, they are."

For the first time in a very long time, I felt absolutely confident in my decision to open my own store. Knowing I had the support and care of this amazing band of people behind me made me proud and made my heart so very full.

"I only wish I could have helped you."

"I know, Mom." I rubbed her arm. "It's okay. Knowing I have your support is what's important to me."

"Oh, honey, you're my precious daughter, and you will always have my support. I know things have been difficult with you having to come home, the divorce, but I didn't want you to uproot yourself."

"Mom, I didn't leave Racine because of you. I left because I wanted to. You needing me was the best sort of impetus, the best shove in the rear. It made me look at everything differently. For the better. Believe me."

"Well, I'm glad something good's come out of it at least. I haven't seen you like this in a long while."

"I haven't felt like this in a very long time. It feels good."

"As it should."

"Sit here, in your grandmother's chair." I patted the cracked leather of the armchair.

"Oh, look at that! You buffed it up. It looks good here."

"I'll make us some tea. I have Earl Grey, some sort of Chai thing Jill likes, and jasmine."

"Jasmine, please."

I helped her settle in the leather easy chair and went to the back storage area where I had a small table with an electric kettle.

"I'm glad you brought Grandma's chair. It's so good to sit in it, use it again, isn't it? I haven't been able to get over to that house at all. Maybe you'll take me one morning? I should go. I'd like to."

"Of course. The house is full of things you should look over. What do you think of Great Grandma's piano over there?"

"Beautiful as ever."

"I just got it tuned yesterday," I said, both our gazes pinned on the freshly polished dark wood upright piano on which Rae, Penny, and I had all taken lessons once upon a time.

"Is this Jill's jewelry? She's been working like crazy, you know."

"Isn't it beautiful?" I placed a mug of tea on the small table by my mother's side. "I wanted to feature local up-and-coming artisans. That was part of my idea for this store. I also wanted to have other more portable and more affordable options available in the store alongside the antiques. Jill's handmade trinkets are perfect."

"I'm glad the two of you are working together."

"Me, too. I need someone I can trust in here. Jill's going to work here part-time for now and then give me more hours once Becca goes to preschool in the fall."

"She's very excited. She's been talking nonstop about it." Mom blew over the hot amber liquid and took a careful sip. "I wish I could come tonight, but I just get too tired in the evenings. It's your big night. I don't want you worrying about me."

"I'm glad you came now to see it. I like this—sitting with you."

Rae set her tea back down on the table. "We're not usually this quiet, are we?"

I laughed. "No."

"That used to drive your father nuts."

"What's that?"

"You and me—loud, stubborn, full of intent to prove our points, day in, day out."

"Ah, he liked opinionated women, Ma. He loved that color in his house."

"He did. See? That's where *nuts* is good, too. I want you to have that kind of nuts in your life, baby. This is important"—her gaze met mine—"but it isn't everything."

"I know."

She grinned, her head slanting toward Willy and Dawes working at the back. "Those Jacks are another breed of men."

"Mom!"

"They are, aren't they?"

"Yes."

"I see it in Grace's eyes. In Jill's, I saw it from the first. Like a fresh drift of snow you wake up to in the morning. Absolutely clean, bright with sparkles as far as the eye can see. She thought she was hiding it from me, but you can't hide that."

"Boner is good to her."

"He is, and it shows. She deserves it. Just like Grace."

"They certainly do."

"So do you, honey. I know Kyle disappointed you in many ways. Maybe he even hurt you. He must have for you to pick up and leave. You dust yourself off and walk ahead. Come what may, let it come. That's what you do, all your life. That's what you've been doing."

"Mom—"

"You need to take care of *you* right now, and all else will fall into place. Hopping into bed with someone is easy. Anyone can give you a good orgasm. You know what I mean?"

"Holy shit, Rae." I plonked my mug down on the table.

"It's true, isn't it?"

"Yes. But if you find someone who can give you a really, really good one…" I said, my insides clenching at the memory of Butler's sensual talents.

"Oh, well then, yes, he's worth a second look. Absolutely." She laughed out loud, and I joined her.

I stretched out my arms and legs and heaved a huge sigh. I wouldn't trade this moment for anything in the world.

"Baby, you have a good head on your shoulders, and you're no flighty young girl, never were to begin with. You'll meet someone else, and you'll know."

"I will. And I'll know," I repeated quietly.

I had already. But I had to let it go.

"You like someone, don't you?"

"Mother—"

"When you turned forty, you complained that things would be so dreary and horrible. But the heart still pumps, and the heart still desires. It still calls." She glanced up at Lock's heart mural. "You'd better listen and pay heed to the call."

"Pay heed to the call, huh?"

"Yes, indeed. Your father and I raised you to be alert and smart, didn't we?"

"You did, Mrs. Reigert." I picked up my tea mug and saluted her with it. "You certainly did."

TWENTY

BUTLER

TANIA HAD GIVEN HER gallery a name. A good name.

The Rusted Heart.

An hour into the opening, and the Rusted Heart was packed.

A huge arrangement of white roses towered over a round wood table at the front of the space where Jill had placed rows of clear plastic cups filled with white wine. A shorter, stocky, dark-haired woman who looked oddly familiar helped her.

The woman suddenly stepped in front of me, a cup of wine in her hand. "Welcome! Would you like some wine?"

"Uh, no. Thanks," I replied.

"Hey, Butler!" Jill smiled at me, stepping up next to the woman. Jill had lost most of her pregnancy weight in the two months since she'd given birth to Grace's baby. Her blue eyes sparkled at me. "Penny, this is Butler from the Club. Butler, this is Tania's sister, Penny."

"Oh, you're Butler!" Penny's eyes flashed at me. Small brown eyes that reminded me of Catch's, not Tania's large exotic dark ones.

"And you're Penny."

"I am," she said, beaming. "Tania's mentioned you a time or two. Good to meet you."

"Thanks. Good to meet you too."

Penny glanced at the sunflowers I clutched in my hand. "Very nice."

I raised my chin at the elegant roses behind her on the table. "Well, they can't match those."

"Tania's ex sent those this afternoon." Penny shrugged. "They're pretty and all, but they didn't make much of an impression on my sister."

"Oh, yeah?" I said.

Penny's lips curled into a grin. "Tania's mingling somewhere in the crowd."

"I'll go find her," I said.

"You do that," said Penny.

A guitarist along with a double bass player, a drummer, and a pianist filled the store with their bluesy music. I'd heard The Innocents play at Pete's one night when Boner and I had hung out. They were good. The perfect soundtrack for the mood I knew Tania was going for.

Nina was talking with Alicia, Wes, and Catch. Mary Lynn and Kicker were talking with Willy, who was showing them around. He had put in plenty of carpentry hours here at the store, he'd told me, helping Tania flesh out the design of her space. They'd made a great team. The bare bones of the vintage structure were still visible, still offering a sense of local nostalgia, while the simple, modern accents did not overpower.

I spotted Tania.

Something dropped inside me, making me stop in my tracks. Her dark hair was sleek, shiny, and very straight. Her makeup was dramatic, her lips colored a deep red. She wore a charcoal-colored dress that hugged every curve and showed off her pale skin and dark hair. Understated and utterly provocative.

Gorgeous.

I hadn't seen her in weeks.

Clip had been over here, helping Willy, and he'd filled me in on what was going on, but I'd kept myself busy. Kept away. Now, the sight of Tania was a balm to that dull ache in my chest. She was every bit the polished woman, the decisive professional, the would-be slayer of my heart and soul.

She lit up the fucking room. The queen in her kingdom.

A blond guy in an expensive suit—extremely polished himself, right down to his fingernails, I'd bet—stood with her. Her arm was through his as he sipped on a glass of wine, and they talked. They looked good together, comfortable. They laughed at something he'd said. *Was it clever? Witty? A clever witty something that I wouldn't understand?*

My stomach hardened, and I clenched my jaw as I brushed past people, pushing through the space.

People admired the paintings, drawings, and old photographs up on the walls, a huge hand-painted canvas circus poster from the fifties dominated one wall. They discovered the bits and pieces on display in the antique cabinets. I recognized a lot of Wreck's collectibles—old signs, oil cans, painted tin boxes, old wooden wagon wheels, original paintings and sketches by Lock. She hadn't included a lot of Gerhard's stuff though; she was saving that for her next show.

Tania had torn through dirty houses, abandoned properties, picked through forgotten junk that was dented, flea-bitten, worn and frayed, ripped at the edges. Yet here, here in her store—under her care and attention, her vision—they glowed. Glowed and were proudly transformed, exposing us to their fragile secrets, their lost worlds, their former beauty.

Revealing a new beauty.

I stopped at a display case with delicate pieces of silver and gold jewelry. *Firefly Wishes* said the engraved label. I smiled. Jill's jewelry.

"Hey, I was wondering if you'd come."

I turned around. Tania aimed a dazzling smile at me, a pink flush racing over her skin. She was excited, happy. Maybe a little high on wine, on her accomplishment. She should be.

Was she high on seeing me?

My chest filled with heat. "I just got back from a run down to Colorado." I sucked in a breath. "I wouldn't have missed this for the world, Scarlett, seeing your dream come true."

"I'm glad."

I handed her the sunflowers. "These are for you."

"Oh, thank you." Her voice came out low. "They're beautiful."

"You like them?"

"They're perfect. I love them." Her eyes met mine and skittered away. Her fingers toyed with the large flower petals. "How did you find these this time of year?"

"I got connections." I winked at her.

Her huge dark eyes took me in, and I was suspended in their liquid magic.

"I haven't seen you in a couple of weeks, and I wasn't sure you'd come." She broke the silence. "I'm glad you did. You're staying, right? I mean, Nina's here."

"I'm staying. Yeah, of course, I'm staying."

Her face relaxed, and the edges of her red, red lips lifted into a smile again.

She slid her free arm through mine. "So, what do you think?"

That peppery flower perfume of hers hit me, and I took it in, my brain blanking, my senses dancing in its breeze. I burned the colors of it into my lungs to torture myself with later.

"What do I think?" I repeated.

"I've been looking forward to your opinion."

"You have?"

"Of course I have, Rhett. You helped me get to this moment. You helped me realize my dream."

Something unfurled inside me at the use of her nickname for me, at her words. Her eyes sought mine, like it was the most natural thing in the world—her asking my opinion, us arm in arm, strolling through an art gallery party.

I liked it. I wanted it.

But it wasn't mine to have.

"I'm glad that you kept the exposed dark brick walls and the forties lighting fixtures. The changes you and Willy made are discreet and clean. The space is offbeat, unexpected. I like it. It all...fits."

"What fits exactly?"

There it was again. That analytical brain. That I-must-know-exactly-what-and-how-you're-thinking demand of this woman.

This *woman.*

"Your eccentric vibe, Tania. Your imagination, which I like. You make it work."

She transmitted that beam of heat again, her cheeks reddening, and I tore my eyes away. I'd pleased her, and she'd liked it.

"I love the Victory bike hanging on the wall in the same state we found it in—rusty and old. And the buffalo horns look amazing over the front door."

"I sold them already."

"Terrific," I said. "I like this furniture you brought in." I gestured at a trio of antique oak cabinets.

"Aren't they great? I don't want people handling certain items, and I also want those pieces to be protected from dust, so I'm glad I found these curio cabinets at my great grandmother's old house over in Pine Needle. My mother owns the house and rents it off and on. Now, it's off, so I went there and shuffled through a number of Grandma Eileen's pieces to see if I could use any that would suit the salon-style concept for my store."

"*Salon* concept?"

She let out a small laugh as she squeezed my arm. "Not beauty salon, but a parlor-like feeling for the store. It's a French term dating back to the seventeenth century. A place where people gather to see art exhibits, hear poetry readings, have great discussions—a meeting place of cultured minds."

"Ah. Like the Jacks' clubroom, right?"

"Right, right. Exactly!"

We both laughed.

"I thought making this space comfortable and cozy with a few choice elements would be a great contrast—"

I leaned closer to her. "The type of ironic contrast you love."

She stopped and held my gaze. "Yes."

Contrasts. The unusual. All that was what Tania was to me— loud and insistent, soft and caring. All of it flecked with ire, streaked with passion.

My eyes swept over the west wall where a huge metal mural hung.

"Shit, those are Wreck's, aren't they?"

She followed my gaze and grinned. "The ones that fell on me. Do you like it?"

She had taken the fifty or so vintage post office postal box doors Wreck had bought from some old hermit in North Dakota who used to be a postal worker, and she'd transformed them into something altogether different. These small brass doors were the size of postcards, each with an eagle sculpted over the number and their small locks. Somehow, Tania had attached them together and hung it on the wall. The woman had vision.

"We laughed at Wreck for spending money on all those little brass doors and lugging them home. Look at that...that's spectacular."

"Thank you," she said in a breathy voice.

We both stared at the striking piece, which gave the wall immense stature.

I took her hand in mine over my arm. "I wish Wreck were here to see it."

"Really?"

"Yeah. He would've loved it. He'd be proud."

She squeezed my hand. "That means a lot to me."

Her hand was warm in mine, and I didn't want to let it go. I didn't.

"I might start weekly poetry readings here next Wednesday and maybe bring the band back on Thursdays. Make it a regular thing. I don't want the place to feel like a typical store or gallery. I want it to feel as if you're entering a place where the unexpected could happen."

"Like an artist's house? A studio?"

"Right. The minute a visitor steps inside, I want him to be taken aback for a moment with a, *Whoa, where am I? Am I intruding in on someone's private special space?* A space where intriguing, mysterious, genius artistic things are brewing. Or have already brewed, as the case may be." She shrugged, her cheeks reddening again. "I want them to feel that initial moment of surprise, of—"

"The buzz. Like at Gerhard and Astrid's house."

Her eyes softened for a moment. "Yeah, that was special."

"It was."

A warm sweetness thickened the air between us, and she slid her arm away from mine.

"This is a classic, huh?" My hand passed over a large studded trunk.

"That's been in my family for generations—it dates back to the mid-eighteen hundreds. My family's hopes and dreams were bundled into this trunk as they kept moving further and further west."

"Ah, pioneer roots?"

"Yes, sir."

"Are you selling it?"

"No way. I brought it over because I like the way it works with the atmosphere tonight. "

"Ah. Good."

"Oh, and the piano The Innocents are playing on—also not for sale. That piano was my great grandmother's, and Mom, Penny, and I had taken lessons on it."

"Looks good under the shelves Willy built you," I said, my eyes darting up at Willy's long thick wooden shelves. "I like those old railroad lamps up there."

"I found those in Nebraska with Grace. A memento of our fun with Creeper. I went back and bought them. I liked them too much."

"Of course you did. Jesus."

"By the way, did you ever catch up with Creeper?" Her forehead puckered. "Or should I be prepared for him to show up and wreak havoc again?"

I touched the side of her face with my knuckles and leaned in close to her. "You don't need to worry about him ever again."

"Okay." She stilled. "I have good news for you, too. My friend Neil is here from Chicago, the art dealer I told you about?"

"Is he the one in the suit you were talking with?"

"Yes." She smiled. A private joke, a treat. "He loves Gerhard's work. He came here to see the pieces for himself and take a few back to Chicago to show at his gallery. He knows a lot of the right people—not just collectors, but museum curators. Things could get big."

"That's terrific. You're making your dream come true, Tan." Something swelled in my chest, and a coil of emotion spiraled up my throat. My eyes darted to the opposite wall. "You framed Gerhard's H-bomb octopus paintings?"

Her shoulder brushed my arm. "Do you like them up there all together?"

"They look good. Like a massive visual LSD trip."

She let out a laugh.

"What?"

"That's a perfect description. You do understand my vibe."

"Oh, I understand your vibes, Tania. Not all of 'em yet though. Not yet."

I wanted to feel her vibes against my lips, under my hands, in my pulse. Crack them open, decode them, revel in their rhythms.

"Hey, you got here. I wasn't sure you'd make it," said Nina, appearing at Tania's side.

"Yeah, I made it," I muttered.

I stared at them both. Such a striking contrast—physically, emotionally.

The one tall, thin, young, bright but bland.

The other...ah, Tania was a woman through and through. A captivating mystery, an intriguing thrill, a demanding challenge. Smart as hell, sensitive to nuances, and sexy as fuck. The kind of sexy that still hadn't stopped making me spin, still hadn't stopped making me crazy to get in there.

"I'm going to go put my flowers in a vase," Tania murmured, stepping away from us.

Away from me.

Tania strode off on her black high heels, my sunflowers in her grip.

TWENTY-ONE

BUTLER

"His NAME SHALL BE WRITTEN in the book of the Lord. And his name shall be—" Pastor Brad nodded at Lock.

Lock glanced at his son who lay cuddled in Boner's arms, Jill at her old man's side.

"His name shall be Richard Thunder Kichú." Lock's steady deep voice filled the small church.

Something pinched in my chest. He named his son for his dead brother, Wreck. I liked that a lot.

Lock and Wreck were brothers from different fathers. Even though they hadn't grown up together and had met further on in their lives, those two brothers had had solid love between them, true esteem.

My throat closed.

I remember.

Wreck and Lock had looked nothing alike although they had the same mother. Wreck was all Anglo like his white dad and mom, and Lock was completely unlike their Anglo mom and more like his Native American dad. But what they shared had been beyond any DNA; it was tangible and unmistakable. That had come from inside, a conscious decision, but it'd also stemmed from their hearts and sung from their souls.

My brother, Stephan, and I'd had that between us, too. We were only a little over a year apart. We'd often fought like dogs, but more often, we'd fought for each other like wolves. He'd had the book smarts; I had the street smarts and the looks. He'd kept his cool; I would lose it on a regular basis. I'd usually get blamed for everything, and he'd been adored. I'd looked up to him, and he'd always stood up for me. But like everything else that had come easy to me—my good looks, my skills with a football, with a surfboard, with a guitar, with girls—I had taken it all for granted. I'd thought Stephan would always be there, that we'd always have each other, no matter the different directions our lives would take.

"You're my kid brother. I should be looking out for you."
"Shut up. It's not such a big deal."
"Yeah, it is, Markus. It is to me. You've got a big heart, tough guy. You don't know how much it means to me that you've always got my back."
"Shut up."
"It's true."
"It wasn't fair, what he tried to do to you. I wanted justice, and I knew how to get it."
"You got it, all right. I just don't want you getting in trouble again. With school, with Mom and Dad."
"Don't worry about me."

"Don't worry about me." That had been my little motto back then. But Stephan had been the only one to ever worry about me.

"Welcome, Richard Thunder Kichú," the pastor pronounced, dribbling water over the baby's forehead.

The pastor gestured at all of us, and we repeated after him, "Welcome, Richard Thunder Kichú."

Grace, her face beaming down at her son in Boner's arms, who slowly rocked him from side to side. A tiny baby fist reached up, and Grace snuck a finger inside that fist, and the little man held on. Jill, who stood on the other side of Boner, grinned. She and Boner were the kid's godparents.

"Dad would like to say a few words." Pastor Brad gestured at Lock, who took his son in his arms from Boner and turned to us, Grace at his side.

"Our son is a gift—*kichú* in Lakota. More precisely, a gift that is given back to one's own. His coming into this world, to us, was a secret wish, a prayer answered and, ultimately, a sacred gift." Lock swallowed hard. "Our son is also like the thunder that rolls through our sky, signaling a storm ahead, a sign of something greater than us that we have no control over. Ever. There may even be no storm—we don't know—but the thunder reminds us of the mystery of the Great Spirit in our lives.

"This thunder reminds us that a greater power works in this world," Lock continued. "A force that has its own logic, authority, and a terrible beauty. And, along with the storms it heralds, it offers us such *kichú*, and we are able to offer *kichú* in return to each other."

Boner tucked Jill's hand in his, his body at attention, his eyes on Lock.

"Thunder fills us with awe when we hear it, even for a tiny moment," Lock said. "And, in that moment, we acknowledge its power and our powerlessness before it. We feel its rumble inside." Lock glanced down at his son, laying his big hand on his baby's tiny chest. "Our son is that thunder in my and Grace's sky."

My chest constricted; my motherfucking heart hurt.

Grace wiped at the tears streaking through her smile. Lock took her hand in his, kissed her forehead, and led her back to the front pew, Jill and Boner following.

My gaze fell to my boots, and I choked down a swell of tears I hadn't known I had.

I felt empty, but that was an understatement.

I felt full, but that was also an understatement.

That I was here at all, to witness this, alive and a part of this circle of *kichú*, was a gift. I rubbed the back of my hand across my mouth. Tania, who was seated in the second row of pews, whispered to Grace's nephew—her late sister, Ruby's, son—Jake and to Jill's daughter, Becca, whom she held in her lap.

Pastor Brad came forward again, clearing his throat. "Richard Thunder Kichú is given new birth through the water and the Spirit. Baptism is the beginning of a lifelong journey of faith..."

Faith, affirmation, covenant, vow, tradition, love.

I closed my eyes and let Brad's words seep through me. Yes, they all made sense to me.

A special sense. A One-Eyed Jack sense.

Hadn't I run after Boner and pulled him from setting himself on fire months ago? That was love, a vow of brotherhood.

Hadn't I gone along with every little crap job Jump could think of for me these past months? That was my covenant with my club, each job a show of faith, an affirmation of my commitment.

Hadn't I created a much-needed bridge for our club to another club, establishing new cash wielding opportunities? That was me continuing the tradition of our brotherhood, moving us all toward something better, something more for the Jacks' future.

165

Nina uncrossed her legs, a leg bumping into mine, and I sank back against the hard wood of the pew.

Hadn't I done right by Nina, who'd needed my help to escape from her private hell? That was compassion, a kind of love.

My eyes slid to Tania once more. Black-haired beauty. Cranky Scarlett.

She rocked Becca in her lap, Jake leaning his head against her shoulder, all three of them listening to Brad.

Tania had bolder makeup on today, like at her art gallery party. She'd made a special effort for this special occasion, enough to accent her beautiful features without going overboard and coming off like a jangly bad chord your fingers had mistakenly stumbled over on a guitar. No, she was a perfectly tuned, perfectly elegant composition.

She turned her head, her gaze meeting mine, as if she'd heard me across the church. The hairs on the back of my neck stood at attention.

Scarlett.

My seductive dream. My other could-be life.

I miss you. I—

Her sexy lips turned up at the ends, a dark eyebrow lifted. She was happy to see me and teasing me all at the same time. I smiled back, enjoying the odd spiral of heat in my chest. She returned her attention to Becca, and something dimmed inside me.

That was too brief, but that was what it was—unattainable and out of reach. A bolt of lightning before me on the highway. Startling. Unsettling. Breathtaking. Then, in an instant, it vanished; it was gone.

"With baptism, we become a part of the body of Christ in the world." Brad's raised voice brought me back to the ritual at hand. "Our name is written in the book of the Lord. We are named. We are commissioned to use our gifts to strengthen His church and to transform the world.

"Richard Thunder Kichú, go forth with the love and the support and commitment of your friends and family gathered here today. God bless you, and may God bless us all. Amen."

"Amen," people repeated out loud through the communal murmuring and shuffling.

Grace took her son back in her arms, and Boner swung an arm around Lock. Jill wiped tears from her face and scooped her daughter up into her embrace. Jake hopped up from his seat, joining Grace, his face craning to check out his baby cousin, with his granddad—Grace's father—at his side.

Grace and Lock had a family. Death, alienation, betrayals— none of it had twisted them in the end. They were the victors.

My eyes clouded; my throat thickened.

I stalked outside of the small church, avoiding the greeting line. I got on my bike and lit a smoke as I watched Tania help her mother into another elderly lady's car. They took off, and Tania turned and opened her car door. Travis came up behind her, saying something, a crooked grin twisting his mouth. Tania swung around, her face drawn tight.

Always ready for a fight, aren't you, Scarlett?

Her shoulders dropped, and she broke into a huge smile, her beautiful dark eyes hanging on Travis.

Son of a bitch.

Tania's face lit up. They talked.

Her face lighting up for me outside that dilapidated house we'd picked over flashed in front of my eyes. Her appreciation of my interest, of any knowledge or history I'd shared with her that she wasn't aware of, our quick way of teasing each other, the jokes—all those moments seemed so far away and so goddamn precious right this very second.

Travis got closer to Tania and said something. Her eyebrows quirked, her mouth twisting in a perfect combination of, *You must be kidding me*, and, *You're turning me on.*

I tossed what was left of my cigarette on the ground.

Once Tania and I had gotten back to Meager and she had found out about me and Nina, I'd thought I'd have a female shitstorm on my hands, its sour aftereffects lasting for weeks, if not months, on end. But I'd been so wrong. Tania was bigger than that. I'd seen her face at the club that day as I entered the clubhouse. Her features had been still, registering what she'd just heard. Then, she'd squared her shoulders, turned her back, and moved on.

It should have been a relief to me. Done and dusted.

But it wasn't.

A deep gouge had ripped through my gut as I was led back inside the clubhouse. Bothered. Disappointed. And fucking confused. Being with Nina was all about no emotional complications, not wanting or needing a real relationship, and knowing I was better off without one. I'd lost Caitlyn. I'd fucked up with Grace. Pain, humiliation, blindness. So much arrogance. Being with Nina was a solution.

Now, I wasn't so sure anymore.

Inside the clubhouse, my brothers and I'd partied, celebrating my return. I'd been so looking forward to that moment, and instead of enjoying myself, feeling the fucking high, I'd felt an odd desolation deep in the pit of my soul that seeped through every cell and vein in my body.

Tania was interesting to talk with, entertaining, thought-provoking, and to top it all off, she was fucking hot. A hot that was intriguing and complex, a hot whose layers I wanted to uncover and explore and get singed from doing it.

In our petty youth, I had kicked her to the curb at Grace and Dig's wedding. I'd flirted with Tania by taunting her and coming on strong, plowing right into her. My hands had grabbed at her flesh, as if I were shoplifting and my life depended on it. And she'd backed out at the worst possible moment. We had been fucking, and she'd panicked, deciding she didn't like what I had been giving her, deciding she didn't want it. Or maybe she didn't want it from *me.*

Back then, she'd always looked at me with hints of distaste, dislike, disgust even. If we hadn't been ignoring each other, we'd been shooting off biting riffs here and there. We'd gotten tangled in each other's barbed wire. She wouldn't back down, and I hadn't quite realized it then, being the self-involved ass I was, but I liked that about her.

In those days, her every glance had been like a scraping over my skin, like she was analyzing me or trying to.

"Let it go, baby. Live and let live," I had told her on several drunken occasions.

She'd only rolled her huge dark eyes at me and taken off in the opposite direction.

So, at Dig's wedding, when she'd stood before me in the repair shed, snarled up in awkwardness—same as me—looking sexy as fuck in that tight dress with, obviously, no underwear underneath, I had gone for it. Or maybe a better description would be that I'd dived for it headfirst.

And she'd taken me up on it.

I had known I was her taste of the lowlife, a secret escapade, a dirty fling, and I'd liked that. That was what most women had wanted out of me anyway. That, I had known how to do and do it well. I'd been with plenty of women, both way younger and way older than me, single and married, regular and rich, all of whom had wanted a bite of the other side. And I'd never said no to providing them with what they wanted. But to toss Tania into that category and to shift blindly into fifth gear with her from the get-go had been stupid.

At Dig and Grace's wedding, I'd been heaving in a tornado of irritation and tension that whole day, and lashing out at Tania had been entertaining, a distraction, a fleeting remedy. I'd wanted to feel like a king again even if it was only for a moment. I got her on that damned couch, and we got busy. Just as I'd started coming, she had pushed at me, panicking. She'd thought better of it, of me. Fuck, I had been a self-centered lay back then. I couldn't say I remembered it much, but I was sure I'd just hammered away at her, getting my rush on.

In the end, I'd gotten left with my wet dick in my hands and hurled bitter words at her for it, letting her know how ridiculous I thought she was before I'd stalked off.

Ugh.

"Butler? Let's go. Come on."

Nina climbed on the back of my bike, her hands latching on to my sides.

I started up my bike and sped out of the church parking lot, swinging by Tania's Yukon. Travis had one arm planted over the door of the vehicle, leaning down toward her open window, the two of them chatting.

Tania's dark eyes darted over at me as I zoomed past in a blur.

TWENTY-TWO

TANIA

"THINGS WITH JUMP any better?" I asked Alicia.

"Nope." Alicia's matte mauve lips pursed together. "He's moved on from feeling bad already. Can't say I have."

"Another shot, ladies?" asked a young blonde with a dozen full shot glasses on the serving tray she held before us.

"Sure," I said, taking two glasses and handing one to Alicia.

The weather had cooperated beautifully for the christening party at the club. A grand buffet table stood at one end of the center of the track, and Alicia and I sat at the other long table opposite, which was for the guests to sit and eat.

Penny's two boys, Nate and Carter chased Becca and Jake through an obstacle course of white chairs on the newly trimmed green grass. All four kids laughed as they punched at the white, blue, and silver balloons attached to the chairs.

Butler and Dready sat on the opposite end of the dining table, talking. With a hand clamped on Dready's massive shoulder, Butler threw back his head and laughed loudly, his body shaking. I tried to look away, but I couldn't. My pulse knocked in my system at the sound of that winner-takes-it-all laugh of his that made you feel as if you'd missed out on something big. His cheekbones seemed more pronounced, and the slight indentations of something like dimples were visible on his face for a moment. Those soft waves of his golden hair shook—a stark contrast to Dready's dark dreadlocked hair—as both men high-fived each other.

The devil inside me wanted nothing more than to torture me today, and I loved and hated every second of it.

Nothing like an impossible crush that just wouldn't die.

I might as well be back in my teens with the way I reacted every time I heard Butler's voice or his name or saw him drive up on his motorcycle. Something would jump and boil inside me and take over my judgment, my reason, my senses. Definitely my senses. I could almost feel his hot breath on my neck on these occasions, like when he'd stared at me in the church earlier. He had unlocked the hidden portal to my carnal self during those hours we had spent together at the motel.

Talking.

Laughing.

Touching.

Kissing.

Coming—Well, me, at least!

I crossed my legs and slammed the lid down on that boiling pot.

Time and time again, I felt compelled to seek him out with my eyes, my ears, whenever I knew he was around. He would match my glances with either a brief smile or a diligent gaze, which would make me mildly uncomfortable because I couldn't tell if these looks were appreciative, friendly, or negative.

But none of that matters, does it? This was an idle game I played with myself. Butler was in a committed relationship with Nina, and that was most certainly that. I was friendly with both of them, but I mostly kept my distance.

Alicia bumped my shoulder with hers. "I've put up with a lot of shit in my time, Tania."

"I know you have."

"At some point, the sewer gets full to capacity and should be emptied. You can't keep plugging up the leaks."

"Oh, totally agree. The stink becomes overwhelming."

She laughed, and we clinked our shot glasses.

Alicia knocked back her tequila and wiped at the edge of her mouth. "Any sense of guilt or wrong Jump might have felt—and I stress the word *might*"—she let out a hard laugh—"vanished within thirty-six hours. And now, I'm the one with the problem."

"Ah, let me guess—that you can't get over it, right?"

"That's right."

"Fuck that."

"Oh, yeah, *fuck that*, is right."

"Maybe you should *fuck that* with a new man," I said.

She laughed, clinking my glass with hers. "I like you, Tania. Have I told you that lately?"

The blonde who'd been passing out shots poured Jump a drink where he was holding court on a long sofa with the president of the Colorado charter of the One-Eyed Jacks.

"For the first time, I really feel like I'm at the end of the line."

"You do whatever you need to do, Alicia."

"For years, I put up with it. I argued, I fought for us, I even fooled around myself to even the score. None of it ever leveled the playing field though. Nothing changed, not really. I knew all this going in. Getting married to him, I knew. But, now, I see my son understanding it, and it's confusing him. Wes is going to be eighteen soon. A man ready to go out into the world and make choices on his own. He already is really. He loves his dad, and it kills me to think that Jump is his role model when it comes to personal responsibility or relating to women. I don't want that for my son. I don't. That hurts more than anything else."

"And you sticking with Jump only shows Wes that all of it is okay."

"Not only that, but also that I'm a fucking failure as a woman, as a wife, and as a mother."

"Come on, Alicia."

"Think about it. All these years, my kid has watched me go from disappointment to disappointment, from artificial high to way down low and back up again. At some point, Wes has made the realization that this is the way a marriage is, that this is the way a man is. And *that* kills me. It's fucking wrong, and I had a hand in that."

I found Wes in the crowd of guests, eating with a couple of his friends. He was a tall teenager with chestnut hair almost touching his shoulders and deep blue eyes. He had his mother's lean frame, coupled with his father's height, and a sullen expression permanently stamped on his face, all of which made Wes a heart-stopper.

"Look at that now."

I followed Alicia's line of sight. The blonde passing out the shots lingered in front of Jump, chatting with him and another biker, while the Colorado president had his hand wrapped around her bare thigh, but her eyes were on Jump, and her smile was for Jump. As the four of them bantered and laughed, the president's hand rose higher under her short skirt, pulling her closer.

"See, right there? That one knows what she's doing."

"What? Flirting?"

"Not just that. Going for the officers. You think she's hot for Jump's body or something?" Alicia scoffed.

How do I say, Of course not, *without offending her?*

Jump hadn't kept up with his formerly fit, muscular self. His bulging stomach attested to that. His arm muscles were still huge, his chest pumped, his legs sturdy. His lone braid ran down his back, now flecked with lots of gray. His face was somewhat swollen and grizzled, which defined his tired, worn appearance, except for those dark eyes of his that would still flick over you with a quick, sharp assessment. Once that assessment had been made, there was no changing it, that was for sure.

But what the hell did I know? Maybe Jump was still The Man in the bedroom.

Jump suddenly got up from the sofa and strode off with another biker from the Colorado club.

Alicia shifted her weight in her chair. She certainly was no has-been/seen-better-days old lady. Her appearance was always polished. Today, her long platinum hair was pulled back in a ponytail with a slightly teased pouf at the top, her heavy eye makeup and perfect dark manicure rounded out her sleek look. Sporting spiked heeled sandals with white skinny jeans and an open-back lilac top held together with thin strips of fabric, showing off an amazing tattoo mural on her upper back, Alicia could give any twenty-something wannabe a run for her money anytime.

The Colorado president lit the shot girl's cigarette. She flicked her mane of golden hair from her face and grinned at him as she drew deep on her inhale, a hand going to her hip.

"Some men think they can walk on water," Alicia muttered.

Grace appeared, shaking her head at me. *A signal to change the subject fast?*

"This spread looks great, by the way," I said. "You know how to plan a party, Alicia."

"She certainly does," chimed in Grace.

"Huh? Oh, thanks." Alicia touched my arm as she brushed past me.

"I've got to say"—I stepped closer to Grace as I admired Alicia's sexy stride through the yard—"I'm tempted to stay because I feel a train wreck coming on, and my evil sensibility would love nothing more than to soak up that spectacle."

Grace sighed. "Right?"

"But I will refrain."

"Oh no. No, no, you can't leave, not yet."

I let out a sigh. *Come on, buy my line of shit, Grace. Make this easy for me for a change.*

"Baby..." Lock embraced his wife from behind, bending his head to kiss her. His one hand stroked just underneath her breasts as they kissed deeply.

I smiled and peeled the empty plastic drink cup from her hand. That hand went to her husband's jaw as she tilted her head back against him. Her pale pink strapless empire-style dress seemed so delicate against Lock's all black clothing. I loved seeing them together. I loved the affection they shared, that physical and emotional need they had for each other.

Real passion. Palpable intimacy.

The blazing afternoon sun slowly seeped into the rich purply blue and burnt coral sky. Flaming tiki torches now lit the field and the music had gotten harsher and louder. Heavy metal was the order of the evening. The family dinner reception had segued into a club party with all the children having gone home to their beds. Penny and her husband, Fred and their boys had taken Becca home with them, and Jake along with baby Thunder had gone back to Grace's with her dad and his new girlfriend. Wes and his friends had disappeared.

I scanned the crowd, entertained by the variety of tattoos, garish sexy outfits, and leather and silver on display. I hadn't been to a club event since Grace's wedding to Dig centuries ago. What a bash that had been. Men and women from over five different clubs had been in attendance. Tables had gotten knocked over, including the fake wedding cake. Once again, Alicia had wisely planned ahead, stashing the real cake in the kitchen and waiting until the last minute to bring it out.

There had been plenty of carousing, singing, dancing, and, yes, surreptitious fucking. As the night had worn on, it had grown much less surreptitious—present company included.

Well, kind of.

And, now, here were most of us again, still standing and still drinking at another club event on Meager soil.

Travis brought me a fresh beer and sat down beside me, stretching out his impossibly long legs.

"Thanks, Travis."

"You bet." He raised his bottle and took a drink, easing an arm around the back of my chair.

Travis was handsome, built, flirty, very charming, and not a One-Eyed Jack. His All-American good looks and southern accent reminded me of my mother's TV chef crush, Tyler Florence, also from South Carolina. Travis, however, was much more alpha commando, less sweet boy next door. Either way, I was sure Rae would love it if I brought Travis home for dinner.

"The stars are amazing tonight, huh?" Travis asked, leaning in close, a whiff of spice and man enveloping me.

I followed his gaze skyward. "They are absolutely beautiful."

"Absolutely gorgeous." He glanced at me, his lips slowly tipping up into a grin.

A woman shrieked loudly in the distance. My stomach clenched at the unmistakable sound of pain, panic, and fear. We sat up, our heads jerking toward the sounds of the woman howling and a man cursing.

"What the hell?" muttered Travis.

We shot up from our chairs, leaving our beer bottles behind and moved in the direction of the crowd gathering.

"Get your hands off her, you fuck! Leave her alone!" a man yelled out.

My chest tightened. *That's my brother's voice.*

I craned my head to see.

Nina twisted in Jump's grip, like a suspended toy tangled in a knot. He had her by the hair, by the hands as he dragged her forward. She was slight, compared to Jump's height and sheer mass.

"Let me go! Let me go!" she shouted.

Bear and Dready held Catch by the upper arms, Catch bucking against their hold.

My heart pounded in my chest, ice filled my veins. I darted toward them, pushing women and men out of my way.

"Catch!" I yelled. "What the hell is going on?"

"Put her down, dammit! What the hell are you doing?" Catch hollered at Jump, his eyes simmering. "Leave her the fuck alone!"

A crowd swarmed around us, and I pushed forward. A steely grip encircled my upper arm, pulling. "Tania!"

Lock.

I pushed back against him. "That's my brother!"

"Hey! Hey! Calm down."

"What's going on?" Jill's voice was raised and thin.

I glanced at her over my shoulder. Her face was pale. Boner had her by the arm. "Get back. Now." He pulled his wife away from the fray before us.

"What the hell is the problem? What happened?" I shouted.

"What the fuck are you doing?" I yelled at Jump.

I glared at my brother. "Drew?"

Catch ignored me. He only had eyes for Nina. His face exploded into a rage, his body jerking against Bear's and Dready's hold.

"Where's her old man?" Jump asked, yanking at Nina's long hair, her head pulling back.

A wall of muscle thudded against my side. *Butler.* His face was set in stone, his eyes diving from his old lady to my brother.

"Did you know he was coming here?" Butler asked me, his voice low.

"No. He's been with Becca at my sister's house for the past three hours. In fact, he should still be there."

"Goddamn it, Jump! You leave Nina the fuck alone!" Catch yelled. "This is all on me! All of it!"

"All of what?" I asked.

My brother shot me a quick look.

He didn't.

Jump's grip on Nina only tightened. "Found the lovebirds fucking," he announced.

My brother's jaw tightened as his eyes trained on Nina, squirming in Jump's grip.

He did.

Butler sucked in air.

"Oh my God." Jill's voice rose behind me.

A malevolent grin creased Jump's face. He was gloating. He kicked at Nina, and she collapsed to the ground on her knees before us, like a wild beast caught at the royal hunt.

Butler lunged at Catch, his fists pummeling my brother. Cracks, pops, thuds, and grunts rocked my ears. Blood spewed from Catch's mouth, his body sagging in Dready's and Bear's hold.

Butler staggered back, a bloodied hand wiping at his chin.

"How you going to deal with your mess, big man?" Jump's voice sneered at Butler. "You gonna teach your bitch a lesson? You gonna kick her out on her ass the way she deserves?"

That was rich, coming from Jump. But I knew he had a point. Screwing around with another biker, a biker from another club, was bad. And said biker screwing around with an old lady from another club, belonging to a biker he knew and worked with, was extra, extra bad. Quadruple fucking bad.

Butler flexed his bloodied right hand—*my brother's blood*—his face grim, as the weight of all eyes were on him. What a combo of public revelation and personal humiliation. After all these years of him being unattached, his new old lady—his hot, fresh young thing that he'd brought all the way out here to South Dakota—had been caught cheating on him.

Butler raised his chin at Dready and Bear, and the men dragged Catch off, away from the track and further into the property where I knew the rocky, grassy terrain met a dense patch of trees on the border of their land.

My brother's grunts faded as my heart banged louder in my chest.

Butler turned to Jump. "Let go of my old lady."

All eyes went to Jump. The amused snarl on his face only deepened. He didn't let go.

"Let. Her. Go." Butler's voice simmered with viciousness.

"Jump!" shouted Alicia.

Jump shoved Nina, and she sprawled onto the ground at Butler's feet. Butler immediately pulled her up. She clutched at him, her chest heaving with jagged breaths and cries.

"He forced me," she spit out. "Catch came out of nowhere, and he-he tried to—"

My blood jammed in my neck. "No! No fucking way!"

Butler wrapped his arms around her, his jaw tight. "It's all right."

Oh no. No, no, no, no, no.

That woman was not going to accuse my brother of trying to rape her. No fucking way. There had to be an explanation.

I pushed past Butler and his old lady and took off for the woods—for my brother. Two massive hands grabbed me and pulled me back into a wall of hard muscle. I recognized the scent of the animal.

"Don't do it, Tania. Do not," Boner hissed in my ear as he held me tight against his chest.

I struggled in his hold. He was leaner and thinner than the rest of the Jacks, but he was very, very strong. "My brother would not try to rape her, for God's sake! That's insane. Makes no sense. She's lying. She's a lying little whore."

His green eyes glimmered as he leaned in closer to me. "Don't make this any harder for Butler."

"Fuck Butler!" I shouted loudly.

Butler caught my feral gaze over his old lady's head.

"Fuck Nina, and fuck you, too, Boner."

Boner dragged me away from the crowd, and I squirmed in his hold.

"Listen to me! Calm down, damn it."

I pushed against his chest.

"Tania!" He grabbed my arms. "The sooner you calm down, the quicker I can get over there and make sure your brother stays in one piece, you hear?"

I stopped, gulping in air. "It's not like they're going to give him a chance to explain himself, are they?"

"No, but I can make sure they don't go overboard."

"That bitch is lying, Boner!"

"Calm the fuck down, and stay with Jill." He squeezed my arms and released them, charging toward the woods.

"Alicia, get Nina inside," Butler muttered.

Alicia led Nina to the clubhouse.

"You gonna let her slide?" Jump asked, his voice raised. "You gonna believe her story?"

"My old lady, my way," Butler replied, his voice leaden.

Jump let out a grunt, his arms folding across his broad chest. "You couldn't give it to her the way she wanted, huh? She had to look for it elsewhere? Too bad she's so stupid that she picked a Flame to fuck. You'd think she'd know better. But, you see, once a Flame always a Flame. You're learning your lesson now at least."

"Shut the fuck up!" Butler's voice boomed.

My breath caught, and needles shot up my spine. Jump only laughed and headed out to the woods where the men were holding Catch.

A cacophony of muffled groans and grunts rose in the distance. Bear's deep laugh howled in the night air along with sickening thuds and a string of curse words and taunting threats.

Nausea swirled in my belly as Butler stalked off toward the woods.

I ran and grabbed his arm. "What are you going to do? Are you going to kill him?"

Butler's grim eyes leveled on mine. "Go home, Tania."

"Don't tell me what to do!" My fingertips dug into his flesh. "You can't kill him. You can't!"

Butler only pressed his lips together, putting his hand over mine on his arm. His eyes were clouded, dark, revealing nothing. He detached my grip from his arm and strode away, leaving me standing alone in the dark.

"Drew, stupid Drew," I muttered to myself, my hands shaking. I balled them into fists.

The music rose in the courtyard. AC/DC pounded in my skull. Men from all the charters of the One-Eyed Jacks ran after Butler, after my brother.

I stepped back and bumped into the buffet table laden with empty food bowls and dishes, strewed with wilting flowers, littered with the small smooth rocks Jill had calligraphed in gold with wishes for the baby.

On the turn of a dime, everything had become ugly.

"Tania?"

I gulped in air and swiveled around. Lenore stood with Jill, the two of them clutching each other, stiff as boards.

"Let's get out of here, Tania," said Lenore. "There's nothing we can do."

The hell there isn't.

"I'm staying. Can you take Jill to my house? My sister should be there with Becca and my mom by now."

"Tania, come with us," said Jill.

"I have to stay."

Lenore's jaw tightened as she took Jill's hand in hers. "Let's get out of here, honey."

"How could he be so stupid, Tania? How?" Jill's voice shook.

"Did you know anything about him and Nina?" I asked. "You talk with her. You—"

"Not a thing. Didn't even suspect. She's been keeping to herself a lot lately, and I thought that was strange." Jill wiped at her hair, pushing it behind her ears. "But how could he do this? Even if he didn't attack her, and I doubt he did—"

"I'm not buying it."

"I don't want to stick around for whatever's coming next," Lenore muttered. "Let's go."

"Lenore's right. You two go. I'll call you, Jill."

"You sure? Please come with us. I don't like this," Jill replied.

"Go."

Lenore and Jill receded into the shadows of the track.

I glanced at the clubhouse. The huge central door was now closed, and six or seven prospects from all the different chapters were smoking and laughing at the entryway. Good times in Bikerland. They were probably laying bets on my brother's survival about now. He was the main attraction at the carnival.

I didn't want to see my brother tortured, maimed, or end up dead at the hands of the One-Eyed Jacks. And I certainly didn't want his foolishness to be the cause for some sort of interclub vendetta yet again. This drama could get out of hand really quickly; and it usually did.

I untucked my cell phone from my tiny crossover bag. I stared at the dark screen.

One night at a high school keg party when we were sixteen years old, I had yelled after Grace as she ran toward the One-Eyed Jacks, toward Dig.

"Grace! Don't you dare!" I'd shouted after her.

She hadn't listened to me, and she'd run over to them to beg for help to save her sister, Ruby, from getting beaten up and probably gang-raped by a group of arrogant football players. I'd thought going to those bikers was only asking for more trouble. They were dangerous. I'd warned her. I'd tried to stop her with logic, with my shout.

But even then, Grace had understood that *to dare, to fly* in the face of the unknown, *to take a risk* had merits, especially if the reason was so very important, and her sister's safety most certainly was.

Life sometimes demanded that you make a leap. No thinking, no weighing rights and wrongs. Only believing.

Believing in your own instinct.

Respecting the boom of that thunder Lock had talked about earlier at the christening.

I had been such a skilled speculator and a comfortable spectator as a teenager and a young woman. Not much of a risk-taker. But that was a long time ago, and I'd grown up since then. The irony was that in recent years, since I'd gotten married, I'd slid back into that passivity, and I'd been bruised by *not* making those leaps, by turning away, by staying still, by not answering that demand.

Now, I was here, in this moment.

Yes, I fucking dare.

I opened up my phone and scrolled down my Contacts list, taking in a deep breath as I looked for his name. A name and number I'd hung on to all these years. I'd never had to call him before to ask for his help, but somehow, I'd known that I just might need to one day.

If there was a time to step over the line I had drawn for myself, it was now.

I tapped on his name.

He answered on the first ring. "Tania?" came that low voice with a hint of a scratch to it. Expectant, suspicious, concerned.

My insides twisted.

Step over the line.

"I'm sorry. I must be bothering you or interrupting—"

"Talk to me."

There it was, still there, that respect, that courtesy, that regard that sliced through all the fog, all the years, and any bullshit.

"I'm at the One-Eyed Jacks' clubhouse in Meager. You need to come here quick."

"Tania, what's wrong?"

I took in a breath.

Yes, I fucking dare.

"I need you."

182

"Let's get some tea." Grace steered me toward the clubhouse kitchen.

"Tea? Seriously?" I spit out.

The commercial kitchen down the long hall reeked of cigarette smoke and the singe of barbecue. Club girls heaped plastic plates and cups into huge black garbage bags. Grace murmured hellos as she opened a cabinet and took down a box of tea bags.

I crossed my arms. "Shouldn't you be home with the baby?"

"My dad and his new girlfriend are at home with him and Jake. She's a retired nurse, so I'm not having any second thoughts about being here for you right now."

"Is Lenore still around?" I asked.

"No, she took off with Jill."

Thank God.

Grace took down two white mugs from a cabinet. "She makes herself scarce when shit goes down. She gets really uncomfortable."

Old scars never really healed. Ugly deep ones at least.

"Yeah, can't blame her," I replied.

The roar and groan of engines rumbled through the open windows. All the women froze.

"Ah, shit, now what?" said one blonde, shutting off the water faucet, ripping off her rubber gloves, and smacking them on the counter.

Grace's jaw set as she stalked off toward the center lounge. I followed her, my heart doing somersaults in my chest.

I sniffed in air. I'd done the right thing, the only thing that would ensure my brother's safety and a quick resolution to the shit-tide he'd brought about between two bike gangs. Clubs. *Whatever.*

The lounge was crowded with murmuring voices, still bodies, some Allman Brothers tune playing very low. A gust of cool night air swept through the room from the open main doors beyond the hallway. I steadied myself on my heels.

Finger and two of his men filled the archway at the entrance to the lounge.

"Motherfudgemycake," Grace breathed.

Finger—dust on his bearded face, a bandana around his head, his long dark hair speckled with gray pulled back in a tie—rested his hands on his hips. His brow was as pronounced as a cliff of jagged granite, the lines of his scarred face still.

"Where the fuck is Jump? And don't make me wait."

His tense gaze darted around the room. No one made a sound. No one moved.

His eyes found mine, and he raised his chin. I swallowed hard.

Grace sucked in a breath. "Oh, you didn't."

TWENTY-THREE

TANIA

"WHERE'S CATCH?" Finger's steely voice filled the space.

The room cleared quickly. Grace and I stood back by the wall of the lounge.

Jump moved through the crowd. "You don't teach your boys any manners?"

One of Finger's thick eyebrows lifted a few degrees. "This is unfortunate."

"Unfortunate?" Jump shot a grimace at Butler, a you-hearing-this-shit look.

"I need to see him." Finger's gaze landed on Butler. "Take me to him."

Butler glanced at Jump, and then he gestured in the direction of the kitchen, which led to the dreaded cellar. Jump narrowed his eyes at the pair of them as they strode out of the lounge, their heavy boots banging on the floor.

Within fifteen long and silent minutes, Butler and Finger returned.

Finger's eyes settled on Jump. "Catch ruin your party?"

"We were having a family celebration," Jump said, his face relaxed.

Shit, he was enjoying this.

Finger's cheeks pulled in, making the deep scars engraved in them more severe. "I was on the road, heading home when I found out. Came straight here."

"Course, you and your men will stay. We've got plenty of food and drink and room for you all to spend the night," said Butler.

Finger slightly slanted his head. An acknowledgment or an appreciation of the bullshit? "Will do."

"A bottle of Jack." Butler motioned to one of the girls.

She scurried off behind the bar. Mary Lynn, Dee, and Alicia darted to the kitchen. They reappeared with plates piled with food and placed them along with cutlery on the center table.

Finger settled in an armchair. The Don had arrived.

His men sat on a sofa and tucked into the roast pork and scalloped potatoes. Finger ignored the food and only drank a swig of Jack from a glass the girl had poured for him, his eyes on me and Grace. The music got louder again. Voices rose.

How things had changed in all these years. Finger was no longer the foot soldier, the ragged prisoner of war, the dreaded messenger, the knife behind the threats.

Now, he is the threat.

He was the architect, the great commander, the respected leader, the sovereign.

Lock, Boner, and Kicker shook Finger's hand and talked with him and Butler.

Why was Butler here, entertaining the VIP houseguest? Why wasn't he with Nina? Had he meted out his punishment already and maybe had locked her in a room while he came out here to hang with his bros and enjoy the rest of his evening?

Butler glanced at me, his lips pressed together. I only averted my gaze.

Lock gestured at me and Grace to come forward.

Grace and I exchanged a brief tight glance as we moved toward Finger.

"This here your old lady?" asked Finger, his eyes taking in Grace.

"Yes, this is Grace," said Lock, his hands on his wife's shoulders.

"We met once. Long time ago."

"Yes, we did," Grace said as they shook hands. "Dig always spoke very highly of you."

Finger raised his glass. "He was a good man."

"He was."

"A man of his word."

"Yes."

"You and Tania are good friends?"

"Since forever."

"She's a good friend to have." He rolled the amber liquor in his glass, his eyes darting to me and back to Grace.

"Congratulations on the baby." He aimed his gaze at Lock. "I apologize for Catch ruining your night."

"Thank you." Lock pressed Grace to his side.

Jump signaled to a couple of the young hanger-on women who hovered in the distance. They sauntered toward Finger.

"Anything you need, Finger, you let me know," Jump said, his forehead creasing.

One girl draped herself on the arm of Finger's chair, the other stood at his other side.

Finger's steady gaze found mine as he drained his glass. "Pour me another, would you, Tania?" he asked, his eyes sliding back to Jump.

"Uh...of course." The bottle on the table was empty. I turned quickly and bumped into Butler. "Sorry," I mumbled as I brushed past.

Another club girl appeared in front of me, as if by magic, and wordlessly shoved a fresh bottle of Jack into my hands, her eyes wide. I went back to Finger, twisted the cap open, and filled his glass. Lock and Grace had sat down on another sofa by his side.

Finger swallowed the liquor and licked his lips as he rested the glass on his thigh. His eyes found Jump's. "I don't like misunderstandings."

"Neither do I," added Jump. "This is done with, as far as the Jacks are concerned. I can't speak for Butler, of course."

"I'm here to make sure shit doesn't get out of hand. Totally understandable what's gone on so far, but it ends here and now," Finger said.

I put the bottle of booze down on the coffee table. "Finger, can I see my brother?"

"He's breathing, Tania. You don't have to worry. Curled up with a bottle. You can see him in the morning over a cup of coffee before we leave."

"Okay," I murmured.

No point in pushing. I was in Bikerland now, and I was simply someone's sister, an outsider.

Jump shifted his weight, a smirk on his face. "Catch is no longer allowed on our club property. I know Meager is his hometown. He's got his mother here, his kid, his sister"—he jerked his chin in my direction—"but he won't be welcome here."

"Fair," said Finger.

Finger took ahold of my arm and steered me to sit on his outstretched long thigh. My breath caught in my chest. There was a hush in the room as I settled on his lap, his arm resting on my hip. Alicia pulled the club girl off his chair, and she grunted, shuffling off with the other girl in tow.

Oh, shitters, what the hell is he doing, and how do I get myself out of this now?

The heat of Grace's eyes scorched my side, but I didn't dare look at her. At anyone. Especially at Butler, who muttered something under his breath.

"Butler, your old lady is Reich's sister-in-law?" Finger handed me his drink, and I took a much-needed sip of the liquor.

"That's right," Butler replied, his hard gaze darting to me, then back to Finger.

"Reich is the VP of my club's national." He leaned back in his chair, a large hand easing down my side. "If he asks me how this night went down, I'll be letting him know."

"So will I," replied Butler, "if he asks."

Finger eyed Butler, his gaze sliding back to Jump. "I've been riding all day. Could use a shower and that bed."

Oh, good, powwow over.

My cue to get out of here fast.

I shot up from Finger's lap, and he rose from his chair, towering over me. I put his glass on the table, and he gripped my upper arm, keeping me close. Grace stared at me, and Butler winced, the corners of his eyes creasing.

Finger's hand wrapped around my neck, and a prickle shot up my spine.

"What are you doing?" I whispered.

His hold on my neck tightened, and he brought me closer to his body, our faces barely inches apart. I took in a breath, my hand clamping onto his wrist.

His dark eyes pierced mine. "I won't have them fucking with you, Tania. You hear? They need to know you're under my protection."

"Am I?"

"Always have been. From the very beginning." His thumb rubbed the back of my neck. "Now that you're back in Meager, I want Jump and the rest of them to respect you, not take any shit about your brother or me out on you after tonight. I won't have that fucker Jump or any of them playing with you."

"But—"

"I'm glad you got Grace, but that ain't enough," he replied to my protest without my even having to spit it out.

"I know them, Finger. It isn't like that."

"You're talking nostalgia. I'm talking here and now. Cold, hard reality."

My teeth dragged across my lip. I knew what he was telling me. The vicious surprise of that biker in the restaurant in Sioux Falls with Butler flashed before my eyes. Jump's sneering gaze this evening and on plenty of other occasions. The knowledge that every Jack here probably had a go at my brother tonight. No, there was nothing left to do but to acquiesce and be grateful.

Oh, shit.

Might as well make it good.

I slid my free arm around Finger's taut middle and pressed into his body. He stayed perfectly still, his eyes on me, as I reached up and touched my lips to his. His hand tightened around my neck as his mouth firmly pressed onto mine.

Our tongues met in a rough argument, a meeting of the minds, a tango performance, a signing of the declaration. I clamped my eyes shut as dizzying cold shudders of pleasure snaked through me with slivers of dread.

Whatdoyathink of me now, Butler?

Finger released me, a hand at my face. "Good girl," he breathed, his warm lips brushing my forehead.

His arm wound over my shoulders, and I leaned into his body. He turned us to face the group, and my mouth dried up.

Grace, Lock, Jump, Alicia, Boner, Dready, Tricky, Dawes, Kicker, Mary Lynn, Dee, Judge, Suzi, Bear, and even the club girls stared at us with a mixture of surprise, veiled suspicion, and alarm.

"Alicia, baby, why don't you show Finger his room?" Jump said, his eyes gleaming at me.

"Of course." A smile blazed over Alicia's face. The perfect hostess.

Butler was a block of stone. Motionless, arms folded, his blue eyes glinting like ice in winter sunshine.

Finger planted a quick kiss on the side of my face. His warm lips might as well have left a burn mark behind on my cool skin.

I glanced at Grace in a farewell gesture, and Finger and I followed Alicia down the hallway.

At the end of the hall, she opened a door for us. "Here you go. You need anything, there'll be prospects in the lounge," she said before leaving us alone.

Finger closed the door behind her. We were alone in the confines of this small room.

"Is this really necessary?" I whispered, suddenly feeling like a day-old picked wildflower struggling to stay upright in a vase.

He locked the door. The click snapped loudly, making my back stiffen, my belly flip.

"Come here."

I went over to him. He slid his hands around my neck and slowly kissed me, his lips nudging mine open. My hands dug into his sides.

"Finger..."

"You wanna fuck?" he said against my lips. His raspy voice growled in *that* way, the way I'd always liked, the way that had always stabbed at my insides with a flare of heat.

So long ago.

His eyes glinted at me. Finger was good at knocking down the elephant in the room, getting it out of the way.

I let out a laugh, my shoulders falling, and his dry laughter rumbled in his chest against mine. He planted a kiss on my forehead, pulling me deeper into his embrace, and I squeezed him back. He released me and went to the bed where he kicked off his boots. I fell back against the mattress, and he stretched out on the bed beside me.

"I guess I'm spending the night, huh?" I said.

"You guessed right." He folded his arms under his head. "Nice to see Maddie again," he said, referring to the fake name Grace had used when we went to Finger's clubhouse many months ago.

"You saw right through that, didn't you?"

"Last thing I expected was to see you along with Dig's old lady walking through my door."

"You recognized her from way back then?"

"You'd mentioned her to me when we first met." Finger removed his bandana and tossed it to the night table. "And I'd noticed her the times Dig and I hung out. He'd introduced us once. I don't forget a face."

"When we came to your club with my niece, Grace figured it was a complication, not needed in the ugly situation with Catch and Jill."

"She figured right."

He stretched his long body on the bed. The springs squeaked, and the pine headboard rattled against the wall. His eyes darted to mine, the edge of his long mouth curling up. I rocked hard into the mattress, and the squeaking intensified, the headboard knocking harder against the wall. I laughed, and it felt good to laugh. Manic laughter, but what the hell? I almost wasn't sure what was so damn funny, but it still felt good.

A low chuckle scraped from his throat as he propped himself up on an arm, his free hand resting on my torso. "How are you really doing?"

"Right now, confused and anxious about my brother and the new shitstorm he's brewed up. I had to call you in. You were going to find out anyway, but I couldn't take the chance that they'd—"

"You did right. Better I handle this now, as it's happening, rather than later when shit blows up and gets out of control, according to every dumb fuck's perception of events."

His hand roamed over my abdomen and slid under my shirt, heating my skin. I squeezed my legs together.

"Well, after tonight, everyone will think differently of me."

"That was the point."

"I imagine the men will keep at least a five-mile distance from me from now on."

"You sound disappointed. Were you after Jack cock tonight?"

I laughed. "Well, that aspiration is shot to shit now, isn't it?"

Actually, that was shot to shit when I first laid eyes on Nina and heard the words, *That's Butler's old lady.* A gong had struck, and I got the message.

Butler's bleak face as he'd watched Jump drag Nina around by the hair earlier flashed before me. He was in pain.

What the hell is he going to do about Nina now? Will they break up? Will he forgive her?

Finger's hand cupped a breast, and my breath caught as he stroked over the material of my bra. For such a fierce lone wolf, he could be gentle.

"Who's the lucky asshole?"

He squeezed my nipple between his thumb and forefinger, and I gasped at the sudden bite of pain.

Gentle sometimes.

"Forget it. I'm trying to." I took in a breath, enjoying the zings of arousal tripping through me, my eyes glued to his.

The slow *rip* of the zipper on the side of my skirt made my lungs bunch together.

"Finger," I whispered.

"Tania." His voice was gruff, hoarse.

"You could have had one of those women in there, if not two or three, no problem, to service your needs. I cut into your action tonight."

"Yeah, what a fucking shame. Make it up to me."

He slid my silky tunic top up my torso and pulled a breast from a bra cup, kneading it, his jaw tightening. My breath stuttered at the harsh look on his face. He lowered his head, taking the nipple in his mouth.

I gasped, my back arching. "Have I ever said no to you before?" I whispered.

"Never." He glanced at me—his face passive, stoic—as he licked, sucked. "Have I ever forced you?"

"Never."

"After you got hitched and I didn't hear from you again, I didn't call you no more, did I?" His voice was even as he stroked me into oblivion.

Tight coils of pleasure wound through me, and heat wrapped around me like warm velvet as my hands fisted the thin quilt. All the pressure of the evening that had built into a tight knot inside my body, my head, now unraveled and built into something else, something that beckoned me to be a part of my destruction.

One ticket. One-way only.

"I missed you," I murmured, squirming on the bed. "Missed this."

His hand slid over my panties, cupping me. "You been faithful to your husband all these years?"

My eyes held his iron gaze. "Yes."

"Still married?"

"Getting a divorce."

His face darkened. "Fuck him."

His hand slid under my panty, his fingers hitting flesh, dragging through me. The silky fabric on my skin flew down my legs and off my feet. The mattress dipped and shook, and I blinked. Finger stood over me at the edge of the bed, snapping off his dirty leathers, a thick eyebrow raised, his intense eyes glimmering.

"All these years later, Tania, and you still fucking do it for me."

A lazy grin curled my lips. "Hallelujah."

His clothes fell to the floor. My eyes took in his naked body, and my face heated.

Finger was several years older than me, which put him in his mid to late forties, and he was still in amazing shape, like I'd remembered. Contoured thick muscles marred by ugly, jagged scars and so many dramatic tattoos were all over his suntanned chest, arms, and torso, hardly a spot of bare flesh left. His body was virile, powerful. A body that screamed experience, strength, capability, threat.

His fingers stroked his cock that stood at rigid attention against his abs.

Yes, I could have that cock right now.

I'd missed that cock. Badly.

Fuck logic, screw sense, damn *goodgirlitis*.

I sat up on my elbows, my mouth dry. "Finger," I breathed.

His hand pumped his cock. "You want it?"

Heat pulsed through my veins. My pulse screamed at me as it zoomed past.

We were picking up where we'd left off eleven years ago.

For years, Finger and I would meet in diners and truck stops and motel rooms down highways all over the Midwest. Once, as far away as New Mexico, when I had been on vacation with a girlfriend, and another time in Nashville, where I'd been on business.

Quick, intense.

We had stayed in touch since the very first time we had met by fateful chance in a gas station outside of Tripp, South Dakota, almost two decades ago after I'd left Meager behind. A moment that had changed my life. But it was years later when it had turned into hook-ups between us.

Frequent hook-ups.

We would hook up to fuck away our disappointments, our missed connections. We'd fuck to reconnect to the trust and sorrow that bound us. We would meet to drop the wizard's curtain for a spot of relief, for however long it would be, either one whole night or only an hour or two. Maybe twenty minutes even, like that time in a restaurant restroom in Indiana.

We'd converse little at each of these encounters. Pleasantries were unnecessary with Finger, and I'd realized it would only serve to make things awkward. We would exchange basic information here and there, always ignore each other's usual moodiness, and let our bodies do what they did, what they needed.

Finger would push me to try new things, and with him, I'd let go of my inhibitions and self-consciousness. I never felt judged with him, like I did with other men. He wouldn't show off. He wouldn't say stupid, superfluous things to compliment me or my body. He wouldn't put on a performance. No bullshit. Ever. Sometimes, it sucked, when I was feeling sorry for myself, but mostly, mostly, I liked it.

Our encounters were a slap of cold water or a soothing hot bath. Either way, they were always good.

And not too many frills either. We didn't kiss very much. He'd hold me down or hold me up, keeping me immobile against him, turning me every which way he wanted. I'd only grip an arm or a shoulder of his to steady myself as best I could during the onslaught. Surrendering to him, to his innate authority felt good. Liberating.

I never expected post-coital soft kisses of affection or delicate caresses, and there were none. Only tight grips, firm holds, and insistent strokes.

From what little he had told me, he would go through girlfriends and old ladies like water. Only with two of them had he not cheated with me, but soon enough, they'd be gone, too. I was sure his emotional coldness was the reason. But all that wasn't for me to judge. We both had our reasons and our demons.

I knew he wasn't a cold, hard bastard inside because all this was about *her* and always would be. Like for me, fucking him was a purely selfish escape, exhilarating for the moment. Reckless, void of responsibility to anyone but me. My secret joyride. A ride removed from the mundane everyday where I dared to take a risk or two or three. I needed that.

I'd fallen in love for the first time in college, but then that relationship had collapsed after two years. That first love wound was no joke. Later, I'd dated, and I'd slept with the ones I really liked and was attracted to, but I'd left those relationships more often than I took them on. No one ever pulled me in with a fever the way I always craved.

Finger and I weren't in love, never would be, but we liked each other as people, were attracted to each other, and shared a kinship that I knew, for me, I'd never felt with anyone before or since. He was a constant I could trust, and that was good; it was enough. There was no question of a relationship between us; there was no way he could fit into my life or me into his, and truly, I wasn't interested in that with him. I honored our way together for what it was. I never expected more, and he appreciated that. Most of all, I respected him, and he knew it and respected me back; that was what really mattered.

Only once, over a shared joint, I'd asked him if he'd seen *her*, his first love wound, and his face had darkened, his body stiffened.

"Yeah, once," he'd said, wincing. He'd gotten out of bed, got dressed, and strode right out the motel room door without another word. He'd climbed onto his bike, making it roar with a ferocity. That old Harley, that cacophonous metal animal, spun him onto the road and into a blur of power and liberty and force.

And forgetting. I'd never mentioned her again.

I'd met Kyle and been totally smitten, and we'd gotten serious quickly. I'd told Finger about it over the phone as I clutched my winter coat against the freezing wind at a pay phone on Michigan Avenue in Chicago eleven years ago and declined his invite to meet after getting his text message.

"You be happy, Tania."

"I will. I want you to be happy, too."

My remark had been met with silence, and the line had gone dead.

Those were the last words we'd exchanged until a few months back when I'd stepped through the massive gates of his clubhouse in Nebraska with Grace and plunged back into Finger World, a world that had now become my brother's, too. Our connection would not ever be severed, it seemed.

I had never asked him for anything in return, yet all through the years, he had offered me his help with anything I might want, like entertainment drugs or money when I was between jobs more often than not, no strings attached. I never took anything from him though. But I knew in my gut that if I ever needed him, really needed him, he'd be there for me.

Like tonight.

Finger rubbed himself with quick, hard strokes. His long cock was stiff in his hand now, the tip engorged, wet. Ready. He licked at his bottom lip.

This wasn't reconnecting though.

This was me being frustrated, angry, pissed, jealous.

And I knew, I knew this was Finger being frustrated, angry, pissed, jealous.

Even though Butler was as good as married and going through a soap-opera drama, I liked him. A lot. I couldn't get him out of my head. And having sex with Finger wasn't going to change that. It would only mess with me.

Furthermore, I wasn't the lonely young woman I used to be a decade ago. I was stronger now. I wanted something real, something I knew was worth waiting for. That was why I was getting a divorce. That was why I was here in South Dakota. And even though a relationship with Butler wasn't possible, the time I'd spent with him as a friend and in that motel bed had shown me that something real, something good, something of worth was possible for me.

I'd moved back home to simplify my life and to be and do the things that I really wanted, to be fearless in that quest, not to take the middle road after eleven years of doing just that. Not to be complacent, under the radar. No, no more. Not any longer.

Finger nudged my legs open with one of his, his large hand pumping hard over his dick.

My breath shorted as he leaned down and kissed me, our eyes on each other, his cock rubbing down my middle to my—

I gripped his arms. "We can't do this. Not now. Not anymore. We had our time, you and me, and I liked it. I fucking loved it. But we shouldn't go back there."

He rose, and I sat up on the edge of the bed and took his hands in mine. I kissed the left, the right. Just above where the middle fingers were missing.

"I don't want to go backward with you. I want you in my life—you are; you will always be in my life—but I need to keep moving forward. We both do."

He pulled his hands from mine.

I tugged at my bra, pulling my shirt down. "You know she's here, don't you? I saw her. Talked to her. She's good friends with Grace now. She has a business here in town. She's—"

"I know." His heavy voice shot through my chest, its dark tone lodging there, filling me with dread.

"Of course you know."

"I've always known." His eyes flared, and my stomach clenched at the sight. "Were you going to say anything?"

"I saw her for the first time a few weeks ago when Grace introduced us. She pulled me aside and asked me not to say anything to anybody. Hell, I don't know what to say when it comes to you two. You had it all, and you both let it go."

"You call that having it all?"

"From where I'm standing today? Right now? You bet I do."

"You called me to come here, knowing she was here?"

I shot to my feet. "I had to call you. My brother's life was on the line."

"You did good, babe."

I rubbed my hands down my face. "Everything's different now. Tell me it isn't."

We stared at each other. Finger reached out, his hand cupping my chin. He leaned down, brushed my lips with his, and planted a gentle kiss on my forehead. He left me and went into the bathroom. The shower turned on.

I fell back on the bed and curled up on the mattress. I squeezed my eyes shut, but those vivid crystal blue eyes still stared at me. Hurt. Fervent. Angry.

Would I ever be able to blot them out?

What was Butler doing now? Fucking his old lady back into submission? Punishing her with his cock? Drowning his pain in booze?

Please, not that.

But it had nothing to do with me. Nothing.

In fact, I was sure the One-Eyed Jacks probably hated me now and would never trust me again. Even Grace was ticked at me.

I turned over on the bed and squashed my face into the pillow. My breathing evened out to the steady drone of the shower water.

Exhaustion.

I gave in.

TWENTY-FOUR

BUTLER

"ARE YOU INSANE? What the hell are you doing?"

Nina shuddered from where she sat on the middle of my bed at the club, wiping the tears from her face. "I know, I know. I'm sorry. We were just fooling around."

"*Just* fooling around?" A blade of fire ripped through the muscles across my back. "You're not supposed to be doing anything with anybody, you little idiot!"

"It started out as flirting, a game."

"A game? A man from another MC is not a game. You know better."

"I know. I do. I just—I've never been so attracted to anyone before." Nina's face crumpled. "Not like this."

"Jesus. There's more to life than fucking and getting off!"

"This isn't like that! It's—I barely understand it. I can't get enough of him. I need him."

"Is it really so difficult for you to keep your fucking panties on?"

"I just want to be with him. All the time. He makes me feel like—"

"Whoa, she feels, ladies and gentlemen! Nina Scott actually *feels* things."

"Shut up! That's not fair."

"Fair? You have no fucking idea," I spit out.

I had chosen to be with Nina because I'd assumed I was done, and yet now I was careening through feelings and emotions for a woman I couldn't have. Was it fair to suddenly feel things I hadn't felt in years? Was it fair to fumble with possibility, curiosity, excitement, and tenderness at the very time that I had all my big plans in place? Was it fair that the one person who made me actually want to wake up in the morning and face the day, the one person who made me realize all that possibility, was, right this minute, in a bed down the hall, fucking someone else? A someone else who was a formidable ally and potential opponent.

Motherfuck.

Nina sniffled, her red eyes wild with emotion. And fear, too. Yes, fear of this new pull in her heart, a heart that had never been clawed at and ripped into shreds before.

Yeah, I knew that fear well.

"What are you saying? You in love with him?"

"Yes," she cried. Tears streamed down her face, her chest heaved.

It's a fucking whirlwind, ain't it, baby?

"Welcome to the real world, Nina, where feelings are genuine, and they are felt right through your goddamn soul. Feelings overwhelm you, and they can drown you, Feelings cut deep, and you fucking bleed. The one thing they aren't is fair."

"I know I fucked up. Fucked up bad. I'm sorry. But I can't...I can't do this anymore," she said through ragged, hiccupy breaths, her arms wrapped around her middle, as if she were freezing.

"Tough shit. You can't just cut and run. We had a deal. You fucked it up."

"I know, I know."

"Do I have to remind you that you have just as much at stake in this as I do?"

"I'm pregnant!"

"What?" That fist tightened in my chest, that nausea rolled in my gut.

"I'm—"

"I heard you!" I steadied myself. "Is it mine?"

She shook her head. "No. No, it's his."

"You sure?"

"I went to this clinic place. I'm seven weeks pregnant. You and I haven't...for a long time now."

"Ah, shit." I leaned over and sucked in a breath. "But you're on the pill. How the hell—"

"Remember when I got sick a couple of months ago, and I had to go on those antibiotics? I forgot to take a pill or two, and I think the medicine interferes with it anyway." She sniffed. "I'm sorry!"

I wiped at the prickle of sweat over my forehead and dragged a hand through my hair. "Sorry gets us nowhere. When Reich hears about you cheating on me—and he will—what are you going to say? You know your sister will be calling you. What are you going to tell her?"

She wiped at the tears on her face. "I'll tell her what I told everyone out there tonight. That Catch came on to me. We were at a party, and he was drunk, and I'd been drinking, too. We flirted, and Catch took it as an invite. Fuck, Deanna knows how I am. This won't be a stretch for her to believe." She bit down on the corner of her mouth, rocking back and forth. "It'll be fine. You'll see."

"Nothing's gonna be the same again. Nothing."

"I'm sorry. Please, I'm so sorry," she wailed.

"Shit had finally settled down with us and the Flames. And now…fuck. You going to keep the baby? I mean, what do you want to do? You going to tell Catch?"

"I want to keep it. I want…" She started crying again.

I sat down on the edge of the bed next to her. "Look, for the time being, you can't tell Catch about the baby. If you do, he's going to come bulldozing over here to get to you. And that can't happen just yet."

"Right." She grabbed a tissue from her handbag and blew her nose.

"You lay low, hang out with Jill, the other old ladies, and be the good girl. No going out at night to bars or clubs anymore, not even a movie. When you hang out with them, I mean, only coffee, lunch, their houses, babysit for them, but that's it. Nothing more."

"Okay." She nodded, pushing her hair behind her ears.

"For a fucking change, you need to keep your mouth shut and be the quiet good girl on the block. Can you do that?"

Her watery eyes met mine. "Yes," she whispered.

"And you're going to have to play the guilty card, too. Be humbled, ashamed, remorseful, so I don't lose face by hanging on to you. You convince them that you want to stay with me, that you're bending over backward for me. That you know you fucked up royally. This needs to stay real, goddamn it. At least for a little while longer. You got that?"

"Yeah, okay."

"Stay the fuck away from him."

"Okay!"

I gripped her chin. "Do. You. Understand?"
She blinked. "Yes. Yes, I understand."
I released her. "I fucking hope so. For both our sakes."

TWENTY-FIVE

TANIA

"TANIA."

I unglued my eyes. Finger hovered over me.

My body jerked up in the bed. "What is it? Did something happen? Is Catch—"

"He's fine. I have to go into town. It's early yet. You stay here with your brother. My men will be here, and I'm counting on you to keep shit cool until I get back. Shouldn't be more than a couple of hours. Depends."

I grabbed his arm, and his eyes narrowed at me.

"Please, be kind to her."

"Tania, all I've ever wanted was the best for her."

"I know," I breathed.

"Listen, you be careful with what you say out there. Don't say shit. After last night, they won't know what to say to you anyhow."

"Right. This should be fun. You know, I'm really surprised you haven't cut my brother loose from the Flames."

"Why? He's a good, loyal brother. He's got balls. He's also good with numbers. Real good."

I swung my legs out of the bed. "My brother?"

"Yeah." Finger shoved on his boots. "He's gotten us out of a few tight spots."

"Oh. Good. Glad to hear it."

"I have plans for Catch. But he keeps fucking up with his bitch dramas. And I don't think this was any ordinary pussy run, but now, he's not giving two shits about much else. Talk to him."

"I will. He's totally devoted to your club—to you, most of all."

"I don't question that. But he's got to keep his goddamn dick in check."

"I don't think this was just about his dick or some grand plan. I think he might actually like her."

Finger adjusted his bandana over his head and tied it in the back. "He needs to focus. I don't want to be questioning his choices anymore. This is getting old."

"I think you know what that's like, saying to hell with it for a woman. *The* woman."

He shot me a sharp glance as he unlocked the door. "You make sure your brother is ready to ride by the time I get back."

The door slammed.

Grace and Alicia sat at the bar, drinking from large white mugs.

"Good morning," I said.

Alicia wordlessly slid a mug in front of me and poured coffee in it. Jump, Bear, and several other Jacks stood, holding their mugs, talking with the two Flames of Hell men. They stared at me.

"Is it?" Grace asked, her tone pricking like a needle on skin.

Here we go.

"The sun is shining. We're alive. That's a big yes in my book."

Grace frowned at me. "Tania…"

I sipped on the strong black coffee. "I know Finger."

"Obviously! Since when? You avoided my questions when we saw him in Nebraska. So, now what? You have an ongoing thing? Or is this new? You've been married for over ten years. Were you—"

"Grace!"

"We're talking about Finger here, Tania," she said, lowering her voice. "The president of one of the most powerful chapters of the Flames of Hell. Not just any ole biker from any ole MC. It's me you're talking to here—the old lady, twice over. Your oldest friend, whom you used to yell at for talking to a biker, let alone liking one, sleeping with one, marrying one. Now, spill!"

"Could you please—"

"And how could you keep this from me?"

"Do I really have to explain *that* to you, Mrs. One-Eyed Jack?"

"*That*, I get, but as your friend, it hurts."

"I'm sorry. Really."

Damn, I hate this.

She took in a breath. "Apology accepted. Moving on. Spill."

I'd prepped the story in my head from the moment Finger had walked out the door this morning. I couldn't tell her the whole truth. I couldn't tell anyone. I'd been keeping it a secret all these years for a good reason, and even though I trusted Grace with my life, I couldn't spill this secret.

"I met Finger through my brother when he first started hanging out with the Flames. I came home just before I got married, and Drew was prospecting then. I went down to Nebraska to see him and tell him my news in person, and that's when I met the Grand Master himself."

Grace folded her arms and stared at me. Alicia drank her coffee, her eyes on me from behind her mug.

I pinned a breezy smile on my face, my gaze darting from Grace to Alicia. "Questions? Comments? Half-and-half for my coffee?"

Grace didn't move a muscle. "What about last night? Don't tell me you only met that one time over eleven years ago and then again when we were in Nebraska a few months ago? That's it?"

"Not exactly."

"Not *exactly*? I should believe that you just caught his eye last night, and he claimed you for his bed, like he would any club girl, and you sucked on his mouth and trotted on after him and—"

"Grace—"

"See? That's not the Tania I know, not unless you wanted him."

"I did. I do. He turns me on."

Literal truth! See? I'm not lying to my bestie.

She shifted her weight, chewing on her inner cheek. That decades old habit of hers hadn't faded.

"Are we going to sit and share our past sex stories, catching up right now on all those many years we were out of touch?" I said.

She pushed her mug away. "What happened out there last night, I don't know if you realize what it meant."

"For God's sake, yes, I've had sex with him before. Okay? But we're not going steady or getting married."

No more, Gracie, please.

"Ah."

"What is it? We can't be friends anymore? The Flames and the Jacks don't break bread together? Play in the same sandbox? Is Flame cock off-limits for me? Am I tainted for you now?"

"Geez, don't make fun," murmured Alicia.

"I'm sorry. Anyway, my brother is a Flame, so I'm in the clear, right? Fucking a Flame should be on the menu for me." I cleared my throat. "Can't Finger and I be...friendly because of that?"

Grace and Alicia eyed me. "Friendly?" they both exclaimed.

Oh, for fuck's sake.

"Finger and I haven't seen each other in a long, long time," I said. "There was always an attraction there." I slid my mug back and forth on the counter. "It was a fling way back then. *Then* being before I got married. Now, I'm not married, and I'm open to flings these days."

I seem to reserve bikers for flings.

Grace's eyebrows jumped. "A fling?"

"Yep, that would be me, flinging."

"Okay."

"Okay."

"Where is Finger anyway? His bike's gone," Grace said.

"Did they want you to ask me and find out?" My voice snapped.

"No." Her eyes flashed at me. "I'm concerned about you. That's what this is, Tania. I've just never seen you be so—"

"Impulsive?"

"Yes! And you being impulsive with *Finger* has me concerned."

"You don't have to worry about me. I'm fine."

Grace frowned. "Ooh."

"What now?"

"That's not good," Alicia said, shaking her head, shooting Grace a look.

"What are you two talking about?" I asked.

"You said fine," Grace said. "*Fine* isn't fireworks. *Fine* isn't heart-pounding. *Fine* certainly isn't fling-worthy multiple orgasms. *Fine* isn't a word I'd use to describe getting it on with a man like Finger. And *fine* is definitely not worth the bed head afterward." She pointed at my still unruly hair. "That being said, I hope fucking Finger was worth being so impulsive."

I grabbed my hairbrush from my handbag. "Who the fuck are you? The orgasm police?"

Alicia laughed out loud.

"I'm your girlfriend!" Grace said. "I look out for your best interests at all times, in all situations."

My face broke into a grin. Hadn't I said the same thing to her when I was being an overbearing bitch after finding her drunk in a post-miscarriage depression at Pete's one afternoon when I first came back to town months ago?

I threw my brush down and pulled her into a hug. "Grace, I appreciate your concern for my orgasms. I really do."

She laughed, holding me close. "You'd better."

I released her. "And how were your orgasms last night? I do hope you enjoyed at least *one*?"

"Three in fact, thank you."

I fluttered my eyelids. "Aw, you're my role model."

The three of us laughed again.

I smoothed my hair into a ponytail. "Finger went into town to Erica's. I told him the coffee sucks here, and I wouldn't be drinking it."

Lie number I-can't-keep-track-anymore-and-I'm-freaking-the-hell-out-now.

Grace grinned, enjoying my bullshittery. "How gallant."

"Isn't he? He really likes me. Or maybe it's just the sex." I winked at her.

"Your eyes do look brighter today," said Grace.

"It's been a *very* long time since they've been this bright, a very long time."

"Oh, boy, that good with Kyle, huh?" asked Alicia.

"No comment. Anyway, I need to see my brother before Finger gets back, and they take off for Nebraska. Could you bring me to the infamous cellar?"

"No, but I'll get someone who will. I'll be right back."

Grace took off, and I heaved a small sigh.

"You really okay?" Alicia asked. "You know you don't have to worry about disappointing me. You ever need to talk…"

"Thanks, Alicia. I appreciate it. So, where's Nina? Is she okay?"

"Butler's got her locked in his room. She sure isn't gonna be too popular around here today, for starters."

"Is she going to have to wear a scarlet letter now?"

Alicia's face scrunched up. "Huh?"

"I mean, punished. Become the club Cinderella?"

"That's up to her old man." Alicia lit a cigarette.

I indulged in images of a repentant Nina in a bikini scrubbing floors and toilets with a toothbrush, taking drink orders while she got swatted on the ass by every male member, cleaning the gutters of the building, hauling garbage.

Grace returned with Butler in tow. "Butler's going to take you to see Catch."

My pulse spiked. Butterflies did a samba in my tummy. "What? No, Butler doesn't…"

Butler stood before me in his post-surfer, road-warrior magnificence. His blond waves were mussed and in his face. His shoulders and arms were stiff, and his jaw jutted at a sharp take-no-prisoners angle. It had been a long night.

"You don't have to, Butler," I stuttered. "You've got a lot going on. There must be someone else who could—"

"Let's go," he said, his eyes hooded.

Grace turned to me, a plastic smile on her face.

Evil girl.

"I've got to go." Grace brushed my cheek with a quick kiss. "I have to pick up more diapers and get back to my son. I'll catch up with you guys later."

"Bye, Grace," said Alicia.

"Bye!" Grace headed for the exit, taking all my bravado with her.

"This way," Butler said, dipping his head in the direction of the kitchen.

I cleared my throat and fell in step beside him.

"You have a good night?" he asked.

Oh, brother, we're going to do this now?

"A what?"

"Last night. I didn't realize you and Finger—"

"You're not the only one who keeps secrets, eh?" I said. "Surprise, surprise."

"You sure that's a good thing?"

"What exactly?"

"Getting involved with Finger?"

"Are you concerned about me?"

"Yeah, I am. You want to hook up, there are plenty of Jacks who'd stand in line for the chance."

"Get out of here."

He clenched his jaw, keeping his attention straight ahead.

Two club girls in cropped T-shirts and shorts sat on the kitchen counter, smoking. Their dark-rimmed eyes followed us as we headed toward the cellar door at the opposite end of the room.

"I just want to make sure you realize what you're getting involved in," he said, his voice low.

"It's just a bit of fun."

"See? Right there."

"What's that?"

"*Finger* and *bit of fun* don't fit in the same sentence, Tania. You have no fucking idea." He tapped on the combination lock pad on the door. It beeped, and he pushed the door open for me with his arm.

I brushed past him. His scent of citrusy soap, coffee, and tobacco was suddenly intense. "Jesus, Butler. Should I be grateful that you're so concerned about me?" I waited on the landing at the top of the staircase.

"Maybe you should."

The door thudded and clicked closed behind us.

I glanced up at him. "Well, I'm not. It's just pissing me off."

"Yeah?" He flew down the stairs.

I followed him. "Yeah! Fuck off."

He stopped abruptly, and I crashed into his massive back. He pulled my arm and pushed me against the wall, the two of us teetering on a narrow step.

"I don't think you want to be doing that!" I said through gritted teeth.

"Finger gonna come after me?"

"Can we stop this now?"

"I'm just getting started."

"You have no right to talk to me about my choice in men. Your choice in women leaves much to be desired!"

Oh, shit, I did not just say that, did I?

You did! You did!

His eyes flared.

"I'm sorry about Nina fooling around behind your back and with my brother, no less. That must hurt."

"Tania—"

I tugged on his arm. "Why the big secret? Why couldn't you tell me about her? We were on the road for almost twenty-four hours together. There I was, spilling my guts about me and my marriage, men, sex, and just about all of it. But you? You couldn't be bothered to mention that you were committed to a sweet young babe named Nina?" I leaned into him. "And then you touched me, kissed me, because you felt sorry for me."

"I told you that wasn't why—"

"Then, why? Why? You obviously love Nina since you haven't tossed her out on her well-deserved ass, like I'm sure all your brothers are expecting you to. You and me though? We hit it off, had a good day. There I was, in the same bed, and you figured, what the fuck, right? You think you can have it all, don't you? Same ole Blondie."

His eyes flashed up at me in the fluorescent lighting, blue nuggets of ice. "Shut up!"

"Don't tell me to shut up, you ass!"

His hands dug into my shoulders, and his mouth crashed down on mine. Vicious anger, stunning lust.

I ignited under his harsh assault.

Our tongues dueled as he shattered me and roused me all at once. My hands gripped his taut sides, our bodies pressing together, a primal instinct of need and unrequited business.

Stop! What are you doing, Jezebel? He's as good as married! This is only him showing you who's boss. Stop! Stop! Stop!

But I couldn't stop. This was Butler, and he felt too good.

My limbs gave in, as if I'd inhaled a drug and it had finally settled into my bloodstream. Yes, Opium de Butler. I clung to his hard shoulders flexing under my hands, his arms surging around me. I gave him everything he was taking and took everything he was giving.

He wrenched away from me, his chest heaving for air, his forehead leaning against mine, his hand still clasped around my neck, as if it were his only source of stability. His addictive scent lingered in my nostrils, his perfect taste in my mouth. A sting whipped over my flesh as my body cried out for more, more, more.

"What are you doing?" I breathed against his lips.

"I don't know." His fingers tensed along my neck, my jaw.

Our eyes searched one another in the half-light. Frustration, despair, anguish.

"That shouldn't have happened," he whispered, his voice rough. "But I'm not sorry."

"I'm not sorry either."

He tugged my head back and met my gaze in the dim light of the staircase. His face was no longer a tightly drawn mask of cool. Now, it was drained, his full lips parted, his jaw slack.

"Something's not right with you, and I want to know what it is," I whispered.

"There's plenty not right with me. Plenty."

"You're upset about Nina and—"

He averted his gaze. "Stay away from me, Tania."

"That's hard to do when you're making snake eyes at me, grabbing me, and using your delicious tongue to show me who's boss."

His thumb brushed over my swollen lips, and his mouth curved into a slight grin. "This fucking mouth."

"Did you miss my mouth?"

The slight grin broke into a huge one, and my insides rippled at the sight.

"Is this really about your old lady screwing someone else or is it more than that?"

He shook his head. He didn't want to discuss it. I reached up and slid a hand over the side of his face, and he leaned into my touch, his eyelids lowering.

This man needed a safe place to rest.

Butler put a hand over mine, and my heart squeezed. Taking my hand from his face, he gently brushed it with his lips. He let go of me and took in a shallow breath, pushing me away from him with a hand to my middle, as if I were unwanted, untouchable, undesirable. He slammed shut the trap door on our dungeon of confusing and colliding emotions.

He swept his hair back, his gaze flicked down the staircase. "You gotta see your brother."

"Butler—"

"This never happened, Tania."

"Right. A lot seems to just happen yet not happen between us, doesn't it?"

His eyes slid to me. "It doesn't *just* happen, does it?"

My stomach hardened. Nothing made sense at this very moment. Not one damn thing.

I turned and stalked down the rest of the stairs. "Which way?"

Butler moved ahead of me down the hallway and unlocked a reinforced steel door at the end of it. He shoved it open and motioned me inside.

My brother—his clothes smattered in blood, his face bruised and swollen, a study in purple, blue, and red—sat on the floor in a corner, his eyes closed, his head leaning back against the wall. One blackened eye squinted at me. "Hey."

I squatted down next to him and put a hand on his leg. "You okay?"

"Dandy. Don't touch me. Everything hurts."

"Want a smoke?" Butler tossed him a pack of cigs.

Catch's bruised eyes darted up at Butler and then went to the pack. He took a cigarette out and tipped it between his lips. Butler flicked his lighter for him. Catch inhaled deeply, his eyes closing for a moment.

"I'll be outside," said Butler. He left the concrete box of a room, closing the massive door behind him.

"Finger went into town for a bit. He should be back soon," I said. "Then, you'll both head home to Nebraska. Are you going to be able to ride on your bike?"

"No." Catch let out a thick stream of smoke from his lips. "But I'll do it."

I handed him a water bottle and two caplets of Tylenol. "Enjoy."

"Thanks." He swallowed the pills, gulping down plenty of water.

"Is Finger going to punish you for last night?"

"Oh, yeah. Can't wait to see what's in store for me when we get home."

Jesus, I didn't want to know.

"Why Nina, for God's sake? You have your pick. How the hell did you...because you knew what was at stake here. Yet you took the risk."

His tired, pained gaze hung on mine. My brother had dared; and he'd felt the heat of the fire. My chest swelled with admiration, with pride, with sadness.

I sat next to him. "Drew, you really like her, don't you? This isn't some anti-Jack ploy, is it?"

"That what you think? Is that what they're thinking?"

"I don't know what they're thinking. They're certainly not talking to me about it. But after the shit you pulled with Jill and Boner a while back, then stealing Dig's gun—what do you want me to think?"

"This ain't that. I like Nina. A lot. Can't get her out of my fucking head." He took a deep drag on his smoke. "She texted me last night. She was bored at the party, wanted to see me. I couldn't resist. I took my chance."

"You came on club property to see one of their old ladies? Drew!"

"I know! So fucking nuts, but that girl spins me out of control. We met at the edge of the property, by this old gate. We started fooling around. Jump was out there, arguing with his kid, who took off, and that's when he saw us. He dragged Nina like a fucking caveman back to the yard. Motherfucker. He had to show her off to Butler and the boys. Shame her—and shame Butler, too, I'll bet. I felt so goddamn helpless, watching her being hauled off like that. I don't know what I would have done if they'd started whaling on her."

"They took it out on you though, huh?"

"Course." He rubbed a thumb across his forehead. "I'm good with that."

"Was it worth it? She's Butler's old lady. She was just having a good time with you, right? She said—"

"It's me she wants, Tan." His eyes were on fire.

"Are you sure?"

"Positive."

"I guess this explains her always dropping by the house to bring Becca gifts and cupcakes whenever you're in town for a visit."

He nodded.

"Way to combine your parental responsibilities with the call of your cock."

He let out a dry laugh, and his head sank back into the wall.

"How long was this going to go on? Was she going to leave Butler for you?"

"You're giving me a headache, Tan, and my skull is already pounding every which way known to man. I was trying to avoid this."

"Honey, you weren't trying very hard. I mean, there was a club party here, and you came over to see her."

"I thought, if they caught us, I could say I'd stopped by to say congrats to Lock and Grace, you know? But, when I saw her, when I'm with her...I don't know...I fuckin' blanked. She makes me crazy." He rubbed his eyes. "Give me another Tylenol, would you?"

Was this true love? Big, fat, and crazy? Leaving you blanked and only wanting more all else be damned?

"No, two pills is enough for right now." I put my arm through his, leaning against his shoulder. "How long has this been going on for anyway?"

"Started when I dragged Jill over here at that party, and Nina and her Flame bodyguard cleaned me up after. He got me back to Nebraska, and me and her kept in touch."

"That's a long time. You really like her."

"Yeah, I do."

"That's good."

"Is it?"

"Why isn't it? You haven't been serious about anyone since Jill. You should be happy, too."

"Happy," he muttered. "I only know I like being with Nina."

"See how that works? That's good."

"I'm glad you think so. Everyone out there sure doesn't."

"They see betrayal and a big, fat hairy mess, which is what it is right now."

"Is Nina okay? Butler hasn't—"

"He's got her locked in his room for now. I don't know anything else."

"Hey, what the hell did I hear about you and Finger?"

"He just wanted to make sure he has me covered with the Jacks since you continue to be so popular with them."

He heaved a sigh. "That's good."

"Is it?"

"Hell yeah."

I leaned my head on my brother's shoulder.

"I'm glad you're here, Tan."

A sparkle of warmth went off in my chest. Years, decades had passed since I'd heard words such as those from my brother, that gentle tone of voice that wasn't dripping with acid.

"Me too." I squeezed his arm.

I wasn't sure how all this would play out or end for my brother and Nina, or for Butler and me. But that churning in the pit of my stomach told me this was only the beginning.

TWENTY-SIX

BUTLER

"Where's Tania?"

I gritted my teeth at the sound of her name coming out of Finger's mouth.

"She's with her brother," I replied.

"Good. I wanna talk to you. Let's take a walk down by the track."

We walked down the side of the hill to the old go-kart track where Tricky and Dawes were testing a rebuilt rat rod.

"I'll get straight to the point," he said.

"You always do."

"Why are you with that girl?"

"Excuse me?"

"Your old lady. Don't tell me you fell hard for her and dragged her all the way out here from Ohio 'cause you couldn't live without her."

I crossed my arms. "Something like that."

"*That* something ain't it."

I didn't say a word.

"It's me you're talking to, Butler, not Jump. You and me have always been able to put our cards on the table with each other."

"I went with my gut on this one."

"You went with your brain. Nina is connected to one of the strongest charters of my MC that's been pushing product from the east into the south. They've been looking to find their own outlet through the Plains to the west, but that's my route, and so far, all these years, no one's fucked with me, especially not them."

"You're complaining about your own brothers? To me?"

"Reich, your old lady's brother-in-law, has been dying to get some play out here. You hooked up with that girl and handed it to him on a silver platter while you hooked up with me at the same time."

"I haven't handed anybody anything, let alone on a silver platter. And I'm not interested in fucking with you, Finger. I worked for you whenever I was allowed to while I was nomad, even did it on the sly when I shouldn't have. I respect you, always have, for years now, and you know it."

"I do know. But don't tell me that Jump let you back on board, here at his club, 'cause he missed your handsome face and witty personality."

I let out a laugh. "He definitely didn't miss me."

Finger made a sound in the back of his throat. "You wanted back into your club. You had to bring something to the table, and you did. That's good. I understand that."

"I had to make up for the losses, the deception under my watch. I was the president of our North Dakota chapter for a good run, and then I went and fucked that up. I let down my brothers. Me, I fucking did that."

"Yeah, and that's a huge fuck-up. But you do something Reich doesn't like—let's say, kick his sister-in-law to the curb—he will come after you. He's a possessive shit on all counts. Business, family. He doesn't need much in the way of an excuse to drop everything and come calling." His neck straightened. "But you knew that already, didn't you?"

I held his resolute gaze. I could've split rocks on that look. "Yeah, I know a few things about Reich. A few things I shouldn't. I did a job for his chapter last year, a job nobody else would touch. That gave me an in with him. An in I took advantage of."

His brow furrowed. "And the frosting on that cake was hooking up with his old lady's sister to keep you and him on the same page?"

"Something like that."

"How long do you think this little deal you've got going with Reich is gonna last, bitch or no?" He let out a dark laugh. "And now that her and Catch have made a spectacle of themselves, you can be sure it's gonna be common knowledge that there's a crack in your *relationship*. That she ain't happy. That you two are done. Someone's gonna try to exploit that rift. Exploit both our clubs."

"I won't let that happen. Nina fucked up, and she knows it. She knows what's at stake. She's keeping low for now."

"Damage is already done, Butler. Add to the mix, the Broken Blades, who have had it raw for you and for me since we got rid of the Calderóns. Notch needed them for his club. Now, he's like a hungry junkyard dog, desperate to keep whatever is left of his club together, desperate for a bone, let alone a good meal. He's fucking rabid. And then you've got Jump on your back. How long until he pulls the rug out from under your sparkly ass? I bet he loved this shit last night, huh?"

"Yeah, he enjoyed it."

"I don't want what we have going on to be fucked with. I'm trying to focus on patching in the Blades right now."

"And you don't think that's gonna stir up trouble?"

"It sure as hell is," replied Finger, "but if I don't make a play now that they're down, someone else will and soon. We can't have outsiders coming in so close to our territories. Jump thinks it's got nothing to do with him. He's living with blinders on."

"Jesus, you and Jump have never seen eye to eye. Two of you have been like oil and water for as far back as I can remember. Hell, Dig and I'd been this close to getting shit started with you, and then the minute Dig died, Jump made sure to break any ties with you. I never knew what the—"

"That's between me and Jump." His suddenly sharp voice cut me off, his eyes stone shutters blocking out all the light, sealing the secrets within.

An old grudge fathoms wide and fathoms deep lay between Jump and Finger. Was it blame, resentment over business? Or something else? Something personal?

Tricky roared past in the rat rod. Finger's chin jutted out, and a muscle pulsed along his jaw as he watched Tricky handle a tight spin on the track.

No, it had to be something else, and that something else was positively caustic in Finger's blood, sizzling deep in his veins.

Finger spat on the ground. "Do not stay comfortable. After last night, shit's up in the air."

I knew better than not to listen to Finger. His predictions had always been shrewd in the past, like a seasoned Roman commander who surveyed the field and could project how the tide in a battle might turn. He always thought five steps ahead, visualized every angle unfolding before him. He gave credence to aftereffects and far-ranging consequences. In my experience, an ordinary leader didn't usually do this; they plowed ahead, their eyes on the prize.

Finger wasn't ordinary.

"You made a good play, Butler. But you'd better sprout eyes in the back of your head to stay above water."

"I had an opportunity with him, and I took it."

He slanted his head at me, his eyes flashing. "You seem mighty confident to me. You've got something on Reich, don't you?"

My spine stiffened under his penetrating gaze.

"And it's good, huh?" He folded his arms across his chest. "I can't get involved. You know I'll have to take his back over yours if it all comes crashing down on your head."

"I know, but you won't."

He quirked a thick eyebrow. "Things just got much more interesting then. Remember, you get Reich ticked at you, don't expect me to save you."

"I know that."

"He might just test us both." Finger raised his chin. "This ain't the eighties or the nineties no more. The landscape keeps changing, brother. Do not underestimate the players on it. Wounded dogs do desperate things to stay alive."

Yes, Notch and his Broken Blades, Reich—they were all wounded dogs, circling.

"Be prepared," Finger continued. "If Reich sniffs an opportunity to make you squirm, he's gonna take it."

Was Finger playing up the drama to get me spooked and get me to side with him? Was he after more of a stronghold here in our territory?

The bigger clubs were always trying to edge out the smaller ones. We were definitely smaller than the Flames of Hell, both in numbers and reach on the outlaw landscape. But no way were we patching in or becoming some sort of satellite lackey, like other clubs were now doing to survive on that map, clubs like the Broken Blades.

"I'm heading out," he muttered.

"Hey, what's with you and Tania?"

He shot me a look. Quizzical at first and then it drained into smug. "What do you fucking think?"

Bastard.

"I don't know what to think, but—"

"But what?" He eyed me, a corner of his mouth tugging upward. "What's it to you?"

Fuck you. I pressed my lips together.

"You worry about Reich being pissed about his girl," Finger said. "You know you can't dump Nina's ass just yet, if that's what you want. Reich will use it as an excuse to come gunning for you and your club, and he'll try to rope me into the party. You got to sit tight, and you got to make her sit tight even if you gotta lock her down to do it. I don't want trouble for Catch or my club. And I don't want any blowback from your club on Tania because of her brother, you hear?"

"Loud and clear."

"Reich is a vengeful motherfucker. He's good at finding ways to make it burn, make it sting."

That queasiness swirled in my gut, the knowledge that Finger was right twisting deep inside me.

We trekked back toward the clubhouse.

"Shit changes fast out in the prairie, man." His voice was low, that scratched quality to it more pronounced. "You've been away a while now. You've forgotten how the glare of the sun can create figments, illusions that just ain't there."

"I haven't forgotten a damn thing."

He tipped his head forward, his scarred cheeks tightening. "You can never be sure what's out there in the wild grasses, lying in wait, lurking."

TWENTY-SEVEN

BUTLER

"WES! WAIT! Where are you going?" Alicia followed her son, who charged past me, out the front bay of Eagle Wings.

"Ma, I've got to get to Zach's."

"Please don't be late for dinner again. Wes? Wes!"

"I heard you, goddamn it!"

"Hey—" I raised my voice. "Don't talk to your mother that way."

Wes only glared at me as he climbed on his bike, started her up into a metallic furor, and took off down the track.

Alicia came up beside me. "He hasn't listened much lately."

"I've noticed. Then again, I didn't either at his age."

A sigh heaved from her lips. "He's hardly ever at home, spending all his time with his friends, mostly that Zach, who isn't one of my favorites. He has some new girlfriend, too, but I don't even know who she is," added Alicia. "He has football, of course, and I'm glad he's keeping busy. I know I've been doing that myself, more than ever these days."

Nina had been keeping busy, too. A couple of weeks had gone by since she and Catch had gotten caught. She did clerical work for Grace at the Eagle Wings office and ran errands for Alicia, keeping the day to day of the clubhouse running smoothly.

Alicia had always been devoted to her club, but to her community as well. She enjoyed showing the town that the One-Eyed Jacks were a respectable, integral part of it. She volunteered at Wes's school, organized various runs for charity with other clubs, and helped Grace with her hospital fundraiser.

"You know, he's missed a couple of afternoons and Saturday mornings with me and Boner at the shop and without calling to even make an excuse. In general, his communication skills have pretty much gone down the tubes."

"Ever since this whole mess with me and his father…" Alicia's voice trailed off, referring to Jump's umpteenth hook-up, this one with two strippers, at a party months before.

The hook-up had led to the club meeting room getting robbed by one of the strippers, who had been put up to do it by Catch. A real fine moment for our club president, both professionally and personally. I couldn't judge, but his old lady—the mother of his kid, who had stood by him and played his game for years and years—certainly could.

"I get that, Alicia. I do."

"Wes is heading into his senior year now, and he's plenty busy. He's going to try for a football scholarship too."

"I'm sure he's going through a rough time with the way things are between you and Jump now."

"If Jump's screwing up his relationship with his son, that's on him. But I shouldn't let my emotions take over in front of my kid or let him know details. It's hard, Butler. Real hard."

"I know Jump's been off on a lot of runs lately, one right after the other."

A sour smile tipped her lips. "He's a busy captain of industry all of a sudden, bringing home that bacon. He came back today, so I'm making it a family event." She crossed her eyes and stuck out her tongue.

I let out a laugh and flung an arm around her shoulders, planting a kiss on the side of her head.

"Thank you," she murmured.

"For what?"

"It's good to know one of you men gives two shits about the other side of the coin."

"Alicia, we all care about you. You know that."

"Are you still gonna care after I leave him?"

"How you deal with your old man is your business, baby." We watched Wes circle the track at top speed. The kid was ready for the Moto Grand Prix. "Look, how about I talk to Wes, find out how he's really doing? I don't want to interfere, but if I can get him to—"

She put a hand on my arm. "I'd like that. A lot. Thank you."

Yes, Wes did remind me of me at his age, but he also reminded me of my brother, Stephan.

My brother, the good guy, the one who'd had it all, and my recklessness had blown that all to pieces. Blown *him* to pieces. And all Stephan had ever done was walk the straight and narrow and give a shit about me. I'd reaped the rewards of my natural talents with minimal effort. Stephan had been all about the effort.

Wes had both natural talents and a responsible work ethic. At least, he used to.

I shifted my weight as Wes shot down the track and headed out onto the road that led off the property and into town. He raised a hand at me and his mother as he sped past.

"Wes! Helmet!" I yelled.

He ignored me.

"Helmet, you idiot!" Stephan would shout out after me when I'd take off after practice.

I rubbed a hand down my chest and across my stomach where that familiar tension bunched inside.

Yeah, Wes used to remind me of Stephan, but now...now, he was looking too much like me.

And that had me worried.

TWENTY-EIGHT

BUTLER

JILL HAD INVITED NINA to Becca's birthday party over at Tania's house today, and she was going.

"Catch isn't going to be there, is he?" I asked her when we woke up this morning.

"No, of course not. Jill said it's a girls-only party." Nina pulled a t-shirt over her head. "I'm going to the salon here in town now, then look for a present. I put it off until the last minute, as usual."

"You need money?"

"No. I still have plenty left from what you gave me earlier this week."

"All right." I swung my legs out of the bed and took in a breath to combat a sudden wave of nausea. Nothing like indigestion first thing in the morning.

Nina left, and I took a shower and got dressed in my sweats. After downing a weak cup of coffee from the pot that she had made earlier, I got on my bike and headed to Eagle Wings at the Club where I was working on a bike rebuild with Boner.

An hour later, I got a text from Finger about a meeting he'd been able to arrange for me with a transport contact of his from Idaho. Finger was in town with Catch and would stop by the club on his own to discuss a few details I needed to be aware of before the meeting.

I called Nina. "Hey. Could you drop off some clean clothes for me? I came here in my shittiest sweats and a ripped shirt, and I've got somewhere to go in a couple of hours."

"Sure. I'll come by on my way to the party."

"Thanks."

Finger arrived at the club. I wiped my hands on a rag and met him as he got off his bike. "Thought I'd come up here in person since Catch had to come for his kid's birthday."

"He's here?" I asked.

A grunt escaped his throat. "Catch is in Rapid City, waiting for the girl party to be over. Then, when they all leave—"

"You mean, when my old lady leaves?"

"Especially your old lady, he's heading over for his daddy time."

"And you came with him to make sure today is all about daddy and his little girl?"

He slanted his head. "That's right."

"You gonna go have some cake and juice, too?"

Is Tania going to sit on his lap and feed him?

He scoffed. "I've got other shit to do while he visits. Let's discuss this meeting. They've been wanting to meet you for a while now."

Finger told me all about this Flames member from Idaho and how he wanted him to work with the Jacks on a new route headed west.

Nina drove through the gates and parked. She got out of her RAV4 and waved a plastic bag in the air that I assumed had my clothes in it. I gestured toward the clubhouse, and she nodded at me, heading inside. Within a few minutes, Nina came back out.

"Sorry to interrupt," she murmured.

"No problem," I said.

"I left the clothes in your room on the bed."

"Thanks."

"Sure. I'm off to the party."

"I'll walk you to your car." I threw an arm around her shoulders as we crossed the yard. "What did you end up getting Becca?"

"A princess Barbie doll."

"Isn't she a little young for Barbie?"

She made a face, as if I had asked why the sun rose this morning. "No. It's a simple Barbie without any fancy accessories. The kid could choke, you know."

"Right. Good thinking."

I gave her a quick kiss. "You come right back here after."

"Here at the club?"

"Yeah, I want you here while I'm out of town. I'll only be a couple of hours."

She made a face. "Fine."

With Catch in the vicinity and me out of town, I wasn't going to take chances that he'd try to see her.

We reached her RAV4 by the front gate, and she got in, slamming the door shut.

"Later."

"Yep," she said.

I strode back toward Finger.

"She settled her ass down?" he asked.

"She's fine."

A slight grin upturned the edges of his mouth, and he let out a grunt as he shoved on his leather gloves. "I'm off."

I glanced over at Nina's car. Her head was bent over the steering wheel. She scowled and got out of the vehicle. Jump pulled in driving his SUV, and he braked. She smiled huge at him, her body relaxing into curves. Jump gestured toward her car.

"Looks like your woman's got car trouble. You gonna fly to her rescue?" asked Finger.

Jump got down from his vehicle and got into the RAV4, settling in the driver's seat.

"Jump seems to be handling it."

"Yeah."

Finger and I tagged fists, giving each other a nod. He swung his leg over his vintage chopper, adjusting himself in his saddle. "Call me, let me know how the meet goes."

"Will do." My eyes went back to Nina and Jump.

Suddenly, Jump's face stiffened from behind the windshield. He propelled himself from the car on an ominous howl, his long braid flying, shoving Nina back as he went. Her designer handbag went flying.

"What the—"

Boom.

The ground shuddered under my feet. Nina's car shook like a fake movie prop, a shell. Orange fireballs rolled and unfurled in the air.

My lungs choked. "Holy fuck!"

Finger was at my side, and we sprang behind a row of bikes, our hands flying over our heads. Charred debris soared in the air and rained down on us, crashing to the ground.

I shot up. "Nina!"

Women screamed, men shouted, alarms blared. Thick black billows of smoke blocked any trace of Nina or Jump. Boner was on his cell phone in the doorway of the office.

I hurtled toward the car, toward Nina, Finger at my heels.

Nina lay facedown at the other end of the car, her one arm twisted awkwardly, blood splattered along the side of her face.

I wrapped my hand around her neck, pushing her tangled hair out of the way.

Her pulse thudded under my touch.

Thank fuck.

Weak, but it was there.

Shit, the baby.

"Ambulance is on its way!" Boner's yell cut through the air.

Finger crouched over Jump who was sprawled on the ground in a heap.

"How's Jump?" I shouted out at Finger, coughing, my eyes burning in the dense smutty smoke.

Finger raised his head. His one gloved hand was planted on Jump's chest, the other pinching Jump's nose.

He was taking him out.

Finger leveled his hard gaze at me, a slight lift to his chin.

Holy fuck.

"Butler!" Boner came up behind me. "How is she?"

"She's out, but she's alive."

I turned back to Jump, but Finger was gone. Gone, like a silent phantom who'd made ominous gestures and then disappeared into the black smoke surrounding us.

Kicker pounded on Jump's chest, giving him CPR. Dawes and Dready worked fire extinguishers, discharging foam over the smoldering vehicle.

The sirens wailed louder and louder, matching the harshness of my pulse pounding in my ears. I struggled to ease my breaths that came fast and hard. My hand flattened over Nina's back. Blonde strands of hair were matted in blood, oozing red. The shoulders of her pink shirt were soaked. I blinked back the sweat clouding my eyes

"Jump's gone. He's gone!" hollered Kicker. Yells. Shouts.

My heart twisted in my chest.

One man dead.

One outlaw president making a shadowy play. Was Finger taking his revenge for ancient crimes, or was this in favor of future maneuvers?

Our president dead.

My old lady down.

Again.

I'd promised Nina she'd be safe with me. I'd promised her, and she'd believed me. She'd believed I was the one who could help her.

"This will work," she'd said back in Ohio.

Caitlyn trembled in my arms on the side of the road in the Black Hills once more. *"Don't let me go. I'm so cold, baby, so cold. It hurts...make it stop...Hold me...don't let me go..."*

My vision blurred. That burning pain tore through my chest.

Alicia screamed from somewhere behind me. "Jump! Jump!"

Another family destroyed.

My jaw clenched against the bile rising in my throat. A heavy, dark swell hovered over me, ready to plunge inside my gullet and wrench every organ up from me, spewing my blood, my poisonous blood.

I knew this darkness; its smell dank, its touch familiar. How could I forget it?

It was damnation.

TWENTY-NINE

TANIA

"YOUR GIRLFRIEND IS A VERY LUCKY WOMAN, Mr. Matthiessen."

Ah, Butler has a last name.

It was a ridiculous thought as I stood here, in the surgical waiting room at Rapid City Regional, with Finger, listening to Nina's doctor tell us how she was doing.

Grace and I had both rushed over to the hospital with Mary Lynn where we found the Jacks along with Finger waiting. Jill and Suzi stayed with the kids and my mom at the house, and they kept the birthday party going.

I still couldn't wrap my head around Jump being dead, but thank God Nina would be okay.

I glanced over at Butler. He was pale, his blue eyes washed with gray under the fluorescent lights. He hadn't spoken a word the entire three hours we'd been waiting with him.

"Ms. Scott sustained internal injuries, but we did manage to stem the bleeding. Her arm was dislocated, and her hip was seriously bruised. She also has a concussion. There were metal fragments, but we went over her and removed them. And the baby is doing fine."

We all froze.

I froze.

My brain froze.

"Baby?" screeched Mary Lynn.

Nina and Butler's baby.

My heart bolted straight out of my chest and *thwapped* me in the face.

Finger let out a heavy breath, his lips twisting. I leaned against him, and his hand wrapped around my arm, steadying me.

"Thank you, Doctor," Butler said, his voice low. He returned to his seat, his head in his hands.

He was in shock, probably feeling like he was losing everything all over again—first, his wife, and now, Nina and their baby. This was why he hadn't kicked Nina to the curb. He was trying to be the bigger man, trying to do the right thing. I choked down the horse pill stuck in my dry throat; it left bruises and a bitter residue behind. I willed my feet to move.

"Hey." I placed a hand on Butler's shoulder. "The doctor seemed confident, right? She's going to be fine. You'll see."

His weary, dazed eyes slid to mine. "Shouldn't have happened in the first place." His voice was flat. He swallowed. "They planted it in her car, Tania."

I wanted to bombard him with questions, but it certainly wasn't the time. Anyway, I doubted he'd share details with me. *For Pete's sake, do I really want to know?*

"Did you call Nina's family in Ohio?"

He only furrowed his brow and gnawed on his lower lip, his head shaking.

"I'll do it, if you want. Really."

"Her bag got thrown clear from the car." He gestured at the Coach bag on the table next to him. "Phone should be in there."

I opened the handbag and found a rose-gold iPhone. "Whose name should I look for?"

"Her sister. Name's Deanna.' rubbing a hand over his face. "I should do it, Tania."

"Let me make the call, get the first words out, and then you can get on the line and do the talking. How's that?"

Butler let out a breath. "There's a passcode." He held out his hand, and I gave him the phone. He tapped out the code and gave me back the phone.

"Deanna. Okay." I fiddled with Nina's cell, tracing over her recent calls. I recognized a number, and the name attached was 'Iron Man'. I clicked on it, turning away from Butler.

Ah, shit.

I tapped on their text messages.

A selfie of Nina clutching her tits. Another of her legs wide open, her fingers getting down to business. Another with those fingers in her mouth, her lips puckered around them.

My breath stalled as I skimmed the texts between Nina and my brother.

Finger stared at me, slanting his head just a few degrees. I took in a tiny breath and went back to Nina's phone.

I tapped on the other text threads I found. More sex texts with porno selfies, but these were to Led, her Ohio Flames of Hell bodyguard, who'd accompanied her to South Dakota when she'd first arrived.

Motherfudgemycake.

Judging from the dates on the texts, Nina had kept him entertained and cozy on his long ride back to Ohio months ago. Shit, the girl was insatiable.

I couldn't stomach any more, so I went back to looking for Deanna's name and number. Finding it, I tapped on her name, and it rang.

"Hey, Neens!"

"Hi, is this Deanna?"

"Who's this?" Deanna's tone sharpened.

"This is Tania. I'm a friend of Nina's here in South Dakota. I'm sorry to tell you, but there's been an accident, and Nina is in the hospital. We're all here with her. Butler was just speaking with the doctor. I'll hand him the phone."

I placed the phone in Butler's cold hand. His eyes softened at me for just a moment as he brought Nina's phone to his ear.

He cleared his throat. "Hey, Deanna."

I went back to Finger.

His brows jammed together. "What's wrong?"

"I just saw Catch and Nina's hot little love texts all over her phone—in full high resolution color. The phone Butler is using right now. You think he's going to like what he sees when he sees them? Because he will see them. They're a little hard to miss."

"Your brother's got it bad for her."

"Yeah, he told me, but newsflash, she's also been sexting with that Flame who brought her to Meager. Led?"

"Good for Goldilocks."

"Where does she find the time?"

He leaned into me. "Keep your voice down."

"Oh please."

Finger's stern face tilted toward mine, his lips at my ear. "Her relationship with Butler is as solid as the wind, Tania."

"What?" I asked, my scalp prickling.

"Butler and Nina—it's fake."

"No."

"Yes. Pure business between clubs."

"What is this?" I sputtered. "The fucking eighteenth century?"

Finger's body went rigid, his eyes flared. A large hand clamped around my upper arm, and he dragged me down the hallway.

Oops.

This might be the twenty-first century, but this was the Land of the Outlaw with its own set of rules, its own way of functioning.

"We'd better stop here—not complicate things."

Butler's tender voice from our night at the motel passed through me, and a chill razored down the back of my neck.

Butler and Nina had never seemed like they were in honeymoon mode. They had never been very affectionate with each other or very demonstrative. So what though? Neither had Kyle and I.

I had tried to put them out of my mind. What was the point of dwelling on it? They were an official couple in Bikerland, and my thoughts on the subject were meaningless and a waste of time.

I took in a breath as Finger pulled me in close to him against the wall. "Keep your voice down."

"Did you hear what the doctor just said? Butler's going to be a daddy."

"What makes you think that kid is Butler's? Could be Catch's."

My mouth fell open. "Oh, shit."

That hadn't occurred to me.

Oh my God. Oh my God. Oh my God.

I glanced over at Butler still talking on the phone.

My hand tugged on the edge of Finger's jacket. "We can't tell Catch about this baby until we're sure. Nina's family is going to be pissed about her getting hurt, aren't they? You think they'll come here and make trouble for the Jacks and for Butler? They'll blame him? Come after him?"

"Sounds right."

"Is there any way you can help him? Do you know who did this? Jump is dead. The president of a club has been murdered. All hell is going to break loose now, right?"

Finger's eyes narrowed. "You're worried?"

"Of course I'm worried. They're my friends. This is my hometown we're talking about."

"I meant, you're worried about Butler?" Finger asked.

I leveled my gaze at him. "Yes, I am. He's a good guy."

The edges of Finger's lips tipped up. "Good, bad—it's all relative at the end of the day."

"It can't be. Some things simply cannot be relative. For you, they probably are. But I don't live that way."

He wrapped a hand around my neck, pulling me in closer. A steely whisper filled my ear. "Shit's either real, or it isn't." His hand squeezed the back of my neck, and he planted a kiss on my forehead. "Relax. I'm going to see what I can do. You make sure the pics on Nina's phone don't get erased. "

His hand stroked the side of my jaw for a moment. "You go support your guy over there. He could use it."

"He's not my guy."

"Baby, you haven't been able to tear your eyes away from him. You went to him in his hour of need, then jumped up and down in the man's defense like you just did? He's your guy."

BUTLER

"SHE SAID SHE'D BE SAFE with you!" Nina's sister, Deanna, yelled at me over the phone. "She trusted you! Oh my God! My old man is going to have your ass for this!"

I shut down the phone and tossed it to the seat beside me and squeezed my eyes shut, burying my face in my hands.

Images of Nina's hair matted in blood, her body a lifeless rag doll, rolled through me.

Just like Caitlyn.

Just like Stephan.

And the pitch of Deanna's hysteria.

Just like my mother.

"He's in a coma!" My mother yelled.

She never yelled. Dad was the one with the temper.

I swallowed hard. "A coma?"

"Yes! Do you know what that is, Markus?" Mom's pale face was streaked with red blotches and wet with tears. "Do you understand how serious this is?"

My eyes went to Dad. "He'll wake up soon though, right?"

"They don't know if he'll ever wake up again." Dad's voice broke, and he averted his gaze, taking in a deep breath. Defeat.

"And even if he does, he'll probably have severe brain damage for the rest of his life." Mom's voice seethed. "Over forty percent of his body is burned." The rage in my mother's eyes, the tension in her limbs, was unmistakable. "He'll never be the same. His spine is broken, and his one leg is so mangled that it will probably have to be amputated. And why? Why? Because of you! You were arguing with him, weren't you? And he lost control of the car. Is that it? Is it?"

"Laura, calm down." Dad pulled my mother into his arms.

"*No!*" *she screeched.*

I flinched at the sound.

"*You were making him go fast, weren't you? You dared him to do it, didn't you? Anything below eighty miles an hour is a crawl to you! It's all your fault! Your fault!*" *She pulled on my father's shirt, pointing at me with her other hand.* "*How can* he *be here, perfectly fine, when Stephan is lying in there in pieces? My boy is broken! Broken!*"

I sat in the wheelchair in the hallway of the ICU—my leg cast stretched out in front of me, my broken arm in a sling, my sprained neck and the long rows of stitches on my chest and back screaming in pain—as she shuddered, fresh tears streaming down her face.

I'd need a shitload of those pain meds the nurses were always offering me to get through this. Yeah, I'd take them up on it now. Load me up, ladies.

"*All he did was try to help you. Again and again and again,*" *she continued.* "*But you don't care. You don't give a crap, do you? As long as you have your good time. What did Stephan ever do to you? Are you that jealous of him? Do you hate him? How could you do this? You're brothers! How could you?*" *Her wails and moans filled the hospital waiting room.*

"*I'm not jealous of Stephan! I didn't do anything on purpose, Ma! I didn't.*"

"*No, everything just happens to you, doesn't it? When are you going to learn that everything you do in this life has consequences? Do you even know the meaning of that word? I don't think you do. Your alcohol level was sky high, as usual. All you ever think about is your good time. Your brother went all the way out there to get you, to make sure you'd get home in one piece. And now—*" *Her voice broke again.* "*I can't even look at you right now!*"

Her bright blue eyes, the color of the sky, the ones she'd given me, were full of strain and anger, a raging ocean. All of it for me. Her blonde hair, something else she'd given me, was pulled out of her usually neat ponytail. Our obvious visible connections didn't matter right now. Now, we were disconnected, divided, detached.

Mom collapsed in my father's arms.

Dad's watery eyes slid to mine. "*You need to leave.*"

"You need to leave," my father had said.

"You need to leave," my mentor and friend had said.

"You need to leave," two of my presidents had said.

Dad, Dig, Buck, my first prez, and Jump had all been right. Their disappointment in me had been deserved.

"*I can't even look at you right now.*"

My mother's words still stung. The others had said as much to me at one point or another.

Now, here was living proof that I was still riding the Fuck-Up train.

I wrapped my arms around myself and leaned over on my knees. Tania was in a heated discussion with Finger. Now, they all knew about the baby.

And me?

I glanced at Tania, her big dark eyes blazing with emotion as she listened to whatever Finger was telling her. I felt so far away from her at this very moment, as if the secret police were yanking me in the opposite direction and throwing me in a Soviet Bloc country with no visa, no return ticket. Doomed. But, of course, no one was forcing me, making me do anything. This was all on me.

No, Tania was better off without me. She had to be. Without me as a friend, without me as a lover.

Without me.

THIRTY-ONE

TANIA

ALICIA WAS STOIC.

Her eyes were glassy and red. But she wasn't a mess. Maybe, as an old lady, she had been preparing for this moment for years. Probably. Her and Jump's son, Wes, stood at her side before the open grave. A legion of bikers had arrived in a long procession through town. A solemn sea of black leather was in attendance at Rock Hills Cemetery on the outskirts of Meager, all these many men paying their final respects to the president of the One-Eyed Jacks, honoring their brotherhood.

Jump's death was a shock to everyone. He'd been a part of the club since before Dig and Boner had arrived over two decades ago and an officer early in his career. Add him to the list of outlaw casualties.

The wind had picked up, and I wiped the hair from my face. The men took turns with a shovel, filling in the grave with earth. The service concluded, and the club members who remained, talked in sullen tones over Jump's open grave. Butler, Boner, Kicker, Dready, and Judge, the president of the North Dakota Jacks, were in the center of the throng, hugging and fist bumping with brothers, all of their faces grim.

I hugged Alicia. I touched Wes's arm. "I'm so sorry."

"Thanks," he muttered, his gaze darting away from me. His face was grim, pale. The boy's once easygoing demeanor was gone, and in its place was etched a tense scowl. A rigid tension kept him standing at his father's funeral. He was a rock for his mother, for his father's club.

"I lost my dad unexpectedly when I was a teenager, Wes, and I understand. I'm very sorry."

He only nodded.

I strolled across the rolling green lawn to where my heart drew me.

"Hey, Daddy," I said, my voice low.

The granite was still clean and fresh, even after all these years—thirty, to be exact. Thirty years without his honking laugh, him yelling at the television over college football and basketball, him grabbing Mom in the kitchen in great big bear hugs.

He'd throw my brother high into the air, and I'd yell, "Dad! Stop! He's going to throw up!"

But he and Drew would only laugh.

Dad had made a face when he caught me putting on makeup the first time. Had it been discomfort, embarrassment? I'd been twelve, going on thirteen, and I'd just gotten my period.

"You're slipping away from me, sugar cube. Growing up fast. Pretty soon, you won't want to hang out with your daddy no more."

"Oh, Dad!" I rolled my eyes at him.

But he was right.

I'd loved helping him on the farm and watching football with him. But I'd started spending hours yammering on the telephone with Grace and our girls or had my nose stuck in a book or a magazine rather than helping out on the farm as much as I used to. I was daddy's girl. We would go into Rapid to his favorite sporting goods store, or go out for barbecue and root beer on his rare free Saturdays, just the two of us. He'd love to go fishing on the lake, or out on his cousin's boat, or—

There was only a slab of granite now. My hand slid over the smooth stone engraved with our family name in big solemn letters.

"Love you, Daddy." The breeze carried my hoarse whisper in the air over his tombstone.

"Hey." A hand swept up my back. Grace's hazel eyes were golden green in the sunlight.

"Hi. How's it going?"

"It's going."

I slung an arm around her waist and pulled her close. "This is terrible."

"Yes, it is."

"Things must be nuts now. I'm worried about you and the baby."

"We'll be fine."

"Is there going to be a war or something?"

"I hope not, but there could be."

"Who's president now?"

"Kicker is until they can sit down and vote. Right now, they need to find out who did this and why."

"Why would someone want to target Nina?"

"That's the million-dollar question."

THIRTY-TWO

TANIA

"WHAT ARE YOU DOING HERE, Tania?" Butler asked me.

Standing in the doorway of his apartment in town, on the second floor of an old two family house, my rehearsed little speech flitted out of my brain like a balloon caught in the jet stream.

"I just—"

His full lips twisted into a smirk. An adorable smirk.

A noise escaped the back of my throat, my shoulders dropping. "I wanted to see how you were doing. I saw you at the funeral this morning, but I didn't get a chance to say hello."

I needed to make sure he was okay. We were friends. He'd listened to my tales of woe, so I could be there for him now.

Simple.

I stared at him in his ripped pale blue jeans, barefoot, a white V-neck T-shirt that showed off the taut contours of his chest and arms. The dark golden scruff along his chin, along the blunt angle of his jaw, emphasized his usual rough and tumble appearance.

Not so simple.

"Things are crazy right now," he said.

"I'll bet."

"I just got back from the club. Big crowd still there. My head was killing me, and I needed a breather."

"Oh, I'm sorry. I don't want to interrupt your quiet time, then. You must be exhausted."

"You're not interrupting. It's good to see you."

"How are you doing?" I asked.

"I don't know if I can answer that right now," he said, his voice husky.

"You don't have to." I held up the canvas tote bag I was carrying with the loaded glass containers. "All you have to do is eat."

"What's that?"

"Homemade food. Roast beef topped with really good Grandma's secret recipe gravy and roast potatoes. Rhubarb pie for dessert. Not sissy food. Manly man food."

He let out a laugh. "You made it?"

"Why? Are you afraid?"

His eyes narrowed. "Maybe."

"I made everything, except for the pie. My sister made that. She's the baker in the family."

"Ah, forget it then." He pushed the door closed in my face, and I burst out laughing.

He swung open the door and grabbed the bag from my hands. "Get in here," came the gruff voice edged with laughter.

I followed him into his apartment.

I gestured at the guitar leaning back against the small navy blue sofa. "I thought I heard music in the hallway."

"It was me."

"It was good."

"It helps."

"I'm glad. Was that Johnny Cash?"

"Very good, Scarlett."

"My dad's favorite. Haven't heard any Johnny in a long time."

My eyes darted around the small living space as I followed him into his very small kitchen where he placed the tote bag on the counter. There were no signs of beer cans or liquor bottles, only an ashtray piled high with cigarette butts on the coffee table by the sofa. And only tobacco smoke lingered in the air. Not weed.

His head slanted, an eyebrow raised. "I'm not drinking or using. Is that what you thought?"

My face heated. "It's completely understandable. There's a lot going on for you right now. I thought a drink though, not—"

He tugged a hand through his blond hair. "If I have even one drink, Tania, it'll lead me down that road again. Coke and booze go hand in hand for me. The more coke I used to do, the more booze I could consume, and the more booze I drank, the more I wanted coke. Whenever I've had a drink this past year, I've really, really missed the coke. And instead of just a couple of drinks, sometimes,

I'd want three or four to take the edge off. At some point, your brain suddenly says, *Oh, yeah, I remember this feeling, and I remember something that feels even better.* Going back would be too easy, but I can't go back there again. I can't."

"Good for you. You're such a strong person. I'm proud of you, if I may say so."

"You may." He rested his hands on the old Formica counter. "I'm not used to being this sane and sober though. Somehow, it doesn't seem natural. Isn't that crazy?"

"You think you're sane now? That is crazy."

He let out a laugh. "My brain function has dwindled some, but yeah."

"Well, your brain needs you to eat." I gestured at the bag.

His lips tipped up, his eyes creased. "Are you a good cook?" He took the two large covered glass containers out of the bag and opened them. "Wow."

"I'm my mother's daughter. I'm a very good cook." I tugged on two drawers in the kitchen. One was filled with screwdrivers and rubber bands, cables and batteries. The other had a handful of basic kitchen utensils and cutlery. I handed him a fork and a knife.

"Sit." I grabbed the lone dish sitting in the drying rack and layered the thick slices of beef with big hunks of potato, spooning just enough gravy over them. I placed the plate of food on the small table and gestured at the chair. "Sit. Eat."

He pulled out the chair and sat down, staring at the food before him. His fingers rubbing the fork. "This looks really good."

"Trust me, it is."

He rolled his lips together, his fingers twirling the fork.

"What is it, Blondie? Did you become a vegetarian? Have I offended your moral sensibilities?"

His free hand fell to his stomach. "I'm not a vegetarian, no. I, um...I haven't had a home-cooked meal in a long time."

My hands reached out and squeezed the rigid muscles between his neck and shoulders. I planted a quick kiss on the side of his face. That forest fresh scent of his shampoo filled my senses, and I pulled away quickly.

"Enjoy it." I sat down in the other chair at the table.

He ate as I nattered on about Becca and my mom, how Boner had become my mom's new favorite son-in-law. How attentive he was—fixing light switches around the house and the garage door opener that kept sticking, to programming her television remote, and bringing her contraband sweet treats from Meager Grand. Boner would take Rae, Jill and Becca out for an early-bird dinner every so often. Butler and I discussed our favorite music. He told me why he admired Johnny Cash, and I waxed lyrical about Carly Simon. I filled Butler in on the doings at the Rusted Heart.

"Jill is helping me with promotion. Flyers, ads, tweets, posts. Social media is an amazing tool." I got up and poured him a glass of cold water, putting it on the table at his side.

He wiped his mouth with a paper napkin. "That was really good. Thank you."

"You're welcome. The rest of the roast beef is in the fridge. It makes a good sandwich." I took his dish and washed it. I released the plate into the drying rack, wiped my hands, and turned.

My eyes widened. He stood next to me, and the weight of his heavy stare made me swallow.

"Thank you," he whispered.

"You're very welcome."

"You should go home, Tania. What would Finger say if he knew you were here right now?"

I folded the damp kitchen towel into a long rectangle and putting it on the counter, pressed my hands over it. "I'm not with Finger."

"You're not?"

"No. It's…complicated."

His eyebrows lifted, and he wiped a thumb across his brow.

"And what would Nina think?" I countered.

"I don't give a shit what Nina thinks."

"Oh, but—"

"It's not my baby," he spit out.

My brain stuttered.

"It's your brother's kid, Tania. It's Catch's baby, not mine."

"Okay." I let out a long breath. "That's good. I guess. I mean, *is* that good?" My pulse suspended waiting for his reply. "Unless you—"

"Hell yes, it's good."

"Then why are you telling me to go home? Are you trying to get rid of me?"

"I'm not—"

"Is this about Grace?"

"What?"

"You and her last year, and she and I being good friends. We all live here now, see each other. It's all too weird for you. Uncomfortable. Am I right?"

"Slow down, Tania." He let out a huff of air. "No, I don't have a hang-up about that, moral or otherwise. Do you?"

"No."

"Look, last year with Grace, I was trying to connect to a spark of something, the me I used to be, the good times we all used to have. I was trying to gain some clarity, too, something finally good to grab ahold of in the sea of shit I'd been paddling in for so long." He dragged his teeth across his bottom lip. "You want real honesty?"

"Yeah, I do."

"I think it was also about the way she used to be with Dig and the way I used to be with Caitlyn. But you can't grab at the past or at sentimental ideas and force them to work in the now. I was kidding myself and being an ass. I was high most of that time. When I felt her pulling away, shutting down on me—oh, I knew it was happening. I ain't stupid—I lashed out at her. Physically even one time. I lost control. Fuck, I had no control."

"Butler—"

"Grace and me would've been easy. At least that's what I thought, what I was hoping for. I've always had a thing for easy, and I latched on to her, like some sort of quick fix and another sweet form of denial. But even if all that club shit wasn't the foundation or the framework for what she and I had and we'd tried for real, I'm sure we both would've been fucking miserable in the end."

His eyes were glassy. He rubbed a hand down his face and looked away.

"I'm not Grace," I said.

His head shot up. "I know that."

"And I'm not in love with someone else, like she was, both times with you. I'm not in love with Kyle. I haven't been for years."

"Tania—"

"I'm afraid of things, too."

He held my gaze. "What are you afraid of?"

"Not of you or what you do. Or what you've done."

"Maybe you should be."

"I'm only afraid of not having lived enough. You hit forty, and things become much clearer, better defined. It's a great feeling, being sure of what you like and don't like, not putting up with shit, but at the same time, you realize that you've now entered the limited time zone. Infinity is no longer stretching out before you. Suddenly, getting out of my marriage because it wasn't good for me, because it wasn't enough, became an urgent necessity, not just a fleeting thought."

"You did that. That's great."

"Yes. And, now, I only want to bite off more than I can chew out of life. I want to chomp it, choke on it, swallow up every last piece. I want to hold it up to the light and admire its sparkle. I want to be in that sparkle. I want to be breathless. Not sigh, not say, *Oh well, maybe another time*. No. There are no more *other times*, don't you think?"

His jaw clenched, his lips pressed together.

"You must be feeling that too," I said. "Does being with Nina make you happy? Really deep down inside satisfied? Does it turn you on?"

His hand went to the back of his neck. "No."

"What does?"

His eyes lifted to mine, fierce and raw. "My bike. That guitar. You."

My breath caught.

"I feel something for you I haven't felt for any woman in a long time, Tania. And I don't know what to do with it."

"You knew what to do with it when you were with Caitlyn, didn't you?"

"I don't want to talk about Caitlyn!"

"Why not? Maybe you should. You can tell me anything. I told you plenty, and you listened without judging."

His mouth pulled together, his jaw firm. "Caitlyn and I were a lot alike. She was as self-indulgent as I was. We both had tempers and fought a lot. Made up a lot." His shoulders lifted and dropped. "Now, I seem to remember only stupid details."

"Like what?"

"She got pissed that I didn't want to pierce my dick."

"Ouch!"

"She didn't see it that way." He let out a laugh. "I'd gotten my tongue pierced, my eyebrow, one of my ears, but not my dick, no fucking way. She was into that shit, but no way was I getting a hole ripped through my Brando."

"Your *Brando?*"

"Yeah, my Brando." He adjusted his jeans at the waist. "Anyway, she threatened to find a guy who had one."

I laughed. "Did she?"

"Fuck no." He lifted himself up to sit on the small kitchen counter. "She also had this thing that she always had to be wearing makeup. She thought she looked ordinary, plain, without it, even in front of me. She'd be up in the mornings, putting her face on, before I'd even gotten out of bed. Never understood that. Used to make me crazy, but she thought that made her more attractive to me, I guess. But that wasn't true. That didn't matter to me, even on the shit days. And there were plenty of shit days in the club back then."

He swallowed hard. "Suddenly, she was gone. It was like I hit a concrete wall, and I was back to square one. Worse actually because her death and the horrible way she died could've been avoided. If only I'd fixed my bike the right way before I took her on it for a joyride, but I had blown it off. I had been in a rush. I hadn't felt like it. Irresponsible. My fault."

"It was partly your fault."

His head whipped up, and he stared at me, his eyes piercing mine.

Had no one ever said that to him before?

"But it doesn't matter how you punish yourself and everyone around you," I said. "She isn't coming back."

"That's right. In rehab, I finally realized that I'd never find her again, no matter how hard I tried. Dead is dead."

"It certainly is," I said.

"Last year, after the thing with Grace and leaving the club again, I finally stopped looking for Caitlyn, finally let her go. Holding on to her was killing me."

Now, that was a confession.

"So, when I tell you that I don't know what to do with these feelings now," he said, "I mean, I don't know."

"You *feel* them, that's what you do, and we explore it together."

"Maybe I shouldn't feel them."

"But they're there."

"They're there," he rasped.

"You can't destroy how you feel or will it away."

"Tania, listen to me. I got my wife killed. I was fucking careless, reckless, and she paid the ultimate price. And now, Nina..." He wiped a hand across his forehead. "That girl almost got killed because of me. I used her to solidify a business deal and look what happened to her. Don't you see? The only two old ladies I've ever had—both of them innocents—were put in danger because of me. But I'm still here, aren't I? What the hell for? If you think all this hasn't fucked with my head, you're wrong. It has."

"Nina is alive and so is her baby. And by the way, my brother is crazy about her. Do you think you're not worth anyone's effort?"

"I'm not worth the risk. The risk it would be to you."

"I care about you, Butler. I—"

"That means a lot to me. It does." His voice was a tortured whisper. "More than you realize, more than you'll ever know."

"I want to know," I breathed. "Give us a chance to know. Please."

He clenched his jaw, the muscle along the sides of his face ticking. "You see something in me you think is worth cleaning, polishing, making shiny. Worth preserving, like one of your antiques. I am an antique all right. Broken casing, rusty insides, faulty wiring."

"Butler, you've faced your failures and your disappointments, picked yourself up and moved forward this past year. That's not easy on a good day, even for us normal folk. But, for you, in your world, I'm sure you've got to keep your shit close to the chest, not let on about any signs of weakness or vulnerability. And you did it. That's a huge accomplishment. You're back here now, to a place that once rejected you. You're back, you're strong, and what's more, you're needed."

He held my gaze, his brow rigid.

"All that for the betterment of your club, for your brothers, right?" I said.

He hopped down from the counter. "You deserve better than me, Tania, better than what I've got. Hell, I don't even have much of anything."

"I'm not asking you to give me anything. Only *you*."

"That's just it, don't you see?"

My eyes bored into his. "I'm starting over from scratch here, too. And I'm far from perfect."

"You're perfect to me," he breathed.

My chest caved in. "Butler—"

"You think that all you have to do is clean, buff, and polish me, put me on shelf with fancy lighting and, bam, that makes me special, too? Makes me worth the inflated asking price?"

"What price?"

"You just don't get it, do you? You're holding me up to your light. But I always fall through on inspection."

I planted my hands on my hips. "What do you think you're good for now? A few one-night stands whenever you get the itch? A fuck buddy? A whore here and there?"

"Sounds about right. I'm here on borrowed time, babe. Have no right to ask for more."

"What the hell does that mean?"

He only turned away from me.

"I think a life like that would bore you shitless," I continued. "I saw you with Nina all this time. Yeah, you were soaring on that high, weren't you? Making do really suits you."

"I don't need much to get by. Hooking up with Nina as my old lady was a good solution. That's what I'm good for."

"I don't believe that." I took a step closer to him. "You need me. I know you do."

My eyes sought his, but he lowered his eyelids.

"Butler—"

He lunged at me, grabbing my shoulders, squeezing tight. "Listen to me, and listen to me good. I've had to accept a lot of truths about myself since I stopped using, Tania. Ugly truths, all of 'em. You need to accept them, too. Every day, there's a war going on in my mind. Part of me wants to use again; part of me doesn't. The hunger, is still there. That urge hits me, and it can get overwhelming. It can last from fifteen minutes up to half an hour some days, but it always feels like a fucking eternity. I fight it. I fight it, and around and around, I go. That disappointment in myself is real. I feel it; it hurts, and it makes moving forward real difficult. Looking in the mirror is hard enough as it is, Tan."

"I want to help you. Support you. I can do that. Let me do that."

He shook me, his eyes blazing. "I assumed this was over for me!"

"What exactly?"

"Being with a woman." He sucked in a breath. "I took my shots, baby, and they didn't end well. Don't you get that?"

"Things are different now. You're different."

"We're different all right, always have been, you and me. We're older now—"

"Screw all that. I have feelings for you, Butler. Big feelings. Good feelings."

"You deserve the best, Tania." His voice was rough, choppy. "That isn't me."

He let go of me and went into his small living room and grabbed a cigarette from the pack on his coffee table. He lit it and took a long drag, his eyes remaining on mine. "I don't have nothing to my name, except for my bike and that snowmobile. I don't have my own home or money saved in the bank. I blew whatever I had up my nose and keeping alive this past year."

I held his simmering gaze across the apartment. "Whatever I had, I blew on getting my store together and buying inventory. We're both starting fresh now, Butler." I shrugged. "You're not a lazy ass, and neither am I, so—"

His phone rang, and he frowned, grabbing it off the table. "Yeah?"

I folded over the damp kitchen towel yet again and wiped at the edge of the sink.

"When was this?" His voice was brittle. He was concerned, annoyed. He paced the room, a hand at his middle. "Do you know who it was? No, doesn't look good. All right, yeah, I'll keep my ears open."

He tossed his phone on the sofa. "Shit."

"Bad news?" I asked.

"There was a fire last night at the Broken Blades' junkyard down in Nebraska. Not too much damage, but it was set on purpose, and now, they're out for blood."

"Did the Jacks—sorry, shouldn't be asking. They think it's you all, right?"

"Yeah, us or the Flames. But we didn't do it. The Blades are high on our suspect list for the bomb in Nina's car."

Banging on his front door made both our heads spin toward the sound.

He picked up his gun from the coffee table and headed for the door, the muscles along his jaw flexing again.

"Open up!" hollered a gruff voice from the other side of the door.

Butler shot me a look and gestured for me to stay in the kitchen. He raised his weapon, and as he looked through the peephole, his hand turned the lock with a bleak click.

THIRTY-THREE

TANIA

A TALL, HEAVYSET MAN in worn biker leather with a thick dark mustache filled Butler's doorway.

Butler lowered his weapon. "Come in."

"Thought I'd see you at the hospital," the man muttered, stepping inside.

"Been there the past two days and nights straight. Came home to get some sleep, something to eat," replied Butler, glancing over at me. "This is Tania. Tania, this is Reich, Nina's brother-in-law from Ohio."

I moved into the living room. My eyes darted to the patches on his colors. *National Vice President, Flames of Hell,* and *Ohio* were stitched on his cut. My eyes darted to the patch with his road name, and a shiver laced my insides with ice.

Reich, as in Third Reich?

"Hello," I said. "I spoke with Deanna on the phone the other day."

"My old lady," Reich said, his eyes scouring me like sandpaper on wood.

"You saw Nina?" I asked.

His lips twisted. "Course I did. Deanna's still with her. I had to get outta there. Hate hospitals."

"What's going on?" Butler's voice was low and steady.

Asphyxiation threatened me in Butler's suddenly tiny apartment.

Reich threw himself onto the sofa, and Butler's phone and the guitar thunked to the carpeted floor. Unfazed, Reich settled back, throwing his arms along the top of the couch.

"You tell me. Explain to me what the fuck is going on out here in this one-horse town? You were supposed to be looking out for her. What the hell? The device was planted in her car? Whose target was she, and why?"

I took a few steps back and bumped into the kitchen counter. I shouldn't be here.

I didn't want to be here.

"The Broken Blades in Nebraska got real unhappy with us working with the Flames of Hell and ripping up their Calderas Group deal," said Butler. "We're betting it's them."

"So, they targeted Nina to get to you? Nice."

"We got a dead prez to show for it," said Butler.

Reich only made a face. He didn't give too much of a shit.

"Jump got Nina out of the way, you know," I piped in. "Nina is alive now, thanks to Jump."

Both men stared at me, as if they'd forgotten I was even there in the first place.

"Tania, you should go." Butler's voice was even, low.

"No, no, no," said Reich, eyeing me up and down. "Why should she go? This your whore?"

"Hey!" My back shot up.

Butler raised his hand between me and Reich. "Tania's a friend, a civilian. She's a friend of some of the Jacks' old ladies, and she's a friend of mine from way back. She's not—"

"Right. Yet she's always at your side, ain't she? That why Nina was crying so much?"

"She's scared after what happened," Butler said through gritted teeth.

Reich's head dipped. "You were cheating on my girl, weren't you? Dragged her out here to this hole in the middle of nowhere, full of promises and dreams, and then you dumped her and did your thing, right? I knew about you from the start, but I figured— she's got a baby coming now!"

"That's not how it is!" I blurted.

"Tania!" Butler snapped at me.

"Why don't you tell me how it is, honey? You seem to know a helluva lot," Reich said on a hiss, his eyes flashing.

"Nina's the one who's been cheating on him with another guy," I said.

"What?" Reich's face creased.

"Not only that, but she and your appointed bodyguard, Led, got to know each other real well on their cross-country joyride over here to South Dakota. Lots of joy. Plenty of joy."

"Damn it, Tania." Butler's sharp tone cut me off.

My gaze landed on Butler. "Oh, come on! Reich's defending her virtue here, so he should know the truth. I guess you've never seen your old lady's selfie collection on her phone?"

Butler's face was a tight mask.

Reich let out a deep chuckle. "The course of true love don't run smooth now, does it?" He leaned forward, his hands clasped together. "What are you all doin' about finding out who's responsible for the attack?"

"We're working on it. We just lost our president. Jump's funeral was today."

"Whose the new prez?"

"The vote's next week," replied Butler.

Reich's head tilted. "They need to make finding the fucker responsible a priority. You all need to get cracking. And I need to take my girl home, where she's safe."

"She's staying," Butler said.

My eyes widened at the seething sound of his voice. At his pronouncement.

"Oh, yeah?" Reich smirked. He seemed downright amused. "Well, I'll be in town a while longer to make sure she's good." He rose from the sofa, heaving a grunt. "I'll let you two get back to your friendship now. I'll be in touch. You can be sure of that."

"Yeah, I'll be waiting," replied Butler.

The door slammed behind Reich.

I let out a heavy exhale.

"Jesus, Tania, you can't shoot your mouth off like that."

"Nina's been fooling around behind your back from the get-go. What the hell? And, on top of it all, my brother actually likes her and wants her ass. What the fuck is going on with you men? Her snatch must be magic."

Butler only lit another cigarette, inhaling deeply.

I grabbed my handbag and the empty tote and headed for the door. "You have a good afternoon. Don't forget to eat the rest of the food in the fridge."

He didn't respond, his thumb twitched over the filter on his cigarette.

I swung the door open. "I'm off."

I tromped down the staircase, each loud and heavy step I took feeding my exasperation.

Outside, in the warm heat of the afternoon sun, I headed for my car, which I'd parked down the block.

A tight grip on my upper arm jerked me back, and I gasped, landing in Reich's stiff chest. His long mustache and harsh scruff, scraped against the side of my face.

"Tania, right?"

"What the—"

He leaned into me. Stale tobacco, old hair gel, and coffee breath assaulted my senses.

"Don't yell, don't make a fuss, and this will all go better. You're coming with me."

"No, I'm not!" I yanked against his hold.

"Feisty. Nice." He pulled me away from my car.

His chin lifted, and one other big man from his club appeared before me on the street, his shadow falling on me and Reich.

I pushed back. "Why? Why me? I've got nothing to do with—"

"Quit shittin' me already. You don't come with me now, I'll make sure lover boy in there pays for it. I got eyes on him."

I jerked away from him once more, but he only shoved me into the bearlike claws of the heavyset Flame.

Reich took out his phone and tapped the screen. "Look out your window, fucker." His voice snarled.

I followed Reich's line of sight to Butler's window on the second floor.

There he was.

His eyes widened, his mouth forming a, *No*, a large palm flat against the glass.

"Don't do this, Reich. You're gonna regret this," roared Butler's harsh voice over the speaker of Reich's cell phone.

"You got that backward, asshole. This is the part where you regret what you've done to me, just like I promised you would. You know what I want. You'd better deliver. Me and your whore got all night." Reich chuckled, shutting down his phone.

He turned on his heel, and I got pushed. We were off.

Adrenaline coursed through my veins with nowhere to go, choking me. My eyes darted to Butler's window one last time.

He was gone.

THIRTY-FOUR

BUTLER

THE RAW TERROR ON TANIA'S FACE tore through me, fisting in my lungs, throttling in my chest, where the familiar knot tightened and tightened.

One more on my watch.

I buckled to my knees, struggling for air. My heart hammered inside me, my pulse thrashed in my neck.

Focus. Do not fucking panic. Focus.

I reached out and gripped the edge of my coffee table and held on, concentrating on my fingers pressing into the wood, as the roar of bikes surged outside, blaring, receding.

Breathe. Breathe. Breathe.

I squeezed my eyes shut as air finally filled my lungs. I widened my eyes, and the warped wood trim on my front door came back into focus.

The door.

The shabby blue sofa.

My guitar.

I leaned back on my haunches and sucked in air slowly.

My phone rang. I reached for it, and losing my balance, I fell back on the floor.

"Shit."

I licked my lips and took in a breath. I rolled over and stretched out my arm. My shaking, unsteady arm. The tips of my fingers flicked at the edges of my phone. *Once, twice, three...motherfuck.*

Got it.

Finger had called me.

Fuck you.

I tapped on Boner's name. The ringer buzzed in my ear as I took in deeper gulps of air. My head swam, and I dragged a hand through my hair, my scalp prickling.

"Butler?"

"Got a problem," I spit out. "Huge problem."

"What is it?" Boner asked. "Is it Nina? Did the doctors say something new?"

"Tania," I bit out.

"Tania? What the fuck? You all right?"

I sucked in more air, wheezing.

"Butler?" Boner's voice hardened.

"Took her—took her from my place. Reich was here, and he took Tania."

"Are you okay?"

"I'll be at the club in five. Be there!" I tossed the phone on the table, my hand still trembling.

I pulled myself up and flicked open the carved small wooden box I always kept on my coffee table. It'd once held a quick, handy supply of coke over the years. Now, it held my medication. The medication I'd been forgetting to take lately.

I pushed a pill between my lips.

I staggered to the table where the glass of water Tania had poured for me earlier stood at attention. I drained it.

My lungs relaxed a few degrees. My head decompressed. I squeezed my eyes shut and then forced them open. The television static in my vision began to fade. Forms took shape once more.

But I could only see that desperation etched on Tania's face as she had been dragged away, those beautiful dark eyes still on me, eyes full of fear.

"He just came in and took her?" asked Boner, his green eyes hard as stone.

"Yeah, wanted to know who'd set the bomb. I told him it must have been the Blades. Then, he accused me of stepping out on

Nina and called Tania my whore. You know Tania; she started defending me, said something she shouldn't have about Nina. And he fucking took her to prove a point."

I wasn't going to share why else Reich was coming after me; that was for another time.

A knock on the door.

"In!" shouted Kicker, a hand swiping through his sleek black hair.

Jill stepped inside, her eyes darting around the room. "I just got off the phone with Nina. She told me where her sister and Reich are staying. The Best Western in Deadwood."

"He's getting a little casino time in with his hospital visits," muttered Dready.

"I told Nina to keep her sister at the hospital with her all afternoon and tonight, like you said," Jill continued. "She immediately turned on the waterworks, and her sister bought it. Deanna even got on the phone and asked me to come by. She sounded overwhelmed. I'm going to go over there now and help Nina create a little more diversion, so I can get the hotel room key for you and make sure Deanna stays put and doesn't go back to Deadwood."

"Good work, Firefly," Boner said. "We'll see you at the hospital parking lot in an hour. Text me on your way down from the room."

"Okay, baby. See you there."

I doubted Reich would keep Tania at his hotel room, but it was a start. How this shit would finish, is what had me in agony.

THIRTY-FIVE

TANIA

THE BROWN BLINDS of the motel room were closed, holding back the heat, the sun, the world.

"I want to freak Butler out. He deserves it for fucking with me." Reich swept his tongue across his teeth. He had just finished tying my hands to the spindles of the chair he'd pushed me into once we'd gotten to his room. The plastic ties bit into my wrists.

"He's been fucking with you?" I asked.

"Butler? Hell yeah. He took something of mine."

"Are we talking about Nina?"

"Yeah, her, too. The two of 'em thought they were smarter than me. Ain't gonna happen the way they wanted it, I can tell you. I'm here to put an end to this shit."

"You didn't come here just to see Nina in the hospital?"

The ends of his mouth turned down. "Fuck, you talk too much, you know that?"

"So I've been told."

"Don't get any ideas. I got three guns, a couple of knives, and a—"

"Oh, I believe you." My gaze roamed over the two suitcases in the room, an expensive facial moisturizer on one night table by the bed. "Won't Deanna be back here soon?"

"You don't want to be alone with me, babe?" He shot me a crooked grin. "Since you're here, we could have a little fun, just the two of us. That there is one big comfy bed."

"Hmm. No, thank you."

He laughed loudly. "Deanna texted me earlier. Nina's all emotional, so she's gonna be spending the night with her. Works out perfect. It's just you and me." He cupped my chin with his meaty hand, his gaze traveling down my chest.

My stomach flipped.

"This was a last-minute decision on my part but a good one." He let go of me, and he went to the mini bar fridge and grabbed a can of beer. "If Butler wants you back—and I'm sure he does— he'll give me back what he took from me. Even exchange." *Snap, psst* went the can top, and Reich guzzled the cold beer.

"Exchange me for Nina?"

Reich wiped a hand across his mouth, eyeing me. "It's time for you to shut the fuck up now. Where's your cell phone?"

"In my handbag."

He opened my red canvas hobo bag and rifled though it. "Fuck, I hate women's bags. Always so much shit. Gives me the creeps."

He whipped out my cell phone and dropped my handbag, its contents spilling out onto the floor. Reich ripped out my phone battery, shoved it in his pocket, and flung the phone on the floor, mashing it with the heel of his boot. I flinched. I could imagine him mashing people dead the very same way. He picked up the pieces and shoved them into his jacket pocket.

He got on his phone. "Hey, it's Reich. I'm in town, and I need a place to take care of a little business. Off the grid." He glanced at me. "For the night."

My stomach twisted.

"You got anything in South Dakota? Don't want to have to cross state lines. Uh-huh. Good. Yeah. Later."

"Are we going on a road trip?"

"That's right."

"Oh, goody. Will there be snacks at least?"

"Snacks, huh? There's an idea. What do you want?"

"Kit Kats, Whoppers, a machete."

His body shook with laughter as he crushed his beer can and tossed it on the dresser top. "Yeah. Let's go." He cut the ties that bound me to the chair and pulled me up.

"Wait! Could I..." I gestured to my handbag and the mess on the floor.

"Make it quick." He released me.

I squatted down and scooped everything back in—my collection of turquoise-blue, pink, and lilac gel ink pens, a lighter, hand sanitizer gel, the trial size of my perfume. My pulse spiked. I always kept a small glass vial with me to dab on my favorite fragrance when I wanted a pick-me-up or was off to meet someone. I'd started this habit in college when I'd be running around campus and Chicago all day and wouldn't get back home until late at night. There was rarely time to freshen up and reinvent yourself for a night out. You had to be mobile, always prepared to step up your game.

I need to step up my game.

"Move it!" Reich snarled at me from the open door.

"All right already." I stood up, gripping the handles of my bag in my fingers, and with a quick pound of my heel—*Crack*—I crushed the perfume vial into the rug.

Thank God I'd worn my old cowboy boots today and not bothered with my summer sandals.

Reich ushered me through the door and out to the parking lot. He pushed me into the back of a small windowless van and taped my mouth. His biker bro sat in the driver's seat. We hit the road, and within fifteen minutes, the groan of a motorcycle surged beside us. *An escort to our private destination?*

An hour or so later, the van doors opened, and Reich's biker grabbed me by the arms and hauled me out. A young red-haired biker stood before me, and I blinked at his colors. The red flames on his jacket made my heart stop. He was from my brother's club. Finger's club.

What the hell?

We were in a wooded area, the late afternoon sun glinting its last rays through the tall evergreens. The call of a bird curled in the sky, and the breeze quivered the long, knobby tree branches. I clenched my jaw, my stomach somersaulting.

The redhead motioned us into a small box of a worn-out wood cabin whose door he unlocked.

"Good work," said Reich.

"You bet," said biker boy. "Anything else you need, give us a call."

Jesus, is Red our concierge checking us into the Flames Four Seasons Hotel?

"Appreciate it," said Reich. "I'll be outta here by morning."

"Sure." The biker stalked out of the cabin without glancing at me.

Was that out of respect for his elder, or was kidnapping women such a common occurrence that it didn't even register?

Reich pushed me further into the cabin, his bro remaining outside. The young biker took off, his engine squealing through the woods where we were hidden. Reich shoved the old wood door shut with a loud thud.

My heart sank lower and lower as the drone of young Red's bike faded.

THIRTY-SIX

BUTLER

I SLID THE KEY CARD Jill had gotten us into its slot in the motel room door. The green light pinged on.

I pushed open the door with Boner at my side, gun ready.

Empty.

"Fuck."

Not that we'd expected him to still be here with Tania.

Boner, Clip, and Dready moved through the room, going through the luggage, opening drawers, kicking open the bathroom door.

My eyes closed, the scent hitting me like a ten-foot wave.

Pepper and flowers and—

I followed it and crouched down in the carpet, spotting the shards of wet broken glass. *Was there a struggle?*

"Is that perfume?" Boner slanted his head. "Smells too expensive for some ten-minute whore he might have snuck in here while his old lady's at the hospital."

"It's Tania's perfume," I said.

I'm coming for you, Scarlett. I'm coming.

"Now, where the fuck did he take her?" I muttered.

"Unless he's got a safe house in our territory, he'll be putting a call into his club here," said Boner.

"That means Finger." Dready raised his chin at me.

I dialed Finger's number. I should have called him from the beginning, but I'd wanted to be the one to handle this, to get Tania safe.

Not him.

"Butler."

It was Catch.

"Why am I talking to you? I'm looking for your prez."

"Finger's out of town with our VP," Catch replied. "As one of his officers, I'm on call."

Fuck, I have to play ball with this jerk now.

"Got a question," I said.

"Let's see if I wanna answer it."

My vision blurred, and I pressed a hand around the back of my neck.

Calm down. He's her brother. You need him.

I gripped my phone even tighter. "You been in touch with Reich, your national VP from Ohio lately?"

"Why should I tell you Flames' business, man?"

"Catch, I think it's safe to say, you fucking owe me. Now, tell me. Has Reich contacted you within the last twenty-four hours?"

Catch let out a heavy exhale. "Yes."

"What did he want?"

"Butler—"

"What the hell did he want?" I yelled.

"He wanted access to a safe house for the night."

"Did you give it to him?"

"Of course I gave it to him. He's the national VP. I set it up and sent one of my bros to take him there. I would've gone myself, but I couldn't get away, had shit to take care of here. He said he'd be there overnight."

"Was anyone else with him?"

"Fuck if I know. Split's not back yet."

"Call him. Find out if he has a woman with him up there. Where is this place anyway?"

"You really just asked me that?"

"He's got Tania, asshole!"

Silence.

"What do you mean, he's got Tania? WHY THE HELL DOES THAT MOTHERFUCKER HAVE MY SISTER?"

The blood rushed through my veins. "You gonna give me the location of that safe house now?"

THIRTY-SEVEN

TANIA

"I NEED TO PEE."

I gestured at the small bathroom on the opposite end of the cabin from where my hands were tied to a hard plastic chair that was blackened with age and dirt.

Two twin beds were shoved against a corner, their thin stained mattresses not inspiring comfort. One large thick brown sofa along with a long plastic table that had seen better days and a dirty, encrusted plug-in hot plate, next to a barely-of-this-century sink, added to the spiffy factor of the cabin.

"Go ahead, hon." He grinned. "I'll watch, and then I'll wipe that pussy myself."

"Oh. Well, I need to...you know..." I slanted my head downward. "My stomach has been acting up with all the excitement. I don't feel too good. Good thing you didn't get me any snacks, huh?"

He scowled. "Ah, fuck. Fine. You stay in there. I got company coming, and I need you out of the way."

"You don't want me serving cocktails and hors d'oeuvres?"

Reich slashed at the ties attaching me to the chair, grabbed me by the upper arm, and shoved me toward the bathroom. "Keep that attitude up and that mouth running, and you just might service cock and serve your cunt."

"Can I have my handbag with me in there?"

He went back for my handbag and tossed it at me. "Here."

"Could you cut these off, just until I'm done?" I held out my tied wrists. "Please?"

His eyes darted up to the tiny wood-framed window in the bathroom.

"I really don't think I'm going to fit through there, do you?" I said.

He muttered something unintelligible under his breath as he took his large hunting knife from his side and slashed the plastic tie around my wrists. "You stay in here. Don't expect any pity or help from my bro."

"Of course not."

He shut the door of the bathroom. I exhaled and slumped back against the small stained counter, clutching my handbag. I waited five minutes and flushed the small toilet. I turned on the water faucet, and shut it off.

A blast of pipes flared in the distance and grew stronger. They cut out, and a hard knock came at the cabin door. The warped door jerked and creaked open, and my heart raced. A new, loud male voice greeted Reich. Pats on backs, chuckles.

I put my ear to the door, begging my breath to slow down, calm down.

"How you doing? Your girl all right? She better?"

"She'll be fine," came Reich's voice. "Nina will be out of the hospital any day now and coming home with me. Something came up, and I'm here for a few hours."

"Well, I'm glad you could meet up before I headed back to Kansas."

I strained to decipher the muttering and small talk.

"What do you have for me?" asked Reich.

"You were right. The Blades are more fucked than when we first talked to them. Notch is desperate for a new lifeline, starving with nowhere to turn now that their hook-up with the Calderas Group is history and they got busted. Now they're interested."

"Thought so. Idiots blew you off months ago when you first contacted them, thought they knew better. And?"

"Pick was impressed with my offer this time around."

The mattress made noises, and more muttering filled the room. Lighters clicked on and off. Cigarette smoke tinged the air. I plastered myself against the door. I didn't want to miss a word.

"Pick is getting the ball rolling with Notch. Meanwhile, Notch is salivating to make a statement to Finger and the Jacks since all that shit went down. Fucking perfect timing, man."

"Good," said Reich.

"Finger's gonna lose his shit. The Smoking Guns haven't been in these parts for decades. Not since—"

"Exactly," replied Reich.

Holy shit, Reich is bringing the Flames' enemies into Nebraska to stab Finger in the back and bolster them against the Jacks? Oh God, no, that meant—

"And Finger?"

"You let me worry about Finger. He's just one man," came Reich's voice. A voice laced with glee. He was making a presentation and relishing his audience's response.

"I'm counting on this to work out, Reich. We've been looking to stretch this way for a while now."

Boom.

My bag stared at me from the floor.

Shit! I'd dropped it.

"What was that? You got a possum in there?"

The wood floorboards creaked and groaned. I froze.

The door unlocked and swung open.

Reich slanted his head at me. "Get out of there."

"Gladly." I scooped up my bag from the floor and brushed past him, heading for the side of the old plastic table.

Reich's guest stepped forward in the shadowy afternoon glimmers of sun in the small cabin. The name Scrib was on a small patch. A grinning skeleton holding two smoking guns was stitched on his leather vest. My insides twisted at the sight.

Scrib stared at me like I was a free bag of his favorite fast food. He pointed a finger at me. "I've seen you before."

"Me?"

"Saw you at the Flames," he said.

"Excuse me?" I mumbled.

"I've been running surveillance on Finger's club this past year. I saw you at his clubhouse. I have a thing for dark-haired women. Yeah, I liked what I saw." His head slanted. "You had a kid with you."

My fingertips dug into the sturdy cotton canvas of my handbag, my heart galloping in my chest. "You're wrong."

"No, I'm not." Scrib's eyes narrowed. "They let you in. They let you out. Seemed like a real friendly visit."

My face heated under Reich and Scrib's hideous inspection.

"Not yapping now, are you?" Reich let out a dry laugh.

"You one of those high class bitches that like it dirty once in a while?" asked the Smoking Gun.

My insides coiled. My mouth dried.

Reich grinned. Satisfaction, but it wasn't from the beer. "Well, Lady Luck has certainly shined her fat white ass on me today."

A smile swept the Smoking Gun's lips. "You get off on Finger's missing fingers?" He laughed loud and hard. "All those scars turn you on, huh? I like bitches like you."

Reich let out a snorting laugh and picked up his beer again, gulping it down.

My stomach twisted and churned.

"You like those designs on his face, do ya? Every time you get off on 'em, it's courtesy of my club." Scrib crossed his arms, his lips curling. The proud warrior retelling old legends.

"You—" flew from my mouth before I could stop it.

"Long time ago, we had Finger back when he was a prospect, chopped off his middle fingers and carved up his face as a lesson to his club."

"That was a lesson?" I blurted.

"Yeah."

"*You* did that?"

He nodded, his eyes flashing. "Then, Finger stole from us and vanished into thin air for a while. He reappeared back at his club, safe and sound. We'd just settled on a truce, so we couldn't go after him the way we wanted, the way he deserved. I don't know though. Maybe it's time that truce expired."

An icy shiver snaked through me, and I staggered back a step.

"You know, Tania, I'm really upset with what happened to Nina. She's very special to me," Reich said. "How do I know that you weren't making her life miserable? I'm sure Butler was. I'll bet that's why she was fooling around behind his back."

"Butler's been a stand-up partner to her the whole time, from what I know."

"Then, why would she be stepping out on him?" Reich asked.

"Oh, that's Butler's fault? Amazing," I muttered.

"Maybe it's your fault. Found you at his place, didn't I? I got me a two for one right here. You a girl with special, hidden talents?" Reich licked his bottom lip.

"You have quite an imagination, Reich. Instead of keeping me here, why aren't you out looking for the idiots who hurt Nina?" I leveled my gaze at him. "Jump sacrificed his life to save her! Doesn't that mean anything to you? Finger could probably help you out."

Both men barked with laughter.

"Okay then. Maybe you don't need to look for who did this." My shoulders stiffened. "Maybe you know?"

Reich's eyes hung on mine, his grin widening. He was having fun.

"Oh, Jesus, it was you," I breathed. "You rigged Nina's car?"

"Tania, you are one smart lady." He winked at me.

"You got Nina hurt. She could've been killed!"

"Serves her right. Twit thought she'd gotten one over on me. Not in this lifetime. She got the message. She's coming back home with me. I made sure of that, and my old lady will pull the rest of those strings."

The full perverse weight of Reich's obsession with Nina, his own wife's sister, made me rock back in my boots. A wave of acid rose in my throat.

He leaned into me. "I get it now. Finger and Butler are buddies, and you're their little go-between. The soup is finally coming together here."

"I'm not anyone's go-between."

He let out a dry laugh. "Yeah, you're just everybody's *friend*, huh? So devoted. Ain't she devoted?"

"I wonder how devoted Finger is to her?" said the Smoking Gun, his hands resting on his wide black belt, his wallet chain swinging at his side.

"Now, that's a good question," said Reich, facing me once more. "Finger's *devotion*." He dragged out the word for emphasis.

Reich traced a line from my lips and down my throat, stopping at my chest. "I think you need a sign of your devotion." Contempt laced his tone.

"Yeah, something real genuine." The Smoking Gun let out a belly laugh.

"Something straight from the source." Reich slapped a hand on the Scrib's shoulder. "His and hers."

The both of them eyed me, as if they were hungry vampires making plans for an unexpected fresh victim. They were looking forward to the feast.

My pulse blared like a screaming fire engine racing down a city street.

I put my handbag on the table and sucked in a deep breath to keep my voice steady. "I don't understand you two." I ran my fingers through my hair and opened my bag. "I'm just caught in your crossfire. All I did was bring Butler some food today, knowing he'd been at the hospital with his injured old lady for days. I was checking in on a friend, nothing more. We do that out here in South Dakota, you know. We're real neighborly." My fingers curled around the lipstick tube, and I removed it from my bag along with my small mirror.

Scrib came up behind me. His heavy breaths heated my shoulder, his hands curling over my hips. I gritted my teeth. He brushed my hair out of his way and rubbed my shoulder with a large hand.

My stomach twisted at our reflection in my tiny handheld mirror, and I smiled. "Please get your fucking hands off me."

His thick black eyebrows jumped. "You crack me up, babe." He turned his head to Reich. "Dude, you—"

I tore open the lipstick tube, pivoted, and jammed the small knife into Scrib's neck with a grunt. I threw all my weight into the thrust, knowing the blade was too small and probably too dull to make a dent in denser tissue.

"What the fuck?" Scrib's arm bashed into me, and my mirror went flying.

He pulled the knife from his neck, blood spurting all over his hands, the whites of his eyes bulging. He lunged at me, and I dived toward my broken mirror on the floor, grabbing a shard. He wrenched my leg and dragged me along the floor, closer to him. I scratched and jabbed at his body with the jagged piece of mirror, and his howls and yells filled my ears.

"Fucking bitch!" Scrib's voice roared.

The room spun, and I flew, landing on the sofa like a tossed doll. A slap tore over my face, stunning me. I gasped for air.

Reich leaned over me, his eyes flashing. "You surprised me. I usually hate surprises, but this one, I kinda liked."

I whipped a knee out at him, aiming for his crotch, but he was too fast. He caught my leg, shoving it back down, his tight grip on my thigh shooting a burning flare of pain all through my limb. His other hand imprisoned my neck.

I was trapped.

"You okay, Scrib?" Reich asked.

"I'm bleeding. Hidden fucking bitch knife!"

That sick smile crept over Reich's lips once again. "Let's return the favor. This is your thing, ain't it, man?"

Scrib grunted loudly, cursing, taking in deep gusts of air.

Reich ripped my shirt open. "I'll hold her down for you."

THIRTY-EIGHT

TANIA

THE BOURBON WASHED over my skin, the burn blaring right through my chest and blowing out my insides. My head fell back, but there was nothing to lean against, no support, no relief.

No nothing.

Their eyes scraped over me. Reich licked his lips. A large hunting knife with my blood on it glinted in Scrib's hand. He took a step back, murmuring a string of curse words to himself, admiring his work as his free hand passed over his crotch.

This shit is turning them on. Cutting me, making me bleed, making me beg for mercy.

"Maybe you want to suck Scrib's cock instead?" asked Reich. "He sure wants you to. He's willing not to cut you any more. Pretty generous offer, considering what you did to him."

I raised my head and focused on Reich's blurry face. "Fuck you."

Reich took his own knife and sliced down my bra, the tip of his blade whispering past my skin. The material gave way, freeing my breasts. I let out a shaky long breath, my stomach clenching.

"Fuck yeah," muttered Scrib.

Reich's damp hand palmed me, sending a jolt right through me. Scrib gripped my shoulder, and brought his blade down on my skin, slicing a short gash into my flesh, stinging me to hell and back.

Blood and sweat trickled down my chest, and a moan lodged in my throat. My joints screamed; my limbs shuddered.

Through the haze, I reached for Becca's sweet face, her cuddling me as she fell asleep. I reached for my baby brother chasing me through the tall sunflowers in the heat of the summer sun.

Daddy's towering gold and green sunflowers.

The sun in my eyes.

Daddy's voice calling out to us.

The thudding drone of his combine in the hot and dusty distance.

Far away.

Reich leaned over and lapped at the blood on my chest, a hand smashing a breast, and I jerked in his hold. He made grotesque noises, his tongue swirling over me. The stink of his hair gel made the bile rise in my throat, and I struggled to choke it back down.

I squirmed in the chair they'd tied me to.

Why haven't I passed out yet?

"Can't say no to tits, bourbon, or blood." Reich laughed hard. Scrib laughed even harder.

Nausea and heat overwhelmed me. The room dipped and dived. A slap cracked over my face, sending my head flying to the right, my neck twisting painfully.

"Don't faint now, bitch. You're gonna suck me off!" came the harsh voice. "And, if you're a good girl, I'll return the favor"— Scrib hovered over me, leaning down—"right up that sweet ass of yours."

The sour smell of his skin, his brutal threat collided in my head, crushed my lungs. I gagged and wretched.

He slapped my face again, and I gasped, needles of pain throbbing over my skin in endless waves. My head swung on my neck like a broken branch.

Scrib fumbled with his leathers, his arched dick in his fist. "I'm gonna come all over that face. All over those tits." He stroked fast and hard. "Oh, yeah. Yeah…"

I couldn't look away from the grotesque spectacle. That had to hurt. I was sure his dick was going to pull off in his hand, like a piece of stressed-out rubber. His mouth twisted in an ugly snarl, grunts escaping his thick lips.

"Open that mouth, bitch."

A muffled *click.*

"Huh—"

Wood cracked and burst. Reich bolted out of my line of vision on a howl. The front door stormed open, knocking Reich back into the room. Fresh air broke through the stifling space, and my lungs surged in response.

A tall figure, his features set in stone, a gun in his grip, flew into the cabin. His cold blue eyes were flames of ice aimed at me.

My brutal angel

Butler.

A loud yell, a gun fired, a massive thud, and Scrib crumpled to the floor at my feet.

"What the hell?" Reich bellowed.

Butler aimed his gun at Reich and hissed. "You just can't resist playing with me, can you?"

"Fuck you!"

"Shut him up!" Boner's voice pounded in my ears.

Dready shoved Reich against a wall, a gun at his chest.

"Shit, Tan! Shit! Motherfuck!" My brother's tense voice rose somewhere above me. His hand cradled my skull.

Drew.

He turned suddenly and launched himself at Reich, shoving his gun up against Reich's forehead. "What the hell are you doing with my sister? What the fuck are you doing?"

"Your sister? She's your sister?" Reich sputtered.

Catch dragged Reich out of the cabin, Dready behind them.

A pair of swiftly moving hands cut my arms loose, and they fell to my sides. My shoulders throbbed. My chest burned.

Butler crouched before me and cut at the ropes binding my legs and feet. My lungs expanded to gain more air, each moment crushing, the pain lashing across my chest, my shoulder joints raw. I met his heavy gaze and tried to swallow as his hands pulled my torn shirt across my chest. I put my hands over his and held them there.

Shouts and yelling blared outside, and Boner and Bear ran out the door, their guns at the ready.

Crack. Crack.

Catch's shouts roared above the others.

A howl and a flash of black made me jack up to my shaky feet. Scrib bulldozed into Butler, pinning him to the floor.

Butler's fists pummeled Scrib's sides over and over again, his boots banging into the old wood plank floor with the ferocious effort. The two of them brawled, the huge knife shuddering in Scrib's grip. His other hand smashed down on Butler's face, while Butler's hand clenched Scrib's arm in a relentless hold.

I have to help him. I have to do something.

A glint of metal on the floor caught my eye. *My lipstick knife.* I grabbed it and swung my arm, plunging it into Scrib's neck on a grunt. His body seized, his blood gushed, his howling wail filled the room. Butler pushed him away, and Scrib dropped to the floor.

"Tania!" Butler grabbed me by the arm, his eyes flashing.

He brought me into his body, and I sagged against him.

He'd come for me.

He held me steady, his arm around me a refuge.

My tender mercenary.

A smile played on Butler's lips, his pale blue eyes gleaming. "Finally got you speechless? What's the matter, baby? No one ever broke down a door to get to you before?"

Warmth tumbled through me at the sound of that smoky, husky voice just for me, the long-held tension draining from my limbs.

"Only you, Rhett," I whispered.

I curled into his chest, shaking in his arms, and he held me tighter in a vise of emotion and mettle.

He lifted me up and swept me outside into the humid haze of dusk.

And I held on tight.

THIRTY-NINE

TANIA

A BARRAGE OF YELLING AND CURSING.

The short slide and adamant click of a gun, heavy footfalls thudding in leaves and branches, thick grunts—all of it jostled inside me.

My fingers gripped the hot metal of the truck door. My insides convulsed, and I threw up on the pine needles and weed strewn rocks.

"Let's go!" Boner's voice.

Heavy arms lifted me inside the airless interior of the truck, a hand on my head. A familiar body, warm skin. Then, it released me.

"You get her to your club and keep her there. I'll be down as soon as I can. Gotta deal with this fucker!" Catch motioned to his men, who got Reich into his van.

I hope he enjoys the ride. I know I did.

"Why the fuck did you let that Smoking Gun go?" Butler got in Catch's face.

"Are you shitting me?" Catch shouted back, his eyes blazing. "I can't do nothing to them, and you know it! Don't you fucking dare go after them. You do, and we are all up shit's creek. This falls on Reich. That Gun came here to see him. He's got a lot to answer for. We start there. You get my sister home. I'm taking this one with me." He banged on the van. "Move!"

Catch's dark eyes slid to me. Our father's dark brown eyes. Eyes now raging with molten iron. I nodded at him from inside Boner's truck. His jaw seemed permanently clenched as he swung on his bike and tore after the van.

Butler got in the truck and took me in his arms as Boner jerked the vehicle back, swung around, and sped off. I wiped at the side of my mouth, acid trailing on my tongue. My vision was blurry, but I didn't fight it.

I gulped and gulped, the gusting air from the window whipping over my face, coolness rushing my skin. I slumped against Butler as I held my shirt together, my limbs exhausted.

A wad of fabric was pressed against my chest, the relentless sting a replay of the horror.

"No!" I swatted at his hand.

"Tania, you're bleeding. Let me do this."

My head sank back, this time against a large shoulder.

The truck barreled over a winding, rocky roadway, and my eyes blinked open. We passed through the open gates of the One-Eyed Jacks' clubhouse and finally came to a jarring stop.

"This way! Take her in here!" Alicia's sharp voice rang out, and my muscles relaxed at the sound.

Butler lifted me and carried me inside to the smell of old vinyl and lemony air deodorizer, the hum of the ceiling fans in the lounge, murmuring voices.

I peered up at a harsh angled jaw and hooded blue eyes. I leaned my face against Butler's sweat and bloodstained T-shirt, his skin underneath blazing with heat. He carried me down a hallway. A door swung open, and my aching body met a soft mattress that squeaked under our weight.

Butler's blue eyes filled my vision, clouded eyes lined with creases. He was worried.

I offered him a faint smile, but it didn't seem to have any kind of softening effect on him.

He took my fingers in his. "Lie back. You're safe now. It's over."

I willed my jaw to unclench, and my gums throbbed. The stinging pain swelled over me again, that burning on my chest. I gave into it and spun on its whirl. I let out a whimper, adjusting myself on the bed.

"Tania? Shit." He opened my hand in his. My skin was slashed from the shards of broken mirror I'd used to stab Scrib. The blood was sticky.

Was it my blood? Was it Scrib's?

"I'm okay, really," I said through gritted teeth.

"Let me get that shirt off you, honey," murmured Alicia.

"I've got her." That growl came up in his voice again. "Get me a first aid kit and make her some tea with a shot of whiskey in it."

"I've got some codeine if you want something stronger, Tania."

"Tea's good," I replied.

"Okay, hon, whatever you want. Be right back." Alicia flew out of the room.

"Butler—"

"Just lie still till we get you cleaned up. Please." His lips smashed together.

I followed his line of sight. My stomach tightened at my ripped shirt, my ripped bra, my skin stained with blood. A moan escaped my mouth.

"Let me do it. Close your eyes," Butler said.

I didn't want to close my eyes. I wanted to watch him, his somber face concentrating on cleaning me up, healing me, making it all better, wiping this hell away.

Alicia burst in with a huge first aid kit and a large black T-shirt. Butler took the kit from her and snapped it open. I closed my eyes and within moments the sting of a liquid over my chest had me squirming. Alicia swept the hair from my face.

"I know. Just a bit more. Hang on." Butler worked over me, his eyes tense, stony. "Thank fuck the cuts aren't deep." The tear of adhesive followed, and he patted the edges of a bandage over my chest. He cleaned the cuts on my hand and gently applied ointment over them.

He turned away, packing up the first aid kit, and Alicia helped me take off what was left of my ripped shirt and bra. She stretched the soft cotton shirt over my head, and we both carefully tugged it down over me. She balled up my ruined shirt in her hands. My pretty black bra.

The madness slammed into me.

Tears filled my eyes, and my chest caved in. I sucked in a breath.

Butler took my hand in his and kissed it gently. "I'm right here, Scarlett. Right here. Not leaving you," he whispered.

Willy stood in the doorway with an oversize steaming white mug in one hand and a bottle of Jack in the other.

"How she doin'?" he asked. That warm voice, a hint of a Texas drawl to it, wrapped around me.

289

I stared at him, his dark blue eyes firmly on mine. Eyes that I'd known for years.

My heart squeezed at the memories of his kindness to me when I used to tag along, against my will, with Grace to the club a generation ago. I was the scared girl desperate to mask her anxiety with an armor of stainless steel cool. From the very beginning, Grace had been right at home among the Jacks but not me. Willy had seen right through me and used to tease me mercilessly, but he spoke my language—a seamless flow of irony and barbs. I'd teased him right back until, eventually, we were both laughing.

Willy's best friend, Wreck had been stern and introverted while Willy was relaxed and easygoing. Of course, Willy liked his women really young, too, so that could have been a part of it, but he was good to me, respectful even, because of Grace, and I'd always appreciated that. And we'd actually enjoyed each other's company.

We'd picked up right where we'd left off when he worked at my store, creating a remarkable array of shelves, platforms, stands, a front desk, while giving me all kinds of design advice and going over my options. We'd made a good team.

"Willy," I murmured.

He handed me the mug and opened the bottle. "How much you need, baby girl?"

"Enough to make me smile again."

"You got it." He poured the booze in my tea and leaned over. He planted a quick kiss on my forehead, his trimmed beard brushing against my skin, a hand at the side of my face.

Warring emotions sprang up like a flooding river sloshing over its banks. I took a careful sip of the hot tea, but it did nothing to control the tide. Tears streamed down my face, and he silently took the mug from my hands and put it on the side table.

Willy sat at the edge of the bed and put an arm around me. His distinct aroma of Brut, cigars, and pine made my heart clutch with the need to have those days of my youth again.

Uncomplicated days even if I didn't think of them that way at the time.

My head fell against Willy's shoulder.

My dad used to wear the same stupid Brut aftershave. After he'd died, my mother had kept his last bottle in her medicine cabinet for years and years. I would ignore it.

A muffled cry escaped my lips.

"Hey, hey, girl"—Willy took me deeper in his arms—"it's all right now. It's over. Over, you hear?"

I sniffled and nodded my head against his shoulder as one heavy hand ran up and down my back.

I hiccuped, sucking in his comforting scent.

"Call Grace," Butler said softly from somewhere above me.

"She took the baby to the pediatrician earlier. I'll call her," replied Alicia. Her footsteps faded from the room.

I peeked up at Willy, wiping at my eyes. "Sorry."

"You drink up and have a rest. Let us take care of you."

I nodded and wiped at my nose with a tissue, and he handed me back his mug of magic potion. I knocked back a healthy slug and forced my lips up into a grin.

Willy stroked my leg. "There you go. I'll check on you later. Okay?"

"Okay."

He left the room, and I downed the rest of the searing liquid. I leaned back against the pillow, letting the warmth seep through my every jagged nerve. Butler stood over me at the side of the bed, hands on his hips, lips pressed together.

"Don't do that," I said.

"Do what?"

"Be mad."

"I'm not mad."

"Okay."

"I'm fucking furious."

"See? You're doing that thing with your lips now, and I like your lips. But not when they're like that."

He slanted his head to the side. "Making jokes isn't going to make this go away."

"It will push it back though. It's a special gift I have."

An uncomfortable silence stretched between us. He shifted his weight, glancing down at his boots.

I thought he needed to stay as much as I needed him to. "Stay with me. Please?"

He moved toward the bed, toward me. I scooted over, making it clear that I wanted him on the bed with me. He climbed on, the mattress dipping under his weight, and he took me in his arms. My heart skipped as I settled into his firm body. His long line of muscles squeezed around me as I brushed my hand over the stony slope of his chest.

"I want to ask you a question, and I want you to be completely honest with me," I said.

"What is it?"

"Do you really want Nina as your old lady, or is that just a business arrangement?"

"That was two questions."

I nudged his leg with my foot. "To be clear—are you in love with her?"

"Third question."

"Butler. Please."

His fingers tucked the edges of the bandage on my chest. "I'm not in love with her. It was an arrangement. She wanted to get away from Reich and her sister, get out of Ohio, and I needed a guarantee on a business deal. We agreed on a year together, and then we'd break it off."

"Oh."

"Oh what?"

"That's interesting."

"How interesting?"

"Extremely, absolutely, very, very interesting."

His fingers traced circles up and down my arms.

"You took something from Reich though, didn't you? Is that the guarantee part?"

His fingers halted, and his body stiffened. "What are you talking about?"

"He told me you took something of his, and he was determined to get it back and teach you both a lesson. And he admitted to me that he's the one who rigged Nina's car."

"Reich?"

"Yes. He's also planning on bringing the Smoking Guns together with the Broken Blades. Remember we had seen those two bikers at the restaurant in Sioux Falls?"

"Ah, Jesus." Butler's head fell back against the headboard. "He'd do that to his own club? To Finger? Fuck, he's totally off the wall."

"He's out for blood. Back to my original question." His eyes met mine, and I continued before I lost my nerve, "Is your deal with Nina still on? Even though things with Reich have literally exploded? Because you need to uncomplicate your life."

He took in a deep breath through his nose and pressed his face against mine. A low chuckle rumbled deep in his chest. "I do. How about you?"

"How about me what?"

"How's your thing with Finger going?"

"I already told you, there's nothing going on with Finger."

"Uh-huh." His sharp tone speared my gut like a fish hook.

We needed to leave it at that for now. Explanations and in-depth analyses weren't necessary at this very moment, and I was too exhausted anyhow. No, only sincerity remained, if we dared. Sincerity would wield an unexpected gentle power, and if treated with reverence, it could bear much and transform even more.

"Can I confess something ridiculous?" I asked.

"Yeah, of course."

"I want my daddy."

"Why is that ridiculous?"

"Because I'm a forty-something-year-old woman whose daddy died when she was barely a teenager."

"So what? You miss him. How old were you when he died?"

"I was fourteen. I should be over it."

"Not if you were close to your dad."

My heart squeezed, and I turned my face into his throat. "I was. Very close. Were you close to your dad?"

"No." He ran his fingers through my hair. "What happened to yours?"

"He had a heart attack one morning while out on his tractor on the farm. It was our little patch of paradise, just past Meager. We lived there until he died. I miss that. I miss him. Anyway, we didn't even know Dad had cardiac issues. I was supposed to be working with him that day, but I'd spent the night at Grace's house instead, so we could watch some video over and over again, play with makeup, and then wake up late the next morning and do it all over again."

"You were a kid, Tan. What would you have done if you had been there? Watch him die, not be able to help him, and then be traumatized for the rest of your life?"

I curled my fingers in his shirt. "He was alone. I would've been with him at least, held his hand, told him I loved him one last time.

Ran for help. There was no one to call nine-one-one. Penny was away on an overnight class trip, and my mom was out of town with my brother, visiting some aunt. She got home and found him later that afternoon, all by himself, stiff in the cab of the Caterpillar."

His fingers stroked mine. "I'm sorry."

"Me, too. It was too soon for Drew to lose him. Way too soon. Penny and my mom were always real close, Drew was the baby, and I was Daddy's girl. After he died, I felt like I had nobody to lean on. I focused on showing Ma that she could count on me, that she could rely on me. Penny was going through her teen rebellion at the time and was much too busy flipping out. I didn't want my mom to worry. I made sure things got done around the house, that Drew was fed and clean, that I pulled in good grades, and didn't get in any trouble."

Butler pressed his lips against my brow.

I swallowed past the mountainous lump in my throat. "Shit, I haven't thought about all that in a long, long time."

He took my hand in both of his and rubbed at each finger, one by one. Tension melted off each digit with his careful stroking. "You still have the farm?"

"No."

"You lost it?"

"No, we sold it to one of dad's cousins. Mom found a good job in Meager, and we moved into town. Life moved us along."

"That's what life does." He ran his knuckles down the side of my face. "Try to get some sleep now."

I settled back down on his chest while he hummed.

"What is that?"

"What?"

"The song you're humming."

He cleared his throat. "It's 'Maybe Tomorrow.' Stereophonics."

"Can you sing?" I asked.

A noise escaped the back of his throat. "I used to be in a band in high school," he said. "Lead guitar and lead vocals."

"Really? So, my instincts about you were right, huh, Rhett?"

"Yep." Butler grinned. "We were fucking good, too. Something else I trashed and stomped on."

294

My fingers rubbed at the base of his warm throat. "Sing it for me." I moved back from his chest, keeping a hand on his stomach. "Please."

He took in a breath, his middle expanding. His rich low voice filled my sore heart, my nicked soul, the thick quiet of the small room. The deeply warm, husky quality of his voice held me still, soothed me, stirred me. The lyrics pleaded, wished, full of grains of hope yet full of bittersweet resignation.

I clung to him, his fingertips pressing into me. This song was me, and it was Butler wanting to find our way home, hoping for a better day, but knowing not to hope for too much.

A tear slid down my face, pooling in my throat. I only wanted to ride the wave of emotions in his voice, feel every lyric, feel this stolen stillness with him as the Jacks were in some sort of full emergency mode beyond the walls of this small room.

He sang the last note and let it go in a deep hum. His fingers played with the ends of my hair.

"Did they touch you, Tania? You've got to tell me the truth."

"There was some groping."

He sucked in a tight breath, his hold on me tightening.

"But that was it," I said. "They threatened me with more to get to me, but they didn't get a chance. It's okay."

"No, babe, it's not okay. Nothing's okay. Don't you see that? Through your association with me, you got punished; you became a victim."

"The craziness started when I stabbed Scrib when he got a little too friendly."

"You what?"

"I stabbed him."

"Say again?"

"I stabbed Scrib."

"With what? You have a concealed weapon on you?"

"Wreck's lipstick knife, remember? It's a sweet little piece."

"Tania—"

"Apart from the aesthetics, I thought I'd keep it handy, just in case. And, boy, did it come in handy. Didn't get me far, but in the end, I used it to get Scrib off of you, too. So, that was very good. Otherwise, you would have been in a hospital bed right about now. Did any of the guys grab it at the cabin? Because I'd really like to keep it."

"Jesus, Tan. I'll ask them."

I picked at a bloodstain on his T-shirt. His hand clamped over mine.

"You shouldn't have been there in the first place. All that's on me, and I will never forgive myself."

"You're not responsible for Reich being nuts," I said.

"He's mad at me, got a beef with me, and he took it out on you. See how that works?"

I held his gaze. "You got me out of there."

"Don't do that."

"Do what?"

"Look at me that way. I'm no savior. I'm the reason you got taken. I'm the reason he hurt you."

"You're not the bad guy here. Reich is. Reich is the one instigating trouble. Reich is the one to blame."

He smoothed the hair from my face. His jaw was set. "You got hurt today, hurt bad."

"Yes, and it was awful, but—"

"Tania, stop. Stop."

"No." I smoothed my hands across his chest. "Listen to me. You are not to blame."

His face was ashen. He was exhausted, worn out.

I ran my hand down his cheek. "Do you feel okay?"

"That depends on what you mean exactly."

I gently pressed my lips to his, and he sucked in a tiny breath at the contact. His face seemed pained.

"Butler." I kissed him again, the taste of him arousing something fundamental in me, something primal breaking free.

His cool forehead slid to mine, our lips a breath apart. He was fighting this.

I kissed him again, and a small groan escaped his throat. His hand fisted in my hair at the back of my head, his eyes wild, his fingers gripping my face.

"Today could've ended very differently." His voice was a rough whisper. "I can't lose you. I can't."

My heart doubled over. "You didn't lose me. You found me."

Oh, I wasn't talking about only today.

"You found me," I said. "You did that."

"I put you in danger yet again."

Butler was on a ledge, and I had to get him down. I had to get him to focus, to hear what I was saying.

"I'm here with you right now, and I can feel you all around me—your heat, your breath, your heartbeat. Now, you show me what you're feeling." I held his tense gaze. "Show me."

He brought his mouth closer to mine, and my lips parted for him, his warm breath heating my skin. I could almost taste him. I was poised on the edge of his cliff.

"Show me," I whispered, my hands sliding up his back, his dense muscles flexing under my touch.

He bent slightly, his tongue swiping through my lips, licking, stroking mine, taking my breath away. His hand wrapped around my neck, and the other fisted in my hair while he tasted, he drank, he savored. He pulled back again, his eyes piercing mine, his breath ragged.

"Show me," I breathed.

Butler took my mouth in a wild kiss, and our tongues found each other again. Raw emotion and aching need surged through me. He unleashed a groan, and a burning heat seeped through my insides at the sound, at the press of his fingers gripping my face. He fed my hunger, and I fed his.

"What are you doing to me?" His thumb stroked the side of my mouth.

"What you've done to me." I kissed his thumb and took his hand in mine. "And your seductive singing voice has only made things worse."

He chuckled, the lines of his face finally relaxing. "Well, in that case, you want to hear my version of 'Riders on the Storm' next?"

"No."

"'Gimme Shelter'?"

I shoved at his side.

"I was kidding. How about 'Wild Horses'?"

"Hmm. Perfect."

His fingers slid through my hair, and I leaned against him and closed my eyes. He sang that beautiful song to me so gently, a sensual lullaby. An ache bloomed inside me for him, for his lost happiness, for the tenderness burning in his soul. I focused on his voice, on his touch, and I willed them to blot out the images of Reich and Scrib dancing behind my eyes. All the tension in my body eased and faded.

Bikes throttled in the distance, and the clamor in the building had now waned.

I sank into Butler's beautifully rugged voice vibrating through his large powerful body, a body that clung to mine. And, in those lingering notes of music, we both clung to a thousand tiny hopes, which seemed elusive as grains of sand.

TANIA

THE SENSATION OF BEING CHASED was overwhelming, and my body jerked awake.

Butler only gathered me in his arms tighter, a hand cradling my head. "Shh. I'm here, Scarlett. I'm the one holding you. I've got you, baby. I've got you."

I trembled, a cold sweat beading on my skin. He caressed my back and sang to me as I curled into his chest. His beautiful voice unclenched the steel clamp of Scrib's eyes from my soul, unleashed Reich's laughter from my ears.

The next time I woke up, I was alone. A quick glance at my phone confirmed it was finally morning.

I sat up slowly in the bed and took in a breath, my feet touching the floor. I shuffled to the bathroom, and stared at my dull reflection in the small mirror. I pulled the V of the huge T-shirt further down my chest and tugged the tape from my skin releasing the bandage.

Grace burst into the room. Her delicate features were an austere mask, her eyes went to the red slashes on my skin.

She led me back to the bed and set about inspecting my wounds, cleaning them. I wrapped my fingers around her wrist. Her hand holding the antiseptic-soaked gauze hovered over my chest.

"I'm fine, Gracie. Thank you."

She resumed dabbing at my skin, her face still tense. "I came by last night, but you were sleeping, and I didn't want to wake you."

"Oh. Thank you."

Had she seen me and Butler together?

"By the way," I said. "I called my mother before I fell asleep and told her that I was spending the night with you and the baby since Lock had to go out of town at the last minute."

Her forehead wrinkled. A slight movement, but I knew her so well.

"Say it already," I urged.

"Just like when we were in high school. Remember when you wanted to spend the night with Trip Hofstedt at his family's cabin in Spearfish, and you told your mother that you were spending the night at my house?"

I let out a small laugh. "Oh, right. Trip was sweet. Good kisser, too."

She shot me a hard look. Not amused.

The door burst open, and our heads jerked toward the noise.

"Tania." Finger filled the doorway, his usually neutral, unreadable face was drawn and tight, his dark eyes fiery coal. One large hand was splayed over the door.

"I'm fine," I said, adjusting my shirt so it covered the cuts.

"That's all she keeps saying," Grace spit out. "*I'm fine. I'm fine.*"

"But I am, honey," I said.

"Sure you are." Grace pitched the gauze into a small plastic bag at the side of the bed. She wiped at her eyes as she shot up and faced Finger. "Take a look. See how *fine* she is. You'll appreciate it."

"Grace, don't," I said.

"I'll leave you two alone." She stalked from the room, her boots stomping on the cement floor.

Finger approached the edge of the bed. His index finger yanked down the loose V of my T-shirt, and I pulled in a breath. His face erupted into a malicious glower.

An *F* was sliced into my skin to match the ones on his face.

"Motherfuckers!" he bit out through his clenched jaw. His eyes darted to my wrists and the red marks around them to the cuts on my fingers.

My stomach rolled. "Finger—"

"That's about me, clear as day!" Finger's jaw tensed, his shoulders one long ridge. "He used you to send me a message, to—"

"Please, please don't start some kind of war over this."

Finger's white teeth dragged over his bottom lip. "War's already begun, baby." His gaze ricocheting around the room with the force of a bottle rocket.

I pushed up in the bed. "They can't find her, can they? One of them was with Reich, and if you—"

"I will take care of this."

"Oh, yeah?" Butler stood in the doorway, arms folded, face stony.

Finger spun around. "They took her from you, asshole. What was she doing with you anyhow?"

"I was at Butler's place because I wanted to be. They took me when I left the building."

"I don't need you defending me, Tania," Butler spit out, his eyes flashing.

"Both of you need to concentrate on getting things right between your clubs. That's how you can make this"—I pointed at my chest wound—"better."

They both stood over me, a savage simmer seething between them, hot and fierce. Two warriors, one dark and one light, from some heretical fairy tale. Their minds were undoubtedly swarming with the same images of revenge seeking—bikes roaring, bloodletting, smashing skulls, breaking bones.

But there was another way to take this.

I touched Finger's arm, and his thick gaze met mine. "I need you to do me a favor."

"Anything," he replied.

Butler let out a huff.

"I need to see my brother."

"Of course," Finger said, tipping his face at me.

"What are you up to, Tania?" Butler asked, his voice sharp.

"In this huge mess, I see an opportunity arising for everyone, something I don't think you see—a first step. I want to make it happen in an unequivocal way."

Butler shifted his weight. "Unequivocal?"

"That's right. Do you need me to define that word for you?" I asked.

Butler's eyes flashed. "No, I don't."

"Finger?" I asked.

"I'll make it happen," Finger replied, a hint of a smile playing on his lips. "In a very unequivocal way."

He shot Butler a pointed look, which Butler flung right back.

"Is Catch far away?" I asked.

"No."

"Good. Get him up here fast. And you," I said to Butler, "let him come here to see me. Please. And I need to see Nina."

"Nina? What for?" asked Butler.

Finger lifted his chin at me as he untucked his phone from his back pocket. "You might not be my old lady, baby, but you sure are thinking like one, and I like it. A fuck of a lot."

Butler shot him another leaden glare.

"There's something else I need to discuss with you. Alone. Sorry, Butler," I murmured.

"You two do what you want. I'm out of here." Butler pulled something small from his back pocket and threw it on the bed. The lipstick knife. "This is yours." He charged from the room, stomping on my good intentions with every step.

"What did you want to tell me?" Finger asked.

I picked up the lipstick knife, wrapping my fingers around it. "There was a Smoking Gun with Reich."

"I know. I heard all about it."

"I recognized his club logo, just like her tattoo—"

"Tania."

"Reich has set up the Smoking Guns with the Broken Blades," I said. "From what they were saying, it's been in the works for a while, but now, the Blades finally said yes to it."

He stilled, his back rigid. "Who cut you, Tania?"

"The Smoking Gun."

His heavy eyes returned to me. "What was his name?"

"Scrib."

Finger's jaw muscles flexed. His eyes lowered for just a moment.

"Scrib told me he's been watching your club since things got touchy with the Blades months ago," I continued. "He recognized me from when I came to Nebraska with Grace."

"Figured you and I were connected?"

I nodded. "Then, I opened my mouth."

I took in every twitch and flash of emotion on his face, in his eyes. Those large dark eyes were now saturated in the vile tones of venom and bile.

"You know how he got that name, Tania?" His voice was low, controlled.

"No."

He took in a deep breath, and my chest constricted.

"He *scribbled* on my face with his knife."

That night, unable to sleep, I tossed in my bed, the sensations of Scrib's knife taunting me, keeping me strung tight. A motorcycle engine blared down the road then cut out. I got out of bed, and, gripping the edge of the curtains, I peered out my window.

My heart skipped a beat. I recognized the blond head of hair, the broad shoulders.

I reached for my phone and hit his name. In the distance, the shadowy figure moved.

"Scarlett?

"Thank you for getting my knife back," I whispered.

"Of course. You not sleeping?"

"Can't sleep."

"Didn't think so. I'm here, baby. You go back to bed. I'm right here."

FORTY-ONE

TANIA

"YOU DOING OKAY?" Nina asked me the second I walked into her room at the hospital.

I closed the door behind me. "Getting there."

"Thank God you're okay. You were lucky. I'm sorry about Reich."

"You have nothing to be sorry about." I sat down on a chair by her bed. "I'm glad to hear you're getting released tomorrow."

"Yeah, I can't wait."

"I need to talk to you about something important."

She pushed her blonde hair behind an ear. "What's that?"

"First off, I know about you and Butler."

"What do you mean?"

"That you aren't really together because you want to be."

"Okay." She shrugged. "So? You've been wanting to jump his bones from the beginning. Think I didn't have that figured out?"

"And I know about your cross-country good times with Led on the way over here from Ohio."

She tugged at the neckline of her hospital dressing gown with her free hand. Her other arm was still in a sling.

"Tell me, why did you agree to come out here with Butler in the first place? I know why he did it. Good business. But what makes a girl like you agree to such a thing?"

Her gaze bounced around the small room.

Nina needed a push, and I was going to give it to her.

"Because the quality time I just spent with Reich made me realize a few things," I said.

"Oh, yeah? Like what?" Her fingers fiddled with the cover of a celebrity gossip magazine at her side.

"He's very controlling, and he especially likes controlling you. He really misses it, too. I think it's more than some power trip."

"Reich's been controlling my fucking life since I was a teenager," she spit out, her neck tensing. "I don't want to end up like my sister, being told what to do and how. Having to look the other way. She loves him and likes the status, the rewards that go with him. It makes me crazy."

"Nina, has he ever touched you? Has he ever—"

"Yes!" Her voice snapped, and her eyes widened. "Yes, he has, okay?"

"Oh God, I'm sorry."

She took in a deep breath. "From the beginning, he'd always been real flirty with me, and I liked it. It was fun; I was flirty myself. I had a crush on him when he was first dating my sister. One day, he took it further. He had just married my sister, and I'd stayed with them one weekend. He caught me fooling around with my boyfriend in their den in the basement. He used to watch us. Watch me. Taking a shower, getting dressed. One night, he came into my room and made me play with myself, and he just watched."

"How old were you?"

"I was sixteen."

I sank in my chair.

"He was rising in the ranks of his club," Nina continued. "I couldn't say a word against him. I was afraid of him. He insisted I live with him and my sister. Deanna was so happy; she wanted me with her. They seemed good together, but I knew he had his share of club whores. But that didn't stop him from making me do things for him. He'd make me strip, bring toys for me to use. In his own house. When my sister was at work or at night when she'd be asleep upstairs.

"I knew he wouldn't let me go. If I ever dated a guy, I had to do it in secret. He'd always find out though. My grades sucked, so I couldn't apply to any colleges and get out of there that way. He wouldn't let me get a job outside the club network either."

"You were trapped."

"Yeah. I dated other club members here and there. But I got scared that he'd set me up as an old lady to one of his boys, and he'd keep me under his thumb, keep me as his toy, and I'd never, ever get out from under him and his club. There were two likely candidates last year."

"Was Led one of them?"

"Yeah, he was. I knew he wanted me. Badly. Then, I met Butler. I came onto him, and we slept together a couple of times. Then I made him an offer."

"*You* did?"

Her cold eyes met mine. "Tania, I would've gone to China if I could, but South Dakota sounded just as far away and just as exotic. Butler belonged to another club, and he was a nomad. When would I get that chance again? Never. I figured I could do my time with him, playing the good old lady for a while. Then, Butler and I would break up, and we would go our separate ways. He was going to help me get to LA or Vegas and get lost there."

"That was generous of him."

"He's a good guy. But I ruined that plan when I got caught with Catch. That put us all on Reich's radar again."

"Is my brother just another good time for you or—"

"I know what you think of me."

"Just tell me."

"Why?"

"It's important."

Her shoulders fell. "I couldn't keep away from Catch. He liked me; I could tell. I can always tell. I liked him, too. A lot. So, I went for it. I know it was stupid and a huge risk, but for the first time in my sorry-ass life, I didn't weigh the risks. I only—"

"Felt."

Her eyes filled with water. "Yeah. I felt all right. But, now, I've ruined everything, and I'll probably never see Catch again. I'm sure he hates me anyway for the lies I told."

Here was this girl, this girl I'd once not had much respect for, this girl who I'd resented, been jealous of, sent poisoned voodoo darts at for months whenever I saw her. She'd suffered and carefully plotted her escape, and with Butler's help, she had achieved her freedom. But then she'd tossed everything in the air for a true moment, a moment full of passion and genuine feeling. She had embraced what she wanted, destruction and death be damned.

I swallowed past the thickness in my throat. "The baby—"

"It's Catch's baby. I want to tell him so bad, but he won't answer his phone. I know he was sent away for a while, and now..." Her hand dropped in her lap.

"I have a proposition for you."

She pulled at her sheet and coverlet. "This should be good. Let's hear it."

"Leave Butler officially and be Catch's old lady."

She stared at me. "What am I? Some Barbie doll that gets passed around?"

"Nina, hear me out. Your fling with my brother is much more than a hook-up or two or five, isn't it?"

"To me it is."

"Catch was on the way up in the Flames of Hell, but recent fuck-ups are ruining that. He needs stability, and he needs to show his president and his brothers that he's not this crazed guy risking everything for some pussy. They like that he's crazed, but he needs to be dependable within that crazy."

Nina remained motionless.

"He likes you, Nina. A lot. He told me himself."

Her face flushed.

"Catch needs an old lady to have his back, someone committed to supporting him and his ambitions. Someone who knows what it takes. You know what it takes, don't you? Let's face it. If you stay with Butler, Reich is going to use your affair against him somehow or against you, don't you think?"

She lowered her gaze to the magazine next to her on the bedspread, rubbing a corner of it with her fingers.

"You want to get rid of me. You're so fucking obvious." She ripped a corner off the magazine cover.

"No. I want to protect you and Butler. And I want what's best for my brother." I sat down on the edge of the bed at her side. "What you and Catch have doesn't need to be a secret or forbidden anymore, Nina. You could explore it, live it, enjoy it out in the open. And, now, there's your baby, too. Fear won't rule your life any longer, and Reich won't be able to use you to stir shit up between two different clubs over bullshit the way he's doing now."

Her legs shifted under the sheets.

My gaze caught hers. "Reich is a cruel son of a bitch, and he's obsessed with you. He intends on taking you home with him, to keep you, and he's not going to let anything or anyone stand in his way this time. Baby or not."

"That's all my sister's been talking about. She's been trying to get pregnant for years. She can't wait to get me home."

"Nina, you can't go back. He set the explosion in your car."

Her head sank back against the pillow, her hand covering her face.

"He didn't care if you or anybody else got hurt as long as his point got made, his rage felt," I said. "I got to experience it firsthand. Look, Nina." I opened my blouse for her to see the marks her brother-in-law and his buddy had left behind.

"Oh my God, Tania! He did that to you?"

"He wanted to piss off Butler and Finger."

"Going after women and kids is wrong, so wrong."

"Isn't it? But he enjoyed every minute of it. Every goddamn minute. I figure, what's that compared to controlling the life of a young girl for years? For forever? He will never allow you to leave again with anyone. He will never take his eyes off you. You will be no better than a prisoner if you go back with your sister. Do you want that for your baby? What if he tries to make you get rid of the baby? Or takes the baby away from you? He's capable of anything."

She swallowed hard, her brown eyes searching mine. "I've never been able to tell anyone. Not my sister, nobody. Only Butler."

I wrapped my hand over hers. "I'm sorry. That's awful. Truly. You did something to get out though, didn't you? You took a chance on Butler, and he helped you. That was brave of both of you. But do you want to keep running from that bastard all your life? You have to protect your baby now, too. My brother's baby."

She chewed her lips as she stared at our hands.

"You and Catch having an affair and getting caught actually works in your favor here, funnily enough. If Reich sees that you're leaving Butler for Catch, he'll know that this time, this relationship, is for real. No more grabbing at happiness in secret whenever you can. Or what you think is happiness."

Her eyes darted up at me. "I get it."

"You give it a chance with Catch, and if it works out between the two of you, terrific. If not, you both go your own way. No worries, no backlash."

"What does Catch say? Have you talked to him? Is he still—"

"He's back, and I spoke with him before I came here. He's in, if you are."

"He is?"

"He's out in the hall with Finger, waiting to see you."

309

Her forehead puckered, and she sank back against her pillow. "He's into this because of the baby though, not because—"

"I didn't tell him about the baby. No one has. He wants you, pure and simple. You have to be the one to tell him about your baby."

Her shoulders dropped, her face visibly relaxed. She was relieved. Pleased.

"I came to see you, because I wanted us to talk first," I said.

"Woman to woman or as a lawyer, negotiating?" Nina asked.

"Both. If you're going to do this, Reich and your sister need to hear it from you. You have to tell them that being Catch's old lady is what you want and that you are taking charge of your life, responsibly, not just running off with some guy again."

"You're right."

"I also came to you first because we're talking about my little brother, and I care about his happiness."

Nina held my gaze.

"I know my brother, Nina. He needs a woman he can trust, not just a woman in his bed, now more than ever, and I think he's ready to appreciate that, especially since he lost Jill over bullshit a while back. He knows where he went wrong there. Where they both did. I think, if you put your cards on the table with him from the very beginning, and be straight-up, stay loyal and honest, you've got a great chance of keeping things good between you two."

"I really don't know what that's like. Sad, huh? Pathetic."

"Nina, there is nothing in this world like mutual respect between a man and a woman. I would say it's the most important thing, even more important than love. Love's easy. It's a good feeling that seeps through you like fine wine and makes you all dreamy and warm. Respect takes thought and care. I'm no expert, but from where I'm standing, it's huge. You'll make mistakes, both of you, but it will be worth it. No games though. No bullshit. That time has passed."

"I want to see Catch." She let go of my hand and shoved the magazine to the side of the bed. "Thank you, Tania," she whispered.

"You're welcome. I'll go get him." I rose from the bed, but her fingers clasped my hand, stopping me.

"You're setting Butler free," Nina said.

"Uh—"

"He's got a deep sadness inside him. He's never let me see it, but it's there. I don't know if anyone will ever get through it and get to him, but I hope you do."

"I'm going to try."

FORTY-TWO

BUTLER

I CALLED FINGER, insisting we meet at a gas stop on Route 385, just over the border in Nebraska.

He tugged off his gloves, his eyes scanning the row of dumpsters, the old air pump, and the rusted out steel drums by where we stood.

We were alone, except for our bikes, a beat-up Dodge pickup, and plenty of garbage steaming in the midday sun.

"Tell me," I said.

"Tell you what?" He pushed back from the grimy wall by the restroom door.

"Why the fuck did you kill Jump?"

He raised an eyebrow. "That keeping you up at night?"

"Yeah, it is."

"An unpaid bill that had to be paid. In full."

"I realized you liked being friendly with me because you knew Jump didn't like me much," I said.

"Yeah." He folded his arms across his chest. "And you were way friendlier with me than I think your national president would have liked, nomad."

"I was. I took the risk. But that's between us. And you liked that. I let you in, and I let you take advantage of that."

His eyes narrowed. "And you got your in with me."

"And I got my in with you, and we pissed off Jump, which benefited both of us. But he was my president, Finger. What did he do to you? You looking to step in, take over the One-Eyed Jacks? Or maybe throw me a bone to distract me, shut me up, install me as your puppet, and drain the Jacks dry until there's nothing left? 'Cause that is not going to fucking happen."

"I considered it, but that's not what I want. Not from your club."

But that's what he's planning for the Broken Blades.

"No, Jump and I were never about the Jacks," Finger said. "It was all Jump." His expression remained neutral, calm, revealing nothing.

"I need to know."

"Is it gonna change anything?" he asked, his tone weary.

"I need to know!"

He tilted his head, leveling his eyes with mine. "Once upon a long time ago, I was in trouble, needed help. I'd gone underground, and I was on the run from the Smoking Guns. My own brothers didn't even know. It was an impossible situation, and I'd put everything on the line, everything, but I had no choice."

I lit a cigarette.

The Smoking Guns were terrors that had risen in the wake of the Flames of Hell's notoriety back in the seventies. They had wanted a piece of the Flames' cocaine pie, a piece of the gun-running, and the easy money rolling in back then. They had also wanted the badass reputation that the Flames enjoyed throughout the country, being one of the first nationally organized outlaw clubs. And, as the Flames had spread throughout North America and then the UK, Germany, Sweden, Holland, so had the Guns.

Stupid confrontation followed epic confrontation. Until one day, the Smoking Guns in Kansas took Finger, tortured him, viciously hacked at him, then sent him back home. The point of no return. The Feds had been watching and waiting for the Flames to retaliate, but the Flames had put the brakes on the bloodshed and notoriety and opted for peace instead. That was twenty years ago. Over that time, there had been mini explosions here and there, some grandstanding, but they had been skin-deep, bullshit posturing.

"Was this before or after they held you prisoner?" I asked.

"After."

"You went back to Kansas? You went on your own to get your revenge on the Smoking Guns for torturing you?"

"No. Things were locked down tight after I'd gotten released, after everyone had smoked their fucking peace pipe. What I did wasn't about my revenge, and that's all I'm going to say about it."

He crossed his arms, his eyes wandering over the dumpsters again.

"Point is, I went in, did what I had to do, and on the way back, I needed help. I was heading for South Dakota to stay out of Nebraska for a while. I was hurt. I needed to lay low. I arranged with Dig to get to a Jacks' safe house for a couple of weeks, and he agreed. When I needed him though, he was gone."

"You mean, when he got killed?"

"No. It was when he got married to his old lady and went on his honeymoon. I couldn't reach him, so I contacted Jump, who was Dig's backup man. And you know what that asshole told me? He said no. I was literally fucking bleeding on the side of the road, and he told me no. *No, I can't help you. No, I can't get you safe. No, I can't take a risk for you. No. No. Fucking no.*"

The muscle along his jaw twitched and pulsed. After all this time, his hate for Jump, for the Smoking Guns, for anyone who had ever crossed him—I was sure—was still raw and brutal, embedded deep. That beast within was alive and beating a barbaric drumroll from within his scarred, blackened soul.

"I was stranded, nowhere to turn. Fucking Guns hot on my ass. If they'd caught me, I would've been wishing I were dead. It got so bad that I almost ended it in the fucking restroom of a gas station on the highway."

"But you didn't."

"No, I didn't." He licked his bottom lip, his gaze pinning me. "I managed. I survived and got done what I had to get done."

"And you've been waiting all this time to—"

"I didn't make life easy for the Jacks after that," Finger replied. "Dig was always a man of his word. We'd been doing small favors for each other here and there. When he found out about Jump leaving me hanging, he was in a rage. He tried to make it up to me, but things cooled off between us. Then he got himself killed." Finger let out a drawn-out long sigh. "But Jump...that fucker. I was never going to forget what he'd done to me." Finger pressed his lips together, his eyes narrowing.

"That was 'cause of me, you know—Dig getting married out of the blue. They'd kicked me out for flirting with his old lady, sent me to the chapter up north. He married her in a flash the next fucking week. Things were crazy for a while there."

Finger let out a dry laugh. "Well, don't expect a thank you from me. Things might have worked out differently. Who the fuck knows?" He rubbed his shoulder. "Doesn't matter now. I got safe. Here I am."

"You're a patient man then."

He shot me a look. "I need to be if I want to get the job done right. Any job. Many times, a situation presents itself—like Reich's bomb at the Jacks' clubhouse and I happened to be there. Purely random. That shit is real sweet when it works out, isn't it? I slipped right in and got done what I'd been wanting to do for years. No big fucking showdown, no fuss, no mess—during and especially after. The best part, Jump was conscious. Looked me straight in the eyes. He knew, and I saw his fear there." A subtle grin broke over his face and then receded.

I exhaled a final stream of smoke, and that goddamn dizzying rush went off in my head, that gnawing need crawled through my veins. I tossed what was left of my cigarette to the ground, crushing it with my boot.

"The next best part, I didn't have to get rid of the body," said Finger. "Your club got itself a new martyr and a fancy funeral, not a vanishing in the dark of the night."

"Oh, we should be grateful?"

"*You* should. Without Jump riding your ass, you got yourself a good chance to rise the ranks again, if that's what you want."

"I only wanted back in. *That* was enough for me. To be in good standing in my brother's eyes, to bring something to the table. Not to take away again. Not that!"

"You accomplished what you wanted, and I got what I wanted."

My pulse banged in my head, and that ache exploded across my skull. "And the blame gets placed on Reich's dirty shoulders, just where you wanted it to, am I right?"

"Patience, my friend, is an important virtue to cultivate. That taste of anticipation brews on the back of your tongue for years, and finally, finally, it transforms into a glorious amalgam of blood, satisfaction, and burning pleasure. It's lingering still." He made a sucking sound with his teeth.

There was a purpose to his madness. A scheme. A huge, fat fucking scheme. He enjoyed bulldozing his enemies in a quiet way. If this shit with Reich was Flames club business and not just about Tania, I had no doubt that vengeance would be taken on a large scale, Napoleonic Wars scale with a legion of troops marching across the agreed upon battlefield.

"And Reich?" I asked. "After what he's done to Tania? What he's trying to do to you and your club?"

He focused on me once more. His eyes were clear now, and there was an odd curve to his thin lips. "What was that word Tania used?"

"Unequivocal?"

He pointed a finger at me. "Yeah, that. Looking forward to making that happen with Reich."

I was sure he was, and I was sure it would be a sight to see.

"You deliver the girl tomorrow," Finger said, that husky scratch underlining his voice. "Tomorrow will be a very, very good day."

FORTY-THREE

BUTLER

"WHY DO WE HAVE TO MAKE A SHOW OF THIS?" Nina eyed the security guards at the Flames of Hell main gate who'd just patted us down and taken my gun and knife.

The four Flames stared at us from their posts at the tall, thick metal fence trimmed in barbed wire that marked the entrance to the property south of Chadron, Nebraska.

"You really have to ask?" I pulled her three suitcases from the back of the truck.

Nina's face was pinched, her lips pressed together, her shoulders stiff, her one arm still in a sling. All through this past year—the plotting together, stealing from Reich, lying to everyone—she'd retained her remarkable cool swagger, her own jazz riff of brassy personality, cocky persona, and pixie dust. Not today. Today, she was worried, anxious.

"I'm just nervous." Her eyes jumped from me to the front door to me again. "Ever since the car bomb. Knowing that he did it. What the hell will he come up with next?"

"I'm here, and so are Catch and Finger. Reich's got no say in your life, Nina. Not anymore. None."

"You realize you've probably said that to me at least a thousand times since we hooked up in Ohio. And look how that turned out."

"It's true now more than ever." I slammed shut the back of the truck and glanced at her. "Hey, it got us here, didn't it?" I wrapped an arm around her shoulders, and she slumped against me, her face in my chest.

She released a heavy breath and pushed back from me. "Let's do this."

"You sure?"

"It's a little late now for that question, don't you think?"

"Never too late."

"This works for all of us, and anyhow"—her hand went to her stomach—"what better reason, right?"

For the first time, there was no confusion, no fussing, no pettiness. She was learning to stand up on her own two feet in the real world for herself and now her kid.

"Thank you." She hooked her arms around my middle. "I mean it. Thanks for everything. God knows what a pain in the ass I've been to you, but I want you to know, I'm really grateful. You saved my life. You helped me realize that—"

"Shut the fuck up already."

She rolled her eyes and planted a kiss on my cheek. "You can never take a stupid compliment. Thank you, okay?" She let out a tiny laugh.

"Yeah." I grabbed two of her suitcases. "Ready?"

"Ready." She grabbed the handle of her small suitcase, wheeling it behind her as we headed inside the Flames of Hell clubhouse past members who stared us down.

The big main room stank of ammonia floor cleaner and dread.

Finger stood in the center by a long table littered with laptops and coffee mugs, his arms crossed, his eyebrows a dark ridge. Catch ambled into the room from a side hallway, his face lighting up. I'd delivered the bride to her shotgun wedding.

"What the hell is this?" Reich eyed us from the sofa where he sat with a group of his men from Ohio, including Led, the bodyguard he had sent with Nina to South Dakota.

Led shot up from the sofa, glaring at Nina, glaring at her suitcases, glaring at me.

I lifted my chin at Catch. "She's all yours."

Catch held out his hand, and Nina raced over to him, wrapping herself up in her new man. They kissed.

"What the fuck is going on?" Reich's voice tightened.

"What the hell is he doing here?" I asked Finger gesturing at Reich.

"Reich's been staying here since your little event," replied Finger.

"Event? Is that what you're calling it? This is bullshit. We've been looking for him for days now. He's gotta answer for killing my prez."

"Butler, you need to leave now," said Catch, his arm firmly around Nina.

Reich's eyes bulged. He rose to his feet, his focus entirely on Nina. "I've been trying to call you, Neens. You haven't been answering your phone. What are you doin', sweetheart?"

Nina only pressed her body into Catch, her arms around his waist.

Catch brushed his mouth against Nina's hair. "Nina's my old lady now, Reich. You got something to say to her, you say it to me. Otherwise, you're done."

"Watch how you talk, asshole!" shouted Led.

"Done? Done? What the fuck? *Done?*" Reich turned to Finger, his face red. "You gonna let your boy talk to me that way?"

"She caused a ruckus with my club and Butler's. But all the drama's over now." Finger shot me a look.

I raised my hands in the air. "I know I'm done with her and her shit."

"Neens, come on now. This is ridiculous. I came out here for you, baby." Reich's tone had mellowed. He wanted his addiction back. My gut roiled at the strange soft look on his face.

"You need to come home with me and your sister and let us take care of you," Reich said. "You need to be with your family, with people you trust."

"I'm her family now," Catch said. "This is where she belongs. With me."

"You told your sister about this?" Reich ignored Catch. "We thought you were coming home with us today. You'd said—"

"I'm staying here with my old man," Nina said, her voice clear.

"Your old man, huh? I've heard that shit before." Reich glanced at me, and I raised my chin at him, not giving two fucks.

"You need to hear it now," she said. "I'm with Catch, and I'm staying with him here in Nebraska. I love him, and I'm pregnant with his baby. I'm not going back to Ohio with you and Deanna. This is my home now."

Her skittish gaze darted at me, and I raised an eyebrow at her. She was doing good. Hadn't missed a beat.

"No." Reich shook his head, his teeth dragging against his lip. "No! Deanna's waiting for us back at the motel. She's waiting for you to meet her there, like you said you would. You lying, cheating little—"

"Yeah, she is a cheating skank. I hope you're proud of her," I said.

Nina's face paled.

"You are such a cocksucker!" shouted Led.

"Shut the fuck up right now! All of you!" Catch's corded neck stiffened like a slab of marble, the lines of his face taut.

"This ain't right," said Reich through gritted teeth.

"You know what's not right?" I stepped forward. "This." I held up the flash drive.

The color drained from Reich's face. "What the fuck are you doing?"

"The right thing, imagine that."

"You're nothing but a two bit thief!" Reich's voice seethed.

"I am. I wanted your cooperation on trade deals out to our territory for my club bad enough to force you. Bad enough to steal from you, blackmail you. I followed your invisible trails and found out your little secrets. You knew that if I told Finger what you'd been doing, he'd wipe the floor of the Flames' national clubhouse with your ass. And you'd not only be out but shamed, backs turned on you. Power taken away. Money gone. And where would the great Reich be then? I don't think those VIP clients of yours would come to your rescue, do you?"

"Clients?" asked Finger, his eyes narrowing.

"Yeah, politicians, big-business millionaires, crime lords, a few celebrities, too."

"What are you talking about? Drugs, weapons?" asked Catch.

I had their attention. Every single Flame in the room had their eyes glued on me. Led was ready to pounce like a junkyard dog.

"Drugs were only the party favors here, the thank-you-for-your-business swag," I replied. "No, Reich catered to one of a kind personal tastes. Snuff films, kiddie porn, gay porn, sex slaves—male and female. All made to order according to clients' likes and dislikes. Reich here is a first rate entertainment mogul. Huge moneymaking business and all of it going into a single pocket. His."

Finger's harsh eyes were pinned on me.

"I know the Flames have a history with a lot of that shit—legendary, in fact," I said.

"We shut it down decades ago after too much heat with the FBI," replied Finger.

"Well, news flash, Reich, your national VP, quietly resuscitated it all on his own. Only, this time, underground, way underground. And this here"—I waved the flash drive that Nina and I had stolen from Reich—"this little stick has the private information of every client on it. Not just names, dates, places, but also all their extra-special tastes and quirky preferences. You can imagine, if this shit got in the hands of, let's say, TMZ, right? The backbone of this business is keeping the info-sharing down to the barest minimum. Reich is their only contact. No go-betweens, no secretaries. Just him. It's key for their confidentiality and his offshore bank account, of course. This shit gets out, he's gonna be burned to the stake in more ways than one."

"That's my business! Mine!" Reich shouted. "You've got no claim on it."

"You had that in your hands all this time?" Finger's tone was clipped, harsh. "What were you gonna do, Butler? Use it to bait me, offer it to me like a fucking carrot, to make our tentative agreements go your way? Get thicker cuts out of us?"

"Why not?" I shot back.

Finger slammed a fist on the table at his side, and my stomach hardened.

I took in a breath. "Reich does have a point though."

Reich's head perked up at me.

"This is none of my business. Not anymore," I said. "It used to be a family issue for me. Nina was my old lady after all, and I got her out from under this animal. But she's not my old lady now. Now, this really isn't my business, is it?"

Reich's lips drew back in a snarl. "Give it to me."

I sent him a grin. "I'm giving it all right."

I tossed the flash drive at Finger, and he caught it, his long fingers curling over it.

"You motherfucker!" Reich exploded

"Yes, I am a motherfucker," I said, making a show of wiping my hands. "And now I'm done with you, too."

Finger gestured to his men, and two of them jumped forward and grabbed Reich by the arms. Finger held out the flash drive, and another Flame took it and hooked it up to his open laptop on the table.

Finger caught my eyes and raised his chin. "Get out."

"You don't expect me to walk away now and leave Reich standing, do you?" I asked.

"You don't have a choice here, Butler," said Finger. "You're one Jack among many Flames and on our property. Unless you've got a death wish, you need to leave now while I still give a shit. I got business to take care of here."

"You lied to me, Finger! He's ours!" I shouted.

The Flame at the computer raised his head from the screen. "It's all here, Prez, just like Butler said. Plenty of fucked-up shit. Long list of names and info. Goes back for years."

A flicker of emotion crossed Finger's face. His version of an excited expression. He eyed me. "Reich is mine. The second you leave, I'm going to blow his fucking head off myself."

Finger turned to another brother. "Have them pick up the old lady and bring her here."

The man nodded and stalked off, his phone at his ear.

"What's going on?" Nina asked Catch, her eyes wide. "Why is Deanna coming here? They're not going to hurt her, are they?"

"It's all right, baby." Catch rubbed her shoulder. "We just need to talk to her about what she knows."

Finger motioned to two of his men. "Get the Jack off my property."

Two Flames grabbed my arms, and I jerked away from them. "Fuck you!"

"Leave, Butler, or we're gonna have problems you haven't even dreamed of," Finger said on a hiss, his ravaged face a forbidding scowl.

His men grabbed at me again.

"You're going to pay for this, you son of a bitch!" Led charged at me, his face red.

Two Flames stopped him in his tracks, yanking him back.

"Never trusted you! Never!" Led shouted, bucking in their hold.

"Oh, don't get me started with you, asshole!" I said. "You always wanted a piece of my woman from the very beginning." I gestured at Nina with my thumb. "You tried so hard, but she never wanted your crooked dick, did she?"

"You didn't deserve her, you son of a bitch!" Reich yelled, lunging toward me, a gun in his hand.

Boom.

A choked gasp.

A split second of silence.

Reich crumpled to the floor, a bullet hole scorching the skin of his forehead. Blood spouted from the raw opening, down his face. Led fell to his brother's side, his hands on Reich's lifeless chest.

"That good for you, Jack?" Finger's steely eyes held mine across the room. "'Cause that's good for me." He slid his gun behind his back. The humid air in the room was thick with gunpowder and sweat. The unmistakable stench of panic and resolve.

Unfuckingequivocal.

"Yeah. Yeah, that's good for me." I muttered, grinding my jaw.

"Get out of my club," Finger said.

I shoved past the Flames and stormed outside the building, my blood beating a wild rhythm through my veins, slamming in my chest.

I got into my truck and started her up as the guards opened the gates for me.

They handed me back my gun and knife, and I took off and left Nebraska behind me.

I leaned my head out the window and took in a gulp of air as I crossed into South Dakota, a grin tugging on my lips.

RIP, Reich.

Nah, fuck you. Rot in hell.

FORTY-FOUR

TANIA

"I LOVE THIS SONG! Come on, Grace, dance with me!"

Grace laughed. "You need a man for this song."

"Psht! A man!" I brought my margarita glass to my mouth and took a long tangy swallow.

Dead Ringer's Roadhouse was packed tonight, always popular on its Friday margarita night. A number of days had passed since my insanity with Reich, and I was doing okay. Well, mostly on the outside. My broken skin was now scabbed over but scarred. On the inside, I was still wobbly and just as scarred. I'd had trouble sleeping. I couldn't concentrate at work. All the same, I wanted to get back to some sort of normal. And when Grace had suggested a night out, as Alicia certainly needed a distraction and a few laughs, too, I was all for it.

Tonight, the tables at Dead Ringer's were full of couples and rowdy groups of both young and old—cowboys, bikers, college types from Rapid, and plain ole townies. The dance floor was crowded, and the band was playing a great selection of classic rock and current country tunes.

Grace and I used to come here when we were in high school, proudly brandishing the fake IDs her sister had procured on our behalf. Ruby had been two years older than us, and she would strut in here like she owned the place—ordering a round of drinks, smoking cigarettes, flirting with whomever she wanted. No apologies, and most certainly, no regrets. She'd been our idol, our mentor in how to cut loose and have a good time, how to own it.

Never in a million years would I have thought that I'd be back here with the One-Eyed Jacks, and the force of nature that was Ruby would be erased from the earth.

I need to get my Ruby on.

The Jacks were having a night out for the first time since Jump's death. They needed something to celebrate. Working with Finger's Flames of Hell was proving to be smooth sailing so far on the one project that had gotten off the ground this past week with Butler at the helm. He wasn't managing the Tingle any longer. This, I had gleaned from Alicia and Grace's conversations when they brought me lunch at the gallery one afternoon.

My brother and Nina seemed to be a good match. They were heavy in love, and she didn't put up with any of his shit, and Catch liked the handful he had at his side and in his bed. He was looking forward to having another child. He'd called me to talk one night, shocking the hell out of me. He'd sounded good over the phone, and I was grateful for this new start between us.

Alicia refilled my and Mary Lynn's glasses for the third time. Or was it the fourth? Her emotions were all over the place, but she'd been trying to keep them in check for her son's sake. Wes, too, was a riot of feelings and tempers, and she matched him one for one, from what I could tell. Yes, she definitely needed and deserved a night out and a good distraction.

Amen to that.

Alicia raised her margarita glass in the direction of the bar behind me. "I remember when he first showed up in Meager. Every girl wanted a piece of that gorgeous ass."

"Who? Who?" I pivoted in my chair.

"Butler," she replied with her trademark throaty laugh.

Along with Kicker and Dready, Butler was perched at the bar, his eyes on us. I hadn't seen or heard from him since that night I couldn't fall asleep and I'd heard his bike down the road. Here he was, staring at me from across a crowded, noisy saloon. My heart did a little dance in my chest.

I raised my glass at him, and he slanted his head, a smile flickering across his lips. Those full, luscious lips. I missed him. I sipped my drink and turned around in my seat once more.

His words echoed in my memory, that sensual tone of voice. *"What are you doing to me?"*

Did he'd regret getting that close? Maybe—

Ah, who the hell knows?

"Those gorgeous blue eyes." Alicia let out a groan. "That almost white-blond hair streaked with sun, that tanned skin…fuck, he was a sight. I'd just started hanging out with the club then. Jump was with Ruby at the time."

"And a couple of months later, Dig and I got together." Grace sipped on her beer.

"Yep." Alicia took a swallow of her margarita. "I had tried it on with Butler, but he only had eyes for one girl—in between screwing everything in sight!" She rolled her eyes and leaned into Grace, laughing.

"I remember that," Mary Lynn said as she sipped on her drink, wiping back her straight brown hair from her face.

"Obviously, he didn't screw *everything* in sight, eh?" I said.

What a shame. Alicia had never gotten her talons into Butler's ass. My back straightened as I downed my margarita. Ha-fucking-ha.

Wait a sec. Was she trolling for sex now with Butler?

No, no, no, no, no. Sorry, girlfriend.

A tall man in his early fifties with wavy salt-and-pepper hair pulled back into a ponytail approached our table. Colorful tattoos covered almost every inch of visible skin along with piercings in his ears and heavy silver jewelry draped around his neck and wrists. "Good evening, ladies. It's been a long while since I've seen you."

"Hey, Ronny!" Grace jumped up and hugged him. "Let me introduce you to my friend Tania. Tania, this is Ronny, the best tattoo artist this side of the Missouri."

"Good to meet you," I said, shaking his large tattooed hand. "I've heard lots of stories about you."

"That's what I like to hear!" he said on a deep laugh. "You're all looking beautiful tonight." His gaze slicked over all of us, settling on Alicia.

"You look terrific, by the way," Grace said, sitting back down next to me.

"Thanks, babe. Feel even better." His hand went to Alicia's arm. "Dance with me, Alicia," His voice was low, almost gentle.

Alicia shot a glance at Grace and stood up. Without a word, she strutted to the dance floor on her impossibly high heels. Ronny winked at me and Grace, and then he followed Alicia.

All righty then.

Ronny took the slight Alicia close against his body, moving her to the music, and they fell into an easy rhythm.

"Ooh," I said, "what's going on there?"

"Very, very long story," said Grace. "I gave him a call earlier and told him he should pop by."

"They look good together," Mary Lynn mused.

"They do." Grace pushed her beer bottle to the side. "I can't get over how good he looks."

"Why?" I asked, scanning the saloon for our waitress, any waitress.

"He was always heavy and bulky. But, recently he had some serious health issues. He went and got himself one of those gastrointestinal surgeries, started eating right and exercising, and look at him now. He must have lost over sixty, seventy pounds at least, and that sparkle in his eyes…never better. He looks freaking hot!" She burst out into peals of laughter.

"He does. But what's so funny?" I asked.

"Because I never thought I'd ever say that about Ronny!"

"Right?" Mary Lynn shook with laughter.

"So, he's the best tattoo artist around?" I asked.

"God, yes. He's had a parlor in Deadwood for decades. He was my first. He gave me my wildflower."

"Ah, right." Wildflower had been Dig's nickname for Grace. She'd gotten a tattoo commemorating it somewhere on her ass.

"And Miller and I went to him for our new ones." Grace's eyes widened. "Are you thinking of getting one?"

"I thought maybe a tattoo would cover up these ugly marks on my chest."

Mary Lynn's eyes lit up. "Great idea!"

"What are you thinking of getting?" asked Grace.

I shrugged. "I'm not sure yet."

"Ronny can do anything. He's done a lot of Lenore's work. And you know that gorgeous piece on Alicia's back? He did that, too."

"Really? That's a masterpiece."

Grace's eyes darted to Alicia and Ronny on the dance floor. "That was a special work of art. Let's just say, he and Alicia have a rich history."

Ronny's hand stroked up and down Alicia's back as he held her close, swaying to the now slower music. They spoke and smiled at one another.

"That is certainly obvious."

"She looks relaxed. I'm glad," murmured Grace.

"Me, too."

"I'm going to hit the ladies room. Be right back." Mary Lynn plonked her empty glass on the table and darted off.

Still no sign of a free waitress, and the empty margarita pitcher was very empty. I scanned the dimly lit cavernous saloon once more. My eyes caught Butler standing against the bar with Kicker at his side, talking, but the blond god's heavy gaze was on me. My insides surged with heat, and I stiffened every muscle against the tide.

Grace had remarked that Butler had also been spending a lot of time at Lock's shop, working on the club's go-kart project with kids from the junior high. He was keeping busy, and maybe he was keeping his distance. The last time we were together, I'd asked him to leave the room so that Finger and I could speak privately. Butler hadn't liked that. Not one nasty bit.

Even though Butler now sat across the vast saloon, that singular rush of crazy shot through my veins.

I smoothed my hair back and faced the crowded dance floor once more. Boner and Jill were dancing slowly, both of them ignoring the fast beat of the new song now playing, only talking, laughing, their faces inches apart, their bodies plastered against each other. Ronny and Alicia continued their tango of reconnection close by.

I'd just managed to disentangle myself from a marriage. It would probably be best for me to keep things light right now. Butler obviously had issues, and boy, so did I. Lenore had the right idea with Tricky, didn't she?

Where is she anyway?

I hadn't seen much of her around the club or at any get-togethers. She hadn't been at Jump's funeral. Her store was only a block down from mine, but I hadn't had the time to check in with her. I would have to get on that.

I blinked at the sight of Lock kissing Grace, hard and deep, his longish black hair falling like a silky curtain around the angles of his face, his hands wrapped around her neck. There was something crude about that kind of kiss in public, and it really turned me on. Blatant possession. Raw need. An I-don't-give-a-fuck, this-is-who-I-am-and-I'm-living-it moment.

A long beer bottle clinked against my empty glass. "Hey, Tania. What's up?"

331

Big brownish-green eyes shone at me.

Travis.

Hot-rod Travis.

Mighty attractive Travis.

Maybe there was something to that *The Secret* crap after all. *Ask and ye shall receive.*

I'll bite.

Thank you, universe!

"Hey, Trav." I grinned, sitting up straighter in my chair, eager to greet the new dawn.

Travis was tall and bulky in that body-building-is-my-hobby kind of way. Dark blond hair paired with those warm eyes, tan skin, and an engaging smile made him swoon-worthy. Let's not forget that Carolina accent. Yes, he was yummy.

Travis winked at me. "You looked so serious there for a sec."

"Ah, just daydreaming."

"Good daydreams, I hope?"

"You want to make them come true?"

He laughed, a hand rubbing down his chest. "Hell yeah."

"Dance with me," I said.

He smiled huge as he took my hand and led me onto the dance floor. "I'm a Southern boy, you know. I take this shit seriously."

"Dancing to a good country song?"

"Not only that."

"Oh? What else?"

He leaned in closer to me, a firm arm snaking around my waist. "Making a beautiful lady's dreams come true."

"Well, that's just what this lady wanted to hear." I laughed as he moved us to the Luke Bryan song.

Travis could dance. His one hand pressed into my lower back, bringing our hips closer together.

"Good to see you smiling again and cutting loose, Tania. It suits you. You doing better since—"

"I'm great. I came out tonight to have fun with everybody."

He raised an eyebrow. "You having fun now?"

"Oh, I most certainly am."

He let out a rich laugh.

Travis and I danced to three more songs, chatting easily over the loud music. We sat back down at the table, and he pulled my chair close to his, throwing his arm around it, as I sat back. His fingers brushed over my shoulder as I wiped my damp hair off my hot face.

A fresh pitcher of margaritas along with new beers were now on our table. We drank and talked and laughed, sharing stories with Grace and Lock, and Jill and Boner. Travis had a wry sense of humor. Grace grinned at me from behind her beer bottle.

Yep, it's all good, girlfriend!

Except for that flaming red-hot laser—or rather, *icy-blue* laser—blasting its special brand of heat through the back of my head.

Yes, Butler, here I am, having fun. Fun, fun, fun. How about you?

Travis's phone rang, and his eyes squinted at the screen. "I've got to take this. Sorry."

I waved at him. "Of course."

Grace and Jill chatted while Boner and Lock were wrapped up in an earnest conversation. The damned pitcher was empty again, as were the chips and salsa baskets. I grabbed a basket and the empty pitcher, pushed back from the table, and strode to the bar. I angled through a sudden gap in a group of four girls and caught the bartender's eye.

I slid the empty basket and pitcher toward him. "Could I get refills for our table?"

"Sure thing! Sorry about that."

"It's all right. Things are busy."

"Tania," Butler said, his voice low.

I cast him a glance. "Hey."

"Having a good time?"

"Doesn't it look like it?"

"Oh, it does. How's Travis?"

My face tilted up at him, and I gave him a smile worthy of a teeth whitening commercial. "Travis is great. He's a good dancer. A very good dancer. Great rhythm. Knows how to move those hips of his."

The edges of his lips twitched. "That's a good talent to have."

"Isn't it? Why don't you come sit with us? I'm sure we could find you someone to dance with."

"There you go, hon," said the bartender, sliding a plastic basket stuffed with tortilla chips and a small ceramic bowl of salsa. His eyes darted to Butler for a second and back to me. "I'll send two margarita pitchers over in a sec—on the house."

"Oh, great. Thanks."

"Let me take that for you," Butler said, moving closer to me.

"You don't have to do that."

"I want to."

"Really?"

His radiant eyes melded with mine. "Yeah, really." That come-hither tone of his reverberated in my lady parts.

"You've been avoiding me."

"You got that wrong, Scarlett."

My heart sparked, tossed up, and landed somewhere between provoked and aroused. I leaned in closer to him, and that fresh citrusy cologne of his mixed with acrid tobacco hit me.

"Prove it, Rhett," shot out of my mouth.

His pale eyes glinted at me in the soft glow from the brass lamps hanging over the bar. "Tania—"

"Butler? Butler?" A young woman swung from behind him, her arms slinking around his middle. "Hey, you!"

Ah, yes, of course.

Butler was once a club president. He must have left a trail of groupies along with his notorious party-animal reputation behind him when he blew out of town. Butler's return and his recent breakup with his old lady must have made the rounds.

"It is you, isn't it?" the woman yelped, squeezing into his side.

How the hell did Grace ever deal with this shit when she was married to Dig?

From what little I remembered, she'd never shown many signs of irritation even though I was sure her guts were churning deep down inside. I used to get annoyed *for* her whenever I'd join them for a night out, and she'd shoot me warning glares for me to keep my cool. Even tonight, I'd noticed the occasional young thing gazing at Lock like she was one-clicking him onto her Amazon Wish List. These men left trails of roadkill everywhere they went.

Now, this girl exhibited not a care in the world that she was interrupting Butler while he spoke with another woman. Nope, nope, nope. Here was proof that the women around here still had their antennae up, excited by Butler's return, and there were plenty of others hoping for Grace's fall and probably Jill's and Mary Lynn's, too. Law of nature, Darwin's survival of the fittest.

The girl giggled as she hugged Butler, her layered coppery blonde hair sweeping from her face.

A piece of my heart deflated. Butler got attention from carefree, sexy young things like this one wherever he went. So, how could he be attracted to me? I had just been there in moments of loneliness, anxiety, when he needed a friend. I was the wild card, the dark horse, the one he could have a serious conversation with when he needed to.

She squealed, "I thought that was you! It's been such a long time. So good to see you!" She waved down the long bar at a group of young women who were staring at us from behind their oversized margarita glasses.

"Lori! Shanda! Amy! Look who's here!" She clapped her hands together. "Things have not been the same without you, Butler. Oh my gosh, are you back for good now?" Her hands slid up his torso.

"Yeah," Butler muttered, removing her hands from his chest.

Her smile was as blinding as her enthusiasm. "That is so awesome!"

#TotallyFuckingAwesome.

She was his type, wasn't she? The leggy young blonde, sporting her false eyelashes, sparkly makeup, and super tight clothes for a night out. The party girl, free and wild as fuck. The biker-adoring chick. Only, she didn't look like some biker skank. She looked like a girl my mother would have wanted my brother to date in high school. Effervescent, wholesome, sweet.

The girl stood on her toes and whispered in his ear.

No, Butler and I were two ships that had passed in the night. Well, twice. The universe had given us those opportunities, and we'd fucked them up, or the timing had been off, or whatever the hell.

I picked up the full chip basket off the bar.

Butler clamped a hand over my wrist. "Tania, wait."

I cast him a downward glance as I peeled my arm away from him, and I moved back from the bar.

Butler jerked his head, scowling at the blonde. "Forget it, Kandace. I'm not into that shit anymore."

"Aw, c'mon!" Kandace wailed behind me. "We used to have so much fun! You used to love to lick the…"

I quickened my stride, so I could get out of earshot of that surely colorful reminiscence. That was certainly black disappointment in little Miss Kandace's voice. She wanted her party-animal biker god back. I glanced over my shoulder. Kandace and the three other girls nattered away at Butler's side, but his pale blue eyes, now stern and stony, were on me. Focused, in control.

Butler the Hedonist was no longer in the building. There was no hint of that untamed, hungry decadence of yore. Only this restrained, quiet self-possession that telegraphed that he had nothing to prove. Wasps buzzed around him, but he didn't flinch or move a muscle. He was impervious.

Butler the Zen Master.

Shit.

I was in deep trouble.

I slammed into a rock wall.

"There you are." Travis took the basket from me, dropping it on the center of the table, as he pulled me into his side with his other hand.

Two waitress appeared, one brandishing two fresh pitchers of margaritas, the other, bottles of beer. Travis filled my glass right away and grabbed a new bottle of beer for himself.

I stood up and raised my glass. "Hey, guys!" Everyone at the table looked up at me. "I'd like to take a moment and say thank you for all your support these past months with my store. I couldn't have done it without you. Thank you for helping me make my dream come true."

Lock held up his beer, a huge grin splitting his face. "Continued success, Tania."

"You rock, honey!" Mary Lynn shouted.

"Here's to you, babe," said Dready.

Everyone raised their drinks and cheered.

My chest swelled. *Enjoy this. This is the best.*

Yes, my new start was a success, my dream a reality. I took a deep swallow of the icy drink, its coolness washing down my hot throat, the intense zip of the alcohol warming my insides.

Travis slung an arm around my waist and pulled me onto his lap.

"Whoa!" I laughed, planting my glass safely on the table.

A chair squawked along the wood-planked floor. Across the table, Butler settled in next to Lock, his steady gaze on me. I slid an arm around Travis's massive shoulders.

Travis was younger than me by several years, but he didn't seem to mind. One of his large hands roamed up and down my

back. Nope, I didn't mind either. This was fun and—ah, yes—
uncomplicated, my alcohol-infused inner ninja whispered in my ear.
Grace grinned at me, and I grinned right back. Suddenly, her
smile froze, her eyes widening at something over my shoulder.
Both Lock and Butler's expressions hardened, their suddenly steely
eyes aiming in the same direction.

"Tania? What the hell's going on?"

My giddy euphoria evaporated at the sound of that voice. I
shifted in Travis's lap, my gaze finding the man standing behind us.
I stiffened in Travis's hold. "Kyle?"

FORTY-FIVE

TANIA

"WHAT ARE YOU DOING HERE?" I asked, lifting up from Travis's lap.

Kyle glared at me.

Was he angry or simply confused?

"I wanted to surprise you. I talked to your mom. She said I'd find you here with your girlfriends." He let out a dry laugh. "Guess you still don't tell your mother everything, huh?"

Travis rose from his chair and stood at my side, a hand at my waist. "Who's this guy, Tania?"

"This is my ex-husband."

"I'm still your husband," Kyle said, his eyes narrowing.

The lines of Travis's body hardened. "Sounds to me like you've got that wrong, bud." His harsh once-in-the-military-always-in-the-military gaze swept over Kyle in his All Stars, cargo pants, designer polo shirt with his brown hair pulled back into a ponytail.

Kyle held his ground, his brows knitting under Travis's inspection. "I need to talk to my wife."

"Why did you come all the way out here?" I asked. "Why didn't you call me?"

"I'm interrupting, huh? Are we really going to do this in front of…your friends?" Kyle's lips twisted as he took in Alicia, Ronny, Kicker, Mary Lynn, Jill, Grace, Lock, a stern Dready, an annoyed Boner, a very amused Butler, and lastly, the steel mountain that was Travis once again.

Travis folded his arms across his massive chest. "You're interrupting. You should've made an appointment with the lady. Until then—"

Kyle scowled. "Who the hell are you? This is between me and my wife. Not anybody else."

"You need to watch the way you talk—" Travis said, slanting his head.

Lock's voice rose from behind us. "Trav!"

Butler leaned back in his seat, studying us, his lips curved in a slight grin. I clenched my teeth at the sight. We were entertaining him.

I planted a hand on Travis's thick arm. "Travis, I've got this. Thank you. Kyle, don't say another word and follow me."

Kyle's face darkened. "Tania—"

"Kyle, please!" I pulled him by the arm toward the end of the bar. "What are you doing here?"

"I was in Denver for a seminar this week. I took a quick flight into Rapid City and rented a car to come out here and see you."

My mouth fell open. That was a lot of effort and planning. "Did something happen?"

"No." He leaned against the bar, rubbing a hand across his jaw. "Everything's great."

"Is Celia okay?"

"Celia's fine."

"Oh. All right. You've lost me."

"Tania! I came all this way to see you, and you're puzzled as to why?"

I shifted my weight under his sour scrutiny. It hung over me like a familiar bad smell.

"Those people over there are your friends?" he asked.

"Yes, *those people* are my friends."

"They look like a bunch of wayward thugs and their molls."

"They are not thugs. They are my friends. Most of them own their own businesses and run charities for their community. Please don't start with your white-trash, blue-collar bullshit."

"I'm just making an observation."

"Well, it's an insulting narrow-minded observation," I shot back.

If the Jacks were wearing their club colors tonight, Kyle would've had a field day, going on about biker gangs. But Dead Ringer's was a colors-free zone to keep the peace among the many different bike clubs who partied here.

What a shame it isn't Bike Night.

Kyle's glare softened. "I didn't come all the way out here to fight. I wanted to say I'm sorry about how we left things the last time we saw each other at home. We shouldn't let go of our marriage over a few piled up misunderstandings. We owe it to ourselves to keep trying. We really should. Come home with me."

I was so done with *shoulds*. They'd exhausted me. Kyle had been trying to delay the divorce with little legal tactics here and there all these months.

"Kyle, both of us have been drifting in this marriage for a long time now. We owe it to ourselves to put an end to it and get on with our lives. Have you ever looked at it that way? It's never too late. Plus, I have my own business in Meager now. You know that."

He glanced back at my table. "You're fucking that big one, aren't you?"

"Excuse me?"

"That's it, isn't it? I mean, you're mad at me for what I did, and now you're acting like some teenager, getting drunk, hanging with the town bad boys, having your good time."

"Fuck you!"

"Excuse me?"

"Look, Mr. Officially Separated—even if I were sleeping with someone now—and I'm not—A, that's my business, and, B, why the hell not? I could use it."

"Here we go."

"It's true! I really can't believe you're here, you know that? And I really don't think it has anything to do with me or with us. I think it's your ego that can't accept the idea that you failed at something, at marriage yet again, at being the perfect husband. News flash, Kyle, none of us is perfect, and we all fail at one thing or another at some point in our lives, often more than once. You don't have to hang on to us just because your parents got divorced, and then your first marriage ended the same way. Maybe you feel like you're a part of some sort of failed chain of destiny. We tried, and it didn't work between us. We grew apart over the years, into different people. And you know what? That's okay."

Kyle's face hardened, his gaze darting back at my table once again.

I touched his arm, and his attention returned to me. "I don't want to fix it, really. I'm sorry, but I don't. Let it go. You can do that, you know. It's all right. Let it go, and get on with your life in

Chicago. I appreciate that you came all the way out here. I do. You surprised me."

"See? I can still surprise you, Tania. So, why don't—"

"Please, Kyle. I can't. I don't want to. Essentially, this is about me. *Me*." I took in a quick breath. "And I have feelings for someone else now."

He visibly flinched, his eyes creasing. "So, you lied to me before—about not fucking someone?"

I winced. Kyle didn't usually use the F word unless he was really angry and extremely bitter.

"No, I didn't lie. It's not Travis, the big guy. It's someone else. The point is, these feelings are there, and they're real. I just haven't acted on them yet. I can't ignore them though. I won't."

Just. Just. Just.

"It's one of them, right? Who is it? Which one?"

"Kyle, you should go."

His eyes searched mine, and the silence strained between us in the midst of a bouncy Miranda Lambert song.

"This is really what you want?" he asked, his face grim.

"Yes."

This was it—that feeling of letting go of a piece of yourself. Something twisted my insides and *whooshed* through me like a hot wind.

"The divorce will be final next week," he said, his voice tight.

"I know."

He cleared his throat and glanced at the floor, his hands smoothing down his shirt. "I'm going to go then. My flight back to Denver is first thing in the morning. I'm staying at a hotel in Rapid City, at the—"

"Kyle."

He only nodded, looking away, his lips pressed into a firm line.

"Good-bye," I murmured.

"Good-bye, Tania." He planted a kiss on my forehead, a hand touching my upper arm.

The faint fragrance of his favorite fabric softener and the scent of his expensive Italian cologne rose between us, and my heart squeezed. Kyle was no longer my wretched present. Now, he was my resolved past.

Two young cowboys jostled past me and joined Butler's Kandace and her friends at the bar.

I turned toward our table. Lock and Grace danced a few feet away. Boner had Jill in his lap, his arms around her, as she sipped on a margarita. Both of them along with Alicia and Ronny laughed at something Mary Lynn, was telling them. Travis stood stiffly, his eyes following Kyle out the main door of the saloon.

Butler stared at me from his seat at the table, the lines of his face relaxed, the edges of his lips turned up.

I sucked in a breath.

I want you, goddamn it. The rest is nothing. Nothing but smoke and lights.

Butler rose from his seat, his jaw set, and he strode toward me. My fingers flexed at my sides as he snaked his way through the crowd, through the clink of beer bottles and the hooting, shuffling through the peanut shells on the floor, his intense gaze never leaving mine. His agile body prowled toward me, closer and closer. My breathing accelerated. He was the moon, and I was being pulled in his tide. A force of physics.

Butler stopped in front of me, looming over me. His hand reached out and took mine, and without a word, he yanked me toward the dance floor.

"Hey—"

He pulled me into his hard chest.

Oomph!

Eric Clapton's guitar opened "Help Me Up."

Shit, a favorite song.

Our eyes met, and my breath stuttered.

Cigarette smoke and that fresh forest and crisp citrus scent of his inflamed my senses. His hand splayed across my back and slid down toward my rear, sending a shiver shimmying up my spine.

"The ex get his reality check?"

"Uh-huh," I managed.

"You seeing Travis?"

"No."

"You like Travis?"

"He's very nice. Very good dancer. Certainly not hard on the eyes."

Butler's fingers tightened around my hand, his other hand burning through my waist, as we moved to the driving beat of the music. "Have you fucked him?"

Shit, that question is very popular tonight!

343

He leaned in closer. "Answer me."

"No, I haven't."

"You want him in your bed?"

"Well, I certainly wouldn't kick him out of my bed if he—"

A hand clenched my ass, and the breath swooshed from my chest. The icy blue of his eyes sharpened, puncturing mine.

"Do you want him? Truth."

"No," I exhaled the only answer there was. "I want you."

The shining truth.

Butler's lips curled into a grin as we danced, his grip easing on me. I nestled closer into him, hoping all this *truth* was a good sign.

His chest rumbled against me. Was that a laugh? I glanced up at him, and my heart skipped a beat at the wicked smile on those chiseled lips of his.

"You want to flirt with other men, Tania?" His deep voice drilled straight into my belly. "You go ahead."

"What?"

He chuckled softly. "You know why?"

"Do I *want* to know why?" My back stiffened under his touch as his lips hovered over mine. I fought his wall of heat overwhelming my sense of logic, any sense of outrage, but it was no use. My body was on fire.

"Because it makes you more turned on for me."

I pushed against him. "You're unbelievable!"

"Tell me it didn't."

"It pissed me off."

"Why?"

"I should be attracted to a man like Travis."

His hold on me tightened, his lips at my ear. "Say his name one more time, and we're going to have a problem."

My nipples hardened at the deep timbre of his voice, the press of his hard body against mine.

"I should be attracted to a guy like *him,*" I said. "He's got the whole package—hot looks, engaging sense of humor, captivating charm. But am I attracted to him?"

Butler raised an eyebrow, waiting for my reply.

"No." I dug my fingers into Butler's hair, my nails scratching the back of his neck. "Instead, I have to go the hard way. Instead, I want you. I want you smiling at me, you dancing with me, you touching me."

He made a noise in the back of his throat and tugged me off the dance floor and down a narrow corridor to the side of the stage.

"Butler? Where are we going?"

We came to a sudden stop in front of a heavy metal door. A loud click of a bolt. He shoved at the door and pulled me inside a small dark room. He pushed me against a brick wall, and our breaths grew heavy, ragged. My back ached against the rough texture, but it didn't matter. His hand seared a path up my chest, my throat, across the line of my jaw, and I turned to jelly. My lips fell open, a whimper escaping. I was pinned to the wall by the hurricane force of our anticipation.

He cradled my face in his hands, our lips breaths apart. There was nothing I wanted more than to feel their pressure, their heat, to lose myself in—

"Tania…" he whispered roughly.

I arched against him, as if our bodies were magnets not to be denied the force between them, and he let out a hiss of air. There was awe, excitement, arousal in that hiss.

His mouth crushed mine, and a thousand particles of light blew up inside me. I surged to my toes and met his demanding tongue with demands of my own.

I broke away from his kiss before I completely turned to mush. "Why didn't you say anything when Kyle showed up?"

He grunted, his thumb tugging on my lower lip. "Did you want me to?"

"I don't know!"

He kissed me again, his tongue exploring my mouth fully.

He was relentless. Brutal. Hungry. And so was I.

I knew it would be like this. I knew it.

His fingers threaded in my hair, pulling my head back, and my scalp stung. His blue eyes reflected the shard of light coming through the half-open door, softly illuminating one side of his face. He took my breath away. Butler the Nordic deity whose otherworldly glare had cast a spell over me through the arctic mists.

"I knew you could handle him, and you had to do it yourself. You don't need me to fight your fights, Tania. I know you're strong enough to do it yourself. I know this. I've seen it before, and I like it. Tonight, watching you be strong, be free, be smart—Fucking. Turned. Me. On."

He nipped at my lips, and I let out a cry.

"Always does, Scarlett."

My heart stuttered, and I pressed my hips into his. "Turn me on some more then."

His hands went to my ass and squeezed as he ground against me, adjusting me against his erection. My eyelids fluttered at the precise friction, at the promise of his hard length.

"What did that fuck want anyway?" His lips nuzzled my jaw, my throat.

"Di-divorce is final next week. He wanted to make sure it was what I really wanted."

"A last pitch?"

"Uh-huh."

"Impressive. And is a divorce still what you want?" His hand found a breast, and he rubbed my already hard nipple through my thin blouse and bra between his thumb and forefinger.

I let out a tiny gasp, squirming against him. "Unequivocally."

He laughed as he bent his head and kissed the other side of my throat, his mouth tickling it with the wet heat of his tongue, his scruff scratching my skin.

I was being drained and given a transfusion all at once. "Kiss me, damn you. I need you to—"

His mouth took mine in a searching, toe-curling deep quest. He pulled back and studied my reaction, that arrogant gleam I knew so well in his eyes.

"God, I like you," I said. "A lot. I—"

He shut me up with another savage kiss, his hands cradling my face.

"Wh-what if…what if I'd gone home with you-know-who tonight?" I asked in between lip sucks and nibbles.

His one hand closed over my throat. "What?"

"Would you have stopped me? Or would you have let me go?"

"That question is null and void," he whispered.

"Why?"

"You wouldn't have gone home with him or anybody else but me, and you know it. You want me to fuck you so bad; I could smell it all the way across the goddamn saloon tonight."

My mouth fell open.

"Again, I've made her speechless." He let out a soft chuckle. "When you want something, Scarlett, you're a single-minded vixen." His husky voice bit down on the consonants and dragged through the word, making everything between my legs pulse.

"I'm a *what?*"

"Vixen."

I wanted to taste that word on his lips, and I kissed him again. His incredible mouth tore away from mine and nuzzled the delicate skin of my throat, the sweet spot behind my ear, sending a dizzying coil springing through me.

"I love your determination, Tan. I count on it. You want me? I'm waiting. Break that door down, baby. I'm ready."

My heart pounded wildly. I never expected to hear this from a man, especially not a man like Butler. Yet, here it was, a declaration of passion, of honesty, of many, many orgasms in my very near future.

My head buzzed. I was light-headed, floating, soaring at a higher altitude than ever before. I was being pushed out of the airplane. Scared out of my wits, exhilarated, intoxicated. Did I even have a parachute?

Who cares?

I relished the warm taste of him, his scent—sunlight and fresh air, his strong body holding me tight, and I held on for the ride of my life.

Parachute be damned.

"All I fucking want is you," his voice rasped.

He took one of my hands and cupped it over the solid length of his erection, and my breath hitched, my eyes finding his burning ones.

"You got me here, baby. You did that," he whispered against my lips, his words burning right through my flesh.

He ignited me in another kiss. My legs shook, and I pressed myself back into the brick wall in a supreme effort to remain standing.

His hands went to my breasts, roughly kneading them together. "So fucking sexy, Tania. Wanna bury my dick in these tits."

I let out a cry and tugged on his hair, bringing his mouth crashing down on mine again. My pelvis ground against his. My trembling body flooded with liquid heat. Every nerve ending tingled with hypersensitivity. The desire to give him all of me was intense. The girl inside me jumped up and down, like when I was a kid and I'd gone to a carnival with my family and had finally won the stuffed animal prize I'd had my eyes on all day.

I got it. Me. I won.

"Butler, you in there? Bro, got a situation. Need you out front!" Kicker's voice boomed on the other side of the door we'd left ajar.

My hands gripped the taut, ropy muscles of Butler's arms.

"Shit!" he muttered against my skin.

He adjusted my blouse, and his brows drew together as he gave me one last heavy look, my stomach knotting under the weight of it. I ran my fingers through his unruly hair, and he reached over and pushed open the door. "What's up, Kick?"

Kicker shifted his weight on his pointy black cowboy boots. "Sorry, man. Finger's here. He's looking for Tania."

I lurched forward, breaking our connection, and Butler's jaw clenched. I pulled open the door wider, the hallway light engulfing us. "What does he want?" I asked.

Kicker's dark eyebrows shot up, a smirk on his handsome face. "You."

Both men stared at me, dousing me with cold water. I squared my shoulders as I moved through the door.

Butler grabbed my elbow, pulling me back. "What the fuck?"

"I won't know what's going on until I talk to him, will I?"

"What the hell is going on between the two of you?" he spit out.

"I need to talk to him."

Butler tilted his head. "God forbid we keep him waiting. He comes calling, you go running."

"Guys"—Kicker shifted his weight, a hand running over his dark goatee—"you want me to tell him I can't find you? That you took off?"

Butler's glittering eyes remained on me. He braced for my response. I braced to give it.

"If he came here to find me, it must be important," I said.

"Really?"

"Yes, really. And I need to find out what it is."

Butler grimaced, raising his hands in the air. "Who am I to stop you?"

"Don't do this, please."

"Oh, *I'm* not the one *doing* here," Butler shot back.

"It's not what you think."

"I'm thinking a hell of a lot of things, Tania."

"Bro!" Kicker's insistent voice cut between us.

"I can't explain it to you now," I said, glancing at Kicker. "But Finger has never lied to me, cheated me, or steered me wrong. He doesn't do things without a purpose. I trust him."

A sneer lashed Butler's face, his lips curling. "That sounds like a long, thick history."

"Are you coming with me?"

"What? Me?" he bit out.

"Can't you trust me here?"

"Ah, I should trust you, but you can't tell me, right? Can't tell me about whatever you and him have had going on or not going on for years now?" His voice grew sharper and sharper.

I let out a breath, my eyes darting down the hallway.

"You can't get into it now, but will you ever?" Butler asked.

"I'd like to. I will."

"Well, that's real sweet."

"Butler, for him to come here looking for me, something must be wrong. Something he needs me to help him with."

He leaned into me. "You'd better not keep the big man waiting then. I'll bet you never have." His rough whisper grated on my skin.

I turned and strode down the hallway, my chest loaded down with bricks. The bricks ripped from the wall he had just had me up against.

Goddamn it.

"B!" Kicker hollered. "Hey!"

Behind me exploded the splintering crash of glass and a thousand black curses.

F⊙RTY-SIX

BUTLER

FINGER'S LEGS WERE PLANTED WIDE, his nostrils flaring, his storm-filled eyes on Tania, as she charged toward him.

She came to a stop in front of him. "What is it? What's wrong?"

A muscle along his jaw flexed. "Where've you been? I've been calling, but you don't answer."

"I've been here most of the night. I wasn't paying too much attention to my phone. Sorry."

His harsh gaze landed on me, the lines of his face tightening even more.

"Finger! Are you going to tell me what's going on, or are we going to stand here all night?" Tania asked, glancing over at me.

He hooked her upper arm and tugged her past our table to the bar. Grace and Alicia stared at them, none too happy.

"Hey! What the hell are you doing?" I tracked after them. "Let go of her!"

Finger pinned me with a ferocious glare. "Get the fuck out of my face!"

"Butler, it's okay. Really—" Tania said.

"The hell it is. I said, let go of her!"

"You stay out of my business!" Finger growled.

"She still your business? She's—"

"Please, Butler! Please!"

"You don't have to do anything you don't want to do," I said.

"Tania, what's going on?" Grace appeared at my side.

"I need to hear Finger out. That's all," Tania said.

"That's all," I said, my tone bitter, mocking. "I've been down this road before, and I ain't doing it again."

Grace stiffened, Tania glancing at her.

"Have at it." I raised my chin. "I'm out."

Tania's eyes widened and she looked away. Was it shock or hurt? The black slime of self-loathing spewed through my veins.

"Let's go," Finger said, his voice curt, harsh.

The pounding against my skull intensified at the tone of his demand. Boner came up on the other side of me, the press of his shoulder against mine keeping me from launching myself at Finger, from getting his hand off her arm.

Biff, the owner of the Roadhouse, got in my face. "Take it off my property. Now. You men know the fucking rules. Years now."

"We're leaving." Finger dragged Tania away.

Away from me.

The woman I had lost myself in moments ago—the feel of her, the taste of her, the promise of her—just the two of us in a stifling dark room off a hall in an old bar, yet it had felt like total fucking paradise. I could still feel her short breaths hot on my chest, her eager hands pressing into my body, urging me, wanting from me.

Wanting me.

One minute, Finger and I have a solid business relationship, seeing eye to eye, and now, here he was, getting in my face over the woman I wanted.

He had killed Jump, and I had helped him kill Reich, so he could gain more power in his club. We had a hold on each other.

And he had some sort of hold on Tania. The one woman who meant more to me than anything. The woman who had claimed my heart, claimed me, body and soul.

"Are you okay?" Grace touched my arm.

My head fell forward, and I let out a laugh. The bitter irony of Grace being the one to ask me that question right at this moment was not lost on me.

My shoulders dropped. "I am done with this shit. So fucking done."

"I don't know what's going on between them," she said. "And I've been wishing I did for a while now."

I tore my eyes away from Finger and Tania exiting the Roadhouse. The two of them were probably charging toward his bike.

Toward fuck knows what.

I ran a hand down my face. "Obviously, it's something, Grace. She's never told you?"

My hands rifled through my pockets. *Where are those fucking smokes when I need them?* I shouldn't be smoking at all, but fuck it. I needed something, and I needed it right the fuck now.

"When we saw you in Nebraska at the Flames' clubhouse, they seemed to know each other already," Grace said.

Damn it. Fucking empty. I crumpled plastic and paper in my fist.

"I'd picked up on that, too."

"She seemed uncomfortable though. I asked her about it on the drive home, but she managed to avoid answering although she admitted they'd had something in the past, a long time ago, but I never knew about it. Then, when he was here at the club the last time, she again refused to discuss it."

"I don't know, Grace. Maybe he's got something on her and he's holding it over her head? Then again, she acts like she owes him, like he's a priority for her."

"She doesn't seem afraid of him or threatened though, right?"

"True. One of the few."

"Whatever it is, they seem pretty comfortable—if that's the right word."

I winced. "I don't know if that makes me feel any better."

"Me either. She never talks about him, and I figure if she's not talking about it, that either means it's really fucked up, or there's some sort of secret involved. In any case, she's extremely loyal, Butler. Whatever it is, she won't just share for the hell of it. With any of us."

I exhaled deeply. Tania's fierce loyalty was one of the things I loved about her.

Loved?

Is that why my heart felt like it was going through the shredder, and the only things keeping me standing were my ribs, my legs, and denial?

"I got the sense that she has a deeper connection with Finger than she does with that husband of hers," I muttered. "Or is that just my crazy talking?"

Grace glanced up at me. "No, it's not crazy. That's what worries me."

A bond. Finger and Tania shared some kind of important bond.

"Grace." Lock stood over his old lady from behind, his arm sliding across her chest, pulling her close to his.

Did Finger and Tania share a bond the same way Grace and Lock had from the very beginning?

Getting involved with Tania, getting attached to her, would only be more of the same disappointment, disillusionment, destruction.

Grace laced her hand in her old man's. "We've got to go. If anything comes up, let me know, okay?"

"Yeah, sure." I raised my chin at Lock. "Good night."

He nodded at me, and the two of them took off, their arms around each other's waists.

I stared after them.

It was meant to be for some of us, not all of us though. No, not all of us. I had accepted that fact at Caitlyn's funeral. I had accepted that fact last year after the debacle of me and Grace as I'd ridden off into my black sunset. *It* would never happen for me again. *It* wasn't in my cards, my stars, my whatever the fuck. That was why agreeing to be with Nina had made sense. Because all that just did not fucking matter anymore. Because I'd finally accepted the message I had been given by fate.

Then, Tania had happened and blown that theory to bits.

And here I was, burning.

Burning.

Burning.

I was such a fucking idiot. Still.

Tania was now scarred with an angry red wound on her chest. The red weals would fade, but the marks would remain forever.

That fucking F.

Failure.

Fuck-up.

Finger.

She was permanently marked from my failure to protect her. And marked with a souvenir of her connection to him. Whatever kind of connection it was, it definitely was something.

That light-headedness kicked in, my breath shortening, the skin across my forehead and down my neck tingling with a cold sweat. I wiped at my damp upper lip.

"You okay?" Kicker laid a hand on my shoulder.

I jerked back at his touch. "Hey. You got a smoke?" I bit out, my gaze averted, my eyes springing in their sockets.

He handed me his pack, and I tore one out, tucking it between my lips. Kicker flicked his lighter on, and I lit up, sucking deep on the nicotine rush, on everything that cigarette was, and on everything it fucking wasn't.

My eyes scraped over the bottles pouring out their seductive potions throughout the Roadhouse, the full glasses being raised in the air, tipped to mouths, the smokes glowing in the dark.

I took in another brutal inhale. My chest squeezed sharply. "I've got to get out of here."

"You need something more?" Kicker asked.

My eyes slid to his.

"Get thee behind me, Satan." My mother's voice echoed in my brain.

She used to say that phrase to tease my father when he would bring home a huge box of doughnuts or her favorite cherry pie. Ma was always on a diet, trying to stay away from temptation, but she loved sweets.

And I loved a different brand of sweets.

Those words were Jesus's reply to his buddy, Peter when he had tried to reassure Jesus that everything would be groovy, if only he'd relax a bit. He'd only wanted to keep Jesus safe and alive, but there was no easy way for Jesus. He'd had to face that cross, and he had known it, no matter how much the human in him might have been tempted to avoid it, desperate to avoid it. Peter had just been making a friendly suggestion, but he hadn't gotten it. He hadn't understood the bigger picture, the danger of what he was saying.

Oh, Kicker got it though, and so did I.

The interim president of my club stood before me, watching me, an eyebrow raised, a glint in his eye.

Was this a little test?

Butler's already lost his temper once tonight. Let's see if the coke fiend is gonna rage again.

"I catch you using—just once—you'll be out on your goddamn ass forever." Jump had told me that first day back at the club.

And he was right. Couldn't be a part of a club as a clown, let alone in any position of responsibility, and you couldn't ride high. They knew I'd never touched the harder stuff—the heroin, the crack—and I hadn't. Those were forbidden. Those were worthy of getting rid of you in an unequivocal way. I'd seen it before. A brother unable to cut himself free from the junk, and the club dealing with it by slipping him pure stuff to OD on. Elimination done right.

Maybe Kicker was only asking a bro to join him in a good time.

Maybe not.

My nerves twitched and snapped inside me.

My exile was fucking over. I had paid the many prices. I'd passed through a year of withdrawal and total abstinence, including booze and pot. Coke withdrawal was a deceptive, deceitful little whore. I had at least another year ahead of me of the mood swings and anxiety, the irritability and bad sleep—all of which would come and go without reason. All it took was one little thing to tick them off, to swing me down low, and I'd have to wrestle my Satan, my adversary, down.

Tania letting go of my hand—*Satan.*

Tania taking off with Finger and his crew—*Satan.*

Kicker inviting me to play—*Satan.*

Howling wind blew through that gaping crevasse in my soul that was still desperate to be filled.

I'm used to that eerie sound, aren't I?

My fingers found the hard outline of the key to my bike in my pocket, and my pulse leveled off. I focused on that one singular craving that made sense to me, the one that came second to none. My music was good, it helped, and I was so grateful to have it in my life again—thanks to Tania—but this, *this* was fundamental.

The drone of my engine, the hot metal vibrating underneath me, my grip on those handlebars, the cold air battering me as I zoomed forward.

No thinking.

Only feeling.

One with the wind.

Inside the speed.

Within the roar.

No thinking. Just riding. Being free.

Free.

"Get thee behind me, Satan."

I took in a deep breath through my nose and stepped forward, heading for the door.

"What I need is the road."

FORTY-SEVEN

BUTLER

I KNEW IT WAS HER, standing in the rain, half on, half off the sagging porch of the old two-family house where I rented out the second floor apartment. The dim yellow light of the front door lamp highlighted her form.

A pull dragged on my heart at the sight of her. Was I annoyed at seeing her here? Was I happy? Fuck, I didn't know.

I pulled up the driveway into the garage and shut down my engine.

She didn't move, didn't say a word. She waited for me.

I moved up the steps.

Pat, pat, pat went the drizzling rain over the hood of Tania's jacket.

"I need to talk to you."

I caught her eyes in the porch light. "About what?"

Her shoulders tensed. "What happened earlier. I didn't like how we left it—"

"But you left it anyway. Left me and took off with him."

"It's not what you think."

I raised my hands in the air. "Let me cut to the chase here. I have feelings for you. Feelings I thought I'd never feel again and ones I wasn't sure I ever wanted to feel because they leave me confused, wanting too much, and fucked in the head. Like right now."

"I'm sorry."

"Don't be sorry." I let out a heavy exhale. "Goddamn, don't be sorry for me liking you."

"I like you, too." She reached out a hand toward me.

I grabbed it, squeezing hard, my fingers digging into her flesh.

She gasped in pain.

"Here's the thing, Tania. I like you as a person; I like you as a woman. I don't want half of you, parts of you. I don't want to just have a good time, have you on my arm here and there, have a laugh at a party over a beer, fuck you, zip up then walk away." I entwined our fingers, pulling her closer in to me. "I want you to want me like I want you. I want you to feel like you can't get enough of me, just like I can't get enough of you. I want you to feel that you can't claw your way in here deep enough." I bashed her hand into my chest. "Because that is how I fucking feel about you."

A tear spilled down her cheek. Was she sorry that it wasn't that way for her? Was she here to explain and say goodbye? The steady rain grew harder, louder.

I released her hand. "I can't do games with you, Tania."

"This isn't a game to me."

"Then, what the fuck is going on with you and Finger?" I wiped the wet, matted hair from my face. "Tonight, you flirting with Trav, you hanging with whoever the fuck else, didn't bother me. I enjoyed watching you have fun, cut loose. But you and Finger? That feels different, sounds different; it fucking smells different. You two are tied in some way. You can't say no to him, and he can't say no to you either. And the thing is, you don't want to. I see it in your eyes, his, too. And that spells disaster for anyone else coming close to the fire to try to get warm. That ain't gonna be me, Tania."

I brushed past her and went to the front door, fumbling for my keys.

"Please, can I come inside?" Her voice shook. "I'll explain what I can."

"Oh, great—what you can?" I unlocked the door and shoved it open.

"Please, Butler. Please?" Her voice was just above a whisper, her posture almost humble.

She wasn't up to tricks or a show or a seduction. This was going to be real. I'd steeled myself against her since I saw her on my front porch, but I wanted to hear it. I did.

I let out a breath and stepped to the side. She entered, following me up the creaky stairs and inside my small apartment. She removed her hands from the pockets of her short trench coat, clasping them together.

"Let's hear the speech," I said, tugging off my wet jacket, throwing it on the peg behind the door. "You practiced it real good for me?"

She wiped the water from her face. "I'm going to take all this sarcasm as a sign that you care and you give a shit."

I toed off my boots. "I'm also a damn sore loser."

"You didn't lose anything, Butler."

I eyed her. "Let's go. I'm waiting to hear the big rehearsed and edited explanation."

"Finger needed my help with a mutual friend of ours."

"A mutual friend?" I grabbed a towel from the kitchen and rubbed my dripping wet hair with it. "You and Finger have a mutual friend? Not your brother?"

"No, not Catch. I met Finger way before my brother had ever even heard of the Flames of Hell. My brother is ten years younger than me. When I first met Finger, Drew had only just started junior high."

I threw the towel at a kitchen chair. "That long ago?"

"Yes. Actually, it all started with you and me."

"What the hell is that supposed to mean?" my voice snapped.

"After you and I had our little hook-up that never was, at Grace and Dig's wedding, I left town a couple months later to go back to Chicago, like I'd told you."

"Right."

"On the road, at a gas stop, I met Finger."

"And what? You had a quick fuck instead of a Slurpee?"

"No." She ignored my sarcasm. "He was in trouble. Finger was on the run at the time. He was injured, and I helped him."

"I almost ended it in the fucking restroom of a gas station on the highway." Finger's voice ran through me.

"He needed food, first aid—"

"And a fuck?"

Her back straightened. "He needed to lay low for a while. He was being hunted down," she said, her voice cool, like a lawyer making her case. "And I helped him."

"I managed. I survived and got done what I had to get done." Finger had said.

"You helped him do that," I said quietly, dragging my hands through my damp hair. "What the hell made you help a guy like that, in that kind of dangerous situation? Back then, you'd never hang out with the Jacks. You were pretty much always uncomfortable around us. But a scarred, injured, on-the-run Flames of Hell Finger, you took under your wing? You took money and time out of your rushing back to Chicago to help a man like that? A man you didn't know? A man you should've been afraid of just by the looks of him?"

Her eyes leveled with mine. "Yes, I did."

I tried to picture the two of them on the run. *This is fucking nuts.*

"Did you realize how dangerous it was?"

"Yeah, I had a good idea. But it was worth it."

Worth it?

I licked my lips and shifted my weight. Dizziness weaved through my head. My damp henley felt like a lead weight on me, and I ripped it off, bunching my wet shirt in a ball and throwing it in a corner. "So, a little while after you and me at the wedding, you met him? Him you fucked though, right?"

"Yes."

I let out a dark laugh. A slap in the face, a definitive kick in the blue balls, delivered twenty years later.

"You couldn't finish what you'd started with me"—I raised my voice—"but him—this scarred, probably bleeding vagrant off the road—you fucked? Him you had a secret getaway affair with?" I dug my fingers into my scalp, the jags of pain satisfying.

"I felt awful about what had happened or hadn't happened between you and me at the wedding. It was a terrible failure. Me, the big talker, and I couldn't follow through with the hot player who had come on to me. I got scared. I felt totally out of my comfort zone."

"It wasn't about being comfortable, Tania. It was about getting wild and getting off."

"Right." She chewed on her lip. "I panicked. I couldn't do it."

My shoulders fell. "Tania—"

"I couldn't do it," she repeated, her voice barely audible. "I felt so self-conscious, so *not* wild and so tense about being able to get off. I looked up at you, and you were charging ahead. Getting into it, going for it. And I...I talked myself out of it. I knew doing it wasn't about you and me being hot for each other as much as it was about other stuff going on in our own heads, and that was fine. I didn't have any illusions. But I felt like I was being pushed off the edge of some cliff, and it scared the shit out of me. I wanted so badly to be this liberated, free woman who took risks, the kind of woman a guy like you would go for, but when push came to fucking shove—"

"And it did."

"And it did." She met my gaze. "I shut it down."

"You backed away from the edge of the cliff."

"And I irritated you, of course," she continued. "I made you angry, and suddenly, you saw me in that same negative way that I saw myself—the ice queen who, deep down inside, was just a ball of fear. The little girl who couldn't step up, couldn't let go. I was embarrassed, horrified, with myself. All my little insecurities were cemented in place. I wanted to run and hide, and I did."

I planted my hands on my hips. "I figured you were playing games, and I wasn't doing it for you after all. That you wanted to kick my ass for the hell of it."

"No, it wasn't that. Not at all," she said. "Weeks later, when I met Finger, it was an opportunity to erase all of that. To step up, to be that wild and free person. To finally take that risk. To set that ball of fear on fire and toss it away and really do something different, something wild, and, yes, even something dangerous. To take it as far as I could."

"Jesus." There was a question I had to ask. "With Finger, was it only then?"

The dreaded answer glimmered in her liquid eyes.

She shook her head. "No. We stayed in touch."

"You stayed in touch?" I breathed.

"Whenever our paths crossed, we would meet up."

My pulse pounded in my neck. I could barely believe what I was hearing. But there she was, in my apartment, her lips moving, going on and on and on.

"How long did it last?"

She swallowed. "Until I met Kyle and things got serious. Almost ten years."

"Ten years? Ten years of you and Finger hooking up?"

"Yes. Off and on." Her eyes held mine. "When I saw him in Nebraska at his clubhouse with Grace, when we saw you there, that was the first time I'd seen him or talked to him since we'd stopped a decade before."

"Were you in love with him? Are you? I mean, is that the real reason why you and your husband didn't work out?"

"No. I've never cheated on Kyle."

"That's not what I asked, Tania. Were you in love with Finger?" I searched her eyes, desperate to see any hints of her hiding, lying. "Are you now, after seeing him again, him now being a part of your life through your brother, through the Jacks?"

"No, I've never been in love with him, and I'm not. It wasn't like that between us. It was very clear from the beginning what it was. I was attracted to him, obviously."

I gritted my teeth. "Obviously."

"Neither of us wanted a relationship. There was never any question. Our lives were and are so different. It was…"

"Your walk on the wild side."

"Yes. My secret life. I didn't have to fake it with him. There weren't any expectations or disappointments."

"Just what? Fun?"

She let out a breath. "More of a relief, actually, something of my own that I did purely for me. A high. That's how I saw it, that's how I see it, and I'm not apologizing for it."

"I'm not asking you to."

We stared at each other across the room in silence.

"I'd fallen in love for the first time in college," she said. "I was so in love with him, but it didn't last, and it took me a long, long time to get over it. That gutting, that sudden void was a shock; a whole new level of loneliness. After that, I hated dating; it seemed so phony to me, and I avoided it. I liked flirting. I liked…I didn't know what I liked. But I knew I hated the messiness of emotions, the confusion, the crossed wires, and on and on. I hated wanting things that the other person didn't want, the not being sure they were being honest with me."

"You can never be sure," I said.

"Do you remember how happy Grace and Dig were together? Remember that?"

"I remember," I muttered. "I remember how it changed him."

Tania's eyes watered. "I'd watched her give up all her dreams of going away to school, getting out of Meager to be with him, to live that love. I saw it as her giving things up, but she saw it as gaining something wonderful. She created a new life with him. They did that, and it was…fantastic." She took in a breath, her eyes piercing mine. "And then it blew up in their faces.

"At school and after I graduated, I was surrounded by so many mediocre relationships. Ones of convenience, ones based on superficial crap, on ambition, on money. But Grace and Dig? My mom and dad?" Her voice cracked. "No, those, the good ones, the really good ones, the ones on my altar? *They* were destroyed.

"After Daddy died, I'd listen to my mother cry every night for over a year, Drew curled up beside me in my bed, and Penny in her teen dream denial. And then, the next morning, my mom would be smiling brightly at the neighbors, carrying on for them, for us. I remember the sudden quiet in the house, and my mother's new abruptness. That's what I remember most about the aftereffects of losing dad.

"Then, there was Dig dead, their baby gone, Grace tied to a hospital bed after trying to kill herself, Ruby screaming in the hospital hallway the next morning. Grace leaving town on her own and trying to lose herself. *Literally* lose herself. Boner was desperate to find her. He tracked me down in Chicago, threatening me, so sure I was hiding her, lying to him. I didn't know where she was. I didn't know."

"And Finger was always there if you wanted," I said.

"Yes. Yes, he was."

My pulse slugged through wet cement all over again. "Shit, who can compete with that?"

"I'm not asking you to compete. There's nothing to compete with anyway."

"You two haven't been—"

"No." She took in a breath and leveled her dark eyes with mine. "That night at the Jacks' clubhouse—when Nina and Catch had been caught, and I called Finger, and he and I spent the night together? You were with Nina, upset she'd been having an affair but hanging on to her. Of course, at the time, I didn't know it was all fake."

"You were watching me, trying to crack my code."

A small smile lifted her lips. "I was. And there was Finger, pulling on me. It would've been very easy to do, to go there with him again. But we didn't. Almost but no. I couldn't. I didn't want to."

I went to the kitchen sink and jammed the cold water knob to the right. I leaned over and drank from the faucet, like I'd just gotten off my bike after a run through the Salt Flats of Utah. I splashed water on my face and wiped at it with a paper towel.

"Tonight was not about me and Finger," Tania said. "He's not hung up on me or making excuses to see me. He needed my help; it was real."

"Why? Why did he need your help? With his gun-running deals? With his meth factory?"

"No, of course not. I can't say right now."

"Of course you can't."

"You have your club business; this is mine. How's that? Now, can you please trust me?"

"And then what? Every time something crawls up Finger's ass, I've got to move to the left and step back, so he can have direct access to you anytime, day or night? I don't fucking think so."

"It's not like that."

"It was tonight!"

"Can't you believe in me?" She swallowed. "I want to be with you, Butler. I like what we have, what's happening between us."

"So did I."

Her eyes winced at my use of the past tense. She bit at her lip, her shoulders sinking.

"There's more to this than what you're telling me, Tania."

"There is. I'm not denying it. But I can't tell you any more right now. I've been keeping a secret all these years, protecting it, like a frame on a painting. I need to keep it safe a little while longer. I'm asking you to trust me."

"I haven't been able to trust anyone for years, baby. Especially myself. Now, this? This is all kinds of no. And I don't want to be in Finger's crosshairs personally as well as professionally."

"I'm not worth it?"

"Goddamn it! You're worth everything!" I yelled.

Her eyes blazed, her lips parted, under the force of those words, the emotion in my voice.

I took in a breath. "But you not being able to share with me, you putting Finger and his club over me and my club? I can't have that. I can't live with that, and you can't expect me to either."

"You're right, but I'm asking anyhow. Because I think what we have is special, and I don't want to lose it."

"You have a funny way of showing it, Tania." I shook my head. I knew I was right. I was. Everything I'd said to her was logical, practical. "Go home. Get some sleep. It's late."

Her lower lip quivered. "I don't want to go home."

I squeezed my eyes shut.

"I want to be with you," she whispered. "I want you."

"You just want to prove something now."

She stepped toward me, her dark eyes flaring. "You and I drove back into the club together that day, and then I heard the words 'your old lady.' I swallowed them down and shoved it *all* away, sealed it up tight—everything I felt, everything I thought, the memories of your every touch, every kiss, every hot breath, every word you whispered on my skin."

My heart thudded in my chest.

"I wanted more," she continued. "But, suddenly, you were taken. You hadn't been honest with me. The night before that, you'd had your hand between my legs, your mouth on mine, and suddenly, you were off-limits. You belonged to someone else. Any possibilities were crushed." Her voice shook, her words burning a hole right through me. "So, I was respectful. I kept away. But, now, you're free, and so am I. Can't we just start again?" She swallowed hard, her eyes searching mine.

Tania emotional, Tania needy, Tania vulnerable.

Tania wanting me like I wanted her.

"Butler," she whispered hoarsely. "I'm trying to claw my way into your heart here."

I grabbed her and crashed my mouth down over hers. She shuddered in my tight hold, and I fucking liked it.

I ripped off her wet coat and tossed it to the floor. I quickly unfastened her jeans and shoved them down her hips. "Off. Now."

Our breathing grew harder and shorter.

She toed off her high heeled sandals. She pushed her jeans down her legs and yanked them off her body, losing her balance as she went. I gripped her arm, and she glanced up at me.

Fear of the unknown, and challenge accepted.

That's right.

She lifted her blouse, her hair flying around her face, through my hands.

I whipped her around in my arms and pressed her back against me. I ripped down her panties and sank my hand in between her

365

legs. She jumped forward like a skittish deer, gasping loudly. I gripped her hips and shoved her back against my dick.

"What's this pussy gonna feel like, taking my cock?" I whispered. "It's all I've been thinking about since I first touched it." I dragged my fingers through her wet heat. "You're gonna fucking take it now."

"Am I?"

"Hell yes."

"Give me your best, blondie."

"Your sweet talk is only making me harder, Scarlett."

"I fucking hope so."

I shoved her facedown on the sofa and got rid of my jeans. I nabbed a condom from the drawer in my coffee table, put it on, and grabbed her again, adjusting her back at an angle. I slicked her wetness over the tip of my cock, and her whimpers and squirming at my touch drove my lust higher. I thrust inside her, keeping it short and shallow. She gasped.

"This is just the beginning. Can you take it?" I said.

"Fuck you!"

I pounded into her, thrusting deep this time.

Her body tensed around me, her sobs satisfying the animal in me.

Yes.

Her head rose up, her neck straining, her shoulders tightening under my onslaught.

"That's it," I spit out through gritted teeth, clenching her incredible ass.

She flinched in my hold, and I shoved her back down and rammed into her, my fingers clamping on her flesh. She grunted loudly, gasping, with every hard thrust. I smacked an ass cheek and stroked it, her skin hot under my hand.

"Your husband give it to you like this?"

"No-no—"

But I bet Finger did. Motherfucker.

I did battle to get images of him fucking Tania every which way from Sunday out from behind my eyes. I wanted to annihilate them forever from her memory.

I fucked her harder, faster, and she let out a low cry.

Tilting my hips, I hit her from a different angle, grunting with the effort. Her cunt fisted around my cock.

"Oh, damn, oh, damn!"

"Got you right where I want you," I said.

"Under you?"

"Yes." I let out a hiss. "And all fucking mine."

I leaned over her and burrowed deeper, rolling my hips, screwing into her. She moaned loudly, and I slowed my pace, dragging out my dick.

"What are you—ah!" Her back arched as I rocked back in, feeling her settle and tighten around me once again. Her back relaxed.

"Don't get comfortable, Scarlett."

I licked my thumb and gently teased her asshole, and it puckered, tensed.

"You like that, don't you? You want that?"

Her muscles relaxed with my words, and she pushed back against me. Her gasps and whimpers made me high, the sound of our fucking sending me soaring. I let go of her ass, dug my hands into her hips, and jackhammered inside her pussy.

No fucking prisoners.

The need to see her, to experience her coming apart in my hands, surged inside me. I pulled out and flipped her over on her back. With one knee on the sofa, holding her legs apart, I drove inside her again, leaning over her.

Her dark eyes were wild now, pulling me in.

"I see you"—my voice was all rough edges—"Fuck, baby."

"Yes, yes." She clutched my arms, her back arching. She shouted something unintelligible, shuddering in my tight grip, throbbing around my cock.

"Tania!" I exploded.

Everything blanked.

Everything.

My resentment, my petty jealousy, my fear.

And only Tania remained.

I collapsed onto her on the couch. She moved to the side and curled into me.

My hand slid over her hip. "For all your bitch sass, you like me taking the lead, don't you, Scarlett?"

Her tongue flicked out to swipe the side of her mouth, her chest rising and falling quickly. "That was cathartic."

I stroked the smooth skin along her lower back and back down her ass. She squirmed against me.

"I think that's the most intriguing compliment I've ever gotten after a round."

"Don't you dare talk to me about going rounds with other women when you have your cock inside me."

"Absolutely right." I took her mouth, my hand stroking a breast. "And my cock loves being inside you."

She laughed, burying her face in my chest.

"You must be really overwhelmed right now by all the pressure, huh? The store, your mom, the divorce. Me."

"Kyle's daughter calling this morning," she added.

"Ah, shit." I pulled out of her and got rid of the rubber.

She turned in my arms and faced me more fully, a leg hitching over my hip. "You took all that away just now. I didn't have to make a decision. I didn't have a chance to analyze. You made me let it all go."

"I have to make you?"

"Sometimes." She curled into me further, her face in my throat. "I think I need that," she whispered, her fingertips tracing a line along my jaw. "I liked that with you. Safe and wild at the same time."

She was being shy, vulnerable, telling me what she needed. Beautiful. *Priceless.* Heat swirled in my chest.

"If you want to come, baby, you've got to let that shit go."

"I definitely want to come. I came right now in a big way, and I want to keep coming."

"I can help you with that." I nipped her bottom lip with my teeth.

She let out an almost inaudible cry. "Yes, yes, you can."

Tania nestled her pelvis against mine, and I chuckled softly, as she released a drawn out sigh at the sensations.

"Secret is, you trusting me to give it to you."

And I so wanted to give it to her. Everything she wanted. Over and over again.

"Interesting." Her lips brushed over my chest. "There's that word again—*trust.*"

"Yeah."

Silence.

She brushed her hair from her face and pushed back from me to sit up. "I need to get home. I can't leave my mother alone at night when she's sleeping. She gets up sometimes and—"

"Right. Of course."

She stood up and found her clothes and got dressed as I watched her from the sofa.

I grabbed my boxer briefs from the floor and slid them on. "You okay to drive? Let me take you."

"No. I'm good. I had lots of coffee before."

Coffee with Finger.

I went to my door, holding it open for her. I followed her down the stairs and outside to the porch. The rain had stopped, the porch steps, the cracked cement walkway glistened in the light of the street lamp.

She raised up and kissed me softly. "Goodnight."

"Goodnight."

Tania got in her car. She pulled out of the road, and her red taillights were swallowed up in the darkness as she drove away. But the sweet press of her lips on mine remained.

FORTY-EIGHT

TANIA

I HATED THREE O'CLOCK in the afternoon with a passion.

Every day without fail three o'clock came, and all I ever wanted to do was close my eyes and lose consciousness. All I needed was a five or ten minute snooze to reboot, but today, stealing a quick nap was impossible. No, I'd gone to the bank to apply for a small business loan. Yippee, oh, what fun it was. Now, I had to get back to the store and tackle the long list of phone calls I needed to make.

First, however, I stopped in at the Meager Grand Cafe, owned by Erica, an old friend from high school, to get one of her mega-size gourmet coffees to get me in gear. Erica's family had once run a restaurant, Drake's Cafe, on the very same spot, a family favorite for generations. Dad would treat us there for dinner on his rare free Saturdays before planting season. Erica had taken over the aging restaurant about six years ago and had transformed it into a coffeehouse extraordinaire.

I stirred the thick dribbles of half-and-half in my steaming hot very tall cup of Tanzania at the condiment counter. The creamy swirls I created on the surface of the black brew were pretty. I took a sip. *So good.*

I chewed on the wooden stir stick. My mind went back to me and Butler at his apartment. He hadn't answered my question of him trusting me. No, that particular thorny issue had not been resolved, had it? The following day he had texted me that he had to go out of town on business, and I hadn't heard from him in three days.

Good sex can either bring people together, or it can cause mighty doses of confusion and awkwardness. I figured he'd call me or come see me when he was ready.

My phone dinged. I put the coffee down and reached into my bag. A text from Grace.

Are u going to answer my calls? :(:(:(Or do u not have cell service in Nebraska???

Cute.

I hadn't spoken with Grace since I'd left Dead Ringer's with Finger. Did she really think I'd ridden off with him into the Nebraska sunset? I owed her an explanation.

I tapped on her name, putting a phone call through. She immediately picked up.

"Hey."

"Tania! Finally. Are you okay?"

"I'm fine," I replied.

"There she goes again with the *fine*."

"Grace—"

"Where are you?"

"Not in Nebraska, that's for sure. I'm at Meager Grand."

"I'd stop by, but I'm on my way to a Mommy and Me class with Thunder. God, I haven't been to the Grand in so long."

"We'll make a coffee date for another time. I can't stay anyway. I'm procrastinating. I have to get to the store and—"

"Don't do this to him."

My neck stiffened. "What?"

"To Butler. Don't lead him on. Don't be with him if it's really someone else you're obsessing over."

"It's not like that."

"That's what it looked like the other night at Dead Ringer's, Tania. To all of us."

"Well, that's wrong."

"I already did that to him." Her voice lowered. "So, please, please don't you do it, too. He doesn't deserve it."

My breath caught at Grace's confession of her sins.

I turned toward the wall, hunching over my coffee. "I agree. He doesn't deserve that. But I'm not obsessing over anyone else. I've been obsessing over *him* for a long time, in fact."

"Over who? You're confusing me, damn it!"

"Butler, damn it!" I whispered loudly into my phone.

"Really?"

"Really!"

"Good! I'm so glad. I was hoping."

"You were?" I asked.

"Yes. You think I haven't noticed? Geez!"

"You care about him that much, don't you?"

"I always have and always will." Her voice was steely. "And I'm not going to let anyone fuck with him, despite good intentions and mysterious doings."

I smiled to myself.

"Tania? You still there? You hate me now?"

"No, bitch. I love you," I whispered. "And I love that you care about him after all these years, after everything."

"I'm concerned about him. The other night at Dead Ringer's, after you left, he was upset and took off alone on his bike. I was worried he might go back to old habits. Now, he's been away for a few days on a run through Wyoming."

"Wyoming?"

"You need sugar with that?"

My pulse skidded at the sound of that voice.

Butler stood next to me at the side counter, his pale blue eyes flickering over me.

My road gladiator had returned.

I cleared my throat. "Um, I've got to go, Grace. Call you later."

"Wait! Who was that?"

"Don't worry about Butler. I just found him. Or he just found me. Bye."

I stared into those heaven-splashed eyes, sending me into a sublime numbness, as my phone dropped onto the counter. "Um, no, I don't like sugar in my coffee."

"You don't say."

"I do say."

His lips turned up at the corners. "Then, why are you hogging the sugar section here?"

"Sorry, could you—" A woman stretched a hand out toward the stainless steel pitcher of almond milk.

I grabbed my phone and shuffled back a step.

"Excuse me," piped up a tall teenage guy with a lock of bright green hair in his eyes.

Butler's hand went around my bicep, pulling me toward him and further into the coffee shop. The place was crowded, not one cozy gray love seat or peachy upholstered easy chair available. He ushered me to the far wall, and we placed our coffees on the strip of wooden bar along the stone facade. He released me from his iron grip, and I rocked back on my heels to steady myself.

"How are you?" he asked, a hand running over the golden stubble on his sculpted chin.

My face heated. Words wouldn't come out of my mouth.

His eyes slowly swept up my body and down again. A searing flare erupted inside me, spreading its heat as it went. Shit, he didn't even have to touch me, and I went off.

"Look at you." His voice was warm, appreciative, aroused.

"I had a meeting at the bank. I had to get out the pencil skirt and heels."

"Is that what they call it? A pencil skirt? I can see why."

"I don't know if my appearance swayed Mr. Hessler, but I tried my very best to impress." I batted my eyelashes.

"I'm sure you did, Scarlett. Did he approve your loan?"

"I don't know yet. I should be hearing from them soon."

His eyes narrowed. "You want me to strong-arm this Hessler guy for you?"

"Well, that's a tempting offer, but no, thank you." I sipped on my coffee.

"You expanding the business already?"

"Actually, Neil and I are buying up the rest of Gerhard and Astrid's pieces. I kept in touch with Dave, the nephew, in Sioux Falls. I did what I could with the cash I had, but now, I need to make up the difference with Neil."

"That's great news."

"It is. Gerhard's work is my next show at the gallery. Neil is working on putting together a private viewing of some of the key pieces to show several museum curators he's been in touch with. I'm very excited that it's all coming together."

He stared at my mouth.

"Butler? What is it?"

"I want us to *come together*."

"Oh God." My grip on my coffee mug tightened.

"I've got to be in *private* with you, too. Something fierce." He plucked my coffee from my hand and plonked it on the bar next to his. He pulled on me.

"What are you doing?"

"Finding some private."

"What about our coffees?"

He dragged me toward the back, and the line of people waiting for their orders parted for us. He banged open a door to one of the two unisex restrooms and swiftly slammed it behind us.

"Lock it," he rasped against my mouth, his hands cupping my face.

He licked my lower lip, and my heart hammered in my chest. *God, how I missed him.*

I reached out, my hand sliding across the smooth panel of wood, grasping the knob. I jammed in the round button with a loud click. His mouth crushed mine, and I opened up to him.

"Hell yes," he breathed in between kisses.

His taste surged in my mouth, and a melting heat seeped through me. Coffee and warmth and man. The ache I had shuttered and bound up for so long now pounded against the doors, and I was setting it free. I danced and was being twirled. I spun on exploding nerves and excitement. I was at the top of the roller coaster, looking down, my every muscle tight. Feverish, exhilarated. My fingers pulled on the thick, soft waves of his hair.

Butler turned me to face the mirror over the sink of the small restroom, his erection firmly up against my ass. Our eyes held our reflection in the mirror. I was helpless in his grip. His hostage.

I loved it when he did this.

I leaned my head against his chest as his hand passed under my jaw, his fingers over my lips. I took his thumb in my mouth on a moan. Animal instinct. Base lust. All of it wrapped into one blaring call of the wild. His other hand went to my breast and stroked it over my thin crepe blouse. My tongue lashed over his warm, salty skin, my mouth sucking on his thumb as if I couldn't get enough of it.

I couldn't.

A tower of heat and pleasure built fast inside me, staking my frenzied heartbeat at the very top of that tower, like a flag snapping in the strong wind.

His hand slid down to my middle and then between my legs where he rubbed over the thin fabric of my skirt. My defenseless body trembled.

His chest was a wall of heat at my back. He tugged his thumb a few degrees out of my mouth, and it pulled on my lower lip.

"You gonna suck on my cock like that, baby?" His eyes were heavy, almost a shade darker now, like molten lapis.

I took his thumb between my lips again. I needed it.

He licked at my ear. "Be a good girl and suck it hard."

A groan escaped my wet lips as they worked his thumb. His breath got ragged, and I liked it.

My eyes widened as he released his thumb from my mouth and turned me around. He tugged my skirt up, yanked my panties off my legs, and raised me up onto the counter. Spreading my thighs, he dropped to his knees. Those eyes glimmered at me as he buried his mouth between my legs.

Hallelujah!

A satisfied noise rose from his throat.

My hand slammed against the tiled wall as my breath caught. His grip on me tightened, his tongue licking, his lips sucking.

The door pulled, thudded, and I froze.

"Oh, sorry!" came a girl's voice from the other side of the door.

Butler's eyes shot up at me, and he kept licking, kept sucking, steadily increasing the pressure.

Hell yes.

I struggled for air. For sanity. For more of his incredible mouth.

"Is someone in there? What's going on?" the voice insisted.

"B-be right out!" I managed.

"Oh, but I'm going in, baby," murmured Butler against my sensitive skin. "Don't make me a liar now." Two of his fingers entered me and moved in quick, short motions, stroking.

"Holy shit." My head fell back as my panting grew even more intense. I moaned loudly, and I didn't care.

There was no more oxygen to be had in this fucking tiny restroom. Oh, who the hell needed air? I only needed my Butler-designed orgasm.

Right the hell *now*.

The door rattled. "Hey! Butler are you in there? What's going on?"

What the hell?

The frantic noise only seemed to set Butler on fire. He removed his fingers and sucked hard on my clit, then pressed against it with the flat of his tongue.

Light exploded behind my eyelids.

I came, jerking in his hold, and he held me down on the counter, his magic tongue continuing its incantations over me. The sensations were extreme, intense, and I welcomed every one. Every single crazy one.

My body went limp, and he kissed the side of a thigh. I attempted to steady myself on the counter, my arms straining, my eyes blurry. Butler helped me off the counter.

I smoothed down my skirt as he adjusted his jeans. He scooped up my panty from the floor and held it out to me on one finger. I grabbed it, stuffed it in my bag, and he kissed me. I relished the taste of me on his mouth. He released me and washed his hands before splashing water on his face and drying off with a paper towel I'd handed him from the dispenser.

Those blue eyes met mine in the mirror, and I blushed.

"Oh, Scarlett," he whispered, taking my hand in his and kissing it. "Look at you, baby."

I grinned through my daze.

Butler clicked the lock and pulled open the door.

"Hey! Get a room!"

Kandace and her three pals, Lori, Shanda, and Amy stood in the narrow hallway. Their eyes widened at the sight of Butler as if he were their favorite book boyfriend unexpectedly come to life.

"I can't help it if I'm always hungry for my woman, Kandace." he replied with a wink, shooting his fairy dust over the four ladies as he steered me out of their way.

"Holy crap, did you really just say that?" Kandace's mouth gaped open. "Yes, you did!"

"Boom," said Shanda.

"I can't even!" exclaimed Lori.

"Damn," murmured Amy.

Their squeals and laughter followed us down the hallway.

"Are they stalking you?" I asked.

"It's been known to happen."

We strode out of Erica's coffee shop, and I gulped in the fresh air, blinking in the stark sunshine. A new day had dawned. Yes, the new dawn of Butler and Tania. To think, when we'd first known each other, we'd continually treated each other with contempt, had no use for one another.

A smile tugged at my lips.

"What are you smiling about?" he asked, getting out a pack of cigarettes. "Or do I need to ask?"

"I was thinking, Dig's probably laughing hysterically behind the pearly gates at this very moment."

Butler laughed. "I'll bet he is. The Ice Queen and his crazy lost boy."

"Lost boy?"

He lit his smoke. "When he and I first met, I was bumming around on different beaches in Northern California, dealing weed, prescription drugs, whatever I could get my hands on to make a buck. All I wanted was to surf, to hang out. He compared me to one of Peter Pan's Lost Boys. That's when he told me to come out to South Dakota with him. He loved the ocean, had never seen the Pacific before. I think it was on his bucket list. He understood that I didn't want to leave it. But it hit me. There comes a time when you've got to go forth into the world and discover more, and I did that, with him. Made me stand up on my own two feet. Made me grow up."

"Eventually."

He hooked an arm around me and pressed his lips against my forehead. "Yeah, eventually." He laughed again.

That rich laugh, that I-don't-give-a-fuck-what-anyone-thinks-of-me laugh was like a favorite song I had forgotten about but was excited to hear again on the radio, totally by chance.

"You know something," I said. "I probably wouldn't be who I am today if it wasn't for you and one of the ugliest thirty minutes of my life in the back of Wreck's repair shed."

"Hmm. Very ugly," he murmured, his eyes narrowing, his lips twitching.

"I'm curious—at the wedding, after you took off from the shed, did you go back to the party and find another girl to screw, like you'd said?"

"No, actually, I didn't." His eyes lit up. "I didn't even go back to partying. I sobered up with water and coffee, got on my bike, and headed back up to North Dakota. Some sort of click had gone off inside me. I knew then that I had to try something different, that I had nothing more to lose and everything to gain. I dug in my heels at my club—paid attention, got involved, listened. I rose the ranks, and best of all, I mended fences with Dig. When I met Caitlyn, I was ready for her."

"Our ugly was good for you, too, huh?" I wrapped my arms around him.

"Yeah, it was." He pulled me in close, brushing my lips with his.

"I wasn't sure I'd hear from you after the other night. I thought maybe we'd gotten each other out of our systems with—"

"A good fucking?"

"A very, very good fucking." I grinned.

"I'm not getting you out of my system, Scarlett. I think I just proved that in the restroom of the Meager Grand." He laughed again and pulled back from me, tucking his lighter back in his pocket. His face was drawn as he exhaled the smoke to the side.

"It's a very nice coffee shop," I said.

"It sure is," he said, his eyes holding mine.

"I like that you felt the urge so strongly that you couldn't wait."

"I got carried away."

I sucked in a loud breath on purpose. "You're still impulsive and hedonistic deep down in there. I knew it."

"You bring it out of me, Scarlett." He exhaled a stream of smoke from between his lips.

Those lips. Taunting me, teasing me, licking me into a fever.

"You mean, I'm responsible for a Butler Renaissance?" I asked.

"Jesus."

"What? You don't like that?"

"I like it. A lot."

My hands gripped the leather handles of my handbag, my legs squeezing together. "Could we perhaps continue this somewhere else? If you're free, that is. I am. I'm free."

"I'm free. You don't have to be at the store?"

"I have a few phone calls to make, but I can take care of them tomorrow. I deserve the afternoon off."

"You deserve a lot of things," he said.

My pulse spiked at the low timbre of his voice, at the promise in his words.

I got in closer and tugged on his shirt. "One thing first though."

He leaned down into me, an eyebrow raised.

"Get back in there, and get me another coffee with half-and-half, and then take me somewhere appropriate because…"

His jaw slackened as his eyebrows shot up his forehead. "Because what?" he breathed, his eyes darting to my lips.

I stood up on my toes and touched his lips. "Because I need to suck hard on that cock of yours."

"Goddamn it, that mouth."

"Oh, I think you like this mouth."

"I do." His glinting eyes narrowed. "I have a feeling I'm going to like it even more, the more quality time I spend with it."

My insides tightened. I released my hold on his shirt and smoothed my hand up his chest, my face heating.

"She's blushing. Fuck, that right there is making me harder than hard, baby."

"I like that."

"Me extra hard for you?"

"No, Blondie. You calling me baby." I wrinkled my nose. "Corny, huh?"

His one hand went to my chin and raised it, his lips brushing mine. Smoke and heat. A charged promise. "I like it, too." He kissed me again—this time, slowly, gently, with his eyes wide open. "Baby…"

His smiling lips moved against mine, his hand cradling the back of my head. My chest swelled with a thick wave of heat.

Breathless never felt so good.

Kandace, Lori, Shanda, and Amy waved wildly from inside the coffee shop, where they sat at the front picture window. Smiling huge, all four gestured at me with a thumbs-up through the glass. I waved at them.

"Get some sugar packets, too." I touched Butler's arm.

"What? Why?" He wiped a lock of blond hair behind an ear. "You said you didn't like sugar in your coffee."

"Not for me. For you."

"What are you talking about?"

"Wouldn't you like to lick it off my skin?"

He stilled, his eyes pulsing. "*Raw* sugar for that white skin, Scarlett."

I bit my lip as he stubbed out his cigarette in the sand-filled can by the entrance.

"What kind of coffee should I get you? Erika's got a hell of a menu, and I want you to have exactly what you want."

"Tanzania, please."

A smile grew on his lips. "Tanzania, it is."

He strode back into the coffee shop. A man on a mission.

Butler returned with a fresh coffee, a cup of ice, lots of packets of raw sugar, and a small stainless steel shaker canister.

"What the heck is that?" I asked.

He raised an eyebrow. "Sweetened cocoa."

"Oh my G—"

"My place. Now."

FORTY-NINE

TANIA

THE SECOND WE GOT THROUGH HIS FRONT DOOR, Butler tore off my clothes and his own with me helping in between drawn-out kisses. He pulled me to the floor of his living room, and his tongue explored every inch of me. He grabbed the packets of raw sugar, ripped one open, lined up the crystals on the curve of my hip, and licked at it. A gentle swipe. My nipples hardened to attention, and goose bumps rose all over my skin. Another longer lick this time in swirling motions, and I gasped for air. My skin shimmered in Butler.

He tapped out another trail of the golden brown crystals around my belly button, my tummy caving in, tensing at the flicking touch of the paper, the sugar grazing my flesh. His tongue nudged the tiny flakes over my pale skin, and the wet heat of his tongue appeased the irritation with luxurious care.

We had all the time in the world, and we were taking it.

He held the canister of cocoa over my chest, my insides heating all over again as the soft kiss of the dark powder landed between my breasts and over my nipples. He licked, and he kneaded. They were his. I was all his.

My damp skin was streaked in chocolate. Butler's hungry eyes flared over me; he had marked me. He raised himself up, his mouth hovering over mine, a groan unsticking from the back of his throat, the rich scent of chocolate thick between us.

"Come get it, baby," he rasped.

I rose up and smashed my mouth to his, my tongue exploding in bittersweet chocolate Butler.

"You taste so, so good," I managed between licks and sucks.

"It's all you on me," he murmured.

He sprinkled more cocoa over my breasts, tossing the canister to the side. His mouth sank over one of my tits again, taking me down into a whirlpool of sensation. He sucked each nipple with long, drawn-out movements of his lips, making each one painfully, ridiculously hard.

He groaned. "Fuck."

My legs went around his waist, locking there. I was desperate for friction, desperate for him.

He glanced up at me from my chest. "Impatient, determined—"

"I thought you said you liked that about me." I laughed.

"I like a lot about you."

He grabbed the cup of ice and as he held my gaze, sucked a cube into his mouth. My insides seized as he crunched on it. His mouth closed over a nipple. The sudden cold had me pulling on his hair. He sucked on more ice and sank his mouth between my legs.

"Butler!" I squirmed.

He pressed a melting cube against my clit then tucked it through my opening where it melted and tingled and melted.

"Oh my God!"

He chuckled as his cold mouth and icy tongue lashed over my skin. My eyes were glued to the thick muscles of his shoulders, arms, and chest as he moved over me. He lifted my hips, and I let out a cry as the hard cool tip of his tongue flicked at my clit, ice melting around it, over and over.

One long, slow, heavy lick.

Flick, flick, suck.

Playful, wicked, malevolent adoration.

I shuddered in his grip, my head dropping to the side. "Oh, shit! You're—oh, oh!"

Butler's hands smoothed over my bare torso, covering my breasts. "Who knew scowling sour Tania would taste so fucking sweet?"

I kicked him with my feet, pushing him onto his back, and he let out a grunt. I straddled him, laying kisses over his sweaty chest, my hands stroking over the firm contours of his muscles. I traced over the gorgeous flaming tattoo on his shoulder and down his arm.

"I love your tattoo."

"Are we gonna chat now, or are you gonna say hello to my dick?"

"So sorry. Will you ever forgive me?" I nestled myself in between his legs.

"Do your best to make it up to me."

I firmly wrapped my hands around the base of his cock, and his breath caught in his throat.

"I'll try." I licked up the side of his stiff length.

His eyes blazed. "Try harder."

I licked the other side of his cock. "Look who's impatient now."

"Stop talking, and do it."

My tongue swirled over the wet tip.

"Tania!" His face drew into a hard frown, his breathing shortened as he watched me take long licks of him.

I finally took him into my mouth, my lips closing over his cock, sucking, pulling back, stroking his velvet hardness.

"Ah, fuck!" A ringed hand dug into my hair, keeping my head close to him.

I worked him faster, my fingers stroking his balls in firm circling motions.

I glanced up at him. His eyes were on me, his lips tense. His cock stiffened in my mouth and throbbed. My neck ached, and I didn't care. I kept the pace and the intensity up.

His head arched back, and he let out a long groan as his cock pulsed in my mouth. I took my time lavishing him with attention, and his small moans, his fingers sifting through my hair rewarded me.

I finally released him. His head stayed back, and his eyes closed tight as his chest heaved.

I raised myself up over his body, my hands planted on either side of him. "Sorry, did you want to spray my face or boobs with your cum or whatever a He-Man does these days?"

He let out a laugh and opened his eyes. He reached up and brushed back the hair from my face. "Scarlett, you working me like that, taking me in, taking every last drop, everything I had to give— nothing like it."

"And I meant every suck and swallow."

"And you meant every suck and swallow." His face softened, a hand stroking down my neck. "You've humbled me to the

385

extreme," he breathed. His lips pressed into a firm line, his jaw tightened.

"Is something wrong? Did I—"

He let out a deep breath. "No. You're amazing. That was amazing."

I lied down next to him and lightly caressed the side of his face. He pressed his hand over mine, leaning his head into my touch, his eyes closing again for a moment.

My heart jumped. With that one simple movement, he'd shown me how he had let me in. I loved being his respite from the circus.

"It hasn't been like that for me in a long while," he said.

"Oh?"

"Yeah."

My hand roamed down to his chest, caressing him over his pounding heart.

"When I started overdoing the blow, getting off got difficult. And, since I've quit, things have been a little different. But this, with you—"

"Yeah?"

"So good. Been a long while."

"What exactly? It being good or—"

"Both."

I raised my head on my hand. "Oh. I thought you and Nina—"

"Not really," he said quietly.

My heart raced. So much for Ms. Hot Twenty-Something.

"Nina and I hooked up a couple of times before we agreed on our deal," he said. "It was fine. Later, after we got together, one time we fucked, I didn't last long enough for her to get off the way she wanted, and she got pissed."

"Did she?"

"She called me an old man."

"She fucking did not!"

"She did." He let out a dark laugh. "She paid for that. Big time."

I bit the side of my lip as kinky visuals flitted through my brain, trying to imagine what that meant. She'd probably loved every minute of it, whatever her punishment had been.

I bet he did, too.

I blinked. *Stop!*

"After that," he continued, "I really didn't want to have much to do with her in bed."

Hmm. Accent on the much.

Tania!

Adrenaline rushed through my veins. Butler was mine for the satisfying. Mine to fulfill sexually, emotionally, in every fucking way, and I wanted him in every one of those ways. I wanted to be the one to fill him up, make his dreams come true. Be his completely. Make him mine.

I stroked his chest, my fingers tracing a circle around a nipple. "Tell me, were you tempted to go further with me that night in the motel?"

He took my hand in his and kissed my fingertips. "Hell yes, but I was trying to be a good boy."

"For Nina and your 'relationship'?"

"Fuck no. For you."

"For *me*?"

"I knew you'd find out about me and her once we got back to Meager, and I didn't want you to think I was some shitty cheater or that I'd used you because I wasn't. That night between us wasn't like that. It wasn't about that for me. I wanted to be inside you real bad, but it felt like stealing, and I couldn't do that. Not to you."

My heart doubled over. "Butler—"

He turned on his side and faced me. "I couldn't lie to you. I'd been lying to myself for years until recently. I finally got out from under that web, sliced it right open. When we got to the club, and I saw that disappointment on your face, I felt like a real shit."

"You noticed?"

"Yeah. I noticed."

"You assumed I'd be disappointed that I couldn't get more of you?"

"Yeah, of course." He grinned at me. He loved teasing me, and I loved it too.

I sank my teeth into his chest, on the swell of a pec.

He let out a long hiss. "Watch it. I like that shit, baby."

My pulse spiked at the heat in his eyes, the raw tone in his voice.

I cleared my throat. "You took a huge chance that night when you touched me. I could've slapped you and kicked you out of the room."

He gently traced a heart-stopping line around my breast with the edge of his thumb. "I wanted you to feel good, like Gerhard's queen did. Adored, beautiful, a sexy-as-fuck and so fucking hot one and only. You were this mixture of elated, sad, and wistful that night. Then, that Blade grabbed you."

"And you went all caveman."

He cupped my breast. "I was protecting you."

Shivers raced over my skin. "Yes, you were. I liked it. I haven't had that in a long time. Not since my dad died. I mean, that *knowing* that I'm safe with a man, that I could face anything if I had him at my side."

His fingers lazed over my skin. "I don't want to be your daddy."

"Are you sure?"

He laughed and kissed me.

"You're strong on your own, Tania. Never doubt that."

"I like you being strong for me, too. Being there for me."

I kissed him. We held each other as we discovered the hollows and soft places over our throats and skin. His hand slid down over my rear end, caressing me there. The heat we generated wrapped around us like the softest warm wind.

"I want to fuck you," he whispered against my ear.

"I don't want you to be anxious."

His face darkened. "About what exactly?"

I planted a kiss on his chest and peeked up at him. "That maybe I'm going to blow the hell out of your cock." I nipped at his flesh with my teeth.

"Fuck, it'd be a great way to go."

His blue eyes glimmered at me as I pushed him against the bed and straddled him. He handed me a condom from the pile at his side. I tore open the packet and fit the rubber on his cock. Positioning him at my entrance, I took him in.

"Ah, shit," he moaned, his head twisting back. "Baby."

His hand slid between us, his ringed fingers forming a V around his cock, providing incredible additional friction for the both of us. I rode him, and the pleasure inside me skyrocketed. My head fell back.

"Scarlett, look at me," he whispered hoarsely. "Look at me, baby. I want to see those beautiful eyes fuck me while you take my cock."

I opened my eyes, and his desire beamed at me, embracing me, swallowing me. I planted my hands on his chest and moved faster over him.

His free hand went to a breast, palming it. He tugged on my nipple, and I cried out. I fell into his abyss, and I never wanted to get out. Never.

Yes, absolute possession.

"You like that, Scarlett?" he whispered hoarsely as his hips drove rhythmically, under mine.

"Yes," I rasped.

Rough tugging, delicate stroking. I was a sculpture he traced his hands over, adoring every curve and pleasuring himself with every touch. He was the sculptor, summoning forth his creation with his hands, his cock.

I was light-headed, exhausted, dancing on a high wire. Alive.

I ground against him, and his breath hitched.

"I can't get enough of you," I breathed.

His hand released my breast and dug into my hip. "Whatever I've got to give, baby, it's all for you. All of it."

I slid my hand over his heart. "I'm clawing my way in there deep."

"I can feel it, Scarlett. Make it hurt."

BUTLER

CLOUDS DRIFTED IN BUNCHES across the wide blue sky, shedding a patch of darkness over the One-Eyed Jacks' property, while the rest of the land stretching in the distance rolled in the sunlight.

"Butler." Alicia's low voice stopped me. She stood stiffly in the shadows at the side of the open front door of the club, a tray of empty juice boxes in her hand, a supermarket bag hanging from one wrist.

We'd finished up painting the go-karts with the kids, and the old ladies had passed out snacks and juice.

"Hey, what's up?"

"I just got a text from Wes. Says he's spending the night with some friends."

"Okay?"

"He would've called me, spoken with me about an overnight, but he just texted me at the last minute, without telling me where exactly he is."

"Babe, I'm sorry about this, but I've got to get going. Got to get to—"

She put the tray down on the long metal console table propping open the front door. "Something's off; I know it. He's avoiding me and all of us."

"Maybe he's really into that new girlfriend of his?"

"I still haven't even met her, still don't know who she is. She's not from around here. She's from Nebraska."

The back of my neck stiffened. "Nebraska? You sure?"

"He mentioned it once. See, Wes has never been so secretive with me before. We've always been up-front with each other, always been able to talk. It's not like him to disappear for hours every day without letting me know where he is or who he's with. Something's going on. A mother knows these things. I'm his mother. I know."

Laughter and screeches from the kids playing tag rose up in the yard. Bear and his small son along with Tricky were leading the teams.

"Alicia, I put in a call to him yesterday, but he didn't pick up, and he never got back to me. He should've been here today."

"Yes, he should've. I just found this on his bike in his saddlebag." She handed me the plastic supermarket bag.

I opened it. Old glass soda bottles, cut up oily rags that stank of motor oil and kerosene, baking soda, petroleum jelly, rubber cement, strips of tire tubing. Fuck me, the kid's been making Molotov cocktails instead of beer bongs.

My eyes shot back to Alicia, her face tight. She knew, and she was worried.

"Please find him. Please," she whispered, stepping toward me. "I don't know what else to say or think at this point. He's been using Jump's bike, and he's out somewhere, doing God knows what. He's angry and confused. Please, you and the men need to find him."

"I'll find him, Alicia. I promise."

She pressed her lips together, nodding stiffly. "Thank you. Let me know."

"I'll be in touch."

She picked up the drinks tray and headed toward the kitchen.

"Butler, let's go!" shouted Dready from the doorway with Dawes and Clip.

"Hey, Dawes!"

Dawes turned around. He shook his blond curls from his eyes, his shoulders standing at attention. "What's up?"

"You still keep that tracking device on Jump's hog?" I asked him.

The Jacks kept devices on all their bikes just in case they got stolen by rival clubs or anyone else. Your bike was your identity, your partner, your soul. You couldn't let anyone fuck with that.

"Yeah, sure."

"Wes is missing, and he's out on his dad's bike. Find it."

Dawes gestured toward the president's office, and I followed him inside. He threw himself down in Jump's old swivel chair and turned on the computer. The room still reeked of Jump. Stale cigarettes, old vinyl, boot polish. Just the creaking of that goddamn chair still sent prickles up my spine, reminding me of all the times I'd been in here in the past—being reprimanded, cursed at, or my hand being shaken, my back slapped. Grins and scowls, disappointment and approval had all been aimed my way within these walls over the years.

A photo of Dig stared at me from the wall dotted with pics of former officers. His ringed hand, cut and bloodied, was balled into a fist, which filled the frame, his face with lips snarled blurred in the background. Determined, stubborn. A Jack.

"Prospect, welcome to the brotherhood. Welcome to the One-Eyed Jacks."

Dig's rich voice came back to me from one of the most spectacular nights of my life, the night I'd patched in and become a One-Eyed Jack.

"There's hope for you yet, bro."

That hearty laugh of his roared in my ears. The slap of his palm against my face, his hand smoothing down the stiff leather of the brand-new vest he'd settled over my shoulders.

"You ready to take it on?"

"Butler?"

I tore my eyes away from Dig's photo and focused on Dawes at the computer once again. I cleared my throat. "What did you find, man?"

"I didn't find shit. I got nothing."

My spine grew rigid. "Why the fuck not?"

"Because the device has been disarmed since last night."

FIFTY-ONE

TANIA

THE BELL RANG over the front door of the gallery. Lenore strode through, wearing a long black tank that showed off the beautiful tattoos swirling over her chest and down her toned arms along with black skinny jeans, topped off with black leather stiletto booties. She sported a number of earrings, and a gorgeous labradorite pendant around her neck. She was an unlikely vision in our small town laden with dusty pastels and cozy prints. Lenore placed a large Meager Grand Cafe iced coffee with a dollop of whipped cream before me on my front desk. *A tasty peace offering?*

I removed my reading glasses. Inputting inventory data nonstop on my computer had screwed with my eyes. "That looks insanely yummy."

"That's cold-brewed."

"Bless you, my child." I grabbed the coffee and took a sip of the richly flavored drink, groaning. I gestured to the rattan armchair next to me. "Sit."

Lenore sat down. "I'm so sorry about the other night at my house."

Finger had come looking for me at Dead Ringer's to help him get through to Lenore. She'd only thrown us both out.

"Are you okay?"

"Yeah. Better. I'm sorry I lost it. You came over because you care, because you were concerned. And I was…a mess. I've been a burden to you. For years now."

"No, you haven't, Lenore. Things are complicated. I get that. But maybe you could give an inch."

"Finger was really angry."

"Being upset was at the heart of his anger. He's trying, Lenore. He's reaching out."

"He hates me."

"No, he doesn't. He can't. I hate all these bad feelings flying between all of us."

"That's my fault."

"I'm not trying to lay blame here." I put my coffee down and took in a breath. "I'm tired. I was up late last night with my mother."

"Is she okay?"

"It comes and goes with the MS. The past few days, she's had a new set of muscle spasms, and we might have to try new medication. She's been depressed lately. She can't knit anymore; her fingers won't cooperate. She loves knitting. It's more than a hobby to her, just like cooking was. How much more is my mother going to have to give up?" I grabbed the coffee and took a hard, long sip from the straw. "She was trying to knit a poncho for Becca yesterday, and she had to give up. She was crying, yelling at herself about everything. I gave the poncho to her friend, Nancy next door to finish. Every time I think we've got this under control, that we're handling it, something new always comes along and blows that illusion out of the water, and we're being dragged back into Shitville."

"I'm so sorry your family's going through this. I have something that can cheer you up."

"Vanilla vodka over ice?" I shook the almost empty coffee cup, the ice rattling within.

"No, no." She let out a laugh. "Too early for that. This is way better. I'll be right back."

Lenore headed out the door into the golden shower of the midday sun. I went back to my inventory program on my laptop, went back to ignoring the heaviness in my heart and the gnawing in the pit of my stomach.

Within five minutes, the bell jangled, and the door cranked open once more. Lenore held up one of her own store's shopping bags, a grin on her face. She was pleased with herself. From the purple Lenore's Lace bag, she drew out a breathtaking orchestration of silk and sci-fi fabric.

"Holy—"

"I know."

From her hands hung an elegant corset of the deepest, richest tone of blood red I had ever seen. I was mesmerized by it, magnetized toward it.

My fingers outstretched and slid over the textures. "It's gorgeous. It's—"

"I made it for you. I'm almost finished with it. One piece. One size. Yours. Try it on."

I pursed my lips, my eyes darting to hers. "Lenore—"

"Ah, Tania, trust me. I know these things. With your skin and hair…"

I took in a deep breath.

She raised a sharply defined eyebrow, her blue-green eyes gleaming at me. "You can't take your eyes off it, can you?"

"Give it here."

She laid it in my arms, as if she were handing over a precious, very delicate antique haute couture museum piece. The fabric deliciously glided against my skin, and I bit my lip as my fingers slid over the webbing of silken material.

"Go," she ordered.

I went in the back storage room and kicked off my shoes and stripped off my clothes. I almost didn't know where to begin.

"Be brave, Reigert. Be brave!" I said to myself.

I carefully stepped into the corset and sucked in a breath, smoothing down the gorgeousness of Lenore's craftsmanship over my body.

"Honey, you need help?" Lenore stepped into the room. "Oh God, Tania. It's perfect."

I stared at myself in the antique full length cheval stand mirror that I had in a corner and swallowed hard. The silk and Lycra-like bands stretched across my flesh, a complexity of glossy texture, seamless workmanship. The corset covered just enough without being crude yet tantalized as it bound my body, revealing all the right curves. Elegant minimalist perfection.

"This color on you—it's even better than I hoped." Lenore smoothed her hands down my back and across my waist. "Fantastic," she murmured to herself.

My hand passed over my hip, and something inside me trembled.

Her eyes met mine in the mirror. "Hon, you okay?" She stood up straight and put her arms around me, her chin on my shoulder. "Tania, what's wrong?"

"You're amazing," I murmured. This is a beautiful work of art. I feel beautiful."

"Babe, you are beautiful. Only you could carry this one off. The color on you is—"

"Stunning. Somewhere between blood and wine."

"Exactly. Your eyes really pop, and your skin is glowing, that dark shiny hair…"

I pressed a hand against my middle. "I don't even mind my tummy."

"Stop. Your body looks great. I think you've lost a few pounds lately. Stressed out much?"

"Just a tiny little bit."

"And don't say a word about that ass. It's glorious," she continued, her hand sliding down the curve of my hip.

I let out a breath and averted my gaze.

"What is it, Tania? What's wrong?"

"I haven't felt this way in a long, long time."

"What way is that?"

"You know what I mean."

She squeezed my hip, and I found her gaze in the mirror once more. "Say it out loud right now while you're feeling that shit."

"I feel like the me I want to be. The me I have always wanted to be but was never usually on the outside—sexy, in charge of myself. Powerful. Bold."

The mirror revealed this different me. Brash, saucy, out there. Here-I-am, take-it-or-leave-me-the-hell-alone Tania. Or the I-don't-really-give-a-damn-because-I've-got-it-going-on Tania.

She gripped my arms. "That's the Tania I know. This one right here. Very powerful. Very bold."

"That's the act I put on for everyone. Or when my back is up against the wall."

"No."

"Yes. There's a part of me that's still a scared little girl. Scared of the dark, scared of twisty roller coasters, scared without her daddy, scared of bikers wielding knives."

Her chin lifted. "That's not the Tania I know. No. This Tania is only scared of being alone, of not being enough."

I bit down on my wobbly lower lip as a tear slipped down my cheek.

She pressed into me. "I know. Don't I know?" Her voice was a hoarse whisper.

"You know."

She wiped the tear from my face. "Hadn't we said no more tears?"

"Tell me you've kept to that deal all these years."

She screwed up her face. "Nope."

"Didn't think so. Me neither."

She took in a quick breath. "It's all right. We're tough, you and me."

I covered her hand with mine. "I'm glad you're in my life again, whatever your name is." I pressed the side of my face against hers in a sudden rush of emotions. "I really, really am."

"Me, too." She pulled back, and a small smile tugged on the edge of her lips. "So, tell me, are you falling for Butler?"

"Yes," I breathed.

Her head tilted. "You're questioning it. Maybe it's too soon after your husband and you need to be on your own for a while?"

"I've been on my own for years and years. That's not what I want."

"Then, what is it?"

"I'm questioning myself. Maybe I don't have what it takes to go the distance."

"That's the fear talking."

"Says the expert."

"We're talking about you now."

"I don't want to screw this up. He and I are both screwed up enough as it is. How many second chances do you get in life anyhow?"

Her eyes flared.

Shit.

I'd always wanted her to stand up and take her second chance, and she'd refused. Refused.

"I've had my fill of second chances. Girls like me have a limited number. You wouldn't understand. Thank your god that you never will."

Those words of hers had haunted me for years after they'd fallen from her lips, her tear-stained face pallid in the headlights of the trucks thundering by us on the side of the road.

I smoothed a hand over the corset. "I want to be with Butler like I've never been with anyone before, ever. But now he knows that I'm keeping a secret from him. A secret involving Finger. I haven't told him all of it. Nothing about you."

She turned me around and leaned her forehead against mine. "You're a good friend, Tania."

She planted a gentle kiss on my lips, and all those sensations flooded back. That fervid urgency, that delicious curiosity, that crazy sweetness, that apprehension of the unknown.

I cleared my throat. "I need to tell you something. Cards on the table. I can't keep it from you, and I don't ever want you to think that—"

"What is it?"

"After you left him, after you…"

"After I broke him, you mean? That last time?"

"Yeah. He and I—"

She held up a hand, shaking her head at me. "You don't have to explain, Tania. I'm glad that he had you in his corner. I'm glad he tried to forget."

I threw my head back. "Dear God, you are so wrong! He did it to *remember*. His passion for you is some kind of fury. A fury whose fangs and claws have sunk deep. A fury that won't let go. A damn tidal wave of love, anger, pain, desolation. A tidal wave that won't quit. And he tortures himself with it."

She stiffened, throwing up the old barricades against my words, against the emotions they would surely invoke. How many times had we done this in the past?

"He got on with his life," she said, her voice flat. "So did I."

"Yeah, he sure did. Just like you did. Oh, there were the usual women. An old lady here, and another one there. They never lasted long though. Not one."

She averted her gaze. "Well, I'm glad he had you."

"We were only two people grabbing at something we couldn't have."

She stepped away from me.

I could tell her now, tell her whom I saw, that the enemy was circling. But it would only make her panic and run again. No, Finger would take care of it, take care of her. *That's why he is in her face now.*

"It has nothing to do with me." She plucked the shopping bag off the floor.

"That is such bullshit, and you know it," I said, raising my voice. "You have to let him in. You have to tell Finger. I won't ever. I made you that promise. But you have to tell him."

She shook her head as she folded the bag and placed it on a nearby box.

"Who's afraid now?" I said. "Finger knows I know more than I've been letting on. Honey, the other night was crazy."

"He was so angry," she said, her voice low. "He got angry at you, too."

"Yes, he did. But that's because he felt powerless. He wants to help you, and he doesn't know how. He's desperate to reach you."

Lenore put her hands over her ears, drowning out the viciousness and the hope.

The howling of her own wolves.

"You still love him," I said.

Her big eyes glimmering like sea water in the sun found mine.

Swim to the surface, Rena.

I pulled her hands from her head, her rings pressing into my fingers.

"Can't you say it? Why can't you say it?" I asked.

"There's no point. Too much has happened."

"No. You have to be brave. You have to be brave enough to act on that love."

Those shrill screams, the ugly words, harsh decisions, stinging tears of our shared past roared between us.

"How brave are you, Rena?" I whispered, lacing our fingers together.

Her eyes held mine. "How brave are you?"

FIFTY-TWO

BUTLER

WES WAS COVERING HIS TRACKS.

I couldn't pinpoint his location, so I'd tracked his best friend, Zach, instead, sending Dawes over to his house in the middle of the night to plant a device on the kid's bike. Bingo. The boys had cut out of football camp today and were in Deadwood, about an hour-plus north of Meager.

A thick blanket of tall evergreens rose around me as I got into Deadwood. I followed the winding road into the center of the historic town nestled in the glorious Hills. Once a frontier gold rush town populated with infamous gamblers and gunslingers, Deadwood was now an American Wild West tourist haven, offering casinos, restaurants, bars, and shops. The streets crawled with people, and the road was clogged with vehicles and a shit-ton of bikes. Another hot summer day in the Black Hills of South Dakota.

I stopped at a red light and scanned the amazing selection of colorful, shiny bikes on my side of the street. Lock's hand-painted version of the One-Eyed Jacks skull with the glinting star shining from one eye glared at me from the gas tank of a Panhead. Jump's Panhead. My shoulders stiffened. The metallic candy shimmer of the paint on his unmistakable Harley danced in the afternoon sun.

Wes was right here.

I hunted for a parking space. I edged into one an elderly man on a trike had freed once his wife had come out of a store. I scanned the streets for any signs of the tall, athletic seventeen-year-old high school senior. The sidewalks teemed with couples, families, and strollers while the shop doors opened and closed, letting out folks, letting in more.

Left. *Nothing.*

Right. *No.*

I scanned the area once more. *Wes.* Across the street, at a diagonal from me. He dumped the remains of what looked like a hot dog in a garbage can and took a swig from a can of Red Bull, wiping his brown hair from his eyes. Wes was an expert dirt-bike racer, a great football player, and now, a rebel with a certified cause.

I'd recognized the signs months before when his parents could barely be in the same room with each other. And now since his father's death, those signs of edginess, irritability, sourness had only gotten clearer, stronger.

I darted across the street and strode toward him. "Wes? What's up?"

Wes's body jerked back. Tense dark blue eyes met mine, narrowing. "Butler. Hey."

"Surprised to see you up here. Didn't you have practice this morning?"

"Nah."

"Really?"

He shifted his weight on his long legs, his shoulders rising and falling quickly.

I gestured at Jump's bike with a slant of my face. "How's she riding?"

"She's a dream."

"Your dad always kept her in good shape. Hope you are, too, now."

A frown passed over his features. "Of course I am."

"Good. What are you up to?"

"Just out with friends. Great day to ride."

We stared at each other. A draw.

"Wesley, this how it's going to be for your senior year? For shit's sake, you're going to be starting quarterback this year. What the hell? You can't be taking off for a good time."

His gaze darted away from me.

"Who are you here with?"

"What's with all the questions?"

"You here with that new girlfriend of yours?"

Wes cocked an eyebrow, rubbing his hands together. "Maybe."

Fuck no.

Maybe used to be my stock response to a whole array of questions.

Maybe I'll drink the whole bottle of Jack.

Maybe I'll fuck this chick who's rubbing her tits up against me along with her friend.

Maybe I'll break the face of this motherfucker who's staring at my old lady's ass.

Maybe I'll fix my bike's cover today.

Maybe I'll sniff more joy powder to keep the carnival in my mind whirling.

I leaned into him. "Don't give me fucking *maybe*. Who do you think you're talking to? I'm the king of maybes. Don't bother making it a good story, give me the truth. And P.S., I know you've been blowing off work at Eagle Wings. Lock was looking for you a while back and then again the other day. He knows something's up with you, but I stopped him from going to your ma. Plus, you blew off the go-kart painting yesterday."

Wes's chin jutted out. Defiance, resentment.

"Where's the girl?" I asked.

"In the restroom, making herself pretty for me."

"Tell me, since you've had all this free time lately from cutting football, cutting your job, what have you been up to?"

He shrugged.

I leaned in closer. "Pyrotechnics, *maybe*? Did you set that fire in the Blades' junkyard?"

Wes's eyes pierced mine. I recognized the fuck-off-I-ain't-telling-you-shit signs.

"Ah, damn it!" I gritted, clamping a hand around his arm

He shoved out of my hold. "You don't know nothing! Nothing! Those fuckers have to pay for what they did to my dad!"

"It wasn't the Blades, Wes." I lowered my voice. "It was Reich, a Flame of Hell from Ohio. He was aiming for Nina and probably for me. Your dad—"

"He was in the wrong place at the wrong time? Collateral damage?"

"Yeah, he was. Look, Reich was punished by his own club for that and for many more sins. It's done now, you hear me? And, as for the Broken Blades, their club is in pieces. They're out there, begging for scraps. The one thing your father hated more than anything else, the one thing he never, ever wanted for our club, was to be taken over, ripped apart, told what to do by another club. And that is what's happening to the Blades. The Jacks played a role in making that happen, and that right there is very sweet."

Wes's eyes filled with water, and I wrapped a hand around his neck. He pushed against me, but I yanked him back in.

"You do not ever go out there on your own. If they'd caught you—goddamn it, Wes. If anything had happened to you—" I caught my breath and pushed down the wave of emotion, that slice of pain ages old and so familiar, searing my middle. "The go-kart championship we're running in a few weeks?"

He glanced up at me. "Yeah?"

"I'm working it with you. We're working it together, whatever Lock has you on."

"What?"

"That's right. One-on-one. You could learn a thing or two about an engine from me, boy. And Lock doesn't have the free time to show you how his designs get done whenever you feel like dropping by. You need to be showing him respect."

"I respect him just fine!"

"Not good enough when you show up once in a while whenever you feel like it, pretend you're listening, and then duck out. Think I haven't been watching you? And another thing—"

"Now what, goddamn it?"

"I'm going to be picking you up from practice and bringing you home from school. Every day."

"Hell no. I got my bike. I don't need—"

"You can ride your bike, but you'll be riding it alongside mine. You got that? Home, school, home again."

"Am I grounded, too?"

"That's up to your mother."

"You gonna tell her about—"

"She's the one who found the shit on your bike and told me about it! You think she didn't know what it was?"

Wes let out a hiss under his breath, his body going rigid.

"We clear?"

He raised his head, an ugly twist to his mouth, his eyes narrowing. He was either going to explode or cry or implode. Any was good for me. He needed to.

I leaned into him. "Right now, you are putting our club at risk. Igniting a war that is unnecessary, dangerous, and very destructive."

Wes grunted, his gaze jumping to my side. "She's coming."

I turned. A petite redheaded girl bobbed toward us from down the street. Her fingers tugged on the open ripped neckline of her cropped tank.

I knew the various stages of girl through woman all too well. I'd been with plenty of jailbait and older women in my time. I'd grown able to make the fine distinctions of age from the way females carried themselves, their expressions, their skin tone, the lines on their faces. This was no woman. This was barely a full-fledged teenager.

"She's just a kid," I muttered.

"She sure doesn't act like a kid."

"That makes it all right?" I grabbed his collar. "What the hell are you doing? What are you thinking?"

He pushed against me. "She's crazy about me."

The girl's pace slowed down under my and Wes's stare, her teeth raking over her highly glossed bottom lip.

"Um, hey," she mumbled, her eyes widening as she looked up at me.

Her gaze darted at Wes for a second and then shot back to me. She gaped at my colors, her eyes widening.

"What's going on?" Her voice came out tiny, low.

I shot a look at Wes and turned back to the girl. "I'm Wes's uncle. What's your name, sweetheart?"

"I'm Lindy."

"Got to get you home, Lindy."

"What? I don't wanna go home! I'm here with Wes. Right, Wes?"

Wes didn't answer.

She grinned unsteadily, still clinging to the dream. "We're going to the ZZ Top concert tonight."

"Oh, yeah?" My eyes slid to Wes.

He only jammed his hands in his pockets.

"Hey, what up? What's going on?"

Zach, Wes's buddy from home, approached us, a plastic bag filled with beer cans hanging from one hand. Lindy blinked at him.

I eyed Wes. "The three of you came up here together, huh?"

"Yeah, we did," replied Zach, slinging his free arm around Lindy, pulling her close.

Lindy shifted, but Zach only held on to her.

"Let go of her, Zach," Wes said.

"What the hell's going on?" Zach shot back, his neck rigid.

"I said, let Lindy go!" said Wes, grabbing Lindy's arm.

Zach jerked Lindy back. "The fuck you say!"

I lunged at the kid, my one hand cuffing his throat, the other releasing Lindy from his grip and shoving her toward Wes. The girl let out a loud gasp as she scrambled away.

"You gotta listen when you're spoken to, boy. And you gotta show me respect when you're in my presence. And you sure as hell don't go grabbing girls who don't want to be grabbed."

"She's—"

"I know all about it." I hooked an arm around his neck and leaned in close to the freckled-face wiry kid with the flashing eyes. He was almost at my height, but he had no strength whatsoever. "Now, shut the fuck up before I rip your tongue out and then drag your ass back to Meager, hanging on to the fender of my bike by your fingernails."

He shoved against me. "You know who my dad is? You—"

"Oh, yeah, I know who your daddy is, you little scumbag. I even know where you live."

His face paled.

His dad, Zachary Kendrick Sr., was a high-ranking member of the local Rotary Club and a devoted golfer who always had gold cuff links on his perfectly pressed shirt, no matter what time of year, and a BMW SUV to ferry himself to his fancy law firm in Rapid every day. His wife—a PTA president—always had a sneer on her face whenever Alicia, Grace, Mary Lynn, and the other old ladies would volunteer for anything from the minor bake sales to the football team spirit club fundraisers.

The kid's cheek muscles spasmed. His eyes darted back to Wes.

My grip on him only tightened. "Look at me. I'm talking to you now. You hearing me, you little piece of shit?"

He only nodded.

"You been drinking? Taking anything?"

"Uh…" He raised the bag of beer cans in his hand. "Not yet. I—"

I grabbed him by the collar and pulled him off to the side, so Lindy wouldn't hear. "What you got on you?"

Zach made a face. "What?"

I shoved my free hand in one of his front jeans pockets. *Empty.* The other pocket. My fingers slid over a plastic baggie with a variety of pills in it. I pulled it out, glancing at it.

"Let me guess. X and a nice roofie you were gonna use on Lindy tonight?"

His lips rolled. "You-you're not gonna tell my parents, are you?"

"And spoil their fairy-tale illusion of their golden boy?" I tossed the baggie in a garbage can to my left.

My fingers gripped his neck, and he gasped.

"This is what I want from you. You get on your bike and get the fuck home. Right now. Bet the University of Texas might not accept you if they hear about how you like to roofie underage virgins, huh?"

His eyes widened.

"That's right. I keep tabs on my town, junior, and the people my family runs with. I'm about expecting the worst at all times. You see how justified I am?"

"The dealer I got it from is probably one of yours anyhow!" he slung back.

My fist pulled on his shirt, ramming him into my chest. "Sorry to disappoint you, shithead. I don't deal in X and roofies. Now, move."

I released him, but he stood still, his lips pressed together.

"You got any more stellar comebacks for me?" I asked.

He shook his head.

"What's going on?" Lindy's shaky voice rose behind me.

"Know this," I continued. "I'll be keeping watch on you, asswipe. You stay away from Lindy and from Wes. Or, along with your shiny future, your fancy bike and your daddy's fancy cars are all gonna disappear. You got that?"

"Yeah, yeah, I got that." Zach stumbled back and stalked off down the street.

I faced Wes and Lindy again. "Now, I've got to get you two home. I got—"

"Oh my God!" Lindy screeched, her eyes focused over my shoulder.

The color had drained from her face, making the makeup she had obviously just applied look like patches of colored chalk blotched on her pale skin.

"What is it?" I asked.

"My dad's here!" She pointed down the block.

I swiveled around.

Fresh from the tobacco shop, not more than twenty yards away, was Pick, the Blade who had assaulted Tania back in that restaurant in Sioux Falls. The Blade whose hand I'd ripped up with a steak knife.

"Pick is your dad?"

FIFTY-THREE

BUTLER

LINDY'S JITTERY GAZE darted back at me. "You-you know my dad?"

"You could say that."

"He's been in Oregon. I didn't think he'd be back until—oh God."

I glared at Wes. "I'm impressed as all hell now, man. I really am."

He was seducing the daughter of a Broken Blade. He and his buddy had taken this underage girl across state lines along with a roofie and entertainment drugs.

Wes had targeted her. He had done his homework.

I turned to the girl. "How old are you, Lindy?"

Her face flushed. "I'm…"

"She's fifteen," Wes replied, his voice flat.

I lasered a hole through Wes's melting armor.

My head simmered on the verge of a volcanic explosion. I could see blood, shards of bone, and brain splattered on the cement at our feet. Tourists yelping as they shot photos of the massacre before them with their fucking cell phones. The town's daily Old West Main Street shoot-out reenactments and that of Wild Bill's Dead Man's Hand, which had occurred just footsteps from here, would seem totally lame in comparison. This biker shoot out would be Deadwood's new tourist attraction, for sure.

"Dad!" Lindy's voice was high. Panic.

"Lindy?"

My spine hardened at Pick's booming voice, at his cold opaque eyes.

"What the hell are you doing up here? What's going on?"

"Daddy!" Lindy lunged at her father's bulky chest. "I came up here with some friends, but we got separated, and this guy was bothering me—"

"Who? This kid?" Pick gestured at Wes, his massive chest surging with air, his nostrils flaring.

"No! No, not him." Lindy pulled on his colors. "This other guy. Wes, here, and his uncle—they stepped in and scared him off. I was just thanking them for helping me."

Pick's fierce gaze blasted over Wes and landed on me. "You telling me the truth, sweetheart?"

She put a hand around her dad's bulky tattooed arm. "My cell phone battery died, and I was just about to call home, using Wes's phone, but, wow, here you are! I'm so glad you're here," she blurted out, her lower lip quivering.

Wes's gaze shifted to his boots.

"You're always doing that shit, baby. How many times I got to tell you to make sure you get the battery juiced before you leave the house?"

"I lost my charger cable again," Lindy murmured. Her eyes went to my patch. "Thank you, Mr….Mr. Butler. You, too, Wes. Thank you."

"You're welcome, Lindy," I said.

She glanced over at Wes and looked away again.

"So good to see you. I thought you wouldn't be back until next week, Dad."

"Things change on a dime, baby. You know that,"

"Usually do." I said.

Pick eyed me. "I came home early 'cause I got a call that there's been trouble on our property."

"Oh, yeah?" I asked.

"Yeah," he replied. "A fire at our junkyard a while back. Petty thefts all this past week."

"Good thing you're heading home."

Lindy leaned against her dad's side, her eyes on me. "Thanks again, sir. I really, really appreciate it," she said, her tone even. "I don't know what I would've done if you and Wes hadn't come along."

"You're very welcome, sweetheart," I said, forcing my mouth into a slight smile. "You take care. Try to keep track of your charger cable."

"I will," she murmured. "Learned my lesson."

"Glad we could help out. Gotta keep our girls safe." I stretched my hand toward him. Ambitious with a heavy dose of presumption, but I needed to seal this into Truce Land. He could accept our neat story, his daughter's passionate and plausible presentation, or he could growl, bite, and rip us all to shreds and move this blip on the EKG of our clubs' lifelines into Code Red territory.

Pick's forehead puckered as he glared at my hand, at what I was offering.

He was making his choice.

Pick met my gaze and shook my hand once, hard.

I nodded. "Well, we're off. Got to get home."

"Bye, Wes," said Lindy.

"Bye, Lindy." Wes threw her and Pick a tight grin.

Wes and I walked in silence side by side.

"Lindy's a good kid. She's not some—"

"I know," Wes said. "She didn't deserve…" He took in a deep breath.

I lit a cigarette. "Thank God I found you when I did. This is how vendettas begin and never fucking end, Wes. Had you gone through with this plan to take advantage of Lindy, there would've been no healing from that—for her or for you. Our colors would've been soaked in blood for years to come, and we would've been sucked into a flaming ball of meaningless chaos."

Wes said nothing.

"You are not that animal, Wesley," I continued. "That is not the man your mother raised you to be."

Wes pressed his lips together in a hard line, his gaze remaining locked straight ahead.

"I get it," I said. "I understand. I do. Wanting revenge, needing to lash out, to hurt because you hurt, because you've been wronged. I respect your passion, I admire it. But you're only fucking things up for your dad's club. *Our* club."

We stopped before Jump's parked bike. Wes's bike.

"I'm going to say this just once, but it's real important," I continued. "You are a born and bred One-Eyed Jack. One day, you might patch in like a brother. But this behavior is not worthy of that patch nor is it worthy of your name or of the reputation your father earned over the years. You want to destroy all that for his brothers, for your mother? For him? His whole life's work for a cruel play? And, trust me, it was a vicious, empty play that you'd have only regretted. There's no way 'round that one. I didn't expect this from you. Wes, got to say, I'm real disappointed."

He jammed his hands in his pockets, his eyes trained on the bike.

My arm hooked around his neck and squeezed. "I've been there. I know, so I can say this to you. These kinds of regrets are too heavy to bear, and I don't want that for you. Ever. You've got your whole life ahead of you, son. You've got a burning heart inside you, and that's good. But you've got to let that burning lead you—not to destroy—but to figure out what exactly you believe in and to stand up for it before it's too late. Never give that a rest, or you'll be lost."

He wiped at an eye, nodding, his gaze meeting mine. There was pain there, shame. And despair.

My heart squeezed. I tossed my cigarette.

"You and me, you got that?" I said.

"Yeah. Got it."

My hand clutched his shoulder, and I pulled him into a hug. "Let me help you. Wes. Let me look out for you."

Wes wrapped his arms around me and held on tight.

FIFTY-FOUR

BUTLER

WES AND I TOOK THE ROAD out of Deadwood and headed home.

"Let's take the long way, take it easy!" I shouted over at him.

He nodded at me, and we swerved off onto Route 14A heading south, which would take us through the Black Hills National Forest instead of the main highway. A much better road to contemplate your sins and transgressions, to meditate, to let it all fucking go rather than debate with the cars and trucks and buses rumbling in your way.

My insides hummed with my engine as we surged over the smooth asphalt, the wind pushing over us both and us ripping through it. My lungs expanded as the road burned under me, the light and heat of the sun fervent, as the elevation descended in the forested hills. That strong aroma of mineral and earth rose around us, shading the crisp fresh scent of the air.

Wes caught my glance and shot me a grin.

Yeah, it was in his blood, too.

We approached a tight curve, and he sped up ahead of me to take it. Two dots appeared in front of us on the road.

Blocking the road. Blocking us.

I decelerated, my hands tightening over the handlebars, my back rigid.

From a blur, the dots became figures that became faces, and now, they finally came into focus.

Led and another Flame on their bikes blocked our road. They raised their arms, guns in their hands.

Bam.

Wes spun out, his bike teetering, tumbling, plunging.

"Wes!"

He sprawled on the asphalt before me, motionless. His bike lay on its side.

I launched off my bike.

Bam. Led fired. *Bam.*

I scrambled through the earsplitting jolt.

Motherfucker.

This cocksucker wanted vengeance.

But Wes was an innocent. An innocent in my care.

My responsibility.

My fucking consequence.

I slid my gun from my back and fired, diving behind Wes's fallen bike.

"Did you think I was gonna leave it like that?" Led charged toward me. "You giving Reich up to Finger? You using Nina?"

Boom.

Crack. Crack.

I twisted back down to the ground. A numbness danced up my arm, and my vision blurred. My chest was being crushed. My heart throbbed loudly in my ears.

Push through, push through.

Wes raised himself up, a gun in his hand. The kid was carrying. His hand shook; his arm wavered. He was injured from his fall.

Everything screeched to a stunning silence.

Wes fired a round, hitting the other Flame. The heavyset man grunted, stumbling back, blood spurting from an arm.

Boom.

Wes howled, his gun flying, skidding across the pavement. "Shit!"

"Wes!" I untucked my second gun, pitching it at him.

He caught it, his eyes hanging on mine for one stinging moment. His dad had trained him. Hell, all of us had.

He turned, sliding the safety. We both aimed.

"Fuckers!" Led charged toward us, shooting.

Another figure drew up behind Led and the Flame, his weapon held high.

What the—

We emptied our rounds into Led. The injured Flame raised his gun from behind his bike and aimed.

Crack. Crack.

The Flame's body jerked forward over his bike. The bike teetered, crashing down.

I lunged at Wes and grabbed at him, my fingers twisting in the cotton of his shirt.

Was he hurt? I had to keep him out of the line of fire.

He's priceless.

I yanked him on the ground and pushed myself upright, pain shooting in my chest, radiating through my neck, my arms straining.

"I'm all right! I'm all right!" Wes's dark blue eyes pulsed with life, with adrenaline, with confidence.

"Stay down," I hissed.

My fingers uncurled and flattened on his chest. His heart beat wildly under my palm.

So fucking priceless.

"Wes!" screamed a girl's voice in the distance, a slight figure running toward us, red hair flying.

Wes craned his neck. "Lindy?"

My shoulders fell, and my lungs constricted tightly, the pain in my chest excruciating. The large figure beyond rushed toward us, a revolver at his side, his features snarled.

Pick.

"Kid all right?" Pick shouted.

The reply stuck in my throat. The banging in my ears so loud...so loud. My heart thrashed in my chest, galloping hard on rocky ground; there was no keeping up with it. My head knocked back, meeting the hard earth. The trees tilted. The blue sky whirled above me.

"Butler! Butler, you okay?" Wes's voice was far away.

Pick hovered over me. Lindy. Wes.

Wes's face faded, and in its place was my brother's face. His voice in my ears.

"You've got a big heart, tough guy."

My hand reached out.

Air. Stephan, I need air...

My heart raced to a finish line that I couldn't make.

Would never make.

"A big heart."

Hands pressed over me.

"He's not shot! Then what the fuck—"

"Something's wrong with him!" Wes shouted from far away.
"Something's wrong!"
Breaths stuttered in my chest, beyond my reach.
I can't breathe. I can't—
My heart hammered in my neck, pounded around my throat.
Squeezing, squeezing everything from me.
I gave in.
"I'm so cold, so cold."
Everything faded.

FIFTY-FIVE

TANIA

MY HANDS SHOOK.

I curled my fingers into tight fists, but it did no good. The trembling and shuddering came from my insides.

Critical condition, Boner had said over the phone.

Heart rate through the roof, had said the EMS worker. *Severe palpitations. Tachycardia.*

In the Emergency Room, they had tried an IV push drug conversion—whatever the hell that was—but that had been unsuccessful.

Unsuccessful.

Boner burst from the hospital elevator doors, long dark hair flying, a small plastic bag in his hands. He threw the bag on the nurse's desk. "I got 'em! I got 'em!"

The doctor had sent Boner to Butler's apartment to find any medication he may have been taking.

Medication.

Prescriptions.

Jill's arm went through mine as we shot up out of our chairs.

"What did you find?" I asked glancing at the nurse who removed several prescription bottles from the bag.

"A lot of shit," Boner replied. "A lot."

Dready planted his hands on his waist. "I had no fucking idea. What the hell?" Dawes and Kicker stood at his side, their arms crossed, their faces drawn.

"Excuse me." The nurse turned to us. "Do any of you know if Mr. Matthiessen was getting his blood drawn and tested regularly to monitor his—"

"No, I don't know!" Boner's green eyes flared. "I don't know anything! He never said a damn word about—" Boner gestured at the pill bottles in her hands. "About—"

The nurse slanted her head. "His arrhythmia?"

"Yeah, that," Boner said.

Butler had a heart condition he'd been hiding from all of us.

I approached the nurse. "What did he have to get tested?"

"With arrhythmia there's the potential to faint and develop blood clots, so he's been on Warfarin, a blood thinner, and Toprol—" She raised a bottle. "—to slow down his heart rate."

"He's a heavy smoker. And he's been under a lot of stress lately!" I blurted.

"Oh. Not good. Plus if he's skipped any doses of his medication and hasn't been getting tested regularly to monitor his Prothrombin time and ratio—"

My brain zoomed back to all the times I'd noticed Butler rubbing a hand down his chest to his stomach, taking in deep breaths here and there, wincing while smoking. All the times he'd seemed tired, worn out, tense. *So many times.*

"Thank you," I muttered and sat back down with Jill.

We waited together.

Emergency surgery.

Alicia and Dawes brought everyone coffee and sandwiches.

My stomach twisted at the memory of the cryptic remarks Butler had made in the past.

"I am an antique all right. Broken casing, rusty insides, faulty wiring."

"I'm here on borrowed time, babe."

Jill threw away my untouched coffee.

Rusty insides.

Faulty wiring.

Borrowed time.

We waited.

He has to pull through. This can't be his end, it can't. Not this, please God, not this.

And we waited.

The hallway doors separating the surgical area from the waiting room swung open, and a doctor emerged holding a tablet. "Matthiessen?"

I darted toward him. "How is he? Is he going to be all right?"

"I had to implant a pacemaker to control his heart rate. He also had a valve problem."

"Fuck!" Dready muttered.

The doctor's glance darted over us, an eyebrow raised. His attention returned to me. "We needed to convert this arrhythmia to a normal sinus rhythm since the IV medication conversion was unsuccessful earlier. It was tricky because he's on the Warfarin, the blood thinner, and he could've bled out very easily."

My eyes widened.

"But he made it through. He'll be fine if he takes better care of himself." The surgeon glanced down at his iPad. "Once his blood pressure, pulse, and breathing are stable and he's alert, he'll be taken to a room. We'll keep him overnight for observation."

"Thank you." I let out a breath. "Thank you."

I sank into Jill's embrace.

FIFTY-SIX

BUTLER

"YOU LOOK BETTER, Uncle B. Much better," Wes said. He and Alicia stood next to me in my hospital room.

Boner and Dready stood on the other side of my bed.

"You're okay, Wes? You're not—" I moved to sit up, and my muscles pulled from somewhere deep inside.

"Relax, man," said Boner, a hand on my shoulder.

"I'm good," said Wes. "It was like I could hear you in my head, and I knew what I needed to do. We had each other's backs. That's what we do, right?"

"That's what we do," I said, my voice hoarse. "You've got good instincts, Wes. Your dad taught you well."

Wes's dark blue eyes were clear. He had a few scrapes and scratches on his face, but he was standing. He was good.

A small smile broke on his lips.

"Come here," I said hoarsely.

Wes leaned down, and I took him in my arms. "Love you, Wes."

"Love you, too," he mumbled into my neck.

I released him. "Like I said, once I get out of here, you and me."

"Yep." Wes nodded, his lips pressed together.

Alicia touched my shoulder. "Thank you for keeping my son safe, for everything. It means the world to me."

"You don't have to thank me," I replied.

"Oh, yes, I do." Alicia's voice snapped. "We all do. And thank God that Broken Blade showed up when he did."

"What Blade?" My mind drew a blank.

"Pick, Lindy's dad," said Wes. "He killed that Flame. Otherwise—"

"You know his daughter?" Alicia turned to her son.

"Yeah, Ma," replied Wes, his eyes sliding to me. "She's a friend."

"It's all good," Boner said. Pick was real cooperative. Everything's sweet and clean."

"Good to hear," I said.

"Oh, I'm sorry." Tania stood in the doorway and took a step back out of the room, her face flushing.

Alicia turned around. "Come in, honey. We're just going. Butler, we'll see you when you get home."

She went to Tania, and they chatted just outside the doorway.

"Oh, hey," said Wes, turning to me. "I forgot to ask you. Before you blacked out, you kept calling me Stephan."

"I did?"

"Yeah."

My hand swept down my chest. "Stephan was my brother. He died when he was about your age."

"Oh, sorry," said Wes, his voice low. He gripped my forearm.

I covered his hand with mine. "You get some rest."

"I will. See you, B." Wes left the room, glancing back at me as he passed through the doorway.

I spoke with Boner and Dready for a few moments more, we said our goodbyes, and then they left. Tania stepped in and clicked the door shut.

My eyes held her full ones. Full of sadness, spilling with emotion.

"Hey you."

"Hey." She tightly clutched the handles of her handbag. She stepped closer to the bed, to me. "You look like shit, but from what the doctor said, it's not deadly, if you take care of yourself."

I let out a laugh. "You know how to make a man feel better, don't you?"

She bit down on her wobbling lip, water filling her big dark eyes.

My insides dropped. "Tania, don't, baby. Don't cry."

"Shut up, and let me feel what I'm feeling."

I held out my hand to her. She took it, and I pulled her closer.

She planted a kiss on my forehead, a hand sweeping through my hair. "I can't lose you. Not now. Not now."

"I'm right here, Scarlett. Not going anywhere." I held her as she cried, hiccuping little breaths. "Get up here, baby. I want to hold you, I need to hold you."

She climbed into the hospital bed and wedged in next to me, sighing. I took in her perfume, the silk of her dark hair against my lips, and I finally breathed easier.

"Why didn't you tell me about your arrhythmia? You must have had a physical wherever you went for rehab, right? Is that when you found out you had it?"

"I never went to a real rehab."

"What?"

"I went to one rehab, but I didn't last too long. Then, I didn't have the money for a real rehab, and what money I did have, I needed to survive on. I did NA. Narcotics Anonymous. I made that commitment to myself and stuck with the program. Went to meetings. Still go."

"You're a strong man."

"Look at me. This is strong? I have a heart condition on top of the addiction issues. Tania, I can make you a hundred promises, sweep you off your feet, but when it counts—when it really counts—will I be able to step up? I'm an addict, and now this. One day, I might fail you. One day, you'll fall, and I might not be able to catch you."

"Stop right there."

"Babe, you can't fly a kite when it's attached to a stone. Kite's got to roll with the wind, move through the sky. You're up there, flying. I don't want your string to break, baby."

"You helped me fly."

"Did I?" I asked.

"Yes."

I let out a breath. "There I was, with this clear idea of what I was doing, what I could handle, where I was heading, and in a diner outside of Sioux Falls all that changed for me. Everything changed."

"For me, too." Her eyes searched mine. "Other than losing you, I only have one fear."

"Tell me. I want you to give all of those to me."

"I feel like I've just come up for air after being locked away in a musty basement. I like the fresh air out here, a lot, and I'm craving it in all sorts of new ways. There's no place in my life for disapproval, skepticism, or hollow criticism anymore. I need to be trusted for who I am, which includes every little inch of my crazy—moods, ideas, my work. All of it. I realize it's asking a lot from you, maybe too much, but I have to ask it of you. I won't allow myself to be crushed or to willingly submit to that ever again. That is a special kind of torture—silent, insidious, soul-destroying."

"I don't want you destroyed, Scarlett. You're soul is too beautiful, too fiery to be crushed."

She blinked at me. This was new for her, hearing that belief in who she was, that admiration. It felt damn good to say it, to see that light in her eyes, that hope blooming where there had once been a deep ache.

I believed it with every fiber of my worn-out heart.

She squeezed my hand, and my eyes went to our entwined fingers. I was one lucky son of a bitch.

"Do you give enough of a damn, Rhett?" Tania wiped at her eyes, a grin pushing up her lips.

"I give way more than a damn, baby." I held her watery gaze. "I want us to know every inch of each other, inside and out, clean and filthy, the pretty and the plain fucking ugly. The sweet and the sour. My cracked corroded parts and all your fragile tiny bones." My fingers tightened over her delicate wrist. "I'm rusty and full of scars inside, and that's as clean as I'm going to get. If that's good enough for you, take it. Take it all."

She brushed her hand down my chest. "You might think you have nothing but rust inside your veins, clogging your heart. But you know what? You and me together, what we have—it creates fresh blood. And that blood will scour the rust in both our hearts, wash it away, bit by clinging hard bit."

She planted a kiss on my lips. "Although, you do realize, rust is a sign of history, experience. It has it's own strange beauty. Some of us appreciate it." A hand swept through my hair.

"That feels good," I murmured.

"You go to sleep, you need rest. I'll keep playing with your hair, Blondie. Don't mind me."

"Hmm." My eyelids sank.

"I can't sing you to sleep though. Sorry." She giggled.

And, on the softness of that sweet laugh, I drifted.

"You didn't have to do it!" Stephan puts his truck in gear, and we zoom down the mountain pass road.

"Yeah, I did," I reply, wiping away the sweat from my hot face.

"I told you not to go near him! Racing on the bluffs? And you've been drinking?"

"Did you see it, Stephan? Did you see me finish?"

"How do you do this shit? How are you going to explain your dented bike to Dad now?"

I shrug, clicking my seat belt in place. "I'll think of something."

"You always do."

"Dude, did you see me cross the finish line and wipe his ass with it?"

"Yeah, I did, Markus. You were amazing. You blew him away." He squeezes my leg. "And I'm so relieved you're in one piece."

I grin. "And, on top of Austen's humiliation, we got plenty of cash." I show him the wad of bills I won.

"Holy shit."

"It's ours."

Stephan only shakes his head at me. Such a worrywart.

"Ah, man, the look on his face," I say. "Pouting on an epic scale. What a dick. I'm so glad you were there. I knew, if I'd told you beforehand, you would've stopped me."

"I knew something was up when you were a no-show at the party tonight. Your band was up there, playing without you. You've never given up a night of playing. Especially a paying gig. They are pissed as hell at you, by the way."

"I had an opportunity. I had to take it. They'll get over it. It'll be fine."

"Well I got out here as fast as I could." He glances at me, his lips pressed together, his wavy brown hair in his eyes. "You didn't have to challenge him. You didn't have to do this for me."

I lean back against the headrest. "Of course I did. That shithead doesn't get to go scot-free after accusing you of cheating just 'cause he got caught. Then, he comes on to your girlfriend? Fuck no."

"I told you to stay away from him, Markus."

"Have you ever known me to back down?"

"No. That's why I told you—"

"Admit it. You're glad I did it."

A grin blooms on his face. "I'm fucking ecstatic."

We high-five, clutching each other's hands for a brief moment. "Priceless!" we declare together, laughing loudly. Our chant since junior high.

We both grin like fools. Deep satisfaction.

"That smile on your face right there just made it all worth it. Even the dent on my bike," I say.

"You're nuts."

"Austen thought he was the shit with that flashy new Yamaha his daddy bought him," I continue. "You gotta know how to ride before you can glide, my friend!"

I howl out the open window, and Stephan only laughs harder.

He squeezes my arm. "You're my kid brother. I should be looking out for you."

"Shut up. It's not such a big deal."

"Yeah, it is, Markus. It is to me. You've got a big heart, tough guy. You don't know how much it means to me that you've always got my back."

"Shut up."

"It's true."

"It wasn't fair, what he tried to do to you. I wanted justice, and I knew how to get it."

"You got it, all right. I just don't want you getting in trouble again. With school, with Mom and Dad."

"Don't worry about me."

"I do worry. Look, you've got to lay low the rest of the season, no matter what Austen and his crew throw at you at school, all right?" Stephan says. "We need you in the game next Friday, and Coach is going to have your ass if you eat another detention."

I tap out a beat on my thighs. I am so ready for that game. So ready. Stephan and I make a great duo on the football field. He makes the plays, and I help make them happen.

"We're in the state semifinals, man!" Stephan hoots loudly. "The semis! You get that?"

"Oh, I get that, and I'm totally psyched. And, by the way, tonight, Joanna Pelton let me know just how psyched she is about it, too."

"What? The Joanna Pelton?" Stephan glances at me. "You're too much."

"I am," I reply, pounding out the beat on my chest. "And she swallowed it all. Every last drop."

"Unbelievable."

"Believe it." I rub my hands down my face and stretch out my lower back. "Shit, I can't keep my eyes open. I'm exhausted."

"Take a snoozer. I'll wake you up right before we get home, so you can get your shit together before you walk through the door. Otherwise, there's going to *be hell to pay. Yet again. And I, for one, am not in the mood for Dad's hard line tonight."*

Stephan flips on the radio, and I close my eyes. He sings along with Van Halen.

I groan. "I hate this song. Change it."

"Tough." He goes back to singing. Van Halen segues into Bon Jovi.

The truck jostles over the rocky dirt road. Nausea rolls through my stomach, and bile rises up my throat. Too many beers, too much vodka, too much adrenaline. My brain swirls and twists in my skull while my stomach does a strange dance. I undo my seat belt and lower my window, leaning my head out, gulping in the cold air. The wet prickles of rain cool my skin.

I swallow hard, a hand sliding down my chest. "Shit, slow down, would you? You're taking these curves way too fast, and there aren't any lights here. So fucking dark."

"You think you're the only Mario Andretti in the family?"

"I'm not kidding, Stephan. I'm gonna be sick."

"Don't you dare puke in my truck."

"Then, slow the fuck down! You bang up my bike that you probably didn't secure properly back there, I'm gonna have your ass!"

"We've got fifteen minutes. You know how Dad is about our curfew. We've already crossed the line a couple of times this month. One more isn't going to fly. I sure as hell don't want to get grounded again, especially on account of you."

"I love how it's always my fault. Usually, it's because you can't tear yourself away from sucking on your girlfriend, and I'm the one covering for you."

"I hate leaving her at the end of the night. You have no idea what that's like."

"Whatever. Oh"—I smack his shoulder—"speaking of which, Jocelyn's mom is under the illusion that her little princess is still a virgin. The other day, I overheard her tell Ma how happy she was that you two were dating, that you're so gentlemanly and respectful, blah, blah, blah. Once again, you made our mother proud in ways I never will. But it's all based on a lie anyway."

"Jesus."

I chuckle, my eyelids sinking shut. "He can't help you now."

The windshield wipers shuffle faster, doing battle with the heavy thrum of raindrops, lulling me to Groggyville.

"What the—"

Stephan jams on the brakes, and the tires scream. My eyes jerk open, my neck stiffening.

A fox with glow-in-the-dark eyes is glued to the shiny wet road before us. The truck lurches and skids. My eyes shoot to Stephan gripping the wheel. He yells. A hideous, horrible sound.

My pulse explodes. The truck spins.

"Stephan!"

We fly.

My breath chokes out from me.

Steel crunches in the black darkness. My head kicks back on my neck, and my lungs crush together. The windshield caves around me, shards of glass slashing my hands, my face.

I soar.

Ripping howls.

Cracking.

Shouts.

Mom!

Blood.

Mom

Pain.

Terror.

Pain.

Blood.

Blood.

Stephan?

FIFTY-SEVEN

BUTLER

I TUMBLED.

"Butler! Honey?"

Tania's voice.

Tania.

Gasping for air, I forced my eyes to unglue.

Tania's dark brown pools of forever held me. "Are you okay? You were having a nightmare. You were calling for Stephan."

My head rocked to the side on the pillows.

The box of a window. The institutional beige Venetian blinds. The curtain hanging around my bed.

Hospital bed.

Hospital.

"Butler?" Her hands swept down the sides of my face, and my muscles eased.

"Here. Drink." She held a Styrofoam cup with a straw out to me.

I raised my head, took the straw between my lips, and drank some water.

"You want to tell me what that dream was about?"

"Not really."

"Too bad. I think you need to."

"It's 'cause of Wes, I guess." I licked at my dry lips. "He reminds me of my brother. A little bit of both of us."

Tania adjusted my pillows. "What's your real first name, by the way, brother of Stephan?"

"Markus."

"I like that. Stephan and Markus. So, tell me about Stephan."

I blew out a breath.

"It might help." She took my hand and stroked it.

My head sank back into the pillow. "My brother was a year and something older than me. More responsible than I ever was. Stephan was a great football player. So great that he was being courted by several top schools for a full ride. It was huge. Dream-come-true huge."

"Did you play football, too?"

"I did."

"Were you good?"

"Yeah, but not great. Stephan was great, and he really loved it. I didn't have the ambitions my brother did either. Didn't see it as a way up or a way out of our mediocre lower middle-class existence. Stephan had the steady girlfriend and the good grades. But I was the pretty one. I was the player, Mr. Easy Come, Easy Go. It all came easy to me, whatever it was—picking up girls, learning my way around a bike and a car at my dad's shop, studying for a test the night before and getting a good enough grade. But Stephan was different. Special.

"This idiot at school who was real jealous of Stephan had tried to get him in trouble with the principal by implicating him in a cheating scandal, but it was all lies. Stephan was so worried about his record, so stressed out. So, I challenged Austen Taymor—I still remember the shit's name—to a bike race by these bluffs we had in our town."

"A duel?"

"Yeah. Stephan had told me to ignore him, but I couldn't. I had to do something, stand up for him somehow. So, I did what I did best. Speed."

"You won?"

"I whooped his ass in front of the whole school—him on a brand-new bike, me on the old bike I'd rebuilt with my dad. I won a lot of money that night, and I stomped on Austen for the whole school to see. He was supposed to retract his bullshit to the principal the next day.

"Stephan heard about the race and came. I hadn't told him about it because I knew he'd stop me. It started raining, and it was really dark. He was rushing, so we'd get home in time for our curfew. Then, some animal appeared on the road, a small one, and he tried to avoid it. He lost control of the truck. We flipped over. I wasn't wearing my seat belt 'cause I'd been drinking and felt sick. I ended up getting thrown clear of the truck."

"And Stephan?"

"Stephan was trapped in the truck, and the truck caught fire. I tried to get to him, but I couldn't. The firemen and the cops got him out, but his spine was broken, a leg smashed, and he had burns. Everything stopped then. The football, the scholarship, the girlfriend, the future. The health insurance. All his plans, his dreams, my parent's dreams. Everything. My parents blamed me, and they were right. It was my fault for racing, for getting wasted, for Stephan picking me up."

"Yeah, but—"

"They were right." My eyes met Tania's. "Then it turned into, *Why Stephan? Why not you?* My parents started seeing right through me, like I was invisible, like I was nothing. I didn't exist anymore in that house. There was a lot to do to take care of Stephan, bring money in, double mortgage, and all. I pulled my weight, but no matter what, I was invisible. They had to put Stephan in a state-run facility, and a few months later, he died from pneumonia and a hundred other complications. It was horrible, it was a relief, it was a nightmare all over again. The blaming and the, *We didn't do enough. We should've done more,* started back up again.

"I couldn't stay in that house. I had two months to go to finish my senior year, and I dropped out. Got on my bike, and didn't look back. Headed further north, up the coast, and just bummed around. I surfed, got odd jobs, sold weed and whatever else I could get my hands on. I convinced myself I was living the good life.

"The Jacks were out west on some run and were joyriding up the coast a bit before heading back here. I tagged along, figured, *What the fuck else did I have to do?*"

Tania's head slanted. "It was more than that, wasn't it?"

"Ah, Scarlett."

"Tell me about meeting the One-Eyed Jacks for the first time."

"What I remember most is looking into those golden brown eyes of Dig's and wanting to be like him. Confident, full of purpose, no shadows hanging over him, and not giving a fuck. And Boner? Oh, man, that cat didn't let anything touch him. The epitome of a free spirit. Totally in the moment, as if he had no frame of reference for anything but what was right there in front of him. I envied that. Boner played it cool and easy, but I could also see the hard glint in his eyes. Dig's, too. It was startling. They were just a few years older than me, but they had lived, and they were living. I was just hanging out, waiting for shit to happen and bumping into it as it did. I didn't know I could want things out of life.

"I got on my fucking bike and came back here with them, prospected, and you know the rest."

"Yes, I know the rest."

"I was Wes once upon a time. I had what he had in the palms of his hands—School, football, and the cover-boy looks to make it all real sweet, but I let it go. Stephan was the good one. Stephan followed all the rules, and it actually bothered him if he ever fell short. Not me. I didn't have that kind of conscience. He did, and he kept me on the straight and narrow, pulling me back in between the lines whenever I strayed."

"Which was often?" she asked.

"Pretty much. Without my brother, I felt lost. In the end, my wrongs, my badness, my unworthiness were all that was left. So, to let all that go, I let *everything* go."

"Did you ever tell your parents that the accident wasn't your fault?"

"They wouldn't have listened, Tania. It just didn't matter at the end of the day. It wouldn't have changed that Stephan wasn't ever going to get better, that he was gone. Their grief was so deep that they couldn't see straight, and so was mine. If it made them feel better to have someone to blame, what the hell?"

"I'm sorry," Tania murmured.

"Almost lost Wes on that road. Because of me. Almost lost Wes. When I saw him spin out. When I heard the gunfire. I saw Stephan again. I saw Caitlyn. Almost lost Wes…Almost."

"But you didn't. You protected him and he protected you. Both of you, together."

"I was a good brother. I was," I breathed.

Stephan grinned at me from inside that truck of his, and a shudder passed through me.

"Yes, you were." Tania's hand stroked the side of my face, and something heavy detached inside me, crumbling.

My body trembled, a cold sweat prickled over my skin. "I was a…g-good brother."

"Yes, Markus, yes, you were. You were a good brother."

She pressed a red button on a cable by the bed.

"I was. I was."

Is that my shaky voice?

"Yes, honey."

Tania took me in her arms and held me as I finally mourned for Markus and Stephan.

FIFTY-EIGHT

BUTLER

THE DRAMATIC SOUNDTRACK to *On the Waterfront* blared from my television set as the credits rolled on the screen.

"The music in this film is amazing, isn't it?" I said. "It's the one time Leonard Bernstein composed for film."

Since I'd come home from the hospital a couple of weeks ago, Tania and I had been spending almost all our free time together. Tonight, I was cooking us dinner while we watched one of my favorite Marlon Brando films on DVD.

"I liked how it ended. Hopeful." Tania put her feet up on the edge of my old coffee table.

I scoffed as I stretched out next to her on the sofa.

"What? You don't think so?" she asked.

"This is the Hollywood version, baby, where Terry Malloy— the has-been boxing contender, the young underdog under everybody's thumb—is finally able to step up and do the right thing, be the best Terry Malloy he could be and forge a new future for his community. Doesn't end this way in the original."

"You've read the book?"

"One of my favorites. *Waterfront* by Budd Schulberg."

"How does it end in the book?"

"In the true ending, last time we see Terry, his pigeons have been massacred after he testified against mob boss Johnny Friendly, and he's saying good-bye to the girl."

Tania sat up on the sofa. "Wait, she leaves in the book?"

"Yeah, she decides to go back to her Catholic boarding school after all. But she's concerned about Terry, hoping he'll escape the hell of their mob-ridden town, too. He's pretty upbeat though about a new beginning, and he's feeling all these emotions for her when they say good-bye."

"They say good-bye?"

"Oh, yes, my little romantic," I said, squeezing her leg. "She leaves, and he goes missing. Weeks later, a barrel washes up in a Jersey swamp. It's filled with lime and a mutilated corpse with a load of stab wounds from an ice pick."

"No!"

"Yep. Terry Malloy ends up being just a bunch of ripped up body parts, never formally ID'd, never claimed by anyone."

"Oh, no."

"Yes, yes. Sucks, huh?"

Tania pouted. "You just ruined my high. I feel an ugly cry coming on."

"Go back to believing in the Hollywood fairy tale. Think of Brando and Eva Marie Saint. Go ahead. Go back to that image of her cheering for him on the wharf, their rosy future ahead of them."

"Can't there be good endings for the battered and bruised?"

I wrapped my arm around her shoulders. "You know, in the book, they barely kiss. They only have that one dance in the beginning. A couple of minutes at best of being in sync, of them feeling those *feelings*. But he felt something, and he knew how good, how special, those feelings were. He knew, and it was the best thing for him. It comforted him, gave him confidence. And that's as close as Terry Malloy got to happy in his whole fucking life."

Her eyes filled with water, and something pinched in my gut. I leaned in and brushed her lips with a gentle kiss, and she softened underneath me. That tender feel of her. Vulnerable. Open to me. A volcanic pulse went off inside me, and I stilled to feel it all.

This is a real high. So damn good.

"A few rays of happiness here and there make life worth all the dull pain. Terry Malloy recognized it and appreciated it in that one moment," I murmured against her forehead. "That's a kind of victory."

"I want more than a moment. I want—"

I pulled back from her. "You want Hollywood?"

Her big dark eyes searched mine. "I don't want a Hollywood fantasy. I want real."

"I used to think that the fact that I was still alive was good enough for me."

Her eyes narrowed. "Don't do that. Please don't do that. Don't be fooled by *good enough*. I made that mistake. I lived *good enough* for what felt like a hundred years. And it's not enough. It barely skimmed the surface. *Good enough* hangs you out to dry."

She pushed away from me, but I grabbed her arm, pulling her back in against me.

"Hey, hey," I said softly. "What is it?"

"When are you going to see that you deserve a happily ever after? A real big juicy one? That it's possible? That you can have it?"

The oven alarm beeped. My roast chicken and potatoes were ready.

Tania sank back against the sofa. "Saved by the bell."

I planted a quick kiss on her mouth and went to the kitchen. I tapped the timer off and opened the oven door. "Looks good."

"It smells really good. I'm starving." She wiped at her eyes and went to the fridge and took out the cabbage salad that she'd made earlier. She brought the bowl to the small table.

I sectioned up the bird. "White or dark?"

"I'm a leg and thigh girl." She winked at me.

"Hmm. Good to know." I placed the meat on her dish and scooped up the golden potatoes with the lemony juice over them. She brought the dishes to the table, and we sat.

Tania put a forkful in her mouth and blinked at me. "Butler, this is really good."

"You like it?"

"No"—she chewed and swallowed—"I love it. How did you do it?"

"At that one rehab I went to, I hung out with this older woman—"

"Of course you did."

"No, it wasn't like that. Gini was about twenty years older than me. She had a problem with pain meds. Gini and I had a lot to talk about. Pain meds were my old pals, too, after the accident with my brother. She was a loner and liked watching cooking shows whenever we had TV time. She used to roll her eyes at the others watching soap operas or talk shows. Very no-nonsense lady. I liked her." I let out a sigh. "I was getting my appetite back. It was a strange new world to me. And I'd never watched shit like that before. I was all animal and nature shows, the guys that live in the swamps, those Alaska shows. Gini turned me on to Bobby Flay grilling, this little Italian woman who was a total powerhouse, that English guy, Jamie Oliver, and a couple of others. Anyway, Gini told me that everyone should know how to make a roasted chicken, a basic, standard classic."

"I have to agree."

"I'd never thought about it before. My ma was not a good cook. No creativity. Made the same shit all the time, and it all blended into one tasteless series of lumps. Meatloaf baked with ketchup on top, dried pork chops with stiff mashed potatoes from a box and a side of frozen peas and carrots, mushy and crusty noodle casseroles with soup can sauces, hot dogs and beans. All insanely predictable, each one assigned to its own day of the week. Over and over again."

"Poor baby!"

"But listening to Gini go on about her family dinners and holidays with such nostalgia and in such loving details, made an impression. She made me see that food could be this connector to good memories of family, friends, big moments in your life. That's something I never had, had no awareness of. I didn't grow up with those flavors, that color, but Gini had, and she'd given it to her family while she could. She showed me how food—*good* food— could help make memories stick, help you touch that joy in high and low times, then helps you recreate it later on. A celebration."

"Did Caitlyn cook?"

"Caitlyn? Nah, not really. She'd experiment sometimes, try out recipes, but nine times out of ten, they wouldn't turn out right."

"Would you give her shit for it?"

I shot her a look. "Hell no. Big deal. She tried, always gave it her all. We'd end up making a sandwich or some eggs and call it a day or go out if we had the cash."

A shadow crossed Tania's face and then faded.

"What is it?"

She stabbed at a potato with her fork. "Nothing," she murmured.

"Baby, tell me."

Her gaze remained on her food. "You were a good husband."

"I don't know. I tried." I touched her leg with mine under the table. "What is it? Tania, tell me."

She put down her fork and ran her tongue across her lips. "If I ever had a fail in the kitchen, Kyle would let me know in precise detail where I had gone wrong. Flavor, texture, salt level—wherever I had missed the mark. He'd point out what I should have done, what I obviously had not done. He'd shake his head and push the food around his plate or chew on a forkful, like he was a martyr enduring some form of torture. Then, eventually, he'd declare it was unfit for his consumption. We'd argue, and sometimes, he'd even leave the table. I'd lose my appetite and end up giving it all to the neighbor's dog or throw it away before cleaning everything all up." She took in a deep breath and slowly let it out.

"Baby—"

She shook her head and swallowed, her eyes remaining on her dish.

That motherfucker.

I wanted to erase that humiliation that was morphing her beautiful face, stiffening her shoulders, streaking her soul. I wanted to obliterate all the negative clouds that fucker had put behind her eyes, the fractures he had created in her heart. The doubts, the mean, the negligence he had singed her soul with.

Here was one of the smartest, most beautiful women I had ever met, and she was shouldering and hiding a mountain of false bullshit that he had molded especially for her. For what? For his own goddamn ego, that was what.

Fuck no.

I slid my leg against hers. "You want my secret roast chicken recipe?" I asked, my voice gentle.

Her face tilted up, the corner of her mouth tugging upward.

Smile, Scarlett. For fuck's sake, I'm gonna put that smile that's connected to that big heart back on your face if it's the last thing I do.

I sliced through a potato wedge. "The recipe is from the Italian lady's television show. I forget her name now. Want to hear it?"

Tania nodded, her lips rolling, her brows still drawn together. "Sure."

"You take butter and garlic, some fresh thyme leaves, some rosemary, grated lemon rind, coarse sea salt, pepper. You mash all that together in one of those pounding things." I gestured with my hand.

"A mortar and pestle?"

"Yeah, that's it, or you could use some mini blender chopper thingy. Anyway, you mash all that together until it's a thick paste. Add Dijon mustard, lemon juice, and olive oil, then, you slather it all over your bird, both under and over the skin. Especially under the skin, in all those hidden little places. Then, you pour more lemon juice and olive oil over the chicken and the potatoes. In the oven it all goes for about two and a half hours. Mid-way, you turn the bird over, and that's it. Done."

She stared at me, her jaw slack.

"What is it?"

"I think I could listen to you describe recipes all day. That growly, husky voice of yours, coupled with all that enthusiasm."

"Huh."

She smiled at me, the tension gone from her beautiful face, and my muscles relaxed. "You did a great job on the bird. It's incredibly good. Really flavorful. I'll be making it."

"Do I get an invite when you do?"

"If you'd like to meet Rae, sure."

"I'd like to meet your mom. Boner knows your mom, right? Of course he does."

"Boner's the new son-in-law."

"Maybe you should get two big birds and have your sister and her hubs, and Jill and Boner over, too, and then we can get the formal intro done that way."

She stared at me, her fork midair.

"What is it?"

She remained perfectly still. "You want to come over to my house and meet my mother over dinner, a family dinner?"

"I've met your sister and her husband at your store parties. And I'd prefer Boner and Jill to Catch and Nina at the moment, don't you think? We'll leave that for another time."

The silent stare remained.

"Unless you think this chicken isn't worthy of meeting your mom?"

"Oh, it's plenty worthy." She slid dark meat onto her fork.

"You should get those Yukon Gold potatoes, too. Boner will flip over those. Guaranteed he has no idea about the different kinds of potato out there."

"Those purply blue potatoes would really freak him out, don't you think?" Tania laughed, and something brightened in my chest.

We finished eating and cleaned up the kitchen together.

I ran my fingers through the back of her hair, the soft silk sliding over my fingers. "Do you have to get home?"

"No. Jill and Becca are spending the night since Boner's out of town. If you need to get sleep though, I'll go." She sat up and moved forward on the couch.

"No, no." My hand landed on her back. "Stay with me tonight?"

We hadn't been together since I'd gotten hospitalized. If I had to spell shit out for her, I would do it. To be clear. Clear as light through a fucking diamond.

"I want you to stay with me tonight. I've missed you. And I have an appetite for you that is not satisfied."

Her dark eyes lit up.

I kissed those lips. "Needs feeding, babe." I stroked her tongue with mine. "Needs satisfying."

"Oh…"

"Could we make a dent in that, you think?"

"Yes, we certainly could. Did you ask the doctor, though?"

"I did. He gave me the green light."

My thumb stroked the side of her throat, and her eyes fluttered. I laid kisses across her jaw.

She let out a soft cry.

I let go of her and went into the living room and made myself comfortable on the sofa, my eyes never leaving her dreamy ones.

"Strip."

Her eyes popped open. She pulled off her socks and tugged off her fancy T-shirt. She undid her jeans, shoving them down those sexy legs of hers. Holding my eyes, she unhooked her bra and slid it off her body, releasing those small but firm, round breasts. My mouth dried as she tucked her fingers in either side of her panties.

"Slowly." My voice rasped.

She tugged them down her legs very slowly, stepping out of them.

She kicked the panties from her ankle, and I shook my head at her as I stretched out my hand. She cocked an eyebrow and leaned over, snatched up her scrap of underwear, and handed it to me. I grinned, holding the damp satiny material in my hand, taking in the heady fragrance of her. Her lust, her desire for me. She blushed, her lips parting. I hung the flimsy underwear on the headstock of my guitar, which stood against the wall at my side. Tania released another low moan at the sight. I gestured for her to come close. She did, standing in front of me.

I held her gaze as my hand slid between her legs and my fingers grazed her very wet sweet spot. She gasped. I held her thighs apart and slowly licked her, my tongue teasing her clit.

Her fingers sank into my hair. "Butler!"

I wanted her to use me.

"Fuck my face, baby." I pressed the tops of my teeth just above her clit, giving her a hard point of resistance. She groaned and whimpered as she ground her hips into my face. My fingers dug into her full ass as she chased her orgasm.

Fuck yeah.

She came, and I lapped at her quivering flesh, holding her close.

"Tania."

Her dazed eyes found mine.

"Go to my bedroom and wait for me on the bed."

Her skin flushed, and she stepped back and strode off into the darkness of my room, the curves of her fantastic ass highlighted by the light we'd left on in the kitchen.

Taking in a deep breath, I ran a hand down my chest. My heart was racing like I was about to lose my virginity. Only that time was a forgettable and pathetic five minutes under the bleachers after football practice. This, however, felt like a game changer. Every time with Tania felt like a new adventure. A step in a new direction.

She wanted to be with me. She knew the risks, and she still wanted me.

My balls tightened. I squeezed my eyes shut, taking in another breath.

I went into the dark bedroom. Her short, choppy breathing was the only sound in the room.

Tania sat on the edge of the bed, her arms taut, her legs pressed together. An actual shiver raced over the back of my neck as I opened my dresser drawer where I kept my bandanas.

No, give her the one you used today. Let her smell you, feel you.

My hand found the twisted cotton lying on top of the dresser, and I grabbed it.

I approached her without saying a word, and I slid the bandana over her eyes. She let out a tiny gasp as I tied it behind her head.

"Butler—"

"Shh…" I ran my hands through her thick mass of dark hair. So dark, it was black, true black. My exotic queen.

She let out a soft moan, her head relaxing under my lazy strokes. I wanted to take my time with her.

Yes, it was good to be sober to drink it all in.

Drink *her* in.

My fingers tickled down her shoulders, her arms, and to her tits. She whimpered as I softly palmed them and squeezed them hard, demanding her attention. Her head shot up, her lips tensed.

My knee nudged her legs apart as I slid a thumb in her mouth, and she sucked on me, making those little sounds from the back of her throat. My cock throbbed in my jeans, my brain misfiring into that intensely happy place of *fuck yes.*

This was anticipation. This was bursting flavors. This was smooth brandy. Expensive whiskey. A gourmet fucking five star meal.

I popped my thumb out of her mouth, and she let out an incredible cry. Want. Need.

I got down on my knees and slid my hands up her thighs, my wet thumb stroked up her slit and swirling around her clit. Her head fell back once more, and she moaned.

"You're beautiful," I whispered against her tits, taking a tip in my mouth, grazing it with my teeth.

She flinched, and I laved her hard nipple with my tongue.

"You're perfect, Tan." I caressed her throat with my lips.

My hands slid down over her hips, and I pulled them forward. I leaned down and blew air over her pussy, and her pelvis arched up.

"You want me, Scarlett? You want what you know I can give you, don't you?"

"Yes, yes—"

"I want to give it to you, baby. Everything you've ever wanted. Everything you need." I pushed her back against the mattress.

She squirmed on the bed, her hands in tight little fists over her head.

I licked her pussy, toyed with her clit, my thumbs pulling her lips apart, giving me full access to every slick little inch. She was a diamond to be adored. My diamond. My black diamond. She tensed, her legs squeezing my sides.

"Easy." I splayed a hand over the cool skin of her hip. "Open wide for me and stay that way, sweetheart."

She did as she'd been told. Wrapping one hand around her quivering thigh, I buried my face between her legs and sucked on her smooth flesh. She moaned out loud, and that raw sound coursed through my veins. My head split open under a blaze of heat. I wanted to give to Tania. Simply give. My fingers pressed into her body, keeping her under me.

"Butler! Stop, please! I'm too sensitive." She twisted in my hold. "It's too much."

"You haven't seen too much yet. This is where it gets good, baby," I insisted with more subtle licks and lashes. I persuaded her with harsher strokes and deeper sucks, sending her over the edge again. She chanted words and sounds, her chest heaving, her arms limp at her sides.

My dick banged against my jeans, and I got up off the bed, ripped them off, then my shirt. I grabbed a condom from my end table, suited up, and went back to her.

I kneeled on the bed, pulled her close, gripped her thighs, and, bending her legs, I spread them wide. I brought my cock to her entrance. "I'm gonna fuck that beautiful pussy that I made so wet, and you're going to fuck me right back. You got that, Scarlett?"

"Yes," she breathed.

I drove inside her. My hungry, desperate cock found its hungry, desperate, and very slick target.

"Butler!"

I pulled out and drove in deeper. "Oh shit, Tan…"

She stretched around me. Her body stilled and then her pelvis rose up to meet me as she let out a low moan.

I fucked Tania. I fucked through the ache and the yearning for her that I'd stashed deep inside myself all this time. I fucked the disappointments from her memories. I fucked the doubts and the pain she still fed like stray dogs, and I fucked those dogs into a corner and stared them down.

I fucked through my own strays.

For both of us.

This was an honesty that wasn't anxious or shaded with denial or had subclauses attached to it for a later date, just in case. I didn't shrink from it like I would a cold blast of frozen winter air on the plains. This honesty only made something inside me pliant, stronger, brighter.

Fucking her now wasn't only about getting us both off, about forgetting or feeling better for a brief moment. With every thrust, I wanted to feel her happiness unfurl around us and keep us both high.

Planting her feet in the mattress behind my legs, she lifted herself up on her arms and quickened our pace, meeting me thrust for thrust.

Fuck yes.

I wanted to show her that she was that glorious woman she craved to be.

I wanted to show her I could be the man she saw, the man reflected back at me in her gorgeous dark chocolate eyes.

I ripped the bandana off of her. Her eyes sought mine.

My Scarlett.

I could trust her, believe in her, as she'd asked me to. It scared the fuck out of me, but I wanted this more than that fear—the fear of losing her, not living up to her, not deserving her, the fear of dying on her. Maybe I had to ride that thin line to get to the other side, to be the man a woman like her could believe in.

"What do you believe in?" asked that voice from my past once more.

I believe in this. In us.

Yes, I could be that man. I could.

"Baby," she rasped, her lips parted, her eyes on fire, her body fucking mine, one with mine.

I am.

FIFTY-NINE

TANIA

"GRACE?"

She grinned at me, a pen in her mouth. "Tania?"

I leaned over her desk in the office of Eagle Wings. "I need new boots."

A grin split her face. She was the one for the job. "Oh?"

"Special boots."

"Intriguing." She put a stack of work orders in a folder and handed the folder to Tricky, who stood waiting. "What kind of *special* exactly?"

I leaned in closer, glancing at Tricky, who ambled into the hallway, going through the folder. "Special fuck-me-now boots," I whispered.

Her eyes widened. "Very, very intriguing. More intriguing than expected."

I laughed.

"Western or high fashion?"

"More high fashion."

"Then, unfortunately, Pepper's is out," Grace said, referring to Meager's very own western boot store, that blessedly had survived all these years. We'd been fans since our youth, as had our parents, and their parents before them.

"Shame, but yes. Not Pepper's. Where else?"

"A snazzy new boutique opened in Rapid last month with brands from LA. We'll go there. It'll cost you though."

"Worth the investment."

"Hmm." She folded her hands together across her desk, her back straightening. "And tell me, Ms. Reigert, may I ask what you're hoping to gain with this investment, specifically?"

"I need to show my appreciation for a very important contract, Mrs. LeBeau."

"Aha!"

"And something else."

"Yes? Yes?"

"I'd like to see Ronny, the tattoo master."

"Seriously?"

"Yes. I have an idea I'd like to run by him, see what he thinks. And then I'll make an appointment for another time."

A grin lit her face. "I'll put in a call now." Grace picked up her cell phone from her desk and tapped on the screen.

"And one more thing—"

Her hazel eyes darted up at me.

"The necklace you had made for Lock—the skeleton key? I need to see that jeweler, too."

"Should I take the morning off from work and see if my dad can stay longer with Thunder today?"

"You assume correctly. You call your dad. I'll go talk to your boss for you."

Laughing, Grace put the phone to her ear. "I'm feeling an urge for champagne."

"That's a good urge, girlfriend. Very good urge. We get all those errands done, I'm buying."

SIXTY

TANIA

I'D MADE THE ROASTED CHICKENS—three, in fact. And I'd bought the Yukon Gold potatoes and thrown in a few sweet potatoes and carrots as well. A huge mixed greens salad and freshly baked baguettes from the new bakery in town, which used local wheat, completed the meal. Under my mother's direction, Jill had set the table with the good china, the crystal glasses, and the silver cutlery.

Rae smiled wide as she shuffled in the dining room with her cane. She'd even put on her favorite gold hoop earrings for the occasion. "Why didn't you set out the cloth napkins, Jill?"

Jill shot me an I-told-you-so face.

"Mother," I said, "I bought these thick formal paper napkins. They look fine. Anyway, we won't have to worry about washing out grease stains or ironing them later."

Rae shook her head. "Oh, Tania!"

"What? I'm trying to play up the low-key, casual aspect of this dinner. You having Jill whip out the fine china, the good crystal, and the silver forks and knives kind of cuts into that idea. Ironed monogrammed linen napkins would only throw the whole thing over the edge. I'm telling you, they wouldn't want to use them. Work with me here, Rae."

"Are you saying, these men would be threatened by a few squares of fabric?"

"Hardly, but that's not my point."

"Oh. You're saying they don't deserve the full extra effort, A-list guest treatment from us?"

"No. No, of course not. That's not what I meant."

Jill's gaze ping-ponged between us.

"Ah. Are you saying they wouldn't be able to appreciate china, crystal, silver, and monogrammed linen napkins?"

"No."

Rae's left eyebrow arched very high. The final pronouncement was to be made. "This is a special occasion. Our house has not seen such an occasion in a very long time. And I would like to welcome our guests appropriately."

Jill and my mother stared at me.

I took in a breath. "Fine."

Jill snorted, covering her mouth with a hand.

My mother only slanted her head. "Fine?"

"You're right, Mother," I replied.

"I think someone could use a glass of wine," Rae murmured. "And it isn't me."

Jill bit her bottom lip and turned to the drawer of the sideboard where the linen napkins were and took them out.

The front door opened, and my sister, her husband, Fred, and Nate and Carter burst into the house carrying shopping bags.

"We're here!" Carter shouted.

"As if you couldn't tell," Penny said on a laugh.

"Hey!" Fred wiped his shoes on the welcome mat.

Becca came running and hopped up and down in between her cousins as they removed their jackets. Penny grabbed them as the boys tossed them off, and she handed them to Fred, who hung them on the coat tree by the door along with his own. Fred headed into the kitchen with the bags.

Penny removed her coat, staring at us, her eyes narrowing. "Oh, oh, oh, what did I miss?"

Jill shook with laughter.

A half an hour later, Boner and Butler arrived in an Eagle Wings pickup truck, the rain falling heavily, driving away the dusk into a windswept stormy evening.

Jill's face broke into a huge grin as they stepped through the doorway, and before she could move, Becca came rushing through the front room, shouting "Grandma! Bo-Bo's here!"

Boner swept her up into his arms. "There you are, Becs!"

They rubbed noses and laughed. She squeezed his cheek with her tiny hand and then the other, and he pretended to try to eat her hand.

"You're all wet!" Becca said.

"And you're all yummy!" Boner replied.

Becca only laughed harder as she pulled on his hair.

Jill took Butler's and then Boner's wet jackets and hung them on the coat tree by the door.

I gave Butler a quick kiss on the lips. "Hi."

"Hey." He grinned. "We brought dessert, as promised." He held up a damp box from the Meager Grand Cafe. "A double chocolate cake."

"Yum. Penny insisted on making her plum tart too."

"My two favorite flavors—tart and chocolate."

My face heated, and I rolled my eyes at him.

"Hey Butler, how're you doing?" My brother-in-law came up behind me and clasped Butler's hand in a hearty shake.

"Hi Fred, good to see you."

"Hi Butler." Penny's eyes positively twinkled as she took in Butler.

"Hello." My mother's voice came up behind me.

"Mom, this is Butler."

Butler held out his hand, and my mother firmly took it in her own. "Pleasure to see you again, ma'am. It's been since the christening, I think?" he said.

"That's right. And what a beautiful occasion that was."

"Good evening, Rae." Boner planted a kiss on my mother's cheek.

"Hello, honey." She squeezed his arm.

"This is for you, Mrs. Reigert." Butler held up a small shopping bag from a store in Rapid.

"How sweet of you." Rae took the bag.

"Oh my gosh, Someone's In the Kitchen is my favorite store!" Penny exclaimed.

"Never been," I said.

"You're missing out," Penny said. "They have a fantastic selection of kitchenware and all sorts of goodies. I have to stop myself from going in there and doing major damage whenever I'm in town. And don't get me started on the Espresso Bar."

"It's a great place, right?" said Butler shooting his sexy sweet grin at Penny.

My mother opened the bag and took out a matching stainless steel salt shaker and pepper grinder.

"They're electric mills," said Butler. "With a touch of a button, the mill does all the work for you. Very simple and efficient."

"They're so attractive," Penny murmured. "I love pink Himalayan rock salt. Oh, and all the peppercorns under the sun are in here. What pretty colors. You see that, Tania?'

I held Butler's clear gaze, my heart thumping in my chest. "I see."

"Thank you so much," my mother said. She handed the bag with the mills to Penny, who rushed off with them to the dining room. "That was very thoughtful of you, Butler. There is nothing like freshly ground salt and peppercorns."

"I agree," said Butler, his lips curling into a smile.

"Well, the food's ready, so let's sit. I'm looking forward to this meal. My daughter followed your recipe to a T, by the way."

"Did she?" Butler winked at me.

Everyone settled in at the table, Penny and I brought in the food, and we ate.

"Tastes really good, Tania," Butler said as he lifted his glass of iced tea in my direction. "Great job."

"Thank you."

My mother slid her fork next to her knife on her dish. "I do love all that lemon with the butter on a roasted bird. And it was crispy on the outside and tender on the inside. Perfectly cooked, honey."

"Thanks, Mom."

"Really good," Boner said as he cut a few potatoes into small pieces and put them in Becca's Hello Kitty dish.

Becca was propped up in a booster seat at the table in between him and Jill.

"You like it, baby?" Jill asked her daughter as she wiped Becca's mouth.

"I like it!" Becca declared, her greasy hands raised in the air.

"Aunt Tania's a good cook," said Nate, glancing up at me, a grin on his little face.

"Thank you, sweetie," I said.

While the kids stretched out and played with their Legos in the living room, Jill and I cleared the dishes, and Penny rinsed them, placing them in the dishwasher. Jill brought out the cake and the tart with smaller plates and dessert forks. I poured the coffee from the coffee machine pitcher into my mother's china coffee pot.

Penny placed the cups and saucers on a tray along with the creamer and sugar bowl. I grabbed the tray. Penny held the coffee pot, Jill had extra napkins, and we headed for the dining room. Jill and Penny froze in front of me at the louvered door.

"What the—"

My mother's voice rose from the dining room. "I know my girls. And they're at an age where they've been bruised and disappointed and learned a number of harsh lessons in life. Now, they know the difference between a good piece of ass and a heart that burns for theirs."

I stilled. Jill turned to me, her eyes wide. Penny's mouth gaped open.

"My girls don't have stars in their eyes. Their eyes are lit from deep within. I see it. It's a rare and special thing. I know. I had that thanks to my husband, and that's what I see in them; it's settled deep in their hearts. Even after all these years without my Joe, it's still there. Penny, has that, and Jill has it now. I've always wanted that for Tania. It's plain to me that you've brought that to her, and I'm very pleased. You are a special man, Butler, and I sincerely hope my daughter will hold on to that with you."

"We will, Rae," came Butler's low voice. "We will."

My heart skipped a beat and a rush of heat flared deep inside my chest.

"It takes work to keep it alive," Rae said.

"That's the best kind of work there is," came Butler's reply.

Penny turned to me and a watery-eyed Jill and mouthed "*Oh my God!*"

I motioned to them both to move out the kitchen door.

"Coffee time!" Penny pushed the door open, and set the coffee pot on the table next to my tray.

Jill sat down next to Boner, her hand brushing his hair back from his face. He whispered something to her, and they shared a quick kiss.

My mother glanced up at me, her eyes clear, calm. "The boys and I were chatting."

"Oh? How's that going?" I asked, pouring coffee, not daring to look at Butler lest I lost all muscle control and the hot coffee went flying over me and my mother.

"Very nicely," Rae replied as I placed the cup and saucer in front of her. I filled another cup and passed it to Butler.

His pale eyes met mine, our fingers touching. He offered me the warmest, most relaxed smile I'd ever seen on him, and my heart melted.

I busied myself with pouring out the coffee, as Penny cut pieces of cake and plum tart for everyone.

"Who wants chocolate cake?" Penny asked, her voice raised.

"Me! Me! I do!" shouted all three kids, bounding back toward the dining table.

We ate dessert. My mother and Becca played with tiny Snow White figurines Becca had by her dish. Fred and Boner heatedly debated Trans Ams versus Camaros, while the boys played with their tablets. Penny and Jill discussed a necklace that Jill was making for her.

Butler leaned back in his chair, that playful, relaxed smile growing on his lips.

"You good?" I asked, a hand on his leg.

He only wrapped an arm around my shoulders, kissed my temple, and drew me close.

SIXTY-ONE

BUTLER

FINGER STOOD UP in our clubhouse lounge, all eyes on him.

We'd just returned from a meeting with his suppliers in Idaho. Everything had gone according to plan, and we were all set to put in motion the second phase of our clubs working together.

"I know it's time for you men to vote on the new president of the One-Eyed Jacks, but before I leave you to your business, I'd like to say one thing."

He glanced at Kicker, and Kicker raised his chin at him.

Finger crossed his arms against his chest. "For years, I'd considered a more long-term plan with the Jacks after the success of several small projects. Dig Quillen, your former VP, was convinced that our clubs working together would be a good thing, prosperous for all of us. But I needed convincing, and the timing never seemed right for any of us. Let's face it, none of us ever trusted each other enough to even sit at a table together. Unfortunately, Dig isn't here to finally see us working together, but here we are."

I pulled in a deep breath and focused my attention on my skull ring, the silver reflecting the light from the long window. The men murmured in agreement.

"But here we are."

I glanced up at Finger, and he met my gaze. Yeah, we were here, but Jump wasn't sitting in his chair at the head of the table. Would this deal have gone down this way if he were still here?

I rubbed my fingers across my forehead, hoping the motion would maybe ease the ache sprinting across my head.

Finger and I had both managed to stay alive so far.

Boner stood in the doorway of our meeting room, his eyes on me. He was still here, too. A fucking survivor, if ever there was.

Did we deserve to be here? To be the ones still living, still sitting at the Jacks' table, still submitting our yays and nays? Who the fuck knew? I wasn't going to waste time thrashing out that futile philosophy of destiny. I knew it wouldn't make any difference.

We were here right now, and it felt fucking good. For the first time in a long while, the sound of my own damaged heart beating didn't annoy me. I was a part of a chain. A link. An important solid link, and I had played a part in keeping the chain strong, keeping it fortified.

"I want to thank Butler here for all his hard work." Finger's rough deep voice brought me back to the room. "For his first steps with the Flames, for seeing past our mutual inflexibility and making this new path possible for all of us. It's a brand-new day."

Hands were shaken, and Finger and his two men left the property.

The door was closed behind them, and we voted. My brothers clapped. I clenched my jaw. A smile grew on Boner's face from across the long, wide, wooden table that had seen decades of officers voted in and booted out. Decisions made and passed. Ambitions come to life.

Kicker, Jump's longtime VP, was voted in as president of the Jacks, and I was voted as vice president. Boner remained as Sergeant at Arms.

Kicker folded his hands together at the head of the table. "We've made new inroads, new contacts, and created a solid firewall against fuckers like the Broken Blades and a number of other fuckers making noise at our gates. Finger's going to take care of the Blades once and for all, and it won't come a day too soon. Working with the Flames in Nebraska is proving to be a huge gig. New business with a club we can count on, all without having to give anything up. Doesn't get any better." He nodded his head at me. "Good to have you back, bro." He slammed the club gavel against the block.

Meeting Over.

A new beginning.

Everyone rose and drifted into the main room. Bottles clinked, laughing, music filled the lounge, but I stayed seated at the great table. I leaned back in my chair and took in the row of photos along the wall, many crooked, badly framed, a few cracked.

Jump, Dig, Dready, and me hiking in Yellowstone. Young Wreck and Willy in their first years as members, holding up a trophy from some bike race down in Florida. Boner and Kicker as prospects, jumping off a ridge into the reservoir. Others were of men from the '70s and '80s, whom I'd never met, but knew their crazy stories. I heard their voices in my ears though, spewing foul curses, roaring with laughter. Men who had fucked up, men who had won big. I felt the shove of their bodies against mine, the thunder of their bikes before me on the road.

My brothers.

We who were all a part of this body. This heritage. A lineage. All of us together, as one, moving forward, always forward.

Our metal bloodline.

Truly fucking priceless.

SIXTY-TWO

TANIA

"DID THE PROSPECTS do exactly as you wanted?" Butler surveyed the new installation at the gallery.

Gerhard and Astrid's work would finally be revealed to the world tonight.

I slid my arm through his. "Jimmy and Teach were terrific. They followed my directions to the letter and took good care of the fragile pieces. Most impressively, they didn't freak out when I kept changing my mind about placement."

"Shit, that is impressive."

"Shut up." I shoved at his side, and he laughed. "Are you keeping track for their Jacks report card?"

"Something like that." He shifted his weight. "This exhibit, which is way more than an ordinary exhibit, looks really good. Makes you want to linger over every weird little detail."

All the H-bomb paintings and the gelatin silver prints I'd bought were up on the walls, and with long hooks, I'd hung Gerhard's glass Christmas tree ornaments on a vintage fifties dress form.

"I'm so thrilled that it's actually happening. Gerhard deserves to have his work seen."

"And the world deserves to see it. This is a huge night for you, too, you know. Not just Gerhard and his babe-a-licious."

"You had a little something to do with this as well. I have something for you to commemorate that." I handed him a small navy blue cardboard box. "It's your piece of this to keep with you always."

"What's this?"

"Open it."

He opened it, and his lips parted at the sight of the silver pendant.

He glanced at me. "The hummingbird skull."

"I had a copy made of the one you found in Gerhard's house."

He removed it from the box, and it hung on its chain between us.

"Those precious, fragile pieces of old bone and tiny skulls," I said. "You noticed them, and you knew what they were. The jeweler loved the skull, by the way. He asked me if he could make more of them from the mold he cast. I think it's macho enough for you to wear—if you want to, that is."

"Put it on me."

"You like it?"

"Put it on me." His voice came out hoarse, low.

I bit down on my lower lip as I took the pendant from him, opened the clasp of the long silver chain, and fastened the necklace around his neck. I righted it over his chest and planted a little kiss on the silver skull, my fingertips stroking over his warm skin.

"Thank you," he whispered.

"My pleasure. Really."

Butler wrapped an arm around my shoulders, his gaze settling on Astrid's crown, a direct spotlight shining on it as it sat in the Plexiglas cube, next to the silver prints of her wearing it. "Love that crown."

"Me, too. It'll be hard to see it go once this show is over. I still remember finding it. God, I thought I'd faint from the shock."

He planted a kiss on the side of my head. "You looked good in that crown."

I snaked an arm around his middle, and a little piece of me glowed deep inside. I loved his compliments. They surprised me, excited me. Would I ever get used to them? Never.

"Oh, I did, huh?"

"Fuck yeah." The husky tone in his voice and the concentrated focus of those aqua-blue eyes made my pulse speed up. His face twitched, a smile curling the edges of his lips.

I eyed him. "What is it now?"

"I was wondering—"

"Here we go."

He narrowed his eyes at me, acknowledging my gibe. "Are you going to wear a tight dress and high heels for the opening tonight?"

"Why?"

"'Cause I really, really like you in a tight dress and high heels."
His hand slid down over my ass.

I pressed against him. "I'll take that under consideration."

"You do that, Scarlett." He laid a deep tongue-ridden kiss on
me.

I melted against him, and a chuckle escaped from the back of
his throat.

"I'm not picky, babe. Heels and no dress, or heels with just
that crown, or heels and nothing else works real, real good for me."

Four hours later, and the opening party at the gallery had begun. I
had invited the Innocents back to play, and their piano player and
bassist were filling the space with a jazzy riff.

I admired the fat tin bucket that I'd found at my great
grandmother's house, which now graced the round wood table at
the entrance of the store. Butler had a huge bouquet of sunflowers
delivered after he'd left earlier. A surprise for me. A perfect one.

"You did good, Tania. It looks fantastic," said Neil, sipping
from the clear plastic cup of wine in his hand. "I have a surprise
for you. I wanted to tell you in person."

I tore my eyes away from my gorgeous, vibrant flowers. "A
surprise?"

"I've got Carl Trenton on my ass about the Gerhard collection.
And, I mean, each and every piece."

I grabbed his arm. "Are you serious?"

Carl Trenton was a contemporary art dealer in New York, who
had a personal passion for American outsider art, which he
collected for himself. Neil had cultivated a friendship with him
back when he worked with the Alden Merrick Gallery.

"I went to New York and showed Carl your photos myself. We
talked. The timing couldn't be more perfect. Last year he left his
hole-in-the-wall space in Chelsea and moved into this huge loft on
the Lower East Side, and he wants to showcase something

different. I pitched him the idea of setting up his gallery like Gerhard's studio with a lot of the original props alongside the artwork."

"And?"

Neil grinned as he took a sip of wine. "After the show is over and you send me the pieces, he's coming to Chicago to see what we have."

"Oh my God, Neil!" I hugged him, spilling his wine.

He laughed. "I tried to convince him to come all the way out here to the Wild West to see this, but that was a no-go." He rolled his eyes. "Anyhow, we've been talking about doing a traveling exhibition, giving the collection a real sense of importance. I want to begin with me in Chicago and then send it to Carl in New York. And—"

"And?"

"And a curator from a major arts center in the Midwest called me back."

"Oh, Neil."

He raised his cup at me. "Here's to you, Tania."

"Here's to Gerhard," I said. "Dave and his family are here from Sioux Falls. I'll introduce you."

"Ah, good."

The Innocents finished their song, and the crowd burst into applause.

"Thank you!" Den, the guitarist and lead singer, spoke. "We've got a special guest performer with us. A friend of ours from right here in Meager."

The brittle strum of an acoustic guitar filled the space, and the bassist plucked a slow, slinking rhythm underneath it. The singer's voice broke through, husky and smooth. Earnest and rough.

My pulse burst, sending a rush of heat through my veins. *That voice.*

I let go of Neil's arm and edged past a couple standing in front of us.

That deep voice growled and declared.

And I saw *him.*

Butler.

Onstage.

Playing his guitar.

Singing.

Singing *that song*. One of my very favorite songs ever, Carly Simon's "Touched by the Sun." That song was me. That song—

My stomach dropped, and shivers raced over my skin as the piano erupted, intensifying the drama. Butler wore a black linen men's shirt, most of the buttons open, revealing his silver hummingbird necklace hanging against his phenomenal bare chest. The lights made his wavy longish blond hair even lighter, setting him apart from the other musicians.

The drummer pounded out a haunting beat beneath. Butler's clear deep voice filled the room, his chords driving through me. His voice was almost gentle and then pleading and determined. I moved toward the stage, as if drawn there by a supernatural force, brushing past people, slipping through the crowd grouped around the small raised platform.

I got to the front and was rooted to the spot, entranced by his smooth-with-a-hint-of-gruff-at-the-edge voice, his sexy and confident stage presence.

Den joined Butler in a gorgeous harmony, his electric guitar grinding out a heated solo. Butler jumped in again, declaring his do-or-die passion. He was thinking and feeling every line, delivering pure emotion. His warm, almost grainy voice gave life to the lyrics, a fervent vow to dream, dare, and soar. He was resolute, adamant, committed, ready to risk, desperate to feel the burning heat of the sun.

He sang the title words, his shoulders rolling with his movements over the guitar, with the driving rhythm of the song. We'd discussed music and our favorite songs many times before. He knew how much this song meant to me; obviously it meant the very same to him.

I sang that triumph with him.

His voice roared, and my heart roared with it. His eyes found mine, and he called, he beckoned, he insisted.

The music swelled as the musicians headed toward the powerful climax, Den's electric guitar wailing, the pianist and drummer flying in. Then, it was only Butler's voice along with his guitar strumming the final splintery chords.

We cheered and clapped loudly. Boner and Kicker's whistles ripped through the room, Lock and Dready joining in.

Butler scraped a hand through his hair. "Thank you. A huge thank you to The Innocents for putting up with me, so I could give my woman a special gift on her big night."

"Anytime!" Den shouted out over the fresh round of applause. "That is one good set of pipes on you, man."

Butler tagged fists with Den and the rest of the band, and then he turned and headed straight for me.

The band started a new song. The thundering drum line burst and rolled through me like a fresh wave of adrenaline and purpose.

My heart beat like that drum.

Butler was coming for me.

My very own rock and roller.

My man among men.

My Rhett.

His lips curved into that wicked, arrogant grin, setting my blood on fire.

He adored me.

And I was a pile of fangirling excitement and swooning mush.

I was going to lay a huge kiss on him.

And let him kiss the hell out of me. In front of everybody.

Crush.

Swoosh.

God, yes.

He released me, an arm holding me close, as the Jacks crowded around us, each brother slapping him on the back, high-fiving him. The excited faces of Grace, Alicia, Lenore, Mary Lynn, and my sister filled my vision.

"That was for me?" I searched his bright blue eyes. "For me?"

"Yeah, that was for you. I haven't sung in front of people in a long, long fucking time. I wanted to surprise you. I wanted you to see that part of me, and I wanted to give it to you."

"Oh, honey, I saw, and I heard, all right. And I loved everything about it."

He leaned into me, his lips brushing my ear. "You gave that back to me when you gave me the guitar, when you believed in me."

I wrapped my arms around his middle. "You were fantastic."

His hand fisted in my hair and tugged my head back. That carnal zing exploded in my ovaries right there.

"Baby, I need to tell you. I—"

I put my hand over his mouth. "Shh!" I grabbed his hand and dragged him into the back room where I immediately unbuckled his huge leather belt.

"What the hell are you doing?" He laughed. Knowing. Turned on. "There's no door here."

"So what?" I pulled down his zipper. "Don't say another word before I make it up to you."

"Make what up to me? I'm lost."

"Our hook-up that never was at Wreck's shop over twenty years ago? We need to appease the bad Karma gods before we do or say anything else."

Yes, yes, I would make this happen before either of us spouted those three little words. With that heated, intense look in his eyes just moments ago, those words that were on the tip of my happy tongue, were most probably on the tip of his as well.

I pushed up on the sturdy butcher-block table I had in a corner and bunched up my skirt. I hooked my fingers in the loops of his jeans and pulled him in between my legs. I was in a frenzy for him, for his cock, for doing it all right for a change. No more looking back over my shoulder.

"Scarlett, wait."

I blinked at him, breathless, willing my hands to stop moving at the waistband of his boxer briefs.

He cradled my face, his lips a breath from mine. "I don't ever want to forget this moment. How this very second feels. This, right now." His deep voice vibrated against my skin. "Not ever."

His hands went to my bare thighs and slid up my skin, taking my breath away. He tugged on my satin panties and ripped them off my legs.

My head fell back. "Hell yes," tumbled from my mouth.

I'd never been so grateful for having gone to the gynecologist and gotten myself birth control. *Ciao, rubbers!*

Butler hooked one of my legs around his torso as I steadied myself back on my arms. His fingers nudged at my opening, swirling through me.

"Fuck, you're ready for me, aren't you?"

"Since I heard you sing those first notes."

A grunt escaped from the back of his throat as he stroked his cock once, twice. He thrust inside me. Slowly, controlled. "Ah, shit,

Scarlett…fuck. Feel so good on me bare." His eyes squeezed shut as his chest heaved for a breath.

"Oh, yes." I raised my hips, taking him all the way in.

He leaned over me and took my mouth and held on to our groans with an unforgiving kiss. He rocked inside me again. "I want you slow. Want to feel every stroke in you. Every fucking one. Deep and tight. Want to feel you come on me."

"Markus."

His fingers painfully gripped my flesh, pinning me to that rough table. "I love you, Tania. I love you."

"I love you, too, baby," I whispered.

I reached for his mouth, and he gave it to me.

He gave it all to me.

The noise of the crowd, the spirited, moody music of The Innocents, our choppy breaths—all of it dinned in my ears. The artwork and antiques we had found together, Wreck's pieces, pieces I had brought from Wisconsin, my great-grandmother's house—all of them here, in the small back room, were silent witnesses to our lovemaking.

I couldn't see his eyes in the dark, but I could see everything in my heart. Butler was there, larger than life. His passion, his strength, his generosity. I trusted the sensations whirling inside me and danced to their beat. The steady, torturous, and sure thrust of his hips into mine, the sliding of our damp skin, his cock filling me, his every grunt as he suddenly quickened his pace were a raucous maelstrom that whipped every dream, every wish, every heartbeat into its vortex, making us one.

We both came within moments of each other, and I bit down on his shoulder to stop from moaning out loud.

I kissed the bite mark I'd left behind. "What do you think, Blondie? Did we put our bad Karma to rest with that?"

He licked the skin under the side of my jaw, and I shivered. "Oh, baby, I think we just cured that great blue wound of the past. But I think you'd better stop calling me Blondie if you want it to stick."

We clung to each other, the two of us shaking with laughter.

SIXTY-THREE

BUTLER

"YOU WOKE ME UP."

"You didn't like that?"

"You woke me up with kisses," Tania said.

"Yeah." My fingers cupped the side of her face. "Again, you didn't like that?"

"I loved it."

And I loved having her here in my bed, at my place.

She ran a hand across the base of her neck, over her sexy collarbone. She was confused.

"You want to tell me what that reaction was about now?"

She bit her lip.

"Okay," I said. "I'll start. *Kyle...*"

She put her fingers over my lips. "Yes, Kyle. I used to complain that he'd never kiss me good morning, but he'd say he kissed me good morning when I was still asleep. He always woke up first, and I'd never realize since I'm such a heavy sleeper."

"Baby, when I wake you up with kisses in the morning or in the middle of the night, you'll feel it. You'll wake up. You'll fucking remember." I rubbed my hand across her collarbone and up her throat. Goose bumps raced over her flesh. "Your body will fucking know."

She squirmed against me. "I sure woke up that night in the motel in Sioux Falls."

"Yes, you did. See what I mean?"

"Hmm." She raised her hips against mine, her lips pressing into my skin.

I ground against her, bringing her hands around my shoulders. "You understand what you got here now?"

"Make me understand some more," she whispered, giggling softly.

Her mouth opened to mine, and I took her in, our tongues tangling, stroking. A laugh bubbled up in my throat.

She pulled away, her dark eyes flashing. "What's so funny?"

I kissed the side of her chin. "I'm glad you like kissing me as much as I like kissing you."

"I love kissing you."

I pulled her in closer. "You know what else I love?"

"I cannot wait to hear."

"I love it when I touch you right here." My fingertips whispered over the smooth skin of her hip, right over her bone, and her body tightened, her breath audibly catching in her throat. "See what happens? You like it a lot; it's a little thrill every time for you. Such a simple thing, slight, delicate even, over a small passage of curves, yet everything about it drives you tighter and higher for me."

"Lordy, I love how you can't shut up after we have sex," she said. "And during sex, too."

"We didn't have sex just now."

"We had lots of sex last night."

"Yeah, we did. Well, enjoy my talking because, who knows? Years from now, I might just roll over after and fart."

She laughed. A hearty, rich laugh.

Years from now.

Her one hand caressed the side of my face, and that wave of warmth slid through me again. I leaned into her palm for a moment. I liked that, settling there in her touch. There was comfort born from surety there. Understanding. No noise. Fucking peace.

We kissed again, slowly, more gently than before. I took her in my arms, and we settled back against the pillows. The window shade flapped and floated in the warm breeze streaming in through the open window.

"What's with the nightlight in the bathroom?" she asked.

"What do you mean?"

"It wasn't on when we went to bed."

"I got up and put it on after."

"Scared of the dark?"

"No, it's this thing Stephan and I had. We shared a bathroom at home. He liked having a nightlight in there just in case one of us woke up in the middle of the night."

"Practical."

"Very. I hated it though. I'd tease him about it. But since he died, I've always used one." I took in a breath.

"I like nightlights," Tania whispered, her hand stroking my arm.

Her gaze fell to the row of medicine bottles lined up on my dresser.

"We haven't really talked about what the cardiologist said yesterday. We fucked about it, but we sure didn't talk about it."

Always insightful, my woman.

"You complaining, Scarlett?"

"Not me, no way. But I'd like to hear how you *feel* about it. We went out to dinner after the opening, came here, and attacked each other. I think you can say a few things about it now, don't you?" She smoothed the hair back from my face.

I let out a breath. "Yeah, I feel great that I have an arrhythmia. That I gave myself this life-threatening condition. When I think about your mother, who, through no fault of her own, got struck with a debilitating, life-sapping, body-strangulating, pretty much uncontrollable disease, and then here I am, responsible for my condition—what can I say?"

"You know what it is. You have a good doctor monitoring your condition. You're being treated. That's positive. Not skipping doses anymore."

"I have to eat better and sleep more."

"That, I can help you with."

"I quit smoking."

"I can imagine how hard it must be after years of doing it."

"It's not's so hard now that this fucked-up heart of mine is beating for you, Tania. I fall into your arms at night, rest my body against yours, and it feels so fucking good. What's tobacco next to that?"

"I want to be that for you," she breathed, a finger trailing over my chest. "I want to be where you rest."

"You are. And you're where I celebrate what I have, what we have."

She blushed, curling into me, her lips brushing over the base of my throat.

I took her hand, and with it, I stroked my dick's hardening length from top to bottom, harder and harder.

"I love it when you do that." Her voice came out hoarse. "I love feeling you, with you."

I twisted on top of her. "Spread your legs wide, baby. My cock can't take the wait."

She threw her head back and laughed.

"You don't laugh when your man's dick is in his hand, and he's telling you he needs to fuck you. Kiss me, Scarlett."

Her eyes gleamed. "Cock or mouth?"

"Mouth is good. Cock would be better."

Her fingers stroked over my hard dick.

"Let's not lose it now," I said on a hiss.

I fell back on the mattress, and she slid down my body. Her mouth took in my tip, her hands digging into my ass.

"Fuck, woman. Stop teasing."

She took me all the way in and swallowed me down her throat, like the hungry girl she was. My jaw clenched, and my lids lowered over my eyes as sweat prickled my skin, low grunts escaping my tense lips. Her hand twisted my base, rubbing hard.

"Ah, baby. That's it. Yeah."

Her mouth worked hard and steady, and I gulped in air.

"Fuck, Scarlett...feels so damn good."

She pulled up and climbed on me, straddling my legs.

Her eyes blazed over me, her hand still working me. "I want you inside me."

"Demanding bitch." I let out a growl and shoved her hand away from my cock. I pulled on it myself, her saliva making it easier, faster. "How do you want me, Scarlett?"

She positioned herself, her hands planting on my chest. "I get to choose?"

"This is all yours."

"Slow first and then hard," she whispered, rocking over my dick, her wet softness killing me with every pass.

I stroked her clit with the tip of my cock, and she moaned, her jaw going slack, her hips squirming at the contact.

"I love this, the very beginning." Her voice had a dreamy quality to it, her large eyes simmering in a glaze. "The very, very first...*ooh*." She bowed her head down as she rocked into me, taking me in.

I lifted her face at her chin, and our eyes hung on to one another's in the same mist. I took in every little sensation—her cries, the tingles, the burning, the fullness of having Tania all around me. The heat of our bodies, us moving together—all of it carried us both somewhere other than this bed.

I pushed up and took her in my embrace as we made love, her arms tightening around me, her gasps in my ear. My own harsh breath jammed in my lungs.

"I love you. I love you," she murmured to me, to herself, to the world.

I held her tightly and thrust inside her, taking her with me.

Into *us*.

SIXTY-FOUR

TANIA

I HADN'T SEEN BUTLER in almost a week. Things had gotten very busy at the store, and he was heavily involved in club business as well as preparing for the go-kart race with Wes and the Jacks. We talked on the phone a lot, texted, sexted, but I missed him. I missed him badly.

However, it had given me a perfect opportunity to get another item on my wish list done. Something special for Butler. For me.

"There is nothing like smoky eyes. Nothing. There. Just right." Jill's eyes scanned my face, her hand at my chin while Grace adjusted the light the photographer had let us use.

Jill, Grace, Lenore and I had spent the morning blocking the glass windows of the Rusted Heart with cardboard, and then we'd set up the "stage" for my photo shoot.

"Ah, Jill! Natural but va-voom-boom all at the same time," said Lenore, who stood behind her, both of them studying me. "Tania, you've got to start wearing it like that every day. Seriously."

"I tell her that all the time. She won't listen," Jill said, crossing her eyes at me.

I blinked at Jill's handheld mirror. They were right. "I think I'll take your advice from here on out, smart-ass."

"Woo!" Jill laughed.

"And your tat healed really well. It's perfect," murmured Lenore.

"I love it," I said.

With Butler away, I'd taken the opportunity to make the appointment with Ronny for the day Butler had left in order to get our design started and have that heal before he saw it.

"Ian's the photographer you use for your ads, right?" Grace asked.

"Yes. He's very good, very professional," replied Lenore. "He does a lot of boudoir shoots, too, if you and Jill are ever interested."

"I only pose for my husband, honey," said Grace. "And his drawings of me would make even you blush."

"Aw, heavy sigh," said Jill. "I get dirty poems written in my honor. If I got a boudoir shot done and gave it to my old man, I can only imagine what raunchy wordsmithery that would inspire."

"I think you should find out, don't you?" I said, laughing.

"Boner's birthday is coming up," murmured Jill, chewing on her lip as she packed up her makeup collection. "Hey, Lenore, I've been meaning to ask you—I love that you pose for your own ads, but you never show your gorgeous face. Why? You're certainly not shy."

"She's all about the mystery," I piped in.

"Yeah." Lenore raised her chin at me, a slight smile on her lips. "Sexy lingerie is all about the mystery and intrigue."

"This is a terrific idea you had." Grace took my arm in hers. "You need a shot of liquid courage, or are you okay?"

"I feel a bit nervous, but I'm excited mostly."

"Good, because I want you to enjoy this. You need to enjoy this. You're gorgeous. A knockout," said Grace, releasing me.

"Thank you. I feel really good about this."

"These photos are going to be amazing," said Lenore. "I might have to use a couple for my next ad."

"Oh, stop!"

"I'm not kidding, Tania," said Lenore. "You can count on Ian's assistant, Alison to help you through the shoot. She's experienced. You sure you don't want me to stay?"

"Really, you all can go." I wanted this moment for me.

"Okay then," said Lenore as she, Grace, and Jill exchanged glances. "Let's go!"

"Thank you, guys, for helping me out."

Jill kissed me on the cheek as she squeezed my arms. "Gorgeous."

"Kill it, babe," said Grace, a hand on my shoulder.

"I intend to," I replied.

"Okay, Ian, we're off." Lenore gave the photographer a wave of her hand from across the room. "Take care of my girl."

"You know I will." He winked at Lenore, and his gaze darted back at his light meter. "Let's do this, ladies. We ready?"

Alison led me around the obstacle course of cables, the light stands, and filters toward the tableau we had set up earlier. My new tall black leather boots made a distinctive clicking sound against the floor.

Ian settled onto his knees in front of us, his camera in his hands.

Alison placed the brass crown carefully on my head, and we adjusted it together. Ian glanced up at me.

I undid the belt on my robe. "I'm ready."

SIXTY-FIVE

TANIA

TONIGHT, FRED WAS OUT OF TOWN on business, so Penny and her boys were camping at the house to spend the night with Grandma Rae. Therefore, I arranged to have my own sleepover at Butler's house. I'd prepared a dinner of broiled salmon, steamed cauliflower, wild rice, and an olive oil vinaigrette with pistachio nuts, packaged it, and brought it with me to his house. I also brought him my gift.

Butler opened the door of his apartment, wearing only athletic shorts that hung low on his lean hips, his feet bare, the skin of his sculpted chest shining with perspiration. His weights were out on the floor behind him. He took one look at me, and that know-it-all self-satisfied smirk slid over his handsome face, uncoiling a shiver of heat over my skin. I took in a tiny breath, savoring the rush.

"Get in here." He tugged me into his living room and kissed me. He pulled back, grabbing the tote bags I was carrying. His eyes widened. "What the hell are those boots you're wearing? Are you my dinner, baby?"

"Dinner is in that blue tote." I presented him with the gift bag. "And this is for you."

His brow creased, a frown shadowing his face. "Do we have some sort of anniversary thing?"

"Nope. I'm not one of those girls who takes notes of the first day we kissed or held hands or watched a full moon, then buys a Hallmark card for every occasion, and freaks if you don't remember every little event."

"I didn't think so." His lips twitched.

"It's a gift for you. That simple. I had to, wanted to, felt compelled to. Accept it graciously."

Butler opened the gift bag and removed a large box that I'd wrapped in a beautiful royal blue and purple wrapping paper tied with a thick gold ribbon.

He stared at the present, swallowing, the muscles of his throat moving with the action. "This is the second time, and…"

"Butler, what is it?"

"This is the second time you've given me a present. I haven't seen a present, wrapped or otherwise, for me in…I don't remember how long." His voice was quiet, the lines of his face drawn.

My heart squeezed. "Baby, open it," I murmured.

He pulled the ribbon off the box, scratched at the paper and ripped it open, his lips pursed, as if he were squelching any kind of excitement. He flung the paper scraps to his side and lifted the 8x10 frame from its box. His body stilled, his eyes focusing on the photograph and widening a few degrees.

"Tania—"

"It's how you make me feel." My heart beat outside my chest. "Because you see me like this."

His gaze darted at me and then back to the photo. "Shit, baby. It's—you're so fucking beautiful. You're incredible."

"I wanted to be your pinup," I whispered.

He swung an arm around my neck and kissed the top of my head as we both looked at the photo Lenore's photographer had taken of me, set off in a ridged white border matte and set in a professional thick black frame.

In the photograph, I wore Lenore's custom-made corset, my black hair long and wavy around my shoulders and down my chest. On my legs were the new high-to-the-knee black leather heeled boots that Grace and I had found in Rapid. Hanging off one shoulder was one of Gerhard and Astrid's velvet throws, almost as if it were a part of me. On my head was Astrid's gold crown with the faux black diamond. In my hand was a sunflower, like the ones Butler had given me at the Rusted Heart's opening parties.

I reigned over a kingdom of pickings—the bone thrones and towers, the gruesome clay masks, the antique Christmas decorations in crystal bowls, Wreck's candelabra, his vintage Harley engines and headlamps and dented, scratched tanks lying around me—my minions, my secret rusted treasures in my field of dreams, my field of plenty.

A field that Butler had helped me cultivate.

Dreams that Butler understood, dreams that he'd lived with me. Found with me. Encouraged in me.

And there were more dreams to dream, more to realize—*that*, I knew with certainty deep in my soul.

"This is my queen," he whispered back.

My heart fluttered, my skin heated.

"This is how I see you, Scarlett. And more. So much more."

Butler's eyes scrunched up for a second. "What's that on your chest? On your—"

His eyes tightened as his gaze snapped at me, those icy-blue stones piercing me. "What did you do?" His voice had deepened. "Let me see."

I licked at my dry lips as I tugged off the thin scarf I had draped around my neck and chest on purpose.

He put down the framed photograph, and his fingers stroked the edges of my new tattoo. "Jesus."

Ronny had transformed the F scar into a B.

"Ronny's going to fill it in more in a few weeks," I said.

He traced the edges of the design on my skin. "And a hummingbird on the side?"

I only nodded.

He bent and planted a kiss over his B on my skin and on the delicate hummingbird entwined in its lines. His lips brushed my throat as his hands cradled my head, tilting it upward. His eyes were shining, the brightest, most breathtaking azure blue. Fresh calm. Startling assurance, clarity.

"The last thing I ever expected was to find you. You're a total surprise to me, Tania. You're the greatest gift for me, baby. And I'm going to show you that every fucking day. I'm going to show you what I see."

A small cry escaped my lips.

He bent and kissed me so very gently. "Love you."

I sighed, my eyes closed. "Say it again."

"I love you, Scarlett."

He picked up the photo. "Baby, these boots with this lingerie number..."

"Hmm?"

"This corset yours, or did you borrow it?"

"Unwrap your other present now."

481

"What other—"

His gaze darkened and didn't roam from mine as he undid the belt on my coat and unbuttoned each button, starting at the top, in swift, precise movements. That dazzling, heady trip of arousal flared through me, liquefying everything in its path.

He swept the coat off my shoulders, and it crumpled onto the floor. "Fucking hell," he breathed, his eyes slowly taking me in from top to bottom.

I wore the corset. And nothing else.

"Get naked," I said.

He did.

My eyes jumped at the sight of his hard length, and he noticed.

"You know how to make my Brando very, very happy and very hard." Butler smoothed his hands down the sides of the silky fabric. "This isn't coming off you just yet."

He stared at me, raw and blatant hunger in his eyes, as he unsnapped the tiny pearl buttons of the panty. His fingers brushed against me, and I almost came right there and then.

He let out a small groan. "I want to fuck my gift package."

"Please fucking do."

He threw me over the arm of his couch and kicked my fantastically booted legs open wide.

He slammed into me.

"Yes!" My fingers dug into the sofa cushion, the throb pulsating through every part of me.

His arm wrapped around my middle and held me up as he plunged deeper inside me. I came quickly, collapsing into the cushions.

He bit my earlobe. "Not done with you yet, my queen."

His slick erection against my flesh along with that husky, hoarse voice summoned my body forth like some sort of call to the animal in me.

"Oh goody," I gasped.

He dragged me down to the floor and pressing my booted legs back against my chest, he pounded into me.

The glimmer in his eyes was unmistakable, the musk of his perspiration, the intensity of his desire making me desperate for more. The wave towered over me again. Never before in the history of Tania had this happened. Violent sensations coursed through me. I wasn't sure where I began and ended.

But I knew who was at the heart of it.

"Markus…"

His eyes held mine, and I was pulled under in the deep blue of his ocean.

There was no going back to average, to routine, to indifference, to settling, to being alone.

No, not ever.

"I see you, Tania. I see you, baby, and you're everything."

SIXTY-SIX

TANIA

"WHAT KIND OF SURPRISE?"

Butler pulled a strap on his saddlebag, fastening it. "Will you get on my bike, so I can get us there first?"

"Does this mean I have to ride on your bike with my eyes closed?"

He raised his eyes skyward and brought them back to me. "Tania, all I'm asking is that you let me take you somewhere special, and I promise you, all will be revealed."

"Okay."

"Okay." He handed me my helmet, and we got on his Harley.

I held on to him, pressed into him, as he took us out of Meager, past the roadside creeks lined with purple and golden wildflowers. We headed east through farmland that lay between Meager and Pine Needle.

My heart beat faster, my breath sped up, and it wasn't from the wind whipping over me or my man's strong body shielding me, as it propelled us forward on his beloved hulk of roaring metal, like a bionic orgasm. No, I had a good idea where we were going, and I hadn't been there in years.

The grasses rippling in the early morning wind stretched to infinity. The vast sky was dotted with soft white clumps of clouds that shed a dappling of darkness here and there over the rolling fields of pale green soy, the gold waves of wheat. I sat up in the saddle. This was dramatic take-your-breath-away splendidness.

And there, there they were, my and my dad's favorite—the glorious sunflower fields. Sunflowers for as long and wide as the eye could see.

I squeezed his middle.

Butler was taking me home. Home to my family's farm, to our sunflowers. Land that had been in my family for generations, Dakotan born and bred folk who tended their land with love and pride, and sweat and tears.

He slowed down his bike on the edge of the road and cut his engine.

I tugged on his jacket. "How do you know that this is the property?"

"I did my homework, baby. I wanted you to see it again with me, and I wanted you to show it to me." He took the helmet from my hands. "You've talked about it, but something in your tone of voice always struck me as far away. I asked your mom, and she showed me the photos of you here on this land, at that farmhouse." He gestured at my great-great-grandparents' sprawling house. The house that I'd been brought to after birth and raised in, the house I'd left after my father's death. The house I hadn't stepped foot in for decades.

He ripped off his gloves and held a hand out to me. My heart chugged through molasses and wine, and I took hold of his warm hand. Together, we walked along the edge of the field.

The sunflowers were at their peak now in early September. The bees were working, and I closed my eyes and listened to their frantic buzzing, the rustling of the thick stalks in the warm breeze.

"I always thought sunflowers would smell more flowery out in the field," he said. "But they smell of green, growing things, and the outdoors. Almost like a resin, isn't it?"

"The petals and the leaves smell like that. The bees can smell the blossoms though. Sunflowers need the bees. We'd bring them in special to pollinate."

"The flowers are huge. I always thought it was odd that they're not harvested at their peak, that they have to be dried up first."

"Most people don't know that," I said.

"I know. Hell of a lot of sunflower farms up north. Been around them for years, ridden through them, but I've never been so up close. Like now." He brought our hands to his mouth, planting a kiss on mine.

"I always liked that a sunflower gets to live out its life naturally on the stalk," I said. "Not cut down early or in its fantastic prime like any other flower. A sunflower gets to go full circle, from seed to strong green stalk, vibrant huge flower to brown, dry, and bowed over. That's when the seeds are ready to harvest. People think the dried out sunflowers are ugly then, but to some of us, it's beautiful."

"I like that, too."

I pressed my body against his. Yes, most people thought the dried sunflowers were spent, done, withered. Wasn't that how Butler and I had seen ourselves on our journeys back to Meager? But we had proven ourselves wrong.

Butler swiped the pollen off his jacket. "Whoa."

"Be careful. The flowers are sticky. If we keep walking through them, we'll be covered in pollen before long. They're difficult to navigate now anyhow."

He squeezed my hand. "I'd rather be covered in you." He threw his arm around me, tucking me into his side, and gently kissed me. He brushed back strands of hair from my face, his eyes soft, faraway.

"What is it?" I asked.

"I want to show you the Pacific," he said. "I want to listen to the crash of the water with you. Swim together. Get you on a surfboard. I haven't been back there in a long, long time."

My eyes flooded and I smiled through it.

We had learned that it was okay to want things, to change things, to make things better.

"Would we go out there on your bike?" I asked.

"Hell yes. Only way to see all that beautiful country. Unless you—"

"Let's do it."

"Really?"

"Yes. Really. I'm sure Jill won't mind running things on her own for a couple of weeks."

Jill had become my partner in the gallery. My business loan from the bank hadn't come through, but Jill and Boner had. They'd made a small but healthy investment in the Rusted Heart. Jill took care of most of the day-to-day tasks and sold her Firefly Wishes jewelry as part of the store's contemporary collection. Her lower-priced faux baubles were extremely popular with ladies of all ages, and her pricier precious metal and stone line was starting to take off. Having someone I knew, loved, and trusted holding down the fort was beyond wonderful. More importantly, sharing that fort and my vision with someone who was just as enthusiastic and devoted as me was extremely satisfying.

Butler squeezed my hand. "Scarlett, I brought you here today to your family's farm for a reason."

"What? Not for sex in the sunflowers?"

He let out a laugh. "Not yet."

"Oh, goody."

He held my gaze, his spine straightened. He was serious.

"Marry me, Tania. I know the ink is still fresh on your divorce, but I want to be with you, in the biggest, most absolute—"

"Unequivocal?"

A grin split his face. "Most fucking unequivocal way possible. So, if that's a piece of paper stamped by the county and the state, let's get on it."

"The paper doesn't matter to me. What matters is that we're together." My eyes stung, and I swallowed hard.

"Am I sensing a but?"

I shifted my weight. "Does this mean you're okay with me not telling you everything about Finger right now? I know it's a lot to ask of you. From the beginning, it was a problem."

"I still don't like it. But, obviously, it's real important to you, so I'm respecting that. I get there are reasons. Believe me. So, I'm taking that leap for you, Tania. For us. As long as you're holding my hand and by my side. As long as you're only mine, forever mine."

"I am, forever and only."

He squeezed my hands. "I believe you, baby."

"I'm honored that you would do this for me. Take this leap of faith."

"I haven't had faith in anything for years now, Tania. You've asked me to do something so against every instinct, every—"

"I know."

I knew. The discomfort, the struggle, had been written all over his face, his body, since we'd gotten together. It was not the best of situations, but in a weird way, we both needed this. He needed to trust, and I needed to be trusted.

I curled my fingers in his shirt. "I promise your faith is well placed. You do it for your brothers every day."

"Yes, I do. Every day." His teeth dragged along his bottom lip. His thumb stroked over my mouth.

"I have to have my mom with me. I can't leave her."

"I know. So, I guess I'm moving in."

I rose up on my toes. "We could knock down the wall between my and my brother's old rooms and add a bathroom. Ta-da—master suite. That is, if you don't mind, if you—"

"You've been thinking about it, huh?"

"Yep."

"I like it," he said.

"And I was thinking that we could take our time with fixing up my great-grandmother's big house in Pine Needle and eventually move there."

"That idea, I really, really like. But first things first."

From his pocket, he took out a small black velvet box and held it out to me. My breath jammed in my chest. "For you."

I snapped open the tiny box. A white gold band with an emerald-shaped black stone glittered in the sun.

"This is why I brought you here, baby. I wanted to do it here."

"It's beautiful. It's—"

"A black diamond on Black Hills gold for my vixen queen. I couldn't give you Astrid's crown, but I can give you this."

I lunged at him, and he lifted me up in his arms on a groan.

The box went flying.

"Shit, the ring!"

"Oh no!"

"Damn it! It popped out of the box—"

We both fell to the ground and searched the dirt, scrambling over the patch of earth.

A dark glittering in a dusty ray of sunlight.

I grabbed it. "Here it is!"

His face tensed. "Are you putting it on or what?"

"Yes! Yes!" I put it in his hand. "You do it!"

He slid the ring of rings on my finger.

"I love it. I—" I caught his gaze.

Enthusiasm and satisfaction were in those brilliant blue eyes that matched the sky above us, a hint of vulnerability in the set of his jaw.

I threw my arms around him and held him close. "I love you, Butler, and I can't wait to marry you."

Right there, on our knees, in the dirt of my forefathers and mothers, with the bees buzzing, the hard sun breaking through the tall sunflowers, rustling in the hot air, waving over us, we claimed our happiness. Vagabonds, the two of us, yet we had brought each other back home; home to one of the most difficult spots on the planet, this beautiful patch of earth.

I held on tight to the man of my unexpected dreams, and he held me even tighter.

Who needed a man who gave you roses?

My man gave me the earth and the sun.

"Scarlett, we've got to get moving."

"Huh? Why? I thought we were going to—"

"Surprise, part two."

SIXTY-SEVEN

BUTLER

"SURPRISE!"

Rae, Penny, and I had organized the engagement party along with Tania's Aunt Charlotte who lived on the farm with her husband, Mac. We'd set up the party in one of the old barns that was no longer being used but had withstood the purges of time and Dakota weather.

All the One-Eyed Jacks were there, as well as Catch and Nina. Tania hugged and kissed every single person and showed off her ring.

"How are you doing, groom-to-be?" Boner held Thunder in his arms.

The kid stared up at me while he viciously chewed on a bright red pacifier, one fist curled tightly in Boner's T-shirt.

"Feels great, man. How's this little guy? He must be the quietest, most no-fuss baby ever."

"He is."

We both aimed our attention at Thunder. He had his mother's luminous hazel eyes and his father's black hair and darker skin. He was gorgeous. Thunder blinked at us, realizing he had our full attention. Those huge eyes of his glittered, swallowing us whole. A gurgle, a smile, and his pacifier popped out of his mouth. He wiggled in Boner's hold.

"He's something," I mumbled.

"I know." Boner kissed the side of Thunder's face.

"You getting the urge?" I asked.

"What?" Boner offered the pacifier back to Thunder, and he gobbled it between his teeth and lips.

"To procreate."

Boner's eyes darted to Jill, who was crouched between Becca and little Jake, her arms around their waists, as Grace took a photo of them.

"I've got it bad, bro, so fucking bad," said Boner, his brow furrowed. "Jill doesn't know it yet though. I can't tell her. I mean, shit, her uterus needs a break."

I laughed, clapping a hand on his shoulder. "Somehow, brother, I don't think your old lady would deny you anything. Especially that." I picked up the thick cotton cloth on Boner's shoulder and wiped at the dribble running down the side of Thunder's chin.

"Hey, congratulations." Wes stood at my side, a slanted smile on his face.

"Wes." I took him in my arms and hugged him hard.

"You deserve to be happy."

"You think?" I asked.

"I know you do. I got a present for you. Tania thought it was a great idea."

I leaned into him. "Does this have something to do with my guitar case disappearing this past week?"

"Yeah." Wes turned to Jake. "Buddy, bring it over."

Grace's nephew struggled with my guitar case in his grip and pushed it at Wes. Wes turned it around. On the front of the case was a hand-painted One-Eyed Jack skull in drippy gothic glory. Its glimmering starlight eye was painted in a wide range of purples, silvers, and light blues.

I stilled. "You did this?" I asked Wes.

"Lock helped me with the basic design, but I took off from there."

"That's incredible, Wes," Boner said.

Thunder gurgled his approval.

I gripped Wes's neck. "You're so talented, and this is beyond words beautiful. Thank you. Means a lot to me. A hell of a lot."

He only pressed his lips together and nodded stiffly. I pulled him close and kissed the side of his face.

"You still coming to our first game on Friday?" he asked, a hand pressing in on my back. "We've got a hell of a starting lineup this year."

"Wesley, I wouldn't miss it for the world."

The engagement party went on all afternoon. As the sun set, Tania brought me into the main house and showed me her old bedroom, a room she'd loved, a room she'd had to say good-bye to when her dad had died and she and her mom, brother, and sister had moved into town. Tania's old room was now Charlotte's knitting and hobby room.

Tania stood at the window. Reds and oranges streaked the huge open sky, the fields gleaming in their glory.

"I loved this view. I used to decorate this window shelf with my little figurines, put my handmade stained glass up here." Her fingers traced down a strip of stained glass with a yellow sun and blue moon on it. "Look at that. Aunt Charlotte kept it. This one's mine." She pressed her face against the windowpane. "I swear, I can still smell my mother's kuchen baking in the kitchen."

I came up behind her and lifted her wrap skirt, moving her boy-short panties out of the way.

"What are you—"

"I'm gonna make you come while you're reminiscing and feeling all that sweet girlie nostalgia. Hands on the window."

Those long fingers of hers splayed on the window, my ring on her hand making a sound against the glass. I palmed her gorgeous ass, bringing it closer to me, and dipped into her wet heat. *Very wet.*

I bent over her back, my lips at her ear. "You ever fool around with anyone in here?"

"No, I was a good girl and a little too young for that at the time."

I unbuckled my jeans with my left hand, my right toying with her clit. "Good."

"But I got started early and played with myself a lot." She took in a breath. "Lots of fantasizing about my dream man."

I grabbed her hips, sliding my cock inside her, and she let out a low moan.

I ground into her deeper. "Play with this."

"Fuck yes," she breathed. "Yes, yes…"

Our breaths fogged the window, and I felt that throb of her around me.

"Fuck your real-life dream man, baby," I whispered, nipping the back of her neck.

She thrust back against me.

"I love you," she breathed. "I love you, Markus. So damned much."

The pale skin of her neck glowed in the warm rays of the setting sun.

"Can't get enough of you, Scarlett. Love being inside you, feeling you come on me." I picked up my pace, my hand sinking over her pussy. "Can't fucking get enough."

She ground back into me. "I hope you never get enough."

Three weeks later, I took Tania on the back of my bike, and we headed for the Pacific Ocean.

I'd had Lenore surprise her with a simple flowing white dress that she'd designed and made for Tania, and Jill had given Tania a lariat style necklace with golden crystals and citrine stones, the color of sunflowers. The long necklace fell perfectly between her braless tits in that loose, slinky made-for-the-beach halter dress.

I bought my woman a single sunflower for a bouquet, and Scarlett and I got married on a beach with the waves crashing on the shore, seagulls calling overhead, the wind joining our promises and blowing them toward that big blue sky.

We kissed as husband and wife and stood there, just the two of us, hand in hand, watching the ocean on the same spot where, years ago and for the very first time, I'd been called forth from the grave, like Lazarus.

Resurrected.

BUTLER

PAST

"I know you guys are from South Dakota. That where you grew up, too?" I asked.

"No, I'm originally from Colorado," Dig said, his tongue sliding across his lower lip. "The mountains."

"Wow. I'd like to see the Rocky Mountains one day. I've always lived by the beach, just a little further south from here. You like it out there? In South Dakota, I mean."

"I do. Very much."

"Oh, yeah? I couldn't be landlocked. No fucking way."

His body visibly tensed next to mine.

"I mean…well, I don't know," I muttered.

Dig stared at me. Hard. His strange almost golden brown eyes drilled into me, and my pulse sprang.

"What *do* you know?" He brought two of his ringed fingers to the sides of his head and tapped. "You're landlocked inside. Inside. And that's a shit place to be." He pointed his two fingers at my face. "I can see it in your eyes."

"See what?"

"That happy glaze that's barely half an inch deep. That lazy smile on your face. Lost Boy." He returned his attention to the ocean.

"What? What did you call me?"

"Lost Boy." He took in a breath of air to deal with his impatience with me, I was sure of it. "Come on, you don't know Peter Pan?"

"Oh, right. Yeah." I shifted my weight.

Dig rested his hands on his hips, perfectly still, listening to the waves breaking, as if they offered him advice. The sea air rustled his dirty blond hair against his face, and he took in a long inhale. "So, what's the plan?"

"Plan?"

"You looking for something out here?"

"Um…nah."

"Why the fuck not?"

My spine stiffened at his words, his sharp tone. "Right now, I'm just—"

Those eyes shot to mine again, and an eerie feeling crawled through my veins. Like he was inside me, reading my fears, poking at my cracks.

"Just *what*?" he asked. "You gonna stay on this strip of beach forever? Surf in a competition here and maybe another one there? Keep pushing dope and whatever else you can scrounge up for kids and yuppie losers? Yeah, you're their idol now, sure. But, in a couple of years, that'll all be over. And none of them are gonna be giving you the time of day, not even the girls. Then, how are you going to eat? Where are you gonna live? How are you gonna look at yourself in the mirror?"

"Wh-what? I don't know." I crossed my arms against his onslaught.

"You don't know. You don't know." He faced the ocean again. "When are you gonna know? You waiting for someone else to know? Because, man, if there's one thing you definitely need to know, it's that nobody gives a shit about you, except for you."

I didn't answer. I didn't know how. He was right. What the fuck *did* I know? I was just a jumble of self-doubt, denial, bravado, and balls. He saw right through me, the asshole.

"Tell me, what do you get out of it?" He motioned toward the ocean with his chin. "What's out there for you?"

I took in a breath, my eyes on the rolling waves I loved so much. "You're out there, and it's like you go into a kind of oblivion. Suddenly, all your life is in this long, long, stretched out wave. You're removed from your past, your present. Everything that's on your mind becomes insignificant. You feel completely removed from the world around you. Nothing matters but you and the board and the wave and the right-the-fuck now."

Dig grinned. He recognized the crazy. "Sounds like how I feel about riding my bike."

"Yeah." I met his penetrating gaze. "You're right. It is the same."

"Me and my brothers have all that, but we also create something new for ourselves on our own terms, something more than just tripping and survival. Something significant. This beach won't give you that. We could, though. I could teach you things, like I've been taught by my brothers," he continued. "You've got good instincts on the water, and you already got good bike skills under your belt."

"I've been working on bikes and cars for years."

"I saw that; it's great. There's more to learn though. Always more to learn."

I wasn't quite sure what he was referring to, but the sudden press of his jaw told me it was serious, something other than, say, construction.

"Why don't you come with us?"

"To South Dakota?"

"Yeah, prospect for the One-Eyed Jacks. Give it your best shot." His lips twitched. "You got a best shot to give?"

"Sure. Of course I do."

"We make our own rules. Live by 'em our way. But with that freedom comes responsibility to each other. We don't break our own rules, because that only leads to death or prison. We ride together, we fall, we pick each other up. That's what brothers do."

I swallowed past the clump of wet sand in my throat and averted my gaze. "That, I know. I know what brothers do."

His hand patted my chest. "Ah, you've got a heart in there, huh? You're trying to hide it, is all."

"It got ripped up," I breathed. "Blood fucking everywhere."

"Yeah, there's always lots of blood. Life sucks ass, Markus, and it's up to you to hang on and ride through it. For me, it's only bearable with good men at my side and at my back. You know what that's like?"

My eyes followed the delicate pinks and soft blues staining the early morning sky over the water. "I used to. Not anymore. Not for a long time now." I glanced up at his hard profile. "What's it like for you?"

A slight smile curled his lips. "One word." Dig leaned into me. "Fearless," he whispered roughly.

A sharp shiver tore up my spine like a razor blade, and I met his gaze. Thrill, danger, unpredictability.

"There's a big raw world out there." He gestured in the opposite direction of the ocean. "And you can be and do whatever you want in it. That makes me fucking high every morning I wake up and realize I'm still alive." He let out a small laugh. It was dark; it was hopeful.

I swallowed, not knowing what to say to that.

"Anything or anybody keeping you here? Except for these waves, that is," he asked.

Keeping me here?

I had no brother, no mother, no father. No girlfriend I cared about. A few pals I hung with, but no one I'd miss—or, more importantly, no one who'd miss me.

No one.

A grin split his face, and he dropped his head back, as if begging the first rays of the sun breaking through the pink-blue sky to bless him. "Out in the Dakotas, we've got plenty of lakes, waterfalls, reservoirs, swimming holes. Which means plenty of girls in bikinis. You wouldn't be missing that, not by a long shot. If that's what's really keeping you here."

"Shit, you read my mind!"

We laughed.

"Well, we got to roll," he said. "Liked hanging with you, Markus."

We shook hands. He slapped me on the back, and I thumped his. My fingers sank into the thick leather of his patched jacket with that incredible star-eyed skull on it.

"Thanks again for the good time and for getting that bike part, man. You saved our asses, done right by us. Appreciate it." He squeezed my arms.

"Yeah, sure."

"We ever come back this way, and you're still around…" He shot me a look.

Was that a veiled insult? A provocation? A challenge?

Dig flicked a hand at me and strode off toward his bike.

My stomach dropped.

Would they ever come back? And where would I be if they did? Still here? Paddling out, hunting the waves, the ride? Working at the 7-Eleven?

He swung on his bike, his crazy-eyed buddy with the wacky nickname and the long dark hair revving his engine next to him.

My chest squeezed, and my skin got clammy.

Wreck, the big guy with the bandana who took care of their bikes and navigated, was at the rear, and their prez, a heavy-set older man, was up at the front. Shit, they rode in a formation. They were a unit. Order, respect, honor.

Dig glanced at me, slid his Ray-Bans over his eyes, and fit his gloves on his hands. Every hair on my body stood on end, as if jolted by electricity, by a once-in-a-lifetime last chance. A signal flare of hope in a dark sky over the ocean, and I was alone on a leaky raft.

He started his engine and hit the throttle.

That blare of disruption, of arrogance, that noise of protest, that declaration of everything he was, that the Jacks were, right there, ripped through the tender dawn and through my soul.

"Hey!" I charged toward him, my heart banging in my chest. "Wait! Wait up!"

Dig grinned from behind those shades.

He knew.

Dig leaned back in his saddle, a hand planted on his thigh, his engine rumbling thunder. That grin of his only grew wider. "You coming?"

BUTLER

NOW

I closed my eyes and made a wish on this very same beach. The beach where it'd all begun and ended for me three times over—when I'd given up, when I'd chased after hope, and now, when I was carving that hope and new dreams into a solid reality.

My fingers brushed over the silver hummingbird skull that hung against my chest.

I held Tania's hand in mine and made that wish of thanks, of gratitude, to *him*, my friend, my brother. I prayed for his peace as the relentless waves of the vast blue crashed and broke before us.

"Butler, you okay?" Tania squeezed my arm.

I held her eyes, which squinted in the sun. Her face was flush with heat. Her white dress billowed behind her in the wind, her bare toes in the sand.

Fuck you, Romeo, and your dagger and your poison. I unlocked that gate myself, I got back into Verona, and got my girl.

I crushed Tania's mouth with mine and kissed my wife.

The next day, I took Tania to see my parents. It had been almost twenty-five years since we'd last seen each other. They were shocked. They were pleased. Tania did all the talking until Mom, Dad, and I got a handle on the situation.

As we sat together in that same living room on that same furniture, my mom offering us those same Italian cookies that were her favorites on those same daisy-trimmed dishes, we relaxed and began to talk.

Tania held my hand and didn't let go.

I took Tania south along the California coastline. We swam in the cold ocean, Tania's body sliding against mine in the water. I got her on a surfboard, and she didn't do half bad for a first-timer.

We'd run on the sand in the mornings, and she'd watch me as I hit the waves. I'd lift the board out of the water and make my way back to her on the beach where she waited for me with a towel, a huge smile on that gorgeous face.

Our last night in California, we hung out on the beach checking out the stars in the night sky, enjoying the sound of the surf. I sang her favorite ballad to her as she nestled into my chest. When I got to the end of "Black," Tania joined in with the background vocals, and we laughed.

In that full, rich laugh of my wife's, the sadness and loss and longing of that song had been erased. There was only joy, because we had that beautiful life together, and Tania was that star in my sky, and I was hers.

EPILOGUE

TANIA

"BABY, YOU DON'T HAVE TO DO THIS."

Butler's eyes flashed at me. "Tania."

He lifted me in his arms, climbed the porch steps, and swept us through the front door of my great-grandmother's Victorian house in Pine Needle.

Our new home.

"Welcome home, Scarlett."

"Welcome home, Rhett."

We kissed.

After we'd gotten back from California, Butler had moved into my mother's house, and we'd used my old room. However, along with my mother, we'd decided that instead of knocking down a wall to create a large bedroom and bath suite, we would instead spruce up the house and put it on the market. We had, and we'd ended up getting a good price on it.

In the meantime, we'd also put our resources to work in my great-grandmother's house. I'd brought Butler and my mother to see it, and Butler had fallen in love with the house.

We'd hired Willy to oversee the contracting and to take care of the finer details. We'd transformed the large formal dining room on the ground floor into a bedroom and bath for my mother and converted the large living room and kitchen—which Mom and Penny and I'd had fun modernizing—into a single great space that was open and airy. The area was easy for Rae to maneuver in, especially once she would have to use a wheelchair full-time at some point in the future.

Along the way in this project, I'd found lots of architectural motifs from my and Butler's sporadic pick travels for us to use in the house and in the large garden. Willy and I'd soon realized that we had a good thing going and put our heads together. I'd amped up those sorts of salvage picks and found him a hell of a lot of one-of-a-kind pieces. He'd used them to create unique furniture and home accents, combining wood and metals, like antiqued bronze and copper and iron. I'd featured his work in my store, and they'd become wildly popular with many professional interior designers from all over the country.

The house had been in good condition, and our renovation had only taken about four months to complete. Up next was building an extra garage for Butler's bikes and our two snowmobiles. We were all moved in. At last, we had our own family home.

Today, a beautiful warm spring day, was housewarming party day. Today was also Thunder's first birthday.

Butler set me down in the entryway, and I peeked over his shoulder. Boner had my mother's arm in his and helped her up the ramp that he'd installed himself by the front steps. Becca came up behind them, holding Thunder's hand. Grace's son toddled through the great room, his tiny feet stamping in the new red high-tops I'd bought him, his eyes wide as he took in the house. He let go of Becca's hand and laughed as he tore around the kitchen island, his long black hair swinging behind him.

"Becca, go get him. Keep him out of the kitchen, so he doesn't see his birthday cake!" Grace laughed, her eyes on her son, as he zoomed past the corner where Butler's acoustic guitar stood on a stand alongside a new electric guitar in between a pair of leather armchairs.

"Thunder! Wait!" shouted Becca, chasing him.

"I already feel the spills coming on," Grace said. "I'm going to get out more paper towels to be ready." She opened the pantry closet.

"They're on the bottom left," I said from the sink where I washed a serving platter. "There should be three jumbo rolls."

"Tania?"

"What is it?"

My gaze darted to the pantry closet where Grace gestured at the ten large containers of Ghirardelli sweet ground chocolate and cocoa gourmet powder.

"What the heck are you doing with so much sweetened cocoa? Have you been baking? You hate baking."

My face flared with heat. "Rae really enjoys a good cup of cocoa, and she got me and Butler addicted. I found a huge sale online. You know me and a sale. I couldn't resist stocking up."

"I'll have to try it."

"Very tasty. Very high quality."

"Uh-huh." Grace eyed me as she ripped open a new roll of paper towels.

I dried the serving platter and handed it to Alicia.

Alicia and Ronny, who were now living together, set up the truckload of food they'd brought from a friend's restaurant in Deadwood. Jill and Boner and Dready had brought the beer from Miner Brewery, a local craft brewery in Hill City, and the wine from its sister company, Prairie Berry Winery. We loved supporting our local businesses.

Aunt Charlotte and Penny had baked an endless array of pies and cakes and beautifully frosted cupcakes for the kids that were spectacularly laid out on the old oak dining room table that Willy had restored.

I cornered Jill by Aunt Charlotte's blackberry buckle.

"What's going on with you, hmm?" I asked, slanting my head.

Her eyes slid to mine. "What do you mean?"

"You haven't touched any booze at all today. Highly unlike you. Highly suspect. I noticed this the other night at Pete's, too."

"I was the designated driver!" She threw her hands in the air.

"And you hate being designated driver, and yet this time you volunteered. Spill."

Jill bit at her lip, putting down her glass of iced tea. She leaned into me. "We're trying to get pregnant."

"Honey!" I grabbed her in a huge hug. "I'm so excited!"

A huge smile blazed over her face. "We talked about it a while back, but I think Boner didn't want to pressure me. He can't wait though, and frankly, neither can I. The timing feels right, especially with Becca acclimated to school now. The business is on steady feet, too, right?"

"Very right."

"We started trying over a month ago. So far, nothing yet, but we'll see. I didn't want to say anything yet."

"Of course." I hugged her again. "Good for you."

"Look at him." Jill picked up her iced tea and gestured across the room with it, toward where Boner sat with Lock on our long sofa, Thunder in his daddy's lap.

The boy screeched as Boner tickled and teased him.

"You see that light in his eyes?" Jill said softly, a wistful tone in her voice. "That's a special kind of joy, and I want him to feel that every day, in his own home, with his own child in his arms. I want to give him that."

"You will. Give it time."

My gaze fell on Wes, his arm around his mother, talking with Butler. "Can't believe that boy is off to college next week."

"University of Arizona, watch out," murmured Jill.

"Amen."

Jill let out a breath. "This is going to be hard on Alicia."

"I know. Butler and I are going to go down to Tucson with her and Wes, help set him up, hold her hand."

"Oh, that's good. Because I can't imagine Ronny can get away now, right?"

"Did she tell you that she finally got him to open a second tattoo shop after all these years, and in Meager?"

"Ronny just told me. I'm so excited." Jill smirked. "There's no stopping her. Ever."

The party ran on. My brother and Nina arrived with their son, Joe. Becca immediately took her little brother in hand and brought him to sit in his grandmother's lap.

"Grandma misses you. You need to come visit more often."

Joe only stuck a finger in his mouth.

Boner brought out Thunder's birthday cake that he'd gotten from the Meager Grand—a double layer chocolate cake decorated with blue and green fondant for wild grasses with two horses grazing on the very top. Thunder was obsessed with horses.

I lit the single sparkly candle and Lock held his son as we all sang Happy Birthday to our favorite little one year old boy in the whole wide world.

Thunder's eyes widened and he hopped up and down in his daddy's arms.

"You ready, Thunder?" Lock asked, his wet eyes glimmering. "Did you make your wish?"

The boy nodded and together with his mommy and daddy, he blew out his birthday candle, and we all cheered.

The party started to wind down once my mother gave sloppy kisses and big hugs to her grandchildren and Thunder and retreated into her room.

An hour later we said our good-byes to our guests. Grace and Lock were the last ones to leave.

Grace and I hugged each other tightly.

"A perfect day in a beautiful house." Her eyes filled with tears.

"Are you crying? Why are you crying?" I whispered.

"Because I'm so happy that you two found each other. So happy for you both. And I'm glad that we're all here together. I found out the hard way—"

"Shh." I hugged her again. "I love you."

"I love you, too." Grace planted a kiss on my cheek.

Lock held his son in his arms while Thunder leaned forward and planted a juicy kiss on Butler's cheek.

"Oh! Thank you," said Butler. "Bye, Thunder." He held out his hand to the birthday boy.

"Bye!" Thunder high-fived Butler, and my husband smiled at him.

"Later, man." Lock shook Butler's hand, his son's arms wrapped around his neck.

Butler rubbed a hand down Thunder's back. "He's tired, huh?"

"Best party ever," said Lock.

"Yes, it was," murmured Butler.

Lock and Grace descended the porch steps, fastened their son in his car seat, got in their truck, and took off, waving at us.

Butler slung an arm around my waist. "Mrs. M, we should hit the hay. We got an early start tomorrow morning on that bike of mine."

"I'm looking forward to Montana. An early night sounds very good. Now with the house totally done and the party down, I am so ready to relax under your magic spell." I squeezed his ass.

"Who said anything about a spell? My magic cock, you mean."

"Your magic cock has me under its spell, baby."

"You're not too tired, I hope."

"Me? No."

"That's good because I didn't have any desserts today. I saved my sweet tooth for you, Scarlett."

I leveled my eyes at him. "Did you?"

He let out a laugh, his tongue lashing out at my lips. "Get upstairs. I'll lock up, put the alarm on, and then I'll bring us some dessert we can share in bed. That was chocolate ganache in that cake, right?"

"Uh-huh."

"Hmm. Get moving."

I darted up the stairs, a huge grin on my face, and I waited for my old man in our brand-new king-size bed.

BUTLER

"Scarlett, it's a '32 Roadster."

"A what?"

"A 1932 Ford Roadster—the inspiration for the Beach Boys hit 'Little Deuce Coupe'?" My pulse raced as Tania's face struggled to register. "Baby, you remember John, the cool dude, in *American Graffiti?*"

"Yeah, of course. He was the ultimate cool dude. Very sexy."

"This is cool dude's hot rod."

Her eyes popped open wide. "Oh my God! That car is an icon."

My hand passed over the rusted hood of the ancient vehicle. "This is so fucking rare. Jesus."

We were in a dilapidated garage piled high with all manner of goodies and junk belonging to an elderly man, a die-hard collector of everything under the sun, in the middle of Montana where Lock had asked us to go and look at a '67 GTO and a '51 Mercury for Eagle Wings. Lock didn't want to leave home so frequently anymore, so he'd asked me and Tania to take a look for him.

In between my many duties as VP of the One-Eyed Jacks, I had started going along with Tania on her out-of-town picks because I really enjoyed it. Also, I didn't want her out there on her own, and we wanted to spend as much time together as possible. We both loved road-tripping, either on my bike or in her Yukon. My old lady enjoyed learning a vast amount about cars and car parts, and bikes and bike parts, and even bicycles from her old man. We worked well together. We zinged together. We also played a mighty round of Good Cop, Bad Cop when cutting deals and negotiating prices with the owners.

It'd all started on a pick in Iowa. I had come across a couple of choice finds, pieces that I'd spotted and recognized amid the rubble—an Indian bike frame from the sixties and an old Mustang grill—and I'd brought them home for Lock and Boner to use at Eagle Wings. They'd been thrilled, so the ball had officially started rolling for the Rusted Heart in the bike and car field, too. Tania had put me on the payroll, and I'd gotten health insurance for the first time in my life.

We were adulting.

Tania had convinced Willy and Clip to start a side business, restoring and cleaning up a wide variety of antiques that we brought home. Instead of sending these pieces off to someone else to fix and paying through the nose for it, the boys would now take care of it. In house and in the brotherhood was the way we rolled.

On the road, Tania and I always managed to mix business with plenty of pleasure. A torch of heat blasted through me with the memory of last night. The motel we'd stayed at had been vacant, except for us, so we'd taken full advantage and gotten loud, noisy, and very creative in our room, in the hallway by the ice machine, in the small swimming pool in the middle of the night.

Yeah, I loved working with my wife.

I took a few pics of the rusted hull of the '32 Coupe with my cell phone and sent them to Lock. Within one minute, my phone rang.

"Man, tell me this is for real!" boomed Lock's voice through my phone.

"It's very real," I replied. "But I'm still pinching myself."

I described the car and its condition. There wasn't much left of the Ford's insides, but the original body and frame, the windshield, and the grill were all there. A piece of heaven.

"Do what you gotta do," said Lock. "Get it."

I got the car and all its pieces for a sweet two thousand bucks. Pulling it out of that damn storage garage took hours and lots of help from a neighbor and his sons. Tania wouldn't let me do any heavy lifting. We called Jill, and she arranged for our amazing treasure to be shipped to Meager.

The next day, on our way home, Tania and I crossed over into South Dakota and then the Meager town limits. We zoomed past the cemetery, the fork in the road that led to Clay Street, the center of our town—at one end, Erica's Meager Grand Cafe, and on the other, the lone, stalwart from a bygone age, the Prairie Pumper gas station. We swung toward the club, and Tania's hands grew tighter around my middle.

Every time we rode down this way through our town, following the winding asphalt that led to the private gravel drive of the One-Eyed Jacks' property, it was a small victory for me.

Going home.

Being home.

Being alive.

The black edges of the mass of evergreens and the ancient worn crags of the Black Hills rose on the horizon, overlooking Meager, as my bike brought us to the top of the drive. That strong scent of pine and birch, edged with a hint of lush green undergrowth, mixed with the crisp air, filled my grateful lungs.

We were home, where we were meant to be.

I opened the throttle a little more, and the pounding of the wind became fiercer, the colors around us vivid. For the first time in a very, very long time, my heart pumped easy, and it pumped free, rich with satisfaction, warm with the afternoon heat of the sun along with my wife's beautiful body pressed against me, her strong heart beating in tune with mine.

Thunder rumbled in the distance, having followed us home since we'd crossed the state line. A magnificent storm was brewing, had been for hours. My eyes darted up at the supercell gathering force, its billowy bulk churning, swirling, in the thick gray sky. Lightning streaked through the dramatic mass of clouds.

Very soon, the storm would break, or maybe it would suddenly change direction. You could rarely predict its course, and a Dakotan accepted these natural laws. You learned to ride when you could and loved it hard when you did. You knew that the storms cutting loose would release their rage and maybe even ruin.

Yet it was in the aftermath, in those ruins that such cruel storms left behind, that we lifted ourselves to see the possibilities once again. We believed that the sunflowers would once more grow, rise tall, and sway against the infinite Meager sky.

THE END

AUTHOR'S NOTE

The work of the artist in this story, Gerhard Von Richter and his wife Astrid, is directly inspired by real life Wisconsin baker and artist Eugene Von Bruenchenhein and his wife Marie. While working at an art gallery in New York City, I was introduced to this genius's life story and work first hand by a dealer from Chicago soon after the artist's house and life's work had been discovered upon the his death. I was very moved by his story and fascinated by his work, and that fascination and inspiration has stayed with me all these many years.

I have pinned as much of the artist's work as I could find on Pinterest, and you'll find it on my Pinterest board for this book. Eugene Von Bruenchenhein's work can be found in the collections of major American museums, galleries, and private collectors.

ACKNOWLEDGMENTS

To Najla Qamber for your artistry and magic. You make my dreams and visions a reality. I can't thank you enough for taking this series journey with me, teaching me new things, flying with me, and offering me a whole new world of possibilities.

To Jovana Shirley, for your professionalism, thoroughness, and for putting up with my many epiphanies!

To Christina Trevaskis for believing in me. For your insights, instincts, articulate and gentle guidance, your generosity, and your friendship. For your wonderful long emails and messages, which I adore. I am so very grateful for your being with me on this journey, and I look forward to much more creativity together.

To Sue Banner. Where would I be without you as a friend and a book person!? I'm shuddering merely considering it…Your professionalism and friendship mean the world to me.

To Linda of Sassy Savvy Fabulous PR for freaking me out, for pushing me off the cliffs I need to jump from, for listening, for your smarts, for the gifs, for spelling it all out time and time again, and for believing in me. And a big thank you to Melissa and Sharon.

To Jenny Rohrach and your amazing Prairie Californian blog. Thank you for taking the time to answer my questions and for sharing with me your insights into life on a sunflower farm in the Dakotas. I love your blog, and your spirit inspires me!

To my beta readers who are dear friends: Natalie (who put up with quite an awkward first draft), Alison (who swallowed chapters like a serial novella at all hours), Lena and Rachel whose keen eyes and pointed remarks, spot on suggestions, and positivity continue to keep me on my toes and push me to do better, reach farther, go deeper, and find the precious details. And Needa, for keeping it real. You ladies are amazing, and I am honored and privileged to have you dive into my rough, raw words and show me the trust that you do in each and every book.

Special thanks to author Needa Warrant whose friendship, sisterhood, opinions, story instincts never cease to humble me. You laugh at me, push me, kick me in the ass, and through all my many ups and downs, pull my hair and hold my hand, all at the same time. Truly something. I love you, woman.

To Alison for being such a wonderful virtual PA over there in the USA and having my back. Love riding this train with you, girlfriend! To Jenn for your friendship and support, for always listening, and the endless love.

To my Cat Callers for the honesty and the laughs we share. Thank you for your support and for making our little corner of Facebook special.

To Ellen, Kandace, Lori, Jo, Sharon, Cindy, Kaylee, MJ, Soulla, Larri, Iza, Shanda, Jan, Amy, Penny, Sammy, Amy F.—you ladies amaze me and blow me away with your big hearts and book passion and messages that keep me laughing. I bow before thee and am thrilled to call you my friends. (Thank you for those coffee shop details, Larri! Wink wink.)

To Milasy & co. of the Rock Stars of Romance for taking the time to read the series and for shouting out about loving these stories and these characters, especially Dig, because #DigForever. An honor, woman! To the amazing Book Bellas, the Dirty Book Girls, Kinky Girls Book Obsessions, Perusing Princesses, iScream Books, EDGY Reviews, Kindle Friends Forever, I Love Book Love, Divas Book Lounge, and so many more—there are no words that are adequate! To all the bloggers and readers and reviewers who have taken a chance on reading my books, on sharing teasers and ads, writing reviews, and sharing the book love, I thank you for all your hard work and the tremendous support. Without you, all this simply does not happen. Thank you for every incredible thing you do.

To authors Willow Aster, Leylah Attar, Daryl Banner, BL Berry, Lorelei James, Shay Savage, Mara White for their support and enthusiasm. It's such an honor and a great pleasure to know you.

To Blue Bayer, for once again generously allowing me to use one of his beautiful, unique jewelry designs on a cover and in my story.

To my family, you are at the center of it all. To my cousin Domna, the medical professional, who provided me with all the details I needed.

Also, I'd like to thank my dear friend, the late Neil Wilson, British art dealer extraordinaire, who I once art "zinged" with all over Europe one crazy summer. And thank you, Edward and the painters and sculptors I got to know at your gallery, for everything all of you taught me about living, creating and "seeing." And whiskey, of course.

As Butler said, "It's a whirlwind, baby." Yes, yes, it certainly is.

xx Cat

FIND ME ONLINE

I love to hear from readers! Please visit me, follow me, come find me out there in the big bad world and keep up with my book news:

Sign up for Cat's Newsletter

My website: www.catporter.eu

Join Cat Porter's Cat Calls Facebook group

Facebook: www.facebook.com/catporterauthor

Twitter: @catporter103

Instagram: catporter.author

Pinterest

Goodreads

Join Cat Porter's Goodreads Group

Email: catporter103@gmail.com

Made in the USA
Columbia, SC
30 July 2017